The Race Through the Sky

CR Baumberger

Editing by Jayne Kirk of Fyrefli Fictionary

Book Cover by 100 Covers

1st edition, 2025

ISBN: 979-8-9928120-0-8

Dedicated to all the girls and women who were told they can't.

Yes you fuckin' can.

"All you have to do is move yourself with your feet across beautiful trails."

Courtney Dauwalter

Chapter 1

Bang.

A surge of energy. The movement of legs. They were off.

Ariel rocketed from the starting line with ease, adrenaline surging through her lanky frame. This floating feeling wouldn't last long, the burn of her effort would eventually catch up. But that was a problem for later. As the mass of runners thundered down the straight away, the crowd of proud parents and friends cheered them on. All the runners' hopes were the same: to qualify for Nationals.

Ariel leaned into the slight downhill, letting gravity take her. The path curved as it led into the lightly forested area at the edge of the course, thinning out the crowd and narrowing the path. Ariel picked up her pace, passing a few runners before the next hill looming ahead. Sitting at the front of the chase pack, she was right on track.

"In one two three, out two three. In one two three, out two three." Ariel repeated the mantra in her head, syncing her breathing with her steps. She did the body scan Coach Bobbi had trained her to do her first day of cross-country practice four years ago. Her lungs were expansive, drinking in the oxygen so her leg muscles could propel her forward. Her calf muscles felt a bit of the effort, but systems were firing on all cylinders. Despite the cold November morning, beads of sweat formed on her face, one running down her forehead past her ear and around her

chin. "Your body cools efficiently." Coach had told her one-time freshman year. Leave it to Coach to always have a positive spin.

The field thinned the farther they went: runners dropping back as their legs tired. But Ariel held strong. And so did Danielle. Her nemesis her entire high school career. While she always gave Ariel a run for her money, Danielle hadn't managed to beat her in any race since their freshman year. Junior year she almost took the State title, but Ariel held her off. Danielle's familiar footsteps sounded off just behind Ariel's right shoulder—her uneven cadence giving her away. Ariel charged ahead, the uneven *thump-thump, thump, thump,* keeping pace.

"Breathe in one two three, out two three. In two three, out two three," Ariel repeated as the chase pack started to speed up, a few of the girls trying to make their moves. As they turned the corner, she got a glimpse of the field behind her. After the pack Ariel was running with, there was a good twenty yards until the next runner- a girl in a yellow and black jersey- and another ten yards behind her was the next group. It didn't seem as though anyone else would be challenging the lead pack anytime soon.

"Halfway there!" Coach Bobbi screamed from her perch against one of the colored triangles outlining the course. Despite the growing burn in her legs being more intense than it should be at this point, Ariel managed a smile. She was in her typical coaching uniform: the team's blue and white warmup set, stopwatch around her neck, and cobalt blue running shoes that looked fresh out of the box. Coach had her thick chocolate hair piled atop her head in her usual messy bun, but she'd added what appeared to be the feathers of a blue and white boa. Every race she added some crazy accessory to make her easy to spot on the course. At regionals it was a massive blue and white jesters' hat with bells. "You're ahead of pace—sub seventeen! Sub seventeen!"

Tingles ran down Ariel's spine, pricking goosebumps on her skin. A finish in under 17 minutes… that would be an Iowa girl's state record. Suddenly the growing burn made more sense. She was ahead of pace, and she wasn't about to let up now. The whole field was running fast with no signs of slowing.

"Your only job in racing is to hurt as much as possible." Coach Bobbi's advice echoed in her head. She'd said it before a meet Ariel's sophomore year: you run, you hurt, you endure, you do your best. It didn't get much simpler than that. Races often come down to who can hurt the best.

She mentally steeled herself for the last half of the race and settled in, finding her breathing again. Her lungs still felt fresh, but the weight in her legs grew.

She suddenly noticed the thump-thump, thump, thump of Danielle's stride wasn't right behind her anymore. Ariel fought the urge to turn around and check where Danielle was. Seconds count in this race, and she couldn't spare one to check where her biggest rival was, lest she give Danielle the chance to catch her. She was on her own at the front of the chase pack, the overall race leaders only a few strides ahead.

As another hill rose to meet her legs, she dug deep and pushed harder, leaving the chase pack and running on the heels of the leaders. While hills were most runners' nemesis, Ariel had made it a point to make them her specialty. She said a mental thank you to the three beloved hills at home that she ran every other morning. Coach hadn't liked her extra training runs outside of official practices, but after Ariel's sophomore season, the hounding stopped as Ariel's race times improved. Ariel was on the heels of the third-place runner, then her shoulder. Her breath was labored, fighting for each inhale. Ariel tucked her chin and pumped her arms, moving ahead of her and towards the runner in second.

The hill crested, and the ground fell. Sweet relief for her legs that didn't last long. She leaned into gravity and hoped to God she didn't trip. She was well into the lead group now, nearly shoulder to shoulder with second place. The pack was tight: bony elbows and colorful shoes a blur.

The finish line appeared on the horizon—the blue timing mats laid out on the ground, colorful triangles outlining the chute.

Here we go. She could see the crowd cheering, waving banners and bells every which way. But she couldn't hear them. All Ariel heard was the sound of her exhales and the swish of spandex.

Thump-thump, thump, thump.

Without looking back, Ariel knew Danielle had joined the lead pack. With the finish line in sight, she felt a surge of fire in her chest. She kicked hard, her legs screaming in protest. Shoulder to shoulder with second place, then with the first-place runner, then no one. She pumped her arms like her life depended on it, eyes laser focused on the large digital clock above the finish.

16:29:12.

Thirty-one seconds to make it across the finish line for that coveted sub-17-minute finish.

Calves on fire, her quads threatened to rip to shreds. Her stomach cramped, nearly emptying itself. The edges of her vision blurred, but Ariel didn't slow.

This moment was hers. She'd worked years for this— this was it. She was going to leave it all on the field or throw up trying. Ariel saw the flash of Danielle's maroon and gold uniform from the corner of her eye, the metallic accents reflecting the sunshine.

A long thin arm.

Blue turning to green turning to black.

Then; nothing.

Chapter 2

"How many stitches do I need?" Ariel asked, her dark blue eyes wide as saucers.

The nurse standing in front of her gave a half-hearted smile. "Probably seven or so. But the doctor will give you a solid number when she gets here."

Ariel turned to her mom, Cheryl ,who was standing right beside her, arms crossed in front of her chest. "Mom. 7 stitches? That means a needle through my skin seven times?!" She felt the panic rising in her chest, like hot water coming to a boil.

"The doc will give you numbing medication, so you won't feel anything." The nurse, who's name badge read Bob, explained. He was an older man with kind eyes and a gruff edge. "And we'll make sure you don't see any of the needles if you don't want to."

"Um, hell no," Ariel said, shaking her head. Her leg bounced uncontrollably. "I don't want any of this. Are we sure we can't just put some glue on it and call it a day?"

Nurse Bob stood, removing his gloves in the fancy way nurses do, turning them inside out and flinging them into the trash in one graceful move. "You can ask the doc, but that cut isn't in a great spot for glue. I'm sorry to be the bearer of bad news."

"You've been great, thank you so much for your help," Cheryl told him before Ariel could freak out more.

"Just press that call light if you need me before the doc comes. Shouldn't be too long," Nurse Bob said, crossing the fingers on both his hands as he strode out of the room.

"Damn, I would've put money on me being the first one of us to get stitches!" said Ariel's twin sister, Sam, moving out of the corner of the room to the chair where the nurse had been.

The tears Ariel had been blinking back poured over her eyelids, streaming down her red, dirt-streaked cheeks.

"I didn't mean to make you cry!" Sam exclaimed, her round cheeks reddening. Usually, she was the life of the party, the one to lighten the mood. But Ariel wasn't ready for the mood to be lightened just yet.

"I don't even know what happened," Ariel said softly, wiping away the tears with her uninjured hand. She examined her bandaged hand- it was twice the size it normally was, and wrapped in the shape of a mitten, individual fingers hidden beneath the gauze they'd placed when she first got to the emergency department. Thankfully, there was no blood soaking through it.

Cheryl pushed herself up to sit on the exam table, the crinkle paper making loud noises as she scooted close to her. She put her arm around her daughter, pulling her into a side hug. Ariel's shoulders shook softly.

"Oh honey, I'm so sorry this happened," Cheryl said, squeezing her.

"What happened?" Ariel asked again, looking up at Sam.

"You got elbowed," Sam said, a fire in her eye.

Ariel held up her gauzy mitt. "I got elbowed and this happened? A sliced open hand?"

Her mom nodded. "You and Danielle were neck and neck. She tried to pass you, and she was too close."

"Way too close." Sam added, standing up. "She clipped your leg too. Look at your shoes."

Ariel glanced down and studied her racing cleats. Sure enough, they were covered in mud and one of the shoe's laces looked like it had been gnawed in half. Her left calf was covered in several large scratches, bruises starting to form around them.

"Did she go down too?" Ariel asked, her sadness taking on an angry edge. Danielle had always been a serious competitor, but never a cheater. "And why don't I remember any of this?"

"You got trampled pretty good, honey," Cheryl said softly, tucking a piece of Ariel's dirty blonde hair behind her ear. Her ponytail had seen better days. "The nurse said the doctor would do a concussion workup on you just to be safe.

Ariel scoffed. "Concussion protocol for a cross runner. That's a new one." She turned her bandaged hand over in front of her face, studying both sides of it. "I take it someone stepped on my hand?"

"Mm-hmm," Sam said. "Pretty sure it was Danielle."

"She didn't go down?!" Ariel exclaimed, jaw agape. "Are you—"

"They disqualified her," Cheryl interrupted, placing a hand on her daughter's shoulder before she could leap from the table.

Ariel caught her breath, puffing out her cheeks with frustration. She sat back down with a thud. "Who won?"

"Tracey Smith, some runner from Wisconsin," Sam said, starting to pace the small room. "You had it in the bag, Ari. You were going to win that whole thing. Until that twat—"

"Language!" Mom said, her shrill voice catching everyone off guard.

"Oh come on, not even this once?" Sam said, rolling her eyes. "She physically abused your daughter and caused her to get stitches. I can't call her a twat?"

Cheryl held Sam's stare, before shaking her head, a small grin turning up the corners of her thin lips. "You can say bitch, not a twat."

Sam grinned. "Deal. Until that bitch cheated. You didn't deserve that at all."

Ariel fell silent, staring at her unrecognizable hand. How had it come to this? She'd done everything she was supposed to: showed up to practice early, stayed late, always ran her hardest for every workout, took breaks whenever Coach said she needed them. She ate what all the sports dieticians said she should eat, stretched when all she wanted to do was go to bed, studied the great runners that had come before her. And yet, somehow, her high school running career managed to end in the emergency room instead of across the finish line.

Suddenly the anemic salmon colored curtain flung back, its metal rings grating against the rod akin to nails on a chalk board. A small woman walked in. The white coat announced she was a doctor but her perfect makeup and dainty frame seemed to say more Dallas Cowboys cheerleader.

"Hi! I'm Doctor Anna, but please just call me Anna," she said, her voice equally as bright as her bleach blonde ponytail. In one graceful move, she pulled the rolling chair out from underneath the makeshift counter that held the computer and sat down in it right next to Ariel's knees. "I hear you're in need of some stitches."

Ariel fought back tears, nodding. She didn't trust her voice not to break, and she didn't want to be known as the girl who lost it because she had to get a few little stitches in her hand. Anna smiled warmly, revealing perfect teeth as expected.

"Not to worry." She patted Ariel's knee, giving it a reassuring squeeze. "I'm very good at my job, so the only thing you'll feel is the little injection of numbing medicine, and the only thing you'll see is a teeny tiny white line of scar tissue once it heals. In six months, you'll barely even remember it happened."

Ariel laughed out loud before she could stop herself. If it caught Anna off guard, she couldn't tell but Cheryl shot Ariel a look that was a mix between shock and "behave yourself". "Sorry," Ariel said, hoping Anna didn't think she was doubting her ability. "I just… this is now officially the end of my high school running career so I don't think I'll forget it as easily as I hope I will."

"Oh, I'm sorry to hear that," Anna said, sounding genuine and not like a doctor trying to placate her patient so she could get on with her day. "I'm sure it will take some time, but you know what?"

"What?"

Anna turned away to prepare whatever god-awful things she needed to do her job. Ariel looked away, not wanting to see any of it lest she run from the room. "As soon as you do your next big thing, this will all seem like a little blip on the road that was always going to get you where you were meant to go."

* * *

A week later, Ariel walked into Coach Bobbi's office and sat down in the bean bag chair loved by all. All the greats that had come before her had sat in this chair: Eleanor Davelle, the first girl from Bondurant to win the State championship; Kate Slavich, the first and only girl from their school to break the sub-17-minute mark. She'd gone on to run at the Olympics. This chair was Ariel's favorite spot to go when she needed an inspirational pick me up.

"Hey, Ariel, give me just a second," Coach Bobbi said without turning around, recognizing the sound of her footsteps. She typed a few things furiously into the computer, then whirled around in her chair.

Ariel held up her hand, showing off a now healing scar. "I got my stitches out today. It feels weird but it doesn't hurt anymore."

Coach nodded in approval. "It looks like it's healing nicely. How are you holding up, though? Aside from your hand?"

Ariel rolled her eyes, sinking back into the chair. "All right, I guess."

Coach Bobbi stood up and stepped around her desk, sitting instead on the folding chair she had placed on the other side. "I'm going to call BS on that. You don't look like you're very happy about it."

"How could I be happy about it? I was supposed to reclaim my title at Nationals, be the first person in history to win four times in a row. I was supposed to go to whatever school I wanted and not have to worry about money. I was supposed—"

Coach held up her hand, stopping Ariel's runaway thoughts. "Let's talk about the facts here. You've still won three State titles, right?"

"Yeah."

"And you won Footlocker Nationals twice?"

"Yeah…"

"And you've already visited a few schools who've given you soft offers, all of them full rides?"

"Mm-hmm."

"So tell me again how not winning this one single race is going to totally derail your post high school running career."

Ariel traced her fingers over the pink and white scar, the only remnants of that day she couldn't remember very well. "But you and I both know that colleges only want you if you're uninjured. As soon as you're hurt, it's game over."

Coach rolled her eyes, leaning back in her chair. "You had a few stitches in your hand, not a torn ACL. Sure, maybe BYU or Stanford might back out, and that's a big maybe. But so what? You weren't wanting to go there anyway, were you?"

"No," she laughed half-heartedly. "I could never see myself at either of those."

"Then there you go," Coach said, smiling. "You're catastrophizing again."

"What? Me? Catastrophize? Never!"

"Yeah, uh huh. Exactly. Now, did you want to talk about what's next? Or did you just want to wallow in poor you?"

Ariel sat up straighter, feeling a little lighter with Coach's walk back to reality. "What's next, Coach?"

"You rest, heal, and get ready for track season. I know cross is where your heart's at, but a good track season will help you solidify more money for school and give you one last good training season before you start your college career in the fall."

"Resting? Gross."

"I know," Coach sighed. "After almost 5 years with you, you still suck at resting."

"But I'm better than I was on day one!" Ariel said, eager to point out how far she'd come. "My first season I was doing fifteen mile runs the day before a meet! Now I only do eight mile runs two days before a meet."

Coach pinched the bridge of her nose between her thumb and forefinger. "Yes, I know. Improved, much more to be learned."

"How about no running for another week? Doctor said I was good to start running again, but I'm willing to give it an extra week just to prove I can," Ariel grinned.

"Deal," Coach said, extending a hand which Ariel took and shook firmly. "But I give it four days and you'll be back out.

Ariel stood up, shaking her head. "Just you watch, Coach. You know how much I like to prove people wrong." As Ariel left her office, it dawned on her that Coach Bobbi may just have been playing her. Coach knew how much she loved to surprise everyone and prove the doubters wrong. Freshman year one of the guys from the boy's cross-country team said she couldn't run the entire Saylorville Lake Hill, a notoriously steep and long local mini mountain, without stopping. She not only did it but did it faster than he had. And when junior year the sports reporters were theorizing her newly developed C-cups would slow her down, she had the fastest season of her life. Oh well. Ariel appreciated that Coach cared enough to use reverse psychology to get her to do what was good for her.

The cold November air hit slapped her cheeks as Ariel walked outside. The sun was already set despite it being barely past five in the afternoon. She'd stayed after school to do some research in the library and talk to coach. She walked briskly to her car and started it, finishing the ten-minute drive home before the heater even had a chance to warmup. Grabbing her backpack off the passenger seat, she dashed from her little parking slab across the driveway and through the front door, slamming it shut behind her.

"Mom! I'm home!" she called, slipping off her shoes on the rug before stepping fully into the mudroom. She hung her coat on its designated hook and walked into the brightly lit kitchen where the smell of something cheesy and garlicy wafted through the air. "Please tell me that's lasagna."

"You'd be right," Sam said. She was perched on a barstool on the kitchen island, textbook and notebook spread out in front of her. "You said five minutes, tops, right Mom?"

"Mm-hmm," Cheryl hummed as she stirred something in a pot on the stove.

Ariel raised an eyebrow at Sam, who shrugged and mouthed, "Something's up, but I don't know." Ariel made herself busy grabbing plates, silverware, and the salad bowl out of the fridge. Cheryl had already cut the lettuce and salad fixings, so all she had to do was empty the Tupperwares into the big bowl, add dressing, and mix. Easiest salad ever. The timer on the oven dinged and Mom removed the steaming hot lasagna, setting it in the middle of the island on a checkered green and white hot pad.

"Have at it girls." Mom removed her waist apron and walked to the bathroom just off the kitchen, closing the door rather loudly behind her.

"What happened? Bad day at work?" Ariel whispered as she cut into the dish.

"No clue," Sam said, closing her books. "She was like that when I got home and when I asked what was wrong she said—"

"Nothing's wrong," they both said in unison, mimicking their mom's soft soprano. They stifled a laugh.

Ariel lifted a plate up to Sam and dished up another one, setting it in Mom's spot. Finally, she dished her own, giving herself a generous helping of both lasagna and salad. Cheryl joined them at the table, not looking either of them in the eyes. After a few awkward moments of silence and cutlery clattering against porcelain plates, Cheryl spoke.

"I lost my job today."

Chapter 3

Later that night, after all had been hashed out at the dinner table, the dishes had been done and homework completed, Ariel snuck into Sam's room across the hall. She climbed up the ladder to the top bunk and crawled into bed next to her twin, pulling the covers up to her chin.

"What do we do now?" Ariel asked after they'd laid in silence for a few minutes, staring up at the plastic glow in the dark stars on her ceiling. They'd put them up there when they still shared a room, probably over five years ago now.

"Beats me… not like we can give her a job."

"I know, but… it just feels like we should do something. I'm going to stop driving into Ankeny every Saturday to go to Porchlight."

"I'm sure the extra four dollars from not buying your jumbo blueberry muffin will save the house." Even though she couldn't see her face, Ariel knew Sam rolled her eyes. It was her signature move.

"Don't forget the gas money. I know it won't save anything, but it'll at least make me feel like I'm doing something. Trying not to be a drain on the household, ya know?"

Sam took a big breath in, her rib cage stretching then releasing with a heavy sigh. "I've been thinking about getting a job for a while, guess now seems like a good time to finally do it."

"You never told me you were wanting to get a job," Ariel said, propping herself up on one elbow. "Where do you want to work?"

"I was thinking Panera. I go there all the time with my friends so the employee discount would be nice."

"Maybe I should get one too…" Ariel had never really thought about getting a job. She knew she'd have one someday. But between school, homework, and running, there just weren't enough hours in the day for her to pick up an after-school gig. She'd been a summer camp counselor, but that hardly felt like a job. It was staying up late, designing fun crafts, teaching kids to ride horses, fun things that Ariel never considered work. And besides, there was no way a camp counselor's paycheck would contribute more than half a grocery bill to the household.

Sam turned her head on the pillow, her eyes inches from Ariel's. "Running is your job."

"But it doesn't pay me anything."

"Not yet it doesn't, but it will."

"It's gonna be quite a while," Ariel explained. "I can't get paid while I run in college."

"For now. They're gonna start allowing that tho!" Sam insisted, rolling her eyes. "And besides, you're going to get a full ride to college, right?"

"Ninety-nine percent sure, yeah."

"That's essentially like making forty to eighty grand a year depending on where you go, since you'll be saving all that money in tuition."

"I guess that's a fair point."

"Yeah, and even though my grades are good, chances are slim I'll get a full ride anywhere. So getting a job now is the least I can do to start paying my way towards that. I know Mom always wanted to help us with college, but if I can take some of that worry off her plate, especially now that she doesn't have a job? Well, I'm going to do it."

"That's very noble of you, Samantha," Ariel teased, poking her in the side and dodging the elbow that flew in her direction. "You bring in some money, I'll pinch pennies. Dream team."

"Dream team," Sam said, rolling her eyes again. "Can I go to bed now? We've got a calculus exam in the morning."

"That's tomorrow?" Ariel said, wide eyed.

"Yes, tomorrow. You'll be fine, it's not that hard."

"Says the math wiz," Ariel said as she shimmied out from under the warm covers and made her way back down the ladder. "You're the brains, I'm the brawn."

"Smartest brawn I've ever met."

Ariel walked to the door and opened it slowly to minimize the creek in the hinges. The small squeak reminded her of one of the last conversations she'd had with her dad. He'd been walking down the stairs as Ariel left Sam's room, flinging the door open and making the hinges cry out in protest.

"Those damn things. Ari, remind me to get the WD40 this afternoon," he said without pausing, already halfway down the staircase. "I've got a work call, but I'm done at four. Remind me then and we'll take care of those suckers once and for all."

"Got it, Dad."

Four o'clock that day came and went, his meeting running over long enough that by the time he was finally finished, Ariel had left for the overnight team bonding party. They'd only had one more conversation after that.

"Hey, Sam," Ariel whispered, stopping in the doorway, the soft hall nightlight illuminating half her face in a yellowy glow.

"What?" she asked, voice muffled by the pillow.

"I love you."

A pause, then a shuffle of sheets as Sam stuck her head up to look over the side of the bunk bed at Ariel . She studied her face for a minute. They were only seventeen, but Sam thought her sister looked older. Her pale skin was still smooth, her dark blonde hair thick and full. But her eyes held more than a teenager's should. She was sure her own looked the same. "Love you too."

* * *

The clanging of the final bell arrived, jolting Ariel out of her concentration on her calculus test. She put her name at the top and passed it up the row of desks, grateful to be done with both the test and the school day. She made quick work of shoving her textbooks and notebooks into her backpack, exchanging them for car keys.

"I'm going to Shelby's, you want the car?" Ariel asked Sam, jangling the keys in front of her.

"Um yes," Sam said, leaning over from her desk and snatching them out of her hand. "I've got a job interview."

Ariel crossed the fingers on both of her hands. "Good luck! Tell me how it goes tonight?"

"Duh." Sam stood up, slinging her bag over her shoulder. "But Mom doesn't know, so shh." She brought her pointer finger to her lips. Ariel did the same, zipping her lips and throwing away the key. The two sisters walked into the parking lot together, Ariel searching for her best friend. Three cars down from her own, Shelby was perched on the hood of her shiny black Honda CRV grooving to the music in her headphones, making her tight blonde curls bounce around her angular face.

"See you later," Ariel said, bumping Sam on the shoulder as she strode past her. Ariel went behind the cars and snuck up on Shelby. She tip-toed up behind her, then pounded on the roof of the car with her fists, making Shelby leap off the hood of her car.

She whipped around, her eyes scrunched together in a mix of anger and fear. When she realized it was Ariel, she grinned, putting her hand over her heart. "Ariel Jane, you about killed me. You could've just waved and said hi."

"But what's the fun in that?"

"I take it you're coming over then?" Shelby asked, raising one eyebrow as Ariel opened the passenger door and slid into the seat.

"Yes! I told you this at lunch."

Shelby thought for a moment, sort of recalling the situation, but not really caring. Ever since third grade, they'd invited themselves over to each other's houses whenever they felt like it. Only twice in their entire friendship did one of them seriously have to say no. The first was when Sam had the stomach flu so bad she pooped her pants, and the other was the day after Dad's accident. Cheryl had felt bad she hadn't let Ariel see Shelby that day, so the next day she made up for it by letting her sleep over. It wasn't a fun memory, but Ariel was grateful for the sleep-over. Shaking the thoughts form her head, she turned up the radio. They blasted the music for the quick drive to Shelby's house.

"Mom, we're home!" Shelby announced into the large open foyer as they walked inside, slinging backpacks in a pile unceremoniously.

A woman who looked like a carbon copy of Shelby with a few more forehead wrinkles appeared in the doorframe separating the sitting room and the kitchen. "Hey girls. Help yourself to snacks. Ariel, are you staying for dinner?" Mrs. Blaine asked, wiping her floury hands on her apron.

"Not tonight," Ariel said, "Mom already made dinner plans for tonight."

"We'll send some leftovers home with you. I made enchiladas, and I made way too much. I'm still not used to cooking when Paul isn't here."

Paul, Shelby's older brother, had moved to college for his first semester. The bottomless pit that was his stomach would easily devour his own nine-by-thirteen pan of enchiladas. Ariel was sure their grocery bill had decreased by half since his move. Ariel followed Shelby upstairs and to her room, bellyflopping on the bed.

"So, what did you want to tell me?" Shelby asked, pulling the bench out from beneath her vanity. "You said this morning you had something to talk about. Did you and Kyle finally kiss?"

"God no," Ariel shook her head, pushing away the warm feeling his name conjured up inside her before her cheeks turned red. "You know that will never happen. My news is much less fun than that."

"You got a B on the chemistry test! Oooo-" Shelby feigned shock and awe. She knew if that happened, Ariel would've come running to her in tears, not casually saying she wanted to talk later. "C'mon, what happened?"

Ariel looked down at her hands, picking at her nails. "Mom lost her job."

The air in the room changed. The playfulness was replaced by concern. Shelby moved onto the bed next to her, draping her arm over her shoulders. "Oh, Ari, that's horrible. What happened?"

"Not sure, she didn't say much. Just that the company was having financial difficulties and that they were having to let people go."

"Isn't your mom their accountant?"

"Yeah, and she knew they were being stupid with their money. There were plenty of times she came home telling me about how she'd tried to tell them about what was going on, but they brushed her off. They ignored her. And because of their own stupid asses, my mom loses her job?" Ariel choked on the tears that were demanding to be let loose. "It's not fair." The injustice of it all overwhelmed her and sobs replaced words. Shelby held her as she cried, letting her friend release what she'd been keeping bottled up all day.

When Ariel took a deep breath and her shoulder relaxed, Shelby spoke up. "That's really fucking unfair. Your Mom deserves so much better than them. Maybe this is the universe forcing her to find the next best thing! She definitely hasn't been happy there. I heard her complain about it all the time, I imagine you did too, yeah?"

Ariel nodded, wiping her nose with the back of her sweatshirt sleeve. "Yeah. And she'd been casually looking, but after Dad died she stopped. Which I get, that's a lot of change and unknown. But now we're here, and this sucks. We have no money coming in and I don't know what our finances look like but growing up they always talked about how we had to budget, watch our spending, that we might have to cut back on things…."

Shelby grabbed her friends face in her hands and held it within inches of her own. "You. Are. Fine. For. Money." she said firmly. "Trust me. There's no way you live in a house like yours without a good chunk of savings."

"You think?"

"I know. No offense, but your family's kinda bougie," Shelby winked. "You're not rich like the Hocker family, but you're definitely richer than us. So, I think you've got some wiggle room."

"Thanks," Ariel chuckled.

"I know this sucks and it's scary, but at the risk of being cliché—"

"It's going to be okay?" Ariel asked, already knowing what she was going to say.

Shelby nodded once in affirmation. "It's going to be okay." She hopped off the bed and motioned to her vanity chair. "Now. I've been watching a new makeup tutorial and I need to try it out. Please, have a seat in my chair."

Ariel rolled her eyes but obliged her friend. As Shelby set up an array of pretty glass bottles and eyeshadow palettes, Ariel felt a wave of gratitude for her friend. They'd been through thick and thin together over the past nine years. She'd been her biggest supporter when Dad died, and Ariel had returned the support when Shelby lost both sets of her grandparents in the same year. But it wasn't just the grief that bonded them, it was the high moments too. Shelby had never been a runner, but she still was at every cross country and track meet. Ariel went to every band and choir concert despite not knowing a saxophone from a clarinet.

"Look straight ahead," Shelby instructed. "And relax your face. You're gonna get wrinkle lines if you look like that."

"Like what? This is just my face."

"Just, take a breath in. Good. Now breathe out." Shelby stepped back to observe her friend's face. "Better."

"Thanks?" Ariel asked, not sure if it was a compliment or not. Shelby got to work spreading the cream-colored lotion over her face.

"What about your Colorado trip?" Shelby asked as she worked. "Isn't that next week?"

"Yeah. I'm still going, Colorado State is footing the whole bill so expenses aren't an issue. I'm not sure if Mom's going though."

"Why wouldn't she if money isn't the problem there?"

"Because she could be using that time to look for jobs and go to interviews."

"Oh, I guess that makes sense. But it takes forever to get interviews. From what I've heard from my dad, it takes a long time to find a new job." Sensing Ariel's tension at this statement, she added, "But that's not always the case."

"I hope not."

"Well, if she doesn't go with, I'll take her place," Shelby said, turning to grab a brush off the vanity. She dabbed it into a rosy, pink powder. "I'll be Mama Shelby."

Ariel laughed at the image of Shelby in mom jeans and a leather shoulder bag, drilling the cross coach about the opportunities for her daughter. "Be careful or I'll take you up on that."

"Oh I'm one hundred percent serious," Shelby said. "I'm sure my mom won't mind."

"Haha, I think she might have opinions on you missing class."

"I'm a straight A student, not much for her to be worried about, is there?"

Ariel held up her hands. "Hey, if you want to be the one to start that fight, be my guest. You're welcome to come along."

Suddenly the bedroom door swung open and in waltzed Kyle. "No one told me there were free makeovers today. What gives?"

"Kyle Hanson, you scared the daylights outta me!" Shelby exclaimed, stomping a foot. "I could've poked Ariel's eye out."

"Sorry," he shrugged.

"Yeah, you would've been getting a bill from my eye doctor if anything had happened," Ariel said, twisting around in her seat. Kyle was dressed in his typical jeans and t-shirt, the bottom of his pants frayed from always stepping on them. No matter how many times his mom had tried to hem them, he never let her. "My mom lost her job."

His demeanor turned from playful to serious. "Ari, that sucks. I'm sorry. What happened?"

Ariel relayed the story to him, already tiring of repeating it. Thankfully, Kyle and Shelby were her only close friends, so after this retelling, she was done. "So now she doesn't have an income and come to think of it, she probably doesn't have health insurance either which means I don't have health insurance which means—" Thoughts of the emergency room and the stitches in her hand flashed before her eyes. How much would that have cost without health insurance?

"Hey," Kyle said, grabbing her by the shoulders. "Look at me."

Ariel looked at his hazel brown eyes, full of a surprising amount of concern.

"You don't have to worry about any of that," Kyle assured her. "First, that's your mom's problem to solve, not yours. What kid thinks about health insurance? Second, my dad's a paramedic. He can give you stitches and fix you up free of charge anytime."

"Ha, thanks," Ariel chuckled. "Good to know I can at least get patched up. But hopefully that won't be necessary. I'm not planning on cutting my hand or breaking anything any time soon."

"Good," Kyle said, nodding. "Now, can we talk about something more fun? I came over here to let loose after that calc test."

"Close your eyes," Shelby instructed Ariel. "Let me put the finishing touches on her and then—"

"Hot tub and ice cream?" Shelby, Ariel, and Kyle said in unison. They broke into laughter, the belly aching, heart healing kind. Friends made it easier to face hard things, and Ariel was grateful for that.

Chapter 4

The conversation at both tables was lively, as was the air in the restaurant. There weren't many patrons at Denny's on a Saturday night, but both the girls' and boys' cross-country teams had enough energy to fill the faux fifties diner with their youthful energy. Ariel did her best to absorb every last bit of it—the buttery aroma of pancakes and bacon wafting from the kitchen, the clinking of silverware on plates hot from the dishwasher, the smiles on her teammates' faces. This was their post-season ritual. Both teams got together for one last post-race meal of diner food and relived the highlights of the season.

"Ariel, how's your hand?" asked Olivia, one of her teammates, from across the table.

Ariel held up her hand, wiggling her fingers. "Good as new. Still a little sore though."

"And ugly," Kyle scoffed from behind her.

Ariel twisted around in her seat, swatting the side of his head with an open palm. The boys team sat directly behind the girls, no table or booth large enough to hold both teams. "No one asked you."

He rubbed the spot where her palm had connected, puppy dog eyes feigning hurt. "I can't believe you'd strike your best friend."

Ariel rolled her eyes, reaching to do it again but this time he dodged her. "You wish you had that title."

"Sorry bro, you'll never take it back from me," Shelby said through a mouthful of apple pie.

Kyle gave her a stink eye. "I still can't believe that you gave that title to her. You've only known each other since what, third grade? Ari...." He leaned forward, resting his hand over hers on top of the chair back. "... there are pictures of us sharing a bathtub."

Ariel yanked her hand away, laughing. "We were barely a year old."

"Exactly! Friends since the very beginning."

"Best guy friend." Ariel conceded.

"I'll take it." Kyle winked, turning back to his own table of conversation.

As Ariel turned back around, she caught the mischievous look in Shelby's eye. "Don't you say anything."

"I wasn't going to." Shelby dropped her gaze to focus on cutting another piece of pie, but not before she made a face at Olivia that communicated a shared opinion.

Olivia elbowed the girl next to her. "Nova, what do you think? Does Kyle have a thing for Ariel?"

"Obviously," Nova said, tucking her short black hair behind an ear. "No doubt about that one."

"See?" Olivia said, grinning. "Nova's a neutral party and even she agrees. Everyone sees it but you."

"Maybe I'm just the only clear headed one here," Ariel said, sticking her tongue out at her friends.

All the girls exchanged knowing glances but didn't say another word about the suspected feelings between

Ariel and Kyle. The two had been neighbors-turned-best-friends since they were in diapers, but the past year things had changed. There were more flirty exchanges and long glances, and Ariel enjoyed the warm fuzzy feeling he gave her every time a touch lingered.

"So, what's everyone's plan for the off season?" Olivia asked, leaning back with her hands behind her head. "Anyone running in the snow to stay in shape for track?"

"Mm-hmm. It's good training for the hip flexors," Ariel said, grateful for the change in subject.

"Well, we all knew you were gonna," Nova said with a teasing eye roll. "But I'm not going to do a dang thing. Maybe in January I'll hop on the treadmill or something. But no way am I running outside in the snow."

"C'mon, we need to be the best relay team this year!" Ariel insisted. "Don't we want to go back and win state instead of take second?"

"Sure, but not all of us can run forever like you do." Shelby shrugged. "I need a break from training. But I promise, as soon as the holidays are over, I'm back at it."

"Fair enough. Olivia?"

"I'm Team Break. Sorry, you'll have to do your runs on your own. You should take a break and see what happens."

"I'd go crazy, that's what would happen." Ariel laughed. "Running is the only thing that keeps me sitting still during school."

"Didn't Coach Bobbi say you're still off running for another week?" Shelby asked, squinting at her.

"I mean..."

"Oh, c'mon!" Shelby chided.

"Yeah, c'mon, Ari," Kyle said, turning around again to interrupt them.

"Eavesdrop much? Mind your own business." She playfully shoved his arm off the back of the booth.

"Never." He threw her a mischievous grin. "You do know even the best professional runners have off seasons, right? Like, they don't run for months at a time."

"That's a valid point," Ariel admitted. "But then again, not all of them do. Maybe I'm just someone who doesn't need it."

"That's not true and you know it, but whatever ya say." Kyle rolled his eyes, turning back to whatever conversation the boys were having at their table.

A team of waitresses appeared, arms full of plates containing a myriad of pies, shakes, and French fries. "Ooo thank God y'all are here," Ariel said, clapping with excitement. During cross country season, she was diligent about her diet: chocolate only on Saturdays, no sodas, and no more than one slice of pizza a week. When training or races got too hard, she just imagined the milkshake and French fries waiting for her at the end of the season.

"Okay, I'm just going to set this all down in the middle and leave you all to figure out whose is whose, all right?" The waitress said. The team nodded in agreement. They waited for her to set down the last of the plates and shakes before they started divvying.

"Chocolate shake and fries," Ariel called out.

"That's mine!" Olivia said, eagerly reaching out.

"Oreo pie and fries?"

"Mine!" Nova claimed.

The rest of the team grabbed their food items. Ariel reached for the vanilla shake and fries, happily dipping a fry in the ice cream. All her worries about what was next melted away. The only thing she had to worry about tonight was if she should get a second milkshake or not.

"Are you guys looking forward to the college day next week?" Olivia asked as she loaded up a fork with so much whipped cream you could barely see the pumpkin pie beneath it.

"Eh, kind of," Shelby said, shrugging. "I already know where I'm going."

"Lucky you," Nova said. "I'm still debating between Iowa State and University of Missouri. Both have recruited me for running but I just don't know what I want to actually study."

"Do you have to know right now?" Ariel asked.

"No, but I'd like to have an idea because Iowa State and Missouri don't have all of the same majors."

"Fair. Do you know what area?"

"Either criminal justice or pre-med."

"Flip a coin!" Shelby suggested.

"That feels a bit reckless, leaving a huge life decision up to a coin flip?"

"The universe will make happen whatever needs to happen," Shelby teased, wiggling her eyebrows.

"What about you, Ariel?" Nova asked, changing the subject away from her.

"Probably going to end up at the University of Colorado. In fact, I have a recruiting trip out there next week."

Olivia ate the last piece of her pie and pushed the plate away. "That's exciting! Why them?"

"They have the environmental science program I want to do, plus their team culture is great. At least in theory. I'm hoping that's still true when I go out there."

"Well, you'll have to let us know how it goes!" Nova said. "I loved my Missouri trip."

Ariel nodded in reply, taking a large bite of milkshake dipped French fry. As the conversation continued around the table, Ariel's thoughts drifted to the upcoming visit. She was excited to meet her potential teammates and see the training facilities. But the idea of being so far away from home made her stomach churn. With her dad's death eight months ago, and now her mom losing her job, everything felt so upside down and she wasn't convinced that one more thing to uproot her life would be a good thing.

"Oh well," she thought. "There's only one way to find out."

Chapter 5

Monday morning came too soon, and it was time to go back to school after riding the high of the weekend.

"Morning," Ariel greeted her mom and Sam as she walked into the kitchen, rubbing the sleep from her eyes. She was shocked to see Sam awake and dressed so early, but then remembered she had an interview after school.

"Are you excited for today?" Cheryl asked, sliding a plate of steamy blueberry muffins in front of her daughters perched at the kitchen island.

Ariel shrugged. She knew what her mom was referring to, but she didn't particularly want to talk about it. It was college day at school. The day where nearby schools set up a booth in the gym so students can talk to their recruiters. Ariel had been speaking to athletic reps since late sophomore year and while she liked the recruiters and their free goodies, she wasn't in a particularly social mood today. But there were a few out of state schools coming today to meet her, so she'd have to shove those antisocial feelings away and put on her best game face. On one hand, it was exciting. On the other, Ariel just didn't want to deal with it today.

"I for one am looking forward to hearing all about it when you get home," Cheryl said when Ariel didn't offer up anything. "It's your college future we're planning for!"

"Oh I know," Ariel said. "Just doesn't seem like it should be this soon."

"You're telling me," Cheryl laughed, shaking her head. "Feels like just yesterday you were running around in your diaper in the front yard, waving a stick in your hand."

"I can still go do that if it makes you feel better. I'll just wear a bathing suit and run around the front yard for a warmup."

"Only if I can film it and put it on Insta," Sam said.

"You wish." Ariel glared at Sam.

"Girls," Mom chided. She gave them both a look, and the tension eased. She glanced at the clock, wiping her floury hands on her waist apron. "I have to get ready for my job interview. You two good to get yourselves to school?"

"Yes, Mom," Sam rolled her eyes. "Just like we have been since freshman year."

"Where's your interview?" Ariel asked, curious. This was the first they were hearing about their mom's plans for the day. Usually, she was more than forthcoming with what her day held.

"A local accounting firm is looking for someone to do their books, be their front office person. Nothing exciting, but it'd be a paycheck."

"Good luck," they said in unison.

Cheryl smiled halfheartedly. "Thanks. Have a good day girls, Love you."

"Love you, Mom."

* * *

"Miss Hart, it's a pleasure to meet you in person." The University of Washington recruiter was much shorter than Ariel had pictured him. He stood all of five feet tall and looked to be ninety pounds sopping wet. After studying his face and hearing him speak, it was easy to tell he wasn't fifty-five, despite his horn-rimmed glasses and sweater vest.

"You too," Ariel said, extending her hand. For what he lacked in appearance, he made up for with a firm handshake, the type her dad would have approved of.

"Take a seat," Mr. Andrews said, motioning to the folding chair in front of the booth.

Ariel obliged, the metal legs dragging on the plastic tarp laid over the gymnasium floor to protect the specially treated wood. As of three years ago, it was a brand-new floor and ever since they'd gone to great lengths to protect it. The one good thing about the tarp was that it dampened the noise in the gym, a much-needed effect when the entire senior class was in the room.

"So let's talk cross! Your performance this past season was stellar. Congratulations on your records. And so sorry about how things ended. I'm sure that's not what you were hoping for."

"No, not at all," Ariel said, shaking her head but smiling. She held up her hand to show off the healing scar. "But thankfully it wasn't my foot, and it was a minor injury at that."

"I wouldn't call needing stitches a minor injury," Mr. Andrews said, cocking one eyebrow. "You've healed wonderfully."

"Thank you. Mr. Andrews, I wanted to ask—"

He held up his hand. "Please, call me Doug."

"Doug, what is the training schedule like and how does it balance with school? If I come to run for UW, that's fantastic. I want to run. But I also want to walk away with my degree. And to do that, there must be some type of balance that's supported by the coaching staff."

"Of course," Doug nodded. He pulled a few papers and a folder out from somewhere underneath the folding table draped in a UW banner. "We have a strong culture of academics within our athletic department, which is not something most schools can say. What are you interested in studying?"

"Double major in environmental sciences and English," Ariel nodded firmly.

"Interesting," Doug smiled. "That's a different choice than most of our athletes. They tend to lean more towards—"

"Let me guess, kinesiology and biomechanics? Athletic training? Physical therapy?"

"You took the words right out of my mouth."

"I like a variety of things. I love to run, but I don't want to run and then go study running for eight hours every day and have to sit through hours of lectures about it."

"Fair enough. Regardless, you'll find that students aren't forced to choose between attending practice and attending lectures. We have practices two times a day, and you only have to attend one during the school year. That way, it allows for more schedule flexibility with what classes you want and need to take."

"That's great to hear. It's important to me that I'm able to do well in school."

"Of course, that's the main reason you go to school."

"I mean, if you're an athlete a lot of the time you go to school so you can continue to be an athlete if we're being honest," Ariel laughed. "What else can you tell me about the program?"

"Well, for you specifically, we think you'd absolutely love the Washington area. I hear you like to train on hills, and Washington has plenty of those. We frequently train on local trails, and not just golf courses. And I know you're no stranger to running in the elements. In fact, when I look back at your race statistics, most of your best times have come during inclement weather."

"Yeah, I've noticed," Ariel said. "I think it's because I just want to be done, and the faster I run, the faster I'm done."

Doug laughed. "Well, whatever it is, it works. As I'm sure you already know, Washington is beautiful, but it sure is rainy. Which for a lot of students can be challenging," he pointed out. "But I know our time today is limited, so I wanted to give you this information here." He handed her a folder. "Inside is my personal contact information. I know you already have it, but in case you lose it, it's there."

Ariel opened the folder and thumbed through its contents. "Is this a plane ticket?" she asked, not believing what she was seeing. She pulled out a thin piece of receipt paper.

"It is," Doug said, a toothy grin spreading across his face. "We want you to come out and tour our campus. I know it's a long way from here in central Iowa, and the plane tickets to Seattle are expensive. We don't want cost to be a barrier to determining if UW is the right place for your running career. We think you would be a fantastic addition to our team, and together we can make some great cross-country headlines."

Ariel examined the ticket for a date but didn't see one. "When is this for?"

"For whenever you're available to come out. I can clear my schedule at a moment's notice for you. Our potential athletes are our number one priority this time of the year."

"What about your current athletes?" Ariel asked, raising an eyebrow. "How do you support them after they've signed with you?"

"That's a great question. We provide world-class training facilities that you have access to twenty-four seven. We pair newer athletes with experienced members of the team to provide a type of mentorship program. You'll have access to athletic training staff seven days of the week, which includes massage therapists. You also have access to the athletic spa with cold soak tubs, sauna, salt rooms—"

"Like Himalayan salt rooms?"

"The one and only," Doug smiled. "It's new, thanks to a grant that we received from an alum."

"That's impressive," Ariel said, shocked at the extent of the facilities. "Let me look at my schedule and talk with my mom about when we can visit. I'm looking at all my options right now, but UW is very high on my list. I look forward to visiting."

"We look forward to having you," Doug said, standing up and offering out his hand again. "And your mom and sister are welcome to visit too. Their airfare will be covered as well."

Ariel couldn't believe it. Not one, but two schools, wanted her so badly they were willing to fly her whole family out just for a tour. "I really appreciate it. I'll be in touch soon."

"Okay, sounds good. Take care."

Ariel walked away from the booth feeling energized. She'd been hearing from recruiters since late sophomore year. This wasn't new territory for her. But now it was getting real. The lengths to which schools were willing to offer amenities to get her to say yes was unbelievable. She'd been begging her mom to go on a vacation for years now, and with her recent job loss, Ariel had all but given up on that dream. And if she decided she couldn't go to Colorado with her in a few days, maybe she could be convinced to go to Washington. She smiled, a warm glow in her heart. The last year had been tough, but the universe always balanced it out.

She had one more school to talk to, and it was the busiest table in the whole place: Iowa State University. More likely than not, over half her class would end up attending.

She made her way over to the booth and quickly spotted the person she was looking for. "Hey Charles," she said, waving her hand above the crowd.

The middle-aged man dressed in a red and gold polo shirt scanned the crowd until he found her. "Hey! Ariel! Come on back, let's talk."

Ariel wove thru the people and around to the back of the table.

"How've you been?" Charles asked, sitting next to her on the bleachers. "Looks like you've already collected some good stuff." He nodded at the full bag next to her feet- overflowing with folders and college swag.

"Oh yeah. Great stuff. Whatcha got for me? I'm interested in baseball hats and good sweatshirts. The kind with the soft lining, not just the smooth outer layer."

Charles laughed. "You joke, but I do have stuff for you." Charles pulled out his own swag bag and handed it to her. "There's a sweatshirt, but not a baseball hat. I'll get you one though."

"I was kidding," Ariel laughed.

"I'll do anything to get you to come run for us," Charles said. "Well, almost anything. What can I do to get you interested in Iowa State?"

"Well for starters you can move the school about five hundred miles away and add a beach."

"You know, I mentioned that at a board meeting, but they all said we didn't have the funds for that."

"Damn. Well, if that's not going to happen. I'll settle for good school/running balance, seven day a week access to a massage therapist, and all my travel to and from meets comped. I can't afford to travel that much."

"Done and done."

"Well that was easy," Ariel laughed. "Should I ask for a private jet?"

"A semiprivate one will work," Charles said. "But all jokes aside, are you considering Iowa State? I know you have some flashier schools interested—"

"I am." She nodded. "To be honest with you, it's not my first choice. But, after all that's happened this past year, being closer to home might be exactly what I need."

"I'm sorry about what happened to your dad," Charles said, his voice somber. "I didn't know him, but my own dad went to school with him. Said he was always quiet, but when he spoke, he was hilarious."

"Yeah, that sounds about right." Ariel smirked. "He was never a man of many words, but the words he did say were… powerful."

"Well, when can we get you up for a full tour and a day on the town in Ames?" Charles asked. "I know we're not as glamourous as Seattle or Colorado, but you know as well as I do there's a lot of charm. And who doesn't like to be wined and dined for free?"

"Can't argue with you there. Maybe end of the month?"

"Sounds like a plan. You have my card. You give me a call with a few days' notice and you all can come up and I'll introduce you to everyone. Your running talent is unprecedented, and we'd absolutely love to work with you. Plus, there's no better story than a hometown girl going to her hometown college and becoming a famous professional runner. You'll have streets named after you in Ames when you make it big."

Ariel smiled, imagining a green and white sign along the streets of Iowa State that said "Iowa State: Alma mater of Ariel Hart, Olympic runner, professional runner." "Thank you, Charles. I'll be in touch."

Filled with gratitude, Ariel walked out of the gym, satisfied with how the day went, but eager for some quiet time to process everyone she spoke with today. The idea of college was exciting. She had no idea where she wanted to go, but she did know one thing. She needed to pack.

* * *

"But Mom, why not?" Ariel begged later that night. "These are essentially all expenses paid trips. We can schedule the one to Washington after the first of the year, which gives you plenty of time to find a job and get settled."

"Yes, I understand that, but it's not like I'll have vacation time. And if I don't have a job, heaven forbid, I'm going to have to be using that time for interviews and applications," Cheryl said, leaning against the kitchen island. She had a blue and white dish cloth slung over her shoulder. Ariel had run home excited to tell her mom all about what she'd learned from the recruiters. The last thing she'd expected was for this conversation to turn into an argument.

"And besides, we're going to Colorado the end of this week, so you can't say we're not going anywhere."

"Yeah, but what if I don't end up liking it?" Ariel pleaded, doing her best not to sound whiney even though all she wanted to do was stomp her foot and pout.

"Then we'll figure it out then," Cheryl said, pinching the bridge of her nose with her fingers. "It's just too much financially right now."

"Don't we have savings to help us get by?" Ariel asked, under her breath before she could even think about what she was saying.

"Not since we had to pay for a funeral," Cheryl snapped back.

Ariel went silent. She hadn't expected her mom to pull the Dead Dad Card ever, much less during this conversation. She felt her stomach churn with guilt, and anger. "I'm sorry. I didn't realize."

Cheryl shook her head, her face softening slightly. "You have nothing to be sorry for. You had no way of knowing that, nor should you be concerned about it." She walked around the side of the kitchen island and sat next to Ariel, draping her arm around her daughter's shoulders. "Look, I'm not saying you can't go. You can go, but you'd have to go on your own. I can't afford to miss work or interviews."

"When did money become such an issue? After you lost your job or after Dad died?"

"It's not really an issue, it's just that—"

"No. Tell it to me straight, that's the least I deserve after everything that's happened," Ariel said, her voice firm. They locked eyes for a moment, Ariel unwavering in her need to know what exactly was going on.

Cheryl sighed. "We were okay after you Dad passed, but barely. The medical bills, funeral, and lawyer fees were a lot, and we lost his income and my income was barely a third of his. And now I don't even have that. I'm not worried about us being able to put food on the table, but I'm not sure if keeping this house is feasible."

It felt like someone dropped a boulder in Ariel's stomach. The thought of losing this beautiful home she loved so soon after losing a parent was too much. She stared ahead at the wall in front of her- a wall she remembered walking through when it was just the studs and wall joists. Playing ghosts and running through the wall framing had been her and Sam's favorite game to play as kids when Mom and Dad dragged them out to the house to check on the progress. And for that all to just be gone?

"I don't feel great," Ariel said, placing her hand over her stomach.

"Do you want some Tums?" Cheryl asked, a worried look on her face. "Or some saltine crackers?"

"No, it's fine. I just want to shower and go to bed. Today was a lot," she said, sitting up. "I'm sorry I didn't understand. I didn't mean to make you feel bad about having to say no."

"Oh, honey, don't even give that a second thought. I never expected you to know all of that, in fact I did what I could to make sure you didn't know. I'm just sorry I can't say yes, because I really want to."

"I know you do."

"And you can still go look at those schools. In fact, I want you to go look at the schools. You need to decide where you want to pursue your education!"

"I know, and I will. But tonight I just want to go to bed and forget I have to make a decision. It's overwhelming sometimes."

"I understand. Well go take a hot shower and I'll come say goodnight before you turn your light out."

"Okay," Ariel said, pushing back and standing up. "I take it you're not coming to Colorado?"

"I wouldn't miss it for the world. We're gonna live it up that weekend!"

"Really?" she asked, skeptical.

"Really. I won't have any interviews that day, and I've already done a lot of work getting applications submitted. We all deserve a little fun." Cheryl winked.

Ariel sighed, the uneasiness in her stomach settling ever so slightly. "I love you, Mom."

"I love you too, honey."

Ariel gave her a half smile before turning around and walking upstairs. As she turned on the faucet and waited for the water to warm up, she couldn't help but let her mind run wild with all the possibilities that their financial hardships might bring. "Lose the house, live in a trailer, trailer gets blown away by a tornado this spring…" She stepped into the shower, hot water scalding her skin until the warmth radiated throughout her body. It would all work out, she reminded herself. It always did.

Chapter 6

The next day, Ariel watched the red second hand on the clock as it crept toward the top of the hour. Fifty-seven, fifty-eight, fifty-nine… the last bell of the day rang overhead, right on time.

"Okay, have a good rest of the day. Tomorrow we'll finish up the last chapter of To Kill a Mockingbird," Ms. Stevens said, flipping her book shut along with her students. Thankfully, she wasn't one of the teachers that insisted she dismissed students, not the bell, so Ariel was always out of the last class on time. Ariel gathered her books and left the room, heading down the hallway to her locker.

Sam had beaten her there, already shoving books in her backpack. Ariel spun the combo lock until it opened and made quick work of selecting the books she needed for homework that night.

"Are you taking the biology book with you?" Ariel asked, peeking into her sister's bag.

"Yeah, I didn't finish that stupid in class assignment today."

"Cool, neither did I. We'll just use your book. I've got the calculus book, so you don't have to bring it."

"Thank God," Sam sighed, zipping her bag closed. She hoisted it onto one shoulder. "Because this is already heavy enough."

"It's a twin perk," Ariel laughed. "We get to split the textbook load."

"We're lucky we're in the same classes."

The girls closed their lockers and made their way through the sea of other students all trying to leave.

"Hey! Ari!" Ariel turned to see Kyle waving at her. He was easy to pick out on account of him being one of the tallest boys in the whole school, his bleach blonde waves adding to the obviousness. He looked like a California surfer boy lost in the Midwest. He wove through the crowd until he was standing next to them. "What're you doing tonight?"

Ariel shrugged. "Going for a run and then doing hours of homework judging how heavy this backpack is."

"Can I come over and do the calc homework with you guys? I suck at it," Kyle said.

"Sure, misery loves company," Sam said, popping a piece of gum in her mouth. "Not sure we'll be much help, though."

"Speak for yourself! I'm not that bad at calc," Ariel protested.

"Oh, come on, you hate it," Sam said, calling her out as they made their way out of the school building.

"Okay, yeah, I hate it," Ariel admitted, shaking her head.

"Then we'll hate it together," Kyle smiled. "See you at home, Ari." He playfully punched Ariel in the shoulder. Ariel laughed and met his lingering gaze as he walked off towards his car at the other end of the parking lot. He never even said bye to Sam.

Sam stared at the side of Ariel's head until she looked at her. "What?"

"You know what. That dude has it bad for you."

Ariel's eyes widened. She shook her head. "Not in the slightest. We've been friends since we were babies."

"No shit, I was there. I've been friends with him since I was 5 too, but you don't see him playfully punching me in the shoulder."

"Okay, one time."

"Uh, no. Not one time. Many times. He's always poking and pushing you. Me? He's never once done that."

Ariel couldn't argue against that. It was getting to the point she couldn't deny knowing about his feelings, or that she had the same feelings for him. But him having a crush on her? The same boy she used to dig up worms with? She contemplated the idea the whole car ride home. On one hand, every time he touched her sent sparks down her spine. She loved spending time with him and they always laughed a lot. But on the other, what if things didn't work out and she lost one of her oldest friends? Was she willing to risk it all? When they pulled into the driveway, she noticed Mom's car wasn't in the garage. As soon as she parked the car, Ariel checked her phone for a text. There wasn't one.

"Did Mom text you?" Ariel asked. Sam was already on her phone, scrolling through messages.

"Um, nope. I take it she didn't text you either?"

Ariel shook her head. "No. That's super weird. Call her."

"Already on it," Sam said, bringing the phone to her ear. While she waited for Mom to answer, she got out of the car and into the house. "No answer."

A bolt of fear ran like electricity down Ariel's spine. Mom was always home by the time they were done with school, and if she wasn't, they knew why well in advance. Had something happened? Images of blue and white police lights ran through Ariel's head, and she swore she heard an ambulance wailing in the distance.

"Hey, Ariel." Sam's firm voice pulled Ariel out of her head and back to where they were standing, safe and sound around the kitchen island. The same kitchen island where she'd been sitting when she learned her Dad wasn't going to make it out of the hospital. What if something happened to Mom? What if they ended up as orphans? Sam's dark blue eyes were full of heaviness. "She's okay. She probably just got stuck in traffic and can't text right now."

Almost on cue, the sound of the garage door opening made them both jump. "Oh thank fucking God," Ariel breathed, the anvil of fear lifting off her heart. The girls waited for their mom to walk into the kitchen a few moments later and when she did, her face was frazzled.

"I know, I know, I'm sorry I didn't text you earlier. And I didn't even see your call until just now," Cheryl started hurriedly. "I just got caught in a lot of traffic."

"It's all good," Sam said, taking hold of the conversation before Ariel could let loose about how scared she was. They were alike in many ways, but Sam always was the cool, calm, and collected one. Even when they were babies, Ariel was the crier and Sam was the self-soother. "Everything okay?"

"Well, um, yes and no," Mom said, not meeting their gazes. She set her purse and briefcase on the counter and stared at the granite countertop.

"What does that mean? How'd the interview go?" Sam asked. She glanced at Ariel to make sure she wasn't about to explode. Her jaw was clenched, but other than that, she seemed to have it together.

Cheryl took a deep breath and looked up. It was clear she had been crying. "It was going okay until the interviewer asked me to drinks afterwards."

"What?!" Sam said, jaw hanging open.

"You mean like work drinks?" Ariel offered. "People do that in the corporate world, right?"

"They do, but that wasn't what this guy was going for," Cheryl said, pinching the bridge of her nose. "I thought maybe but then he put his hand on my thigh."

Sam's jaw hinged even further open if that was possible. Ariel felt her face redden.

"Are you kidding me!?" Ariel asked, the first to recover from the shock of what their mom had just told them. "What an ass."

Sam moved from the opposite side of the island to next to her mom, pulling her into a hug. "It'll be okay."

"I know it will be," she said softly. "It's just a shock. Especially for my first interview? That's not what I had in mind." Ariel joined in the hug, holding her mom and sister close. "Let's go sit down."

The women made their way to the living room, crowding onto the love seat together. They sat in silence for a few moments, all of their thoughts racing.

"What now?" Sam asked softly.

"Did you report him?"

"I did," Cheryl said, a bit of brightness coming back in her voice. "Who knows what will happen, but I sure as hell wasn't silent about it."

"Good," Sam said. "Hopefully the next person they interview won't have to deal with that douche."

"Hopefully not," Mom said with a sigh.

"I'm going to try again, but I think I won't go on another interview until after our trip," Cheryl said, sniffing. "I need a bit of a vacation after all this… stress."

"You can say bullshit, Mom," Sam encouraged.

Cheryl laughed. "I know I can, I just don't want to."

"I think you do," Sam said, eyeing her skeptically. "C'mon. Just this once. Say this is bullshit."

"It's bullshit, for sure," Ariel said, egging her mom on.

Cheryl's thin frown broke into a semblance of a smile. "It is some bullshit, isn't it?"

"There ya go!" Ariel and Sam said, excited their mom was letting loose. In their entire seventeen years on the planet, they'd only heard her say a curse word twice. And that word had been "ass" when someone rear-ended their car.

"It does help a little," Cheryl chuckled. "This is some grade A bullshit."

"Yeah it is!" Sam laughed. "And don't worry. I'm working on getting a job so I can help with bills until you find a job."

Cheryl shook her head. "That's great, honey. But I only want you to work if you want to. I don't want you to worry about bills. We still have money to put food on the table, gas in the cars, and make the minimum payments for the house. We just can't do much else."

"Like what else? We don't spend that much I didn't think," Ariel said, trying to comprehend the gravity of the situation. It didn't feel real. Just like when she got the news that Dad had been killed by a drunk driver, it felt like a bad dream. She'd thought getting a job would be easy for her mom. The news was always talking about how good the economy and job market was.

"Just be glad cross country is over," Cheryl laughed. "Whoever said running is a cheap sport clearly was not a runner."

Ariel laughed. "Yeah, those shoes do get expensive. What can we do to help?"

"I don't want you two to worry. I also didn't want to keep you in the dark. Looking for a new job is hard. But we're going to be okay. I want you both to just focus on your schoolwork, and we can talk about maybe not driving as much to help save on gas money."

"We'll ride with Kyle to school," Ariel said immediately.

Sam gave her sister a knowing glance but didn't say anything.

"Oh, that reminds me. Please don't tell your friends," Cheryl asked. "I know this is a lot, but I don't want the whole world to know, okay?"

Both girls nodded in agreement. Ariel felt a small pain of guilt, having already told both Kyle and Shelby. But she was sure her friends would keep the secret, and they wouldn't judge them one bit. Mom smiled at them.

"Are you guys good with spaghetti for dinner? I stole some Texas Toast from that company's breakroom freezer."

"Mom!"

"What?" she laughed. "After what that guy did, the least they could do was give me some damn garlic bread."

All three broke out in bellyaching laughter until tears of joy were streaming down their faces. It felt good to laugh, even in the face of devastating news. A ring of the doorbell interrupted their laugh session.

"Oh, Kyle's coming over to do homework with us," Ariel said. "Sorry I forgot to tell you."

Cheryl wiped away the tears from her cheeks. "That's fine, he's always welcome."

"Come in!" Ariel screamed at the top of her lungs, making Sam cover her ears.

"Jeez-us, you can't just go open the door?"

"No, that's too much work," Ariel teased. Kyle heard her and let himself in, kicking his shoes off on the welcome rug. He'd exchanged his old t-shirt he'd worn to school for a forest green Henley, his fresh cologne making Ariel's heart race.

"Take a chill pill, Ariel," she scolded herself mentally. "Now is not the time."

"Hi, Mrs. Hart," he said, giving her a nod. Upon seeing their tear-streaked faces, he paused. "Is everything all right?"

"Yes, Kyle," Ariel snorted. "They're tears of joy."

He laughed and shook his head. "Okay I'm not even going to ask. Can we get started on this calc homework before my brain quits on me?"

"Yes, you guys get to work on that, and I'll get dinner started," Mom said, slapping her knees as she stood up from the couch. "Kyle, you want spaghetti tonight?"

"I want spaghetti every night," he said.

Cheryl made her way into the kitchen and Sam, Ariel, and Kyle all pulled out their calculus textbooks and worksheets. Normally this was Ariel's least favorite subject, but tonight she was grateful for the distraction and the ability to do it with some of the people closest to her.

Chapter 7

"I got the job!" Sam said, bursting through the front door waving a denim and tan baseball hat above her head. Ariel was stretching on her yoga mat in front of the TV. She looked at her sister between her knees in her downward facing dog pose.

"Seriously? Who would hire your crazy ass?"

"Panera." She tossed her purse aside and skipped into the living room, throwing the hat on the yoga mat for Ariel to see. "The one on the north side of town, so we need to talk about me using the car. I figure since you like to run everywhere, I might be able to have it after school? When it starts to snow, we'll figure that part out. But for now I think that'll work."

"Yeah, that's fine. Wow, that was fast," Ariel said. She got herself out of the downward dog and sat in easy pose, admiring the hat of her sister's brand-new uniform. The idea of her sister at a job, acting professional, was hard to wrap her mind around. "And they hired you? Did you have to do an in-person interview?"

Sam snatched the hat back and placed it on her head, pulling her long blonde ponytail through the back of it. "Yes, I did, and they loved me, thank you very much."

"When do you start?"

"Next Tuesday. I'm just working two nights during the week, and then all day on Saturday. But during the summer I'll pick up more hours."

"Now I feel like a slacker," Ariel laughed.

"You have your running to focus on. That'll earn you more money through scholarships than you ever would earn at a job," Sam pointed out, plopping down onto the couch. "But me? I have to boost my resume with other things. My extracurriculars aren't as impressive as yours."

"I suppose you have a point," Ariel admitted. "Still, that's great you can help Mom pay some bills. I could probably manage to get a job too…" she trailed off, trying to brainstorm where she could work. Growing up in a small town was great, except for when it came to getting a job that wasn't at the grain elevator. Sure, she could work anywhere in Ankeny she wanted, but the gas money would end up taking most of the paycheck, so in the end it would be a wash.

"Seriously, just focus on your running for now. You've got recruitment trips, plus track season. And no one's gonna want you to run for their school next fall if you trade your training for bussing tables."

Ariel nodded. "I mean… you're not wrong."

"Of course I'm not wrong," Sam said, a smug look on her face. Her narrow nose crinkled between her eyes like it always did when she smiled or had a mischievous look. "How're you feeling about not being at Nationals this year?"

Ariel sighed. "It feels weird, but I've done a good job not thinking about it. When I do it makes me sad."

"I'm sorry I brought it up, but I figured it must be on your mind. And you know what our family shrink says—"

"If you want to heal it, you've got to feel it," Ariel repeated the therapist's mantra, refraining from rolling her eyes.

"Will it affect your school choice at all?" Sam asked, tucking her legs underneath herself on the couch.

"I feel like I'll have my pick of schools despite not being at Nationals. Not to sound arrogant, but the past four years of running outweigh one bad race, especially because I lost because someone tripped me, not because I ran poorly. I'm more worried about our immediate home situation than my college future. That's pretty set in stone, but this isn't."

"Well, you get through the rest of this school year and if after graduation you still want a job, we can look at getting you a job."

"I can look for a job whenever I want, with or without your permission," Ariel said, sticking her tongue out.

Sam held up her hands in surrender. "Obviously. You do you, boo."

"Does Mom know you got the job yet?" Ariel asked, changing the focus back on Sam.

"Not yet, but I don't see why she'd have a problem with it. She sounded pretty neutral the other night. It won't interfere with school, and it won't make me need to drive more."

Ariel wasn't sure how Mom would take it. It was one thing to think your daughter might get her first real job, it was another when it happened.

"Girls! Come here for a second," Cheryl called from her office upstairs.

"What's up?" they both asked, walking into the room.

"I want to show you this," Mom said, scooting her chair back so they could all see the computer screen. The Excel spreadsheet before them contained lots of numbers and categories.

"Is this a budget?" Ariel asked.

"That's exactly what it is," Mom nodded. "We've always had it, but now that you are almost adults, I figured it was time to teach you a little about money management."

"That sounds exciting," Sam said.

"You don't have to make fun of it," Mom started, but Sam cut her off.

"No, I'm serious. I want to learn how to be good with money. I'm lookin' to be a millionaire someday."

Cheryl laughed—grateful Sam was interested. She started explaining all the columns, the amounts, and what they meant. "You see this number down here?" She pointed to a light green box in the bottom right-hand corner of the screen. "This is how much money we have leftover at the end of the month. Right now, it's green because of my income and the life insurance payout from your father. But next month, it'll probably be red due to my loss of income."

"Does that mean we won't be able to pay the mortgage?"

"No, because that's accounted for up here." She pointed to the line items listed out in the body of the spreadsheet. "But it does mean that we can't spend any extra money on groceries or going out to eat. We're going to have to get creative with what we have at home."

"Or we can use some of the money from my first paycheck to buy pizza," Sam nonchalantly added.

"What do you mean?" Cheryl asked, turning to face her.

"I got the job!" Sam said, nearly bouncing with excitement. Ariel couldn't help but smile, it wasn't like her sister to get this excited about something.

"That was so quick," Cheryl said, taken aback. "That's really cool! Where are you working?"

"The Panera right up the road. I start Tuesday."

"And it won't interfere with your schoolwork?"

"Nope," Sam said firmly.

With her worries addressed, Mom grinned. "I'm proud of you, Sam. That's wonderful. You save that money for your college."

"And pizza every now and then for us," Sam reminded her. Ariel glanced at Sam, an odd welling of pride in her chest. She knew her sister— she would contribute half her paycheck to the general household fund, the other half to her college fund. Their mom would never ask her daughters to help pay the bills, but she'd be grateful for the help. With Dad gone, it was their time to step up and help run the household, lest they not have a household at all.

Chapter 8

Sam stood in front of her bed, staring at the multiple outfits she had laid out on her bed. "How long are we staying again?"

"Not long, we fly back Monday night," Ariel replied from her perch on the lounge chair in the corner of the room. "So you don't need a whole suitcase full of outfits."

"It's like you can read my mind." Sam picked two of the outfits and returned the shirts to the closet, the pants to their appropriate drawers. "What's the weather going to be like?"

"Cold and sunny."

Sam walked back to the closet and picked out several sweatshirts and a few different colored beanies. "You know, next time we go on vacation, let's go somewhere warmer."

"This isn't a vacation," Ariel said, tossing her phone aside. She'd been waiting on a certain someone to text her back and she was sick of staring at her phone.

Sam shrugged. "Sounds like the closest thing we've had to a vacation in years."

"I mean, maybe it is for you and Mom. I've got to bring my A game" Ariel said, stretching her arms above her head. "But at least we're gonna escape the state! When was the last time we went anywhere?"

"Six years ago, when we went down to Florida to visit Grandma and Grandpa."

"Okay, so I guess we can count this as a vacation. Partial for me," Ariel laughed. "It's not the most relaxing when I have to socialize and meet a bunch of new people. Especially because I have to impress them."

"Fair enough. At least you're more social than me. I'd die."

"This is true. Do you want help packing?" Ariel asked, bouncing from foot to foot. "I've got a ton of nervous energy I'd love to channel into organizing something."

"You can do it for me," Sam said, holding out her sweatshirts. "Actually, no. I don't trust your style judgement."

"That's probably a wise choice," Ariel laughed, not offended in the slightest. Her t-shirt and running tights style was not at all in line with her sister's much more fashion forward choices. Sam was always on top of trends. She almost never wore t-shirts and jeans unless the jeans were faded and strategically ripped and the t-shirts cropped. Sam had attempted to teach Ariel the basics of how to put an outfit together, and Ariel had really tried, but she just couldn't find the effort to maintain it in the morning when it was so easy to grab her favorite outfit and call it a day.

The great thing about her lack of fashion prowess though, was that it made for easy packing and light luggage. Ariel sauntered back to her room to finish packing and when she was done, she set her backpack beside her desk. She flopped on her bed and pulled out her phone.

"All packed for the UC trip this Friday!"

True to form, Shelby replied seconds later. *"Jealous! Bring me back some 'special' gummies."*

"You've never done an ounce of weed in your life."

"Yeah, cuz I haven't had access to edibles!"

Ariel rolled her eyes. Shelby was too much the goodie-two-shoes and she knew it. "Tell me about it tmrrw. I'm tired."

Ariel clicked through her phone and brought up Kyle's number, texting him the same news. He must've been on his phone because he responded immediately. "Congrats! That's cool. Where you staying?"

"No clue, but it's near UC. I'm excited to tour and meet the team."

"They'll love you."

Ariel felt her cheeks flush. *"Thanks. Gonna be weird thinkin of running somewhere new."*

"I bet. But you'll love it."

"Thanks. Tell you more tmrrw."

"Sounds good. Night!"

Ariel plugged her phone in and laid it on the nightstand, her head abuzz with anticipation for the weekend. She was packed, her friends were informed. Now all she had to do was make it to Friday.

                                    * * *

"Get in loser! Let's go!" Ariel yelled, leaning across the passenger seat. "I wanted to be on the road fifteen minutes ago!"

Sam moved leisurely, grabbing her suitcase, and arranging her backpack. She gingerly held two reusable Starbucks cups in her hand. One for hydration, one for caffeination, she always said.

"Ariel, be nice!" Mom demanded as she slid into the driver's seat. "We have plenty of time."

"The plane doesn't wait for us, you know," Ariel said, crossing her arms across her chest.

"Oh, I know," Sam said, settling into the back. She arranged her cups in the middle console, making sure they were snug. "But I really like those dramatic scenes in holiday movies where people run through the airport to get to their flights. It makes it so much more exciting."

"Well, it's the Des Moines airport, so it'll be more like a jog than anything. It'll take a lot to make that exciting," Ariel said as Cheryl put the car in reverse and backed down the driveway.

"I mean, we're going to be there three hours early anyway because someone's neurotic," Sam said, giving her the side eye.

"The last thing I want is to miss this flight," Ariel said, watching the cornfields pass out the window. "This is my future we're talking about."

"Girls," Mom interjected. "This is going to be a very long three days if this is how it's going to be. I know we haven't vacationed in a hot minute, but they're supposed to be fun."

"Fine," Ariel said, taking a deep breath and trying to focus on the fact that in a few hours, they'd be in Colorado, surrounded by mountains and people who loved the outdoors.

"I guess," Sam agreed. "While you two are touring the school, can I go do my own thing?"

"If by own thing you mean wander the campus on your own? Sure," Cheryl said, turning the keys and backing out of the garage. "But you're not going off in downtown Denver without us."

"The school's in Fort Collins, Mom," Ariel reminded her.

"Either way. You're not wandering around a random city by yourself."

"But-"

"It won't take that long and then we can go do whatever you want to do," Cheryl said, eyeing Sam through the rearview mirror. "Deal?"

"Fair enough I guess." Sam turned on the radio and pushed buttons until the music on her phone started playing. A slow jam with a reggae beat came on.

"I know we have different music tastes, but can we pick something a little more upbeat, please?" Ariel asked. "I can't stand the slow rap you listen to."

"Slow rap? You mean R&B?"

"You know what I mean. The chill, low-fi, rap stuff that people who wear beanies and those woven chevron sweatshirts listen too? The Rastafarian types."

"Wow, way to stereotype."

"I'm not saying it's a bad thing!" Ariel said. "I'm just saying that's who that music makes me think of. And chill out vibes isn't what this trip calls for! It calls for pump up, excitement!"

"I mean, I think it's appropriate vibes for this trip. We are going to Colorado."

"Yes, but not to smoke weed and walk around art galleries all day—"

"Now there's an idea," Sam said, raising an eyebrow. "That might not be what you're doing, but now that you mention it…. Mom can we go to a weed shop?"

"Absolutely not," she laughed. "Besides, you couldn't even get in. It's twenty-one and up."

"Yeah, but you can get in and get us some stuff to try," Sam pried. "They've got tons of fun edibles now. Cookies, gummies, brownies, you name it!"

"And how do you know about this stuff?" Cheryl asked, one eyebrow raised suspiciously.

"Because I go to public school?"

"Good save," Ariel laughed.

The traffic to the airport was minimal at three in the afternoon on a Friday as most people were still at work. And thankfully parking was plentiful. Cheryl quickly found a spot close to the terminal walkway.

"Everyone have everything?" Mom asked, grabbing her one bag out of the backseat.

"That I do," Sam said, grabbing only one of her cups.

"You bringing that?" Ariel asked, nodding to the container she'd left behind.

She shook her head. "Already drank it all."

"Girl, you're going to be peeing like a racehorse the whole flight."

"I'll be fine," Sam said, waving her off. "Let's get this show on the road! Vacation has started!"

The women made their way across the parking structure and into the airport terminal building. When they reached the top of the elevator, they saw the security line had all of ten people in it.

"See? We didn't need to get here this early," Sam jibbed. She popped the handle out on her bag and started weaving her way through the black-roped walkway. Ariel did a mental checklist as they made their way to the back of the security line. Driver's license, running shoes, sunglasses, toothbrush....

The small line moved quickly and soon enough they were presenting their boarding passes and IDs to the TSA agent, who thoroughly looked them over. "Have a safe trip," he said in a flat monotone that made one certain that he didn't care if you had a safe trip or not.

They moved quickly through security. Ariel was waiting for her bags on the other side of the scanner, crossing her fingers that her bag wouldn't be pulled aside. She had a knack for getting flagged. When she was ten, her shoes had been flagged and had to have them swabbed and sniffed by a bomb squad dog. Ever since then, something of hers always set off their sensors, and she was convinced that she was on a watch list somewhere.

Much to her delight, her bag continued down the conveyer belt, and she plucked it up before anyone could change their minds. She found a bench out of the way and reorganized her things while waiting for Mom and Sam.

"Wow, did you really make it through without setting off their bomb squad dogs?" Sam asked, equally surprised.

"I did! It's a good sign, we're off to a great start."

"Let's hope the rest of this trip goes the same way! My goal is to score some weed while we're out here."

"Samantha Jean, you're seventeen," Cheryl exclaimed having overheard her daughter's conversation. "Since when did you become obsessed with weed?

"I'm not, I'm just kidding, Mom," Sam rolled her eyes, her face slightly reddened.

"I'm sure. I'm keeping a close eye on you," Cheryl teased, wagging her finger.

Sam rolled her eyes but didn't say anything else.

Ariel laughed. "That didn't quite go the way you thought it would go did it?"

"We're going to Colorado. If I can't make jokes about weed, this is going to be a very long and stressful trip for you, Mom."

"Yes dear," Cheryl said, shaking her head. "You can make whatever jokes you like."

"Well thank you. And anyway, I'm not the wild child here. We all know that's Ariel's wheelhouse."

Mom and Ariel looked at each other and burst out laughing. "Girl, save some jokes for later. C'mon, let's go find our gate."

"Not much to find," Ariel said, standing up and slinging her backpack over her shoulder. "It's gate A4, you can see it from here." She pointed down the left side of the hallway and sure enough, there was gate A4.

"We can get the good seats so we can hear the gate agent and watch the planes take off," Cheryl said as they made their way down the one main hallway that made up the entirety of the airport. There weren't many people sitting around at any gate, but with less than two hours until flight time to go, the seats near gate A4 were starting to fill up. Luckily, there were able to snag three seats next to the window.

Ariel set her stuff down on the chair next to Sam and looked around. Despite only having flown two other times in her life, airports were one of Ariel's favorite places to be. The amount of potential they held was palpable. People traveling to see family they haven't seen in years, couples going on that honeymoon they scrimped and saved so hard for, best friends flying to Miami for a bachelorette party. Here, people were stripped of the boringness of daily life—no nine to five jobs they hate, no obligations at home. Here, they were heading to a new world, a new place and going to do new things. It's all Ariel ever wanted. The anticipation of something new, something great.

"I'm going to take a few laps," Ariel announced, standing up. "Will you guys watch my bag?"

"Mm-hmm," Sam and Mom said simultaneously, both buried in their phones.

Ariel shook her head and took off down the concourse. The Des Moines airport had expanded recently, but it still only had six gates, making her stroll a short one. She took her time though, enjoying the smell of fresh coffee and pastries from the corner coffee shop that thankfully hadn't been turned into a Starbucks. The Chive and Table restaurant wasn't open yet, but you could smell the bread and pizzas baking. The airport was busy but not packed. When she reached gate six, she turned around and headed back down the way she came.

She watched people as she went. A mom walking with two small boys was pushing a third boy in a stroller. The boys followed her quietly, looking around with wide eyes, and she was certain that this was their first time in an airport. Ariel imagined they were going to meet up with their father. Maybe they're a military family and they're flying out to meet his ship when it arrives in port in Jacksonville, Florida instead of waiting for him to make his way home to them. The thought of a heartfelt homecoming made her smile.

An older couple, probably in their sixties, held hands as they strolled slowly along the concourse. The woman in a teal sweater with a red scarf. Her husband—presumably—in a red shirt with a teal tie. They looked like they'd been married for decades and still loved each other enough to hold hands and wear coordinating outfits.

A group of younger men in army fatigues huddled around the seats in front of gate C4. Ariel chuckled at the irony of the gate assignment. They were smiling and laughing, probably trading insults that passed as jokes between them. They were on their way to basic training by the looks of it: fresh buzz cuts with a number one or two, fully packed rucksacks, and an innocent look in their eye not unlike that of a deer you see in the woods.

All of these people, full of anticipation of where their plane would take them, all sorts of adventures waiting on the other side.

She passed their gate, and Sam and Mom hadn't moved. Mom was reading a new book from the library she'd gotten for the trip and Sam was scrolling on her phone. Instead of stopping, she made another lap, watching people and making up more stories as she went.

A middle-aged man with the most defined grey under eye circles she'd ever seen rushed past her heading the other direction- pulling a leather suitcase behind him. A leather suitcase with wheels, that was a new one. She made up his backstory: a public defense lawyer from New York. He was here to visit his ailing mother and now he has to rush back for court tomorrow. He'll be back in a week to see how she's doing because his dead beat brother is no help.

Right behind him was a young family. A mom and dad who looked like they were out of a Home and Garden magazine in their matching athleisure wear. Their three kids, all under the age of twelve, in matching Disney t-shirts. The one daughter wearing Minnie Mouse ears. No doubt where they were off to.

She heard them before she saw them, and they looked exactly like they sounded. The boisterous voices belonged to a large group of college-age bros, all of them with skin the color of snow. They practically walked out of a stereotypical rom com movie about Spring Break. Their polos were all Hawaiian themed, one of them tossing a beach ball around in the middle of their seats. Ariel was sure their suitcases were full of beer bongs, weed paraphernalia, swimsuits, and condoms.

Right next to them was a group of nuns. Ariel turned her head, so they didn't think she was laughing at them. The vast contrast of the two groups was comical. As loud as the frat boys were, the nuns didn't seem bothered in the slightest. They were hunched over their Bibles, habits tucked dutifully out of the way. This is what made airports the best- literally everyone from all walks of life peacefully coexisting in the same space. Where else could that happen?

"Attention on the concourse," the overhead paging system echoed. "Flight 433 for Denver will begin boarding in fifteen minutes."

Ariel made a quick pitstop in the bathroom before rejoining her mom and sister.

"Y'all better go pee now," Cheryl said. "I'll watch the bags while you two go."

"Already went," Ariel said, sitting down next to Sam. "You guys go and I'll watch the bags. Especially you, Sam. You've gotta have to pee with all that coffee."

"Yeah, I kinda do, actually," Sam said. The two got up and left Ariel with the bags.

"Attention on the Concourse, Flight 433 to Denver is now boarding those with active military IDs and parties with children three years old and younger, those two groups please approach the gate."

A small handful of people made their way to the gate and started boarding. Soon after, groups one and two were called.

"Did we miss our group?" Cheryl asked, reappearing just in time.

Ariel shook her head as she gathered up her things. The groups prior to them boarded quickly, and their group was called to board.

As they made their way towards the gate and towards their seats, the energy of the day buzzed in Ariel's chest. She was excited, and a little nervous, for her first serious college visit. She was looking forward to getting to know Coach Angela a little more, and to meet some of her potential future teammates. But in the back of her head was a nagging worry that she wouldn't be enough to make the cut. The words of her mom rang in her head. "You've already made the cut. If you hadn't, they wouldn't have just paid $1,800 for plane tickets for you and your family to visit. They've already made up their minds. You don't have to convince them of anything. They're trying to convince you." Ariel smiled at the thought: her mom was right. She was excited to see the school, and to tour where she'd be taking most of her classes. While she was most excited for the running, she was also looking forward to higher education. And the scenery. Living somewhere with mountains had always been a dream of hers, and now it might be coming true.

They reached row twenty-eight and the three girls filed in, Ariel on the window seat, Mom in the middle, and Sam on the aisle. Ariel popped her headphones in and settled her head against the window, watching the airport workers move about while she listened to an inspiring podcast about a woman runner who was beating the men, Courtney Dauwalter.

* * *

"Right there, that's our turn off," Ariel told Mom, who was busy driving their rental car. We're taking I-25 all the way up to Fort Collins."

"Roger that," she said, flipping on her turn signal. "Oh wow. Girls, look at the mountains now."

Sam and Ariel turned to look out the window. Sure enough, the mountains lining the horizon were awash in the soft oranges and pinks of sunset, the snow on their peaks reflecting the colors in a magnificent way.

"I want to move here," Sam said, eyes wide with awe. "This is beautiful."

"Isn't it?" Cheryl agreed, stealing a glance whenever traffic would allow her.

As they turned onto I-25 they went through a little town, not too unlike the small towns in Iowa. It was small and sleepy with enough for the locals, and even then it seemed like it might not have much to offer. Old brick buildings lined the probably-once-bustling downtown, and there were a few restaurants along the way: Mojo Taqueria, Smokin' Daves BBQ, The Lyons Dairy Bar. If it wasn't for the rocky peaks casting shadows on the town, Ariel would've sworn they were in the Midwest with restaurant names like that. They were through the town in the blink of an eye, befitting most small towns and off they went into the crevices of the mountain.

"We really live in the ugliest place our parents could've picked, don't we?" Sam said. She had her head practically out the window as she tried to get the best view of the canyon walls.

"Right? Why'd we have to live in the land of farmers?" Ariel asked her mom. "We don't even farm!"

"Beats me," Cheryl shrugged. "I'm not the one who moved us there. It's just where I ended up with roots."

"Well, we should start putting roots down elsewhere."

"Maybe you can be the first to start," Cheryl said, glancing over at Ariel. "I'm not moving. I'll come visit you though."

"I'm glad you'll visit at least."

With the sun now fully set, darkness descended around them, obscuring the natural beauty of the land. The lights from the surrounding suburbs and cities lit the way. Ariel watched the lights pass out the window, trying her best to stay awake. An hour after they'd left the airport, the three were checked in and settled into their hotel room.

"I'm starving," Sam groaned. She was already in her pjs and snuggled underneath the duvet. "Can we get room service?"

"Honey, the Holiday Inn doesn't have room service," Cheryl laughed. She walked over to the sleek black desk along the far wall and opened the top drawer, pulling out a binder that looked like it had seen better days. "But they do have delivery menus from restaurants around which is just as good."

She tossed the binder on the bed and the girls rushed to flip through it.

"Pizza," they both said in unison.

"Pizza it is," Cheryl agreed. "Sounds great." The rest of the night consisted of showers, pepperoni pizza, and indulging in the cable TV shows they never got to watch at home. By the time it was almost eleven, they all agreed they better try to sleep.

"You've got an alarm for six tomorrow?" Ariel asked as she popped her retainers in. "We can't be late and I want plenty of time to find our way around. Their campus is big."

"Yup, alarm is set. And you know I'll be up anyway," Cheryl said.

"I know. I'm just paranoid." Ariel said as she threw the covers off and stood up. "I've gotta pee."

"Again? You just went five minutes ago," Sam groaned, flopping back against the pillow.

"I'm a nervous pee-er! You know this." Ariel closed the door behind her. She barely peed, her bladder empty. She ran the sink and splashed warm water on her face to help calm the jitters in her stomach. When she reemerged, all the lights were turned off but thankfully the path to the bed was clear.

"No more bathroom breaks," Sam mumbled.

"I'm good now," Ariel lied.

"Goodnight girls," Mom said.

"Night, Mom," Sam and Ariel said. They turned off the lamps and did their best to sleep.

Chapter 9

The next morning, Ariel was awake at five-thirty. She could see the bathroom light was on through the crack underneath the door, and she knew Mom was most likely awake, perched on the sink reading her book. She rolled out of bed and tip-toed over, so as not to wake the sleeping Sam.

"Knock, knock," Ariel whispered as she opened the bathroom door. "I figured I'd find you here." Just as she'd predicted, Mom was sitting on the sink, her legs propped against the opposite wall as she read her book in one hand, Styrofoam cup of coffee in the other.

"Hey, how'd you sleep?"

Ariel shrugged. "Eh, about as well as I sleep before race days. I'm too excited."

"Fair enough." Cheryl smiled. "They have breakfast out downstairs already. Do you want to go get some?"

"Um, yes. Yes, I do."

Ariel threw on her sweatshirt and flipflops and they made their way down to the hotel lobby. Ariel loaded up her plate with cheesy scrambled eggs, medallions sized pancakes, and a cup of yogurt. She eyed the coffee but decided against it, opting instead for orange juice. Cheryl assembled a bowl of oatmeal and toppings and refilled her coffee. They decided to eat in the lobby rather than in the dark with a sleeping Sam.

"How're you feeling about today?" Cheryl asked.

"Good, actually," Ariel said through a mouthful of pancakes. "I'm excited to meet the team. What're you and Sam going to do while I'm off with them?"

"I found a cute art gallery that's right off the campus, so we're going to go check that out. Depending on how long you take, we might find a park and a café somewhere as well."

"Sounds nice. Tomorrow, can we go check out downtown Fort Collins? I'd like to see at least a little of the town I might be living in while we're here."

"Sure thing."

The two women ate their breakfast, chatting about the mountains and planning out visiting schedules. While the decision wasn't officially made, Ariel was excited about Colorado. Even in the short time she'd been there, having just seen the airport and the hotel, she loved the aura of the place. People were just as nice as Iowa, there were breathtaking mountains, and the air smelled of alpine air rather than hog crap and corn.

"Well, shall we go wake the beast?" Cheryl asked, finishing the last dregs of her coffee.

"Only if you're doing it." Ariel laughed.

"Deal." Sam was notoriously difficult and unpleasant to wake up in the mornings. She'd been that way since she was a baby. Ariel had more than one vivid memory of being sent to wake her sister from her nap, only to run down the stairs crying because Sam had pulled her hair or hit her after waking up. Luckily, she wasn't physically violent anymore, just cranky.

A short while later, after everyone was up and dressed, Cheryl was parking the car in the large parking lot outside of the campus library. It was a stout building, a rotunda in the center of it flanked by rows of floor to ceiling windows.

"It looks like a nice campus," Cheryl commented. "Even with all the bare trees. I bet it's just stunning in the spring when everything is in bloom."

"Too bad most of the school year is when things aren't in bloom," Sam said. Ariel didn't take her attitude personally. This was her baseline until after noon.

"Where are we meeting Coach Angela again?"

"Just out front of the library here," Ariel said. She opened the door and stepped outside. There was a cool breeze to go along with the sunshine, and she was grateful for her scarf and beanie. From the parking lot, she couldn't see Coach Angela. "Let's walk up there."

The group made their way towards the front of the library, where lots of students were coming and going. It was almost Thanksgiving break which meant it was midterms for the college students. Ariel tried to glimpse their faces as they hurried along. They didn't appear too stressed, something that gave Ariel a little relief from her anxiety about going to college next year. Towards the end of the building Ariel spotted Coach Angela walking towards them, her long dark hair blowing in the wind behind her. She waved to grab her attention, and Coach nodded in recognition.

"Hi, Ariel. It's great to see you again," Coach Angela greeted them as she approached. "And you too, Mrs. Hart. I take it you're Sam?"

"I am," Sam said in her best monotone. "Nice to meet you."

"Same to you," Coach Angela smiled, giving Sam's hand a firm shake. She didn't seem to notice Sam's gruffness. But then again, Ariel was sure Coach Angela had enough bubbliness in her personality to make up for it. "Did you find the place all right?"

"Very easily. This was probably one of the easiest college campuses to navigate."

"Good. I would agree, the people who planned this University did a great job of it. Shall we go on a little tour? I wanted to show you around the main academic buildings, dorms, student centers, and then we'll go look at the athletic facilities and meet the team. Sound like a plan?"

"Sounds great," Ariel said, doing her best to contain her excitement.

"Sam and I will stay with you all through the athletic facilities. After that, we're going to go check out the Curfman Gallery and then to Café Bluebird for lunch. We'll meet up with you guys when you're done."

"Sounds great. I highly recommend their Colorado Street Tacos for savory, and their Mandarin Orange French toast if you want something sweet."

"You should bring me back something," Ariel winked. "Blueberry pancakes would be ideal."

"Noted," Cheryl smiled.

"Shall we start in the library and work our way around?" Coach Angela asked, pointing towards the large glass doors.

"Sounds great."

Coach Angela led the small group through the library and the main buildings on campus. Ariel took it all in, wide-eyed at the thought that this time next year, this might be her school. And not just her school, her home. The people walking through campus all walked in groups, chatting with their friends on their way to whatever important class they were headed to. Despite the early November timeline, the campus still had greenery in the form of large evergreen conifers lining walkways and outlining the large greenspace known as the Quad. It was a large campus, but walking it was within reason. As they exited the last building, Ariel saw the athletic building across the way.

"The nice part about the science building is it's right next to the athletic facilities," Angela said, holding open the door as the three walked out. "You're wanting to study something in the sciences, right? Remind me again."

"Yeah, environmental science," Ariel said.

"You'll have a lot of classes in this building then. It'll make your campus commute easier. Shall we head to the athletic department and meet the team?"

Ariel nodded. "Let's do it."

"All right, this is where we leave you," Mom said. "Have fun. Call me when you're done, okay?"

"Will do," Ariel said, a little embarrassed. She hugged her mom goodbye despite not wanting too and followed Coach Angela into the building.

There's an unmistakable smell of rubber and sweat that accompanies any indoor athletic training facility and this one was no different. If you had blindfolded Ariel, she could've told you right away where they were. A loud banging made her jump. Coach Angela laughed.

"Racquetball courts are open to everyone and they're very popular. Anytime you're in here you'll probably have people playing. You'll get used to the sound quick enough."

"Good because that scared the crap outta me." Ariel laughed; grateful Coach didn't seem put off by her jumpiness.

"So on the first floor, you've got your racquetball courts to your left and locker rooms are to your right. They have tons of lockers, showers, toilets, and a great area for getting ready if that's your thing. Since you'll be an official athlete for the college, you'll get a designated locker." Angela pointed out everything as they walked down the wide hall. "And here is our indoor track. It's full sized, so one lap is a quarter of a mile."

"That's fantastic," Ariel smiled. "I hate track workouts, so the fewer laps I have to do, the better."

Angela laughed. "Back in my college days I was the same way. I did track events, but I never liked them. We'll go upstairs next."

As they ascended the stairs, Ariel could hear weights dropping on the floor, plates rattling against the barbells as they were replaced onto the racks. At the top, the stairs opened into a large weight room filled with all the free weights and machines you could imagine.

"Wow, this is expansive."

"It is," Angela agreed. "The only downside is that this serves as our athletic training area as well as the main gym for the general student body. Sometimes it sucks to have to share the space, but thankfully the space is so large often times you don't even notice that you're sharing with all thirty-three thousand students."

"Coach!" someone called from behind them. Angela and Ariel turned around. "Hey, Tiff." A tall lanky woman approached them and high fived Angela.

"Tiffany, this is Ariel. She'll hopefully be joining the team next year."

"Hi, nice to meet you," Ariel said shyly, sticking her hand out.

Tiffany shook it vigorously, a large, toothy grin on her face. "I've heard about you. You're the girl who took Nationals three years in a row. You set all the records in Iowa from what I hear."

Ariel turned red. "That I am. I didn't think anyone outside of Iowa would've heard about that."

"Oh- anyone in the running circle has definitely heard of you. Or at least what you've done," Tiffany said. "How's your hand? I still can't believe what happened. They should've let you run Nationals. Wasn't your fault you got elbowed."

Ariel shrugged. She agreed, but she tried not to let her thoughts dwell on it lest resentment started to brew. "My hand healed great. It still hurts a bit though; I need to stretch the scar tissue out or something because it still feels tight."

"Good thing you don't need your hand too much for running," Coach Angela said. "But I'm sure some of our staff PT's can help you with that."

"That'd be great," Ariel said. And here she thought she was going to be stuck with a painful hand the rest of her life.

"I'm excited you're here," Tiffany said, redirecting the conversation. "We've got an awesome team, and a great coach. And I'm not just saying that because she's right here. The assistant coaches are great too. Have y'all been to the spa room yet?"

"We were just headed that way. We're planning on meeting the rest of the team there."

"I'll walk down with you," Tiffany said. The group turned around and made their way back down the stairs. "So what do you want to study while you're here?"

"Environmental sciences and English," Ariel said. "I want to be a journalist who focuses on conservation efforts."

"That's kinda cool. Like Jane Goodall?" Tiffany asked.

"Haha, similar." Ariel smiled. "What do you study?"

"Athletic training. When I can't run competitively anymore, I want to help women who can."

"Cool."

Angela pushed open the big double doors that separated the entrance lobby and the gym from the athletic spa. "Welcome to The Spa!"

As far as spas go, this one was nothing to write home about. Unless you're a collegiate athlete. Instead of calming music and dim lighting, the room was filled with bright fluorescents and punk rock played on a portable speaker someone placed on one of the padded massage tables in the far corner. On one wall were several tin tubs, Ariel assumed for cold therapies. In the middle of the room was an assortment of large, comfy furniture where a small group of women were lounging. On the opposite wall stood a large wooden structure.

"Is that a sauna?" Ariel asked, mouth agape.

"Sure is," Tiffany nodded. "We do cold baths, then straight to the sauna. Then to the massage tables if Mariana is around. She's our athletic trainer. She'll work out all your knots and make you cry while she does it."

"Sounds relaxing?"

"It is once you're done," Tiffany nudged her in the ribs. "And the strawberry kale smoothies are to die for."

"Ladies!" Coach Angela called out as they approached the group of women. "I'd like you all to meet Miss Ariel Hart. We're trying to convince her that Colorado State is the place she wants to continue her running career."

A chorus of heys followed. "You're the girl from Iowa," a woman in a green crop top interjected.

"That's me," Ariel nodded, smiling from ear to ear. She wasn't used to people knowing who she was or where she was from. "I feel like I need that on a shirt. I like Iowa, but I will say, Coach Angela and the mountains have done a really good job at convincing me to leave the state."

"The food is phenomenal out here, too," a woman sitting on the arm of the couch said.

"McKenzie's right, the food scene is great here. And running through the mountains after years of running through cornfields is life altering," another woman said. "I would know, I'm from Lincoln, Nebraska. I'm Shelley."

"Nice to meet you, sorry you're from Nebraska." Ariel teased.

"Made it easy an easy decision to come here though." Shelley smiled. "Speaking of, Coach was talking about us taking you out on a little run this afternoon through the foothills. Is that something you'd be up for?"

"I would love to," Ariel said, her heartbeat quickening. "There's a reason I wore my athletic clothes today."

"You mean you aren't like the rest of us who live in them?" McKenzie asked.

"Oh no, I totally am," Ariel laughed. "My Mom tried getting me to wear a dress for this, and I had to convince her no, this is an athletic tour not an interview for a full ride scholarship."

The small group laughed. "Well that settles it then. We're all ready to go if you are?" Tiffany asked.

Ariel nodded. "How far are we going?"

"Five easy miles sound all, right? You've gotta remember we're at elevation here too, so don't be surprised if it feels a little harder or you're a little slower than you're used to."

"How high up are we?" Ariel asked, cocking an eyebrow. "I thought it was just five thousand feet?"

"It is," Tiffany assured her. "But even that will make a difference, especially when you're coming from whatever sea level Des Moines is at."

"I think it's only like 800 feet or something."

"Exactly, you'll feel it. But once you get used to it, it makes you superhuman everywhere else."

"I like the sound of that. Let's go!"

Ariel nodded goodbye to Coach Angela, and she followed the group outside to the front of the building. The day was beautiful, only a slight cool breeze in the air. The sun shone bright overhead.

"Do clouds exist here?" Ariel asked, pulling her sunglasses over her eyes.

"Only sometimes," Tiffany laughed. "There's this trailhead right at the edge of campus. It won't take us up to the tops of any mountains, but it has great views of them."

"Good enough for me." Ariel smiled. She jogged in place a little, kicking her heels up to her butt to wake up her legs. She was eager to move after the sedentary travel day.

"You ready?" Tiffany asked, stretching her long arms overhead.

"Born ready," Ariel said. "Lead the way."

Tiffany and Shelley started off towards the direction of the mountains. Ariel fell in line with McKenzie, and the rest of the team followed. They started slow, letting Ariel take in the town surrounding campus as they made their way towards the trails. The homes surrounding the campus were quaint brick structures that reminded her of her grandmother's house. The trail wove through the houses and treelined streets. Even the busiest of streets were cute.

Eventually, the trail led them away from the town and into a more forested area, the concrete path giving way to packed dirt and gravel. The shaded path was nice, but it blocked the mountain view. As the group picked up the pace, they rounded a bend in the trail, and it opened up again. The mountain views were large and imposing on the landscape.

"Woo, you weren't kidding about the elevation," Ariel huffed. Her lungs burned with the extra effort despite the pace being slower than what she was used to.

"Yeah, you'll adjust after a few months," Tiffany laughed, not a bead of sweat on her face.

Ariel dared a glance at her watch. Much to her horror, they were on a nine-minute pace: a speed that would typically have her yawning. "A few months?!"

"I adjusted after a few weeks," a woman towards the back of the group spoke up.

"Yeah, but you're from the mountains of California," Tiffany laughed. "You were already halfway adjusted."

"I'll figure it out," Ariel laughed, trying not to let her breathlessness show. "But this is no joke. I swear I'm not this unfit." Suddenly, her mind was filled with thoughts about how slow she was, how pathetic she was running. They were barely even trying and Ariel's lungs felt full of cement, her legs of lead.

"We know," McKenzie said, clapping her on the back. "We all had that transition moment when we first got here of 'Oh shit, I swear I don't suck'. Just keep running through it and eventually you'll feel like yourself again."

"Woo! It feels great out here," Shelley yelled, kicking up her heels. "Ladies, we pick up the pace, add a few extra miles, some elevation gain, and we'll be training for Leadville!"

"Some elevation gain?" Tiffany said. "Try twenty-two thousand feet of gain."

"I'm def not ready for that," Ariel huffed, shaking her head.

"None of us are," Shelley said. "But being on dirt trails instead of cement just makes a gal feel alive!"

Ariel had to admit, running on the softer service was doing her knees wonders. Every now and then, her knees would start to protest during her training, and she'd have to move to running on the golf courses or anywhere she could find smooth grass. But the trail made it easier. Her watch beeped, alerting her they were done with two miles already. She did a mental scan of her body: lungs on fire, knees fresh, calves loose, feet fine. When she realized the only thing giving her grief was her lungs, she loosened up a bit. Her legs felt better than they'd had in weeks. The dirt must have some magic cushion in it.

"Coach would have a fit if we all came back and 'We're like 'we're going for Leadville!'," McKenzie said. "I'm running it after I graduate."

"What's the Leadville?" Ariel asked, curious about this word they kept throwing around.

"You've never heard of Leadville?" Tiffany asked, mouth agape as she fell back to run with her in the middle of the group.

"Nope." As they rounded a bend in the trail, the ground got softer. The trail was littered with pine needles, the scent of Christmas filling every breath Ariel took. Memories of warm Christmas mornings by the fire suddenly appeared, bringing with them a sense of home.

"It's only the most famous ultramarathon in the world," Tiffany explained, snapping Ariel back to reality. "It's infamous for being the highest race in the world."

"How far is it?"

"One hundred miles, and the tallest pass on the course is twelve thousand six hundred feet above sea level."

"One hundred miles is crazy, but one hundred miles at that high of altitude is certified insane," Ariel said, eyes wide. "I'm dying at just five thousand. I can't even imagine higher."

"Give yourself a few months, then we'll see what you think," Shelley winked.

"It's in this old mining village every year. If you were staying longer, we'd take you up there. When you come back, we'll go check it out. It's a cute little town— we go up there for training runs sometimes. You can't beat the scenery."

"Can we go after I adjust to the elevation? I mean, it sounds great but I'd rather enjoy it than focus on trying not to puke," Ariel said.

"Oh it is. Hope Pass is the best. The week of the race, the town gets flooded. You get to meet a lot of the celebrities of the ultra-racing world, and it's a big boost for the economy."

"How much is the prize money, like ten grand?"

"Haha girl, you've got to get with the program," Tiffany laughed shaking her head. "Usually, there's no prize money. But this year, one of the race founders died and left like half a million for the first-place winner. Usually there aren't a ton of the elite athletes because there's no prize money, but this year? The field of runners is going to be absolutely stacked."

"Five hundred thousand?! That's a shit ton of money," Ariel exclaimed, almost tripping. "That's enough to buy a house…" she thought to herself.

"Mm-hmm. They've started doing fundraisers and some races have prize money, but this amount of money for an ultra-race is unheard of."

"That was generous of the founder to do that." Ariel couldn't fathom that amount of money, much less that the only thing you had to do to earn the money was run. The ground started to fall, the trail leading down the large hill they'd just climbed up. The group's pace naturally increased for the final mile, pushing so hard no one felt like talking anymore. When they arrived back at campus a mile later, Ariel flopped on the grass underneath a bare willow tree.

"Y'all weren't kidding about the elevation, hot damn," Ariel said between breaths.

"You'll get there," Tiffany laughed. "So, are you comin' to join us next fall?" She asked, hands on her hips.

"Well, I don't want to make any promises… but…" Ariel shrugged.

"When you do decide, just know we'd love to have you. I think we can all agree that you'll fit in great here." All the women nodded in agreement.

"Thanks," Ariel smiled. She had envisioned today going well, but not that she'd be welcomed with open arms by the entire team.

The group stretched together underneath the tree, cooling down from the workout.

"Do you have plans for tonight?" McKenzie asked as they made their way back to the student center.

"Yeah, my mom and sister are here, and we wanted to go explore the town a little bit."

"Go to the Gardens on Spring Creek," Shelley said. "It's one of my favorite spots in town."

"Will do."

Ariel glanced at her watch. It was nearly five o'clock already. "I've gotta get goin'. It's been great meeting you all. Thanks for showing me around."

"Any time," Tiffany smiled. "We hope we see you again."

"I have a feeling you might," Ariel smiled back. She started back towards the library, where they had agreed to meet up. As she walked, she dialed her phone.

"How was it?" Cheryl exclaimed, picking up immediately.

"It was great, Mom," Ariel squealed, trying to contain her excitement so as not to embarrass herself. "I'm ready for you guys to come get me."

"We'll be there in fifteen."

Sure enough, fifteen minutes later, Mom and Sam pulled up. Ariel hopped in the car, prepared for Mom's barrage of questions. "Yes, it was a great time. Yes, all the girls were nice. Yes, I think I might want to come here next year."

"Well hello to you too," Cheryl laughed.

"Ugh, you stink of sweat," Sam said, pinching her nose.

"Yeah, I went for a run with the team." Ariel tried to embrace Sam in a hug but she pushed her away with one hand, pinching her nose with the other.

"How'd that go?" Cheryl asked.

"Honestly, I was slow. Running above sea level is an adjustment. But everyone said I'll get used to it and be just fine, so I'm trying not to let it get to my head."

"Sounds like a good idea," Cheryl laughed. "I'm glad you had a great time and you liked everyone on the team."

"Me too," Ariel said. "How was your guys' day? I'm sorry it took longer than I thought, time kind of got away from me with the run and all."

"You ran as a team, eh?" Sam said. "Does that mean you've made up your mind?"

"Not yet," Ariel said.

"We had a good day," Cheryl said. "That café was great, there are a lot of cool parks around, and Sam liked the art gallery."

Sam pulled herself forward and leaned into the front seat. "They had some original Grant Wood paintings!"

"I'm glad to hear it," Ariel smiled.

"What's the plan for the rest of the night?" Cheryl asked.

"Get dinner and hang out at the hotel pool?" Ariel asked. "That run kind of kicked my butt and I'm all sweaty now so I could use a shower."

"Do you want to go to the hotel first?"

"No, we're already out. If we go back to the hotel, I'm going to not leave again," Ariel laughed.

"Sounds like a plan."

The group swung by a Thai restaurant on the way back to the hotel and picked up to-go. Later that night, Mom had gone off to bed, leaving Sam and Ariel in the hot tub with the promise they'd come to the room by ten.

"Any hot boys on campus today?" Sam asked. She leaned back in the water, letting the jets blow her long blonde hair around.

"Honestly, I didn't pay much attention. I was so nervous about meeting the team."

Sam sat up, a puzzled expression on her face. "You? Nervous? Since when?"

"I dunno, it's intimidating meeting people who're competitive runners like you are," Ariel said, absentmindedly running her hands through the water. "I love my teammates at school, but I've never really had someone to compete with on the team."

"I guess," Sam said. "But these people clearly want you. Like Mom said, they paid good money to bring you here to convince you."

"I looked like a fool running with them today," Ariel confessed. "They barely broke a sweat and I was fighting for my life."

"Psh, I bet you're over exaggerating."

"Not really," Ariel shook her head, small water droplets flying from the ends of her hair. "Elevation sucks."

"Didn't you say one of them was from Nebraska? I'm sure they all understood."

"They did…" Ariel trailed off, knowing her sister was right. Leave it to Sam to reground her and shut down the negative voice in her head. "You know what else?"

"What?"

"They mentioned this race in Leadville. Apparently, the prize money this year is half a million dollars."

"What?!" Sam yelled, her voice echoing off the pool walls.

"Shhhh, you'll wake the whole hotel!" Ariel exclaimed, looking around to make sure no one heard them. They were the only ones still in the pool area, but she wouldn't have been surprised if the people in the poolside rooms had heard her sister's exclamation.

"Sorry!" Sam whispered, sitting up and splashing water. "But half a million dollars?! That's crazy. Do you have to run naked to get this money?"

"No," Ariel snorted. "You run a hundred miles at like thirteen thousand feet of altitue. So, really hard. But not impossible. And the scenery is stunning because you're literally in the middle of the mountains. It was pretty enough today running around the foothills. I can't even imagine how great it is up there."

"One hundred miles?" Sam repeated, mouth agape. "I'd rather run naked."

"Crazy, right?" Ariel said, trailing off.

Sam was silent for a moment, staring at her feet underneath the water. "Do you think you could do it?"

Ariel's heart leapt. "I do. I'm glad you had the same idea! I thought I was insane for even letting the idea cross my mind."

"Why? You have a proven track record of being a kick ass runner. You're quite literally the top high school runner in the country."

"Yeah, but there're a lot more runners out there than high school girls."

"Hold on a sec." Sam climbed out of the hot tub and grabbed her phone and a towel off the table. She returned with it and sat on the edge, her feet in the water while she vigorously typed something into the phone. "Look at this."

Ariel took the phone from her hands and studied what she'd pulled up on the screen. It was an excel spreadsheet with all her race times in one column. In another column were the names of other runners who Ariel recognized along with their times in the same races. She looked up at her sister. "What is this?"

"That's a spreadsheet I've been keeping since you started cross your freshman year," Sam explained. "It compares your races times to the top twenty D1 women's cross-country athletes in the same events and guess what?"

Ariel studied the spreadsheet of numbers and shrugged. "What?"

"Your times are faster than all but two of them."

"Huh," Ariel handed the phone back. "Are you sure?"

"Hell yes I'm sure," Sam said, feigning offense. "I worked hard on this!"

"Why did you start making it?" Ariel laughed, shaking her head.

"Call it twintuition. I had a feeling you might one day doubt yourself and need your sister to pull your head out of your ass. Can you imagine what that prize money would do for us?"

Ariel could imagine it. It's all she'd been thinking about since the run. They could pay for their college educations, they could buy more reliable cars, they could go to Europe. And most importantly, they could keep their house.

"You should run it," Sam said softly. "If anyone has a chance at making history, it's you."

"It's going to take so much training… I'm going to have to train harder than I've ever trained before."

"What do you have to lose for trying?"

* * *

Their Sunday spent exploring the city of Fort Collins had flown by way too quickly, and they were waiting in the security line at Denver International Airport. Ariel was originally dreading the return home. But with her newfound goal, she was eager to get back and get to work.

As they were in line to board the plane, she got one last glimpse of the mountains, imprinting it on her memory until she could return. She imagined running in those mountains—the air thin and cool, the sun intense, the scenery imposing and taking what little breath you had left.

"I'm going to do it," she whispered to herself.

Chapter 10

"I mean, I guess." Kyle said, shrugging. Ariel brushed in front of him as they walked into the classroom and took their usual seats in the front left corner. Ariel yawned. It was only third period, five more to go.

"Well if you're not going to go to Trevor's party, do you want to go to the Icebox after school at least?" Kyle pleaded.

"I have—" Ariel started.

"Just for an hour," Kyle said, interrupting her before the excuse could escape her lips. "Everyone knows that you don't have to study. And cross season is over, so you can't use that as an excuse."

"Fineee," she conceded. "Twist my arm why don't you."

"That's my specialty."

The bell rang and the rest of their classmates sat down.

"All right, everyone," Mr. Maffin said, taking his place at the front of the room. "Pull out your biology workbooks from last week, please."

Ariel opened hers to the next unfinished page. She took a deep breath and settled into her favorite class, but try as she might, her mind wouldn't focus. Memories from the past weekend's trip to Colorado kept coming back.

She'd dreamt of the mountains every night and on her morning runs, the frost covered ground of the plowed cornfields just didn't feel the same. Yet, she couldn't see a world where she didn't have both mountains and her childhood home in her life. Maybe she didn't have too. And she couldn't wait to tell Kyle and Shelby her plan.

* * *

The Icebox was bustling with the usual after school crowd of teenagers. If you didn't hang out at the Icebox after school, you probably worked there. It was the only ice cream place in town and was one of three or four places for teenagers to work without driving thirty minutes into Ankeny. The restaurant was Ariel's favorite—the red brick walls with a wood burning fireplace on the far side of the room surrounded by comfy faux-velvet chairs made it feel grand and cozy. The front of the building was all windows, illuminating the ice cream counter with natural light. There were two large ice cream coolers full of original flavors. The most popular being their homemade Rocky Road, but Ariel preferred the salted caramel brownie. In the summer, strawberry lemon was her go to.

Kyle, Ariel, and Shelby sat in their favorite booth tucked away in the back corner next to the fireplace. Kyle had his usual banana split, Shelby her waffle cone filled with vanilla chocolate chip and monster cookie dough ice cream. Ariel took a bite of her caramel brownie, savoring the rich sweetness and contemplating how to bring up her big idea.

"Did you guys hear the latest rumor about DJ and Kylie?" Shelby asked.

"No, what?" Kyle asked.

106

"They got caught making out behind the baseball dugouts when they were supposed to be in study hall," Shelby said, wiggling her eyebrows.

"Getting hot and heavy were they?" Kyle asked.

"From what I heard, their pants were nearly off."

"Well, that's embarrassing for them and for whoever found them," Kyle said.

"Principal Danner found them."

"Embarrassing, but props to them," Kyle nodded, raising his cup for a solo cheers.

"That's so awkward though. Like… I wouldn't wanna be caught doin' it behind the baseball dugout," Ariel said.

"I mean, you gotta get it where and when you can." Kyle shrugged.

"I guess. Still, that's gross," Shelby said, scrunching her nose.

As the two of them discussed the merits of a quickie behind the bleachers versus finding a place to park in the dark, Ariel contemplated whether to tell them about her decision. On one hand, having support of her friends would be great. And Ariel was notoriously terrible at keeping secrets, especially one this big. But if they weren't supportive, she'd be devastated. She didn't have a counter argument for Shelby's prying, practical questions. She just knew she had to do it, whether it was practical or not.

"You're awfully quiet about this matter," Shelby said, elbowing her in the ribs. "What would you pick? Quicky on school property and get caught by the principal, or higher quality sex in a parked car but risk getting caught by the cops?"

"None of the above." Ariel shook her head. "Take a blanket out to the middle of Saylorville woods."

Kyle nearly choked on his ice cream—eyebrows raised to his hairline.

"Oh, now that's a game changer," Shelby declared, sitting up tall. "Wait, have you been holding out on us?! What have you been up to?!"

This conversation was quickly going the wrong way, so Ariel decided to just rip off the band aid. "I have something to tell you guys something."

"You're pregnant!" Shelby exclaimed.

"What? Hell no," Ariel said. "Why in the world is that your first guess?"

Shelby shrugged, licking her cone. "We were just talking about sex, so it seemed like a logical next step in the conversation."

"What's your news?" Kyle asked, regaining his composure. He leaned forward, elbows on the table, chin in his hands.

Ariel glanced from Kyle to Shelby, Shelby to Kyle, trying to read their expressions. "I'm going to enter the Leadville 100 Ultramarathon."

Shelby's eyes widened. "Like, thee Leadville 100? The one in Colorado?"

"The one and only," Ariel said, nodding firmly. "It's next June. Also, how do you know about it? I only just heard of it."

"My cousin does ultras. She's tried to get in for a few years now but never gets her name drawn in the lottery." Shelby said, pushing back from the booth. "But wow… why in the world are you going to do that? And so soon?"

"I mean, that's practically a year away," Kyle said. "She's got plenty of time."

"Thank you for the support, Kyle," Ariel said emphatically.

"I don't mean to be unsupportive," Shelby said, waving her off. "I'm just surprised, that's all. And I have a lot of questions."

"I figured," Ariel said, leaning forward and folding her hands together. "Hit me with them."

Shelby thrummed her fingers on the table in front of her. "Why do you want to run a hundred miles?"

Ariel was caught off guard by the simplicity of her first question. "Because why not?"

Shelby scrunched her eyes at her friend. "Nope. You always have a why behind things. What made you suddenly want to do this?"

"I want the prize money," Ariel admitted. "Half a million."

"Dollars??" Kyle said, jaw dropping to the floor. "That's a lot of money."

"Exactly," Ariel nodded. "You know how my mom lost her job?" Shelby and Kyle nodded. "Well, this way we could pay the mortgage off and not have to worry about losing the house."

"Is it that serious?" Kyle asked quietly.

"Maybe," Ariel said. "But the point is, with this, it wouldn't be."

"Okay, you want the prize money. How do you plan on doing it? After all, the best runners in the world are going to run this race. Tons of them don't finish every year. How on earth do you plan on even coming close?"

"Gee, thanks for the vote of confidence," Ariel said, hurt by her friend's skepticism.

"I think what she's asking is, what's your plan?" Kyle said, trying to soften the tension. "We don't doubt you could do it, we just know it's a lot."

"Yeah, what he said," Shelby said, nodding at Kyle.

"I plan on training like I've never trained before. And I plan on having a great team behind me," she said, alluding to her next point.

"You mean like a nascar pit crew?" Kyle asked, perking up.

"That's exactly what I'm talking about. I need a crew of people I trust. I was hoping you'd both be part of the crew, and maybe even help pace me?"

"I'm down," Kyle said, slapping his hand down on the table.

"Does that mean I have to run a hundred miles too? Because if so, I'm out," Shelby said, waving her hand.

"No, you'd just run part of the course with me. Your job would be to keep me on course and make sure I eat and drink."

"Oh, in that case, sure!"

Ariel smiled. That had been easier than she'd expected. "I was also thinking of asking Coach Bobbi to do it with me too. Kinda be a coach and a crew. Do you think she would?"

"Of course she would! She's always looking for ways to help runners even after they've graduated," Shelby said. "She's run a few ultras too, ya know."

Ariel's eyes widened. "No way."

"Yes way."

"How have I never known this?!"

"Beats me," Shelby shrugged, spooning her ice cream around. "Especially since she's been your mom's best friend since before you were born. I don't see how that never came up."

"I have some questions for Mom first thing when I get home," Ariel said, still in utter disbelief. How could the two biggest pillars in her life never have mentioned Coach Bobbi ran ultramarathons? Seems like that would've come up in a conversation or two over the years.

"Holy shit, this will be a huge year for you then!" Kyle said, a smiling widening on his face, revealing perfectly aligned teeth, courtesy of braces. "You set records and won State for the fourth time in a row, you're going to graduate, and then race the Leadville 100!"

"Not just race it, win it." Ariel corrected him.

"Professionals run that race," Shelby reminded her.

"Thank you, Captain Obvious. You already pointed that one out," Ariel said, rolling her eyes. "Amateurs run it too."

"Has an amateur ever won?" Kyle asked.

"Not yet," Ariel shrugged, unbothered.

"And that doesn't intimidate you?"

"It invigorates me," she said, leaning back in her chair, arms wide open. "What better opportunity than to be the first amateur, the first woman, and the youngest person ever to win? Besides, it seems like I have a knack for setting records. What's one more?"

"I admire your loftiness," Shelby said. "But I don't want you to get in over your head and be disappointed when you don't win."

"Again, thanks for the support." Her best friend's words stung. "A runner wins it every single year. Why not me?"

"I can think of a million reasons," Shelby said.

"Yeah, that was a rhetorical question," Kyle said, jabbing Shelby in the arm. "Way to be supportive."

"I'm just trying to be realistic," she said in her defense. "You two are dreamers which is awesome, but someone has to keep you grounded otherwise you'd be off running marathons on every continent and then you'd be dirt poor living in a refrigerator box somewhere."

"Or I would have so many sponsors I'd live in a mansion," Ariel countered.

"That's the attitude to have!" he beamed, throwing an arm around her. Ariel felt her face flush— a warm feeling grew in her stomach. "You have such a bleak outlook on life sometimes, Shelby, ya know that?" Kyle said, scrunching his nose in disapproval. "Lighten up a bit, would ya? Your best friend since third grade just announced she's going to try for probably the coolest achievement anyone in our class could go for except qualifying for the Olympic team or something—ooo you should try for that too!"

Ariel laughed. "They don't pay out like the ultramarathons do."

Shelby cocked an eyebrow. "If you're in it for money, why not just get a job?"

"Because jobs don't pay half a mil. At least not the ones I could get."

Shelby sighed. "Can I ask one more potentially downer question before I move in to full support mode?"

"Go for it," Ariel said, leaning forward, resting her elbows on the table.

"If you do win—"

"When," Ariel corrected.

"When you win," Shelby restated, rolling her eyes. "What does that do to your eligibility to still run in college?"

"Honestly, I'm not sure." Ariel admitted. "There's a lot of change going on right now with athletes maybe being able to be paid. So until the NCAA decides on that, it's a little up in the air. Either way, I'm willing to risk it. This is huge."

"Okay... so long as you're aware of the risks."

"I appreciate your concern, but I am," Ariel said, nodding curtly.

"So what's your training regimen look like?" Kyle asked, taking another bite of his banana split and turning the conversation in a more positive direction.

"Not sure other than lots and lots of miles. That's what I was hoping Coach Bobbi will help me with. Which, knowing now she's actually done some of these before, I think she'll know just what to do."

"Do you think she'll be supportive?" Shelby interrupted. "It sounds like this might affect your track season. Or are you not going to run that?"

"I haven't decided about track yet," Ariel said.

"She might be hesitant at first, but I think she'd warm up to the idea," Kyle said.

"That's kind of what I'm hoping will happen," Ariel admitted.

"How long do people take to run these ultramarathons?" Shelby asked.

"It depends. The world record for the fastest one is like twelve hours. But thank God that's not where most people hang out. Depending on the course, it can take anywhere from sixteen to over thirty hours."

"Running?! For thirty hours?! God, what fresh hell is that?" Shelby shook her head. "I like running, but God not that much."

"Yeah, the one thing I'm dreading is the sleep deprivation."

"I love how that's the thing you're dreading and not the hundred miles you have to cover," Shelby laughed.

"Ooo you are not a night person," Kyle said, shaking his head. "You go downhill fast once you've been up longer than like thirteen hours."

"Remember when you fell asleep on the bleachers at after prom last year?" Shelby laughed, picturing the sight of her friend snoring despite the loud music and bright lights.

"I know, I know," Ariel said, rolling her eyes. "But I'm hoping the adrenaline from the race will keep me wide awake."

"What about altitude?" Shelby asked, finishing the last bite of her waffle cone.

"That was going to be my next topic," Ariel said, biting into her ice cream. She turned to Kyle. "Can we get your parents to let us go to your cabin in Colorado for Spring Break?"

"Probably only if they come with, but if you're okay with that," Kyle said, nodding in approval.

"The more the merrier, I love your parents," Ariel said.

"Are we partying or training?" Shelby asked, one eyebrow raised.

"Both," Ariel said. "But I'll be training mostly. No matter how many hills I run, nothing will make up for the elevation difference between here and Leadville."

"Will one week of training really make a difference though?" Kyle asked, his voice gentle.

"Yes and no. It won't get me acclimated to it, but it will give me an idea of how I'll react," Ariel explained, folding her arms in front of her on the table. "Plus, it's an excuse to get away for spring break!"

"I'm in," Shelby said. "As long as you don't make me wake up at four in the morning to train with you."

"No, I'm not that mean," she laughed. "But I might have you meet me at noon to bring me food or something while I'm out running."

"Noon is fine," Kyle nodded. "I think a Colorado spring break sounds great. Your mom and Sam should come too, I know my parents will invite them."

"Oh I'm not going without Sam," Ariel laughed. "She'd kill me."

"It's settled then, Spring Break, we're heading to Colorado!" Ariel cheered, tapping the table with excitement.

"That's so far from now," Kyle groaned.

"It'll be here before we know it," Ariel said. She glanced at the watch on her wrist. "I really need to be getting home. I've got a load of homework to get ahead on for next week."

"Nerd," Kyle scoffed. "Why don't you stay a bit? Sounds like this might be one of the last real days off you have for a long time."

"I've enjoyed it enough already," she laughed, standing up. "Besides, you two have a party to start planning for when I win this thing. And I know how Shelby is when it comes to parties, we'd be here until midnight."

"Fair enough," Shelby agreed, cocking her head. Ariel could practically see the party details running through her head: what color combinations? What's the menu? Party games or pool time? You never knew what you'd get with a Shelby party— she always wanted to throw sophisticated parties. Ones that you'd go to when you're twenty-six and had money: perfectly decorated, dress code, themes. But unfortunately, most high schoolers weren't interested in wearing coordinating outfits and bringing a dessert. All they wanted was something with alcohol content and a red solo cup. And loud music.

"See you guys tomorrow."

"Bye!"

Ariel grabbed her ice cream bowl off the counter and dropped it off at the station on her way out the door, giving a wave to the man behind the counter. As she got in her car, the sun was starting to set, casting the bare trees and buildings of their little downtown square in a golden light. Everything had been so serious the past year, and things were finally starting to feel exciting again.

"I'm going to win Leadville, our home is going to be ours forever…." she thought. She couldn't help but smile as she thought of her home. She never knew how much she loved it until she knew they might lose it. She'd always assumed it'd be there forever and that one day after her parents had passed on, she'd inherit it and move back in. By then, all the evergreen trees they'd planted for wind cover would be fifty feet tall. The apple, pear, and peach trees would be mature, bearing plentiful fruit every spring and summer. There'd be so much that they'd have to give boxes and boxes of the fruit to neighbors, even after they'd canned enough to fill the root cellar. The garden would take up a whole acre, and they'd only have to go to the store for cheese, bread, and chocolate. The basement would be finished, complete with a mini movie theater and gaming station.

She pulled into her parking spot on the concrete pad to the left of the driveway. She stared out the windshield, the conversation with her friends replaying in her head as she stared at the trampoline in the yard, its metal legs reflecting the golden light of sunset. She'd spent hours on that trampoline playing with friends, sharing secrets, even sleeping out when the summer nights were warm enough. It'd been a centerpiece of her middle school years. She sighed, hoping this view would never change.

"It won't change. I'm going to win that race." She said to herself.

She gathered her backpack off the passenger seat and headed inside to start her homework.

Chapter 11

Ariel sat at the computer, staring at the small rainbow circle cursor hovering over the blue and white "enter" button. Round and round it went. "Can you guys step back? I can smell your breath."

"Does it smell like ham?" Shelby asked, breathing a hot breath right in Ariel's face. "I had a ham and cheese sandwich for lunch."

"Ew, gross," Ariel exclaimed, covering her mouth and nose with her elbow. "You're disgusting."

"Mine probably smells like Pepsi," Sam said, adding her breath to the mix.

"Imma punch you," Ariel laughed, turning in her seat to swing at her twin.

"You're so predictable," Sam laughed, dancing away.

"Why isn't it loading?" Shelby asked, leaning in even closer to stare at the screen.

"Because it's not noon yet," Ariel said, pointing to the clock in the bottom right-hand corner of the screen. "We have two minutes."

"Longest two minutes of my life," Shelby moaned, pacing around the edges of the room.

"Of your life? You're not even the one applying!"

"Yeah, but I get secondhand emotions easily, you know that."

"Yeah yeah, whatever you say."

Ariel stood up and stretched her arms above her head, then down to touch her toes. She let her head hang, clasping opposite elbows and swinging gently side to side. "Someone tell me when it changes."

"Hey, where's Kyle? Wasn't he supposed to be here?"

"He was going to, but his dad needed help at the bike shop," Ariel said. As if on cue, Ariel's phone buzzed with a text from Kyle.

"Let me know when you get signed up! You're gonna rock it."

She smirked and typed back. *I'm just signing up for the chance at signing up. It's not a big deal.* She sent off the message and caught the look Shelby was giving her. "What?"

"What did he say?"

"How do you know it was him?" Ariel said, shrugging.

"You smirked and blushed at your phone. What did he say?"

Ariel rolled her eyes. "He just said to let him know when we get signed up."

"Will y'all just kiss already?"

"He doesn't like me, and I don't like him," Ariel said, laughing. "You've been giving us shit for years and nothing has come to fruition. Isn't it about time to give it up?"

"Nope," Shelby said, smiling a toothy grin. "Ron and Hermione were friends for years and look how they ended up."

"They weren't even real," Ariel insisted. "Is it noon yet?"

"It's twelve-o-one!" Shelby said, leaning over to look at the clock.

"Ah!" Ariel dashed to the computer and sat down, hitting refresh on the page. Mercifully, the spinning circle was replaced with a cursor and she clicked on the "Apply" button which redirected her to a new page. She filled out the entry form as quickly as she could type. A few minutes later, she hit the submit button and held her breath while the page reloaded. A few tense seconds later and the screen refreshed, revealing an exclamatory "Confirmation" on the page.

"Oh, thank God, I've gotten in. I'm signed up!" Ariel sighed, leaning back in her chair, her heart pounding in her chest. If just signing up for lottery gave her this much adrenaline, she wondered what it would be like to actually toe the starting line.

"Woohoo!" Shelby exclaimed, jumping up from the bean bag and hugging her friend. "You did it! You're in!"

"Just in the lottery though," Ariel reminded her. "I very well might not get into the race."

"When do you find out if your number was picked?" Sam asked.

"January. AKA forever," Ariel said, draping herself dramatically over the chair.

"Time will fly, it's already December." Shelby said. "We've got finals, and then Christmas!"

"This is true, Christmas will be a good distraction," Sam said. "Presents, cake, lights, trees, all the fun things."

"You're right," Ariel nodded. "I'll drown my sorrows in baking."

"Perfect," Shelby smiled. "Now, text Kyle so he doesn't get mad and then let's go downstairs. Whatever your mom is cooking for lunch smells heavenly."

"It's beer cheese soup and chili," Sam said, pushing herself up out of bed and climbing down the ladder. "We make it every Sunday in December."

"Hell yeah, did she make her sourdough bread too?"

"She always has fresh sourdough around," Sam said.

Ariel picked up her phone and shot off a quick text, which got an immediate reply. "*Congrats! You'll get in. I feel it in my bones.*" She couldn't help but smile when she saw his name pop up on the screen. It felt great knowing she had a team of support behind her. She tucked her phone back into her pocket and followed Sam and Shelby downstairs for lunch.

"So, girls, I have some news for you," Cheryl said later that night as they were cleaning up the dinner dishes. Cheryl was washing, Ariel was drying them, and Sam was putting the clean ones away. Shelby had said her goodbyes and headed home to finish homework, leaving the three to themselves.

"We're moving to the beach," Sam guessed.

"Hah, fat chance of that," Cheryl said. "No, your Aunt Erin is coming for Christmas."

"Ahhh are you serious?!" Ariel exclaimed, almost dropping the plate she was drying. "When does she get in?"

"She'll get here next week and stay until after the new year."

"Oh, that'll be fun," Ariel smiled.

"Agreed. We haven't seen her in forever," Sam said.

Aunt Erin was their favorite aunt. Mom's youngest sister was the aunt that every kid dreams of having. the one who takes trips to exotic lands and returns with the best presents to go along with her crazy stories. One of Ariel's best memories was when she returned from her month-long stint in Africa and Aunt Erin gifted her with a small stuffed rhino, along with an envelope detailing the real rhino a donation made in her name had adopted. All these years later she still got emails with updates about Reba the Rhino. Aunt Erin also had one of the coolest jobs: geological researcher. Ariel couldn't remember what exactly she specialized in, but whatever it was granted her the opportunity to travel to far-off places and get paid for it. The only downside to Aunt Erin was the fact she lived in California, meaning they only got to see her once a year at most. When they were younger, she'd made the trip more frequently, but the past few years they hadn't seen her at all. She'd made the trip for Dad's funeral but hadn't stayed long.

"Why's she coming this way for Christmas?" Ariel asked.

Cheryl shrugged. "She said she wants a white Christmas, but I think it's to check up on us."

"That's fine by me. What does she want to do while she's here?"

"You'll love this," Mom said, handing Ariel another dish to dry. "She said she wants a traditional Christmas. So the whole nine yards–lights, reindeer in the yard, a live tree."

Ariel did a happy dance. "Yes! I mean, I would've made you do all those things anyway, but now that she's coming you can't give me grief about it."

"Yeah, yeah, I thought you might appreciate that," Cheryl laughed.

Christmas had been a big deal all their childhood, and it was still Ariel's favorite holiday. Not because of the presents, but because of the rituals. Hunting for the perfect tree and bringing it home, decorating it, more dinners at Grandma and Grandpa's house, an afternoon spent putting up Christmas lights followed by hot chocolate and fried cheese, choking down the Christmas Eve oyster stew after sitting through an hour and a half of church, Christmas morning cinnamon rolls. And since Dad's side of the family essentially cut all ties after the funeral, there would be no oyster stew or dinner at Grandma and Grandpa's house. This fact filled both Ariel and Sam with an immense sadness. But the news of Aunt Erin's visit lifted her spirits. There was hope after all.

* * *

The next day after school, Ariel made her way down to Coach Bobbi's office. It was time to have the conversation that she'd been putting off for weeks. She knew she couldn't avoid Coach forever, and it wouldn't be long before Coach started barging into classrooms or her house to get a solid "yes or no" answer regarding her track season. She knew Coach was already suspicious as to why she hadn't signed up, and that suspicion was going to turn into action real quick.

Thankfully, most sports were already practicing in the gym or the weight room, so no one was milling about in the hallway. Coach's door was slightly ajar, and Ariel could see her sitting at her computer, reading something. She gently knocked on the door. "Hey Coach, you got a minute?"

"Hey, Ariel," Coach Bobbi said, sitting up and turning her swivel chair to face the doorway. "I've always got a minute for you. What's up? Are you coming to finally tell me what we're doing this year with track?"

"Haha," Ariel laughed nervously. She sat in the bean bag in the corner, the same chair she'd sat in many times over her high school years. "Yeah, I suppose I am."

"Hey, look," Coach said, leaning forward to rest her elbows on her knees. "I didn't mean to be so pushy. I know this year has been hard on you. It just shocked me when you weren't the first to sign up like you usually are and I was concerned. It's not like you not to jump at a chance to run."

"Yeah, you're right," she said, picking at lint on her leggings. "I appreciate you caring. I've had a lot to think about, and that's kind of what I wanted to talk to you about. I want your opinion on something, kind of your help too."

"Shoot. Whatcha got for me?"

She took a deep breath and launched into the explanation she'd practiced for weeks in front of the mirror, and then in front of Sam. She explained about the financial situation, her desire to do something life changing, to find herself post grief, etc. Ariel was grateful for Sam's speech team experience, otherwise this monologue would've been a list of logos but no pathos. Which would've been great, but unconvincing with no emotional appeal, and she knew she needed that to get Coach on her side. While Coach was generally supportive of lofty goals, this one pushed the gambit and Ariel knew she needed every bit of luck and strategy on her side.

"And that's why I want to run the Leadville 100, and that's why I want you to help me do it. Not only do I want you to help me, but I need your help. These runners I'm going against, they're professionals. And they have teams of professionals running their support crews and pacing them. So, I'm going to need my own set of pros."

Coach Bobbi leaned back in her chair, intertwining her fingers behind her head, elbows splayed out to the side. "Well, I'm no pro," she said without missing a beat. She fell silent for a few minutes, turning over the well of information Ariel had just laid in her lap.

"And Shelby said you used to run ultras," Ariel said, unable to stand the silence any longer. "How did that never come up in conversation?"

Coach's stoic face cracked a small smile, her eyes bright. "Back in my day, yeah, I ran a few."

"Come on, you've got to tell me more than that. What did you run? How many have you done?"

"I did a few fifty milers, but only two one hundred milers," Coach said, shrugging as if what she just listed off wasn't impressive. "I never placed in the hundreds, but I did get third overall in one of my fifty milers."

"That's incredible! Why did you never mention it?"

"It never came up, I guess."

Ariel rolled her eyes. "You can't tell me, in all the decades of knowing me, all the conversations we've had around running, running careers, etc. that that wouldn't have come up?"

"You're only seventeen, I've known you one decade and some change. I swear, I wasn't hiding it or anything," Coach laughed, leaning forward to rest her elbows on the desk. "I'm not one to brag about my accomplishments and it never really did seem relevant. Until now I suppose."

"Right, which is why—"

Coach held up her hand. "Are they really offering half a million dollars to the overall winner?"

"Sure are," Ariel nodded. She studied Coach's face for any hint of what she was thinking. But as usual, her poker face was stable, revealing nothing other than that she was listening. "One of the founders died and that was what he wanted in his will."

Coach shook her head. "That's way more prize money than has ever been offered in ultrarunning. Hell, that's more than any professional sport outside the NFL. You know what that means, right?"

"That when I win, I'm going to be rich?" Ariel answered, half joking, half serious.

"That's a huge goal on a regular year. But this year? With that kind of money on the line? Every pro that's ever been pro is going to be there."

"That's the beauty of the lottery though," Ariel said, trying to suppress her smirk. She had practiced this argument plenty of times. "It gives everyone a fair chance, at least as fair as it can be."

"You do know the elites get reserved spots sometimes, right?"

"Yeah, but only a small amount and per the race website that amount isn't changing this year."

Coach Bobbi sighed, rubbing her temples. "Kid, you've got an answer for everything, don't you?

"Sure do. Because I've thought this through."

"You know the odds of you finishing the race are low, and that the odds of actually winning are less than one percent, right?"

"I'm well aware," Ariel said, sitting up tall. "And I don't care. I know all the statistics are against me. The race has a forty-five percent finisher rate, even getting in is difficult. But it's these exact odds, the shear impossibility of it, that makes me want to do it. And it's what's going to make it work, even if I don't win."

"How do you figure?"

Ariel leaned back in her chair; arms open wide. "What news outlet wouldn't want to pick up this story? Local Midwest running legend attempts one of the hardest ultramarathons in the US? C'mon. Just the publicity alone might be enough to launch me somewhere. What's that saying? Shoot for the moon, and even if you miss you land amongst the stars?"

Coach cracked a smile. "You're crazy, you know that, right?"

"My mother reminds me of it every day."

"Well… I honestly don't know what to say," Coach said, rubbing her hands together. "You know how unlikely it is to win and even to finish the race?"

"Yes."

"And you know that training for this is going to be incredibly difficult, and that the risk for injury is high and you might not even make it to the race?"

"Yes."

"And you know that I am in no way a professional runner. I'm simply a lowly high school cross country and track coach, and English teacher."

"You're not lowly, but yes."

"And you know you can train for this and still compete in track and field this spring?"

Ariel smiled. "No, I didn't actually, that's why I was hesitant about it. But if you say it's all right, I'm game."

"Good," Coach said, breathing a heavy sigh. She turned towards her computer and brought up the track and field sign up. "We really need you in the 4 x 800 meter relay."

"I'm a little concerned I won't be up to par if I'm focusing on my distance and not the track events. Are you sure I can do both?"

Coach leaned forward, resting her elbows on her desk. She glanced around as if to make sure no one overheard them, but there was no one else in the room. "Look. If you were any other runner, I'd say hell no. You have to focus on one. But you on your worst day is still better than anyone else on this track team. I don't mean that to play favorites, it's just a simple fact. You have a gift for running most don't."

Ariel felt her cheeks blush. "Thanks, Coach. I appreciate that."

"It's true. Here, you can sign up from my computer while we keep chatting." Coach stood up and gave Ariel the chair so she could operate the computer. Instead of sitting, Coach slowly walked around the small office.

"What more is there to chat about?"

"Oh. So much," Coach Bobbie said. "We need to make a training plan, a nutrition plan, we should probably also get you another sports physical… have you thought about who else might help crew? Also, do you want a pacer?"

"Coach, take a breath," Ariel laughed. "We've got time to answer all of that. But to give you some peace of mind: I'll figure out the crew and the sports physical, you figure out the training plan and nutrition stuff. And yes, if you'd pace me at some point that'd be great. But I know nothing about pacers so I'll read up on that."

Coach nodded. "I can do that. I'm going to have to start running more seriously haha. I'll see if any of my old running buddies in Denver will be around too, maybe they can pitch in if we need back up."

"I mean, if you're willing to see what connections you have, that would be great. Trust me, the more support we can get, the better off we'll be."

"Oh, don't I know it," Coach said. "Which reminds me of one other thing. What about Colorado State? You do realize that if you win any prize money in this race, that makes you ineligible for any NCAA participation? You'll lose all your scholarships."

Ariel swallowed. "That's only if they don't approve of athletes being able to get paid. It certainly seems like that's where we're headed."

"I mean… it's not certain yet. Are you willing to risk that?"

A small feeling of doubt played in the back of Ariel's mind, but she pushed it away. "Yes. This is far bigger than college scholarships if that's what it comes to. But I don't think it will."

"Have you at least told the coach at Colorado State about it?"

"She's on a need-to-know basis," Ariel shrugged. "And I figure she only needs to know if I win the prize money. Because if I don't, it changes nothing. And if I do win and the NCAA rules athletes can be paid, it also changes nothing."

Coach gave her a stern look but dropped the subject. "This is a mountain. If we're going to take it seriously—"

"Which we are," Ariel interrupted.

"Which we are," Coach repeated. "Then I'll call in all the favors I have. But you have to promise me one thing."

"Anything," Ariel said, not taking her eyes off the computer screen. She finished filling in the last few spots on the form and hit submit. "I'll get you the signup fee tomorrow after I talk to my mom."

"Don't worry about it," Coach said. "Wait, Cheryl knows about this, right?"

"Sure does."

"Okay good. That was going to be my first point, but that's taken care of. But you have to promise me that if you're hurt, or we determine that it's unsafe for you to keep training or racing, you have to listen to me and know when to quit, okay?"

"Done," she said, rereading the signup form on the screen and not really listening.

"No, I need you to look at me," Coach said, standing next to her. "You're a great runner, but you don't know when to quit. And that's been fine in high school, but it won't always be fine. It could get you hurt and ruin any running career you might want to have. I need you to look at me, and pinky promise to me that you'll listen to me if I say you need to stop." Coach held her hand out, pinky extended.

Ariel laughed. But Coach's face was stoic and serious. "I promise," Ariel said, reaching out her pinky to seal the deal. But Coach yanked it away.

"You're serious?" she asked, lifting an eyebrow.

"I am. I know I need to learn when to quit, that's part of why I need you."

"Okay," Coach said, nodding and wiggling her pinky. "I believe you now."

Ariel looped her pinky around Coach's and they shook, sealing their pinky promise. "You didn't before?"

"I mean, I seventy percent believed you. But now I'm one hundred percent."

"Ha, okay." Ariel stood up from the desk and picked her backpack up off the floor. "Thank you for being so supportive. I was worried to talk to you about it."

"Well, like I've said since you were a little kid. I'll always support you how I can. Even if what you're doing is crazy."

"I appreciate it." Ariel smiled. "I better get home. I've got a mountain of calculus homework to do for tomorrow."

"Yes, go, get after it," Coach said, shooing her out of the office. "Which reminds me, your grades can't drop because of all this, capisce? You never known when you'll need those for a scholarship."

"<u>When</u> I win in the prize money," Ariel winked. "There'll be enough left over from paying the mortgage I won't need a scholarship, academic or otherwise."

Chapter 12

The morning sky was still dark and silent, the only sound the soft crunch of gravel under Ariel's feet as she ran down her usual route. Grateful the snows had held off, she cherished the winter mornings she could actually get out and run. Soon, the snow and ice storms of January would come, making the roads too slick to run on before the sun rose, the icy temperatures and wind transforming her favorite route into an ice rink. But that was still a few weeks off, thankfully.

As she ran, her mind drifted to the looming race and everything it would entail. The idea of it lit a fire deep in her belly, an excitement that she couldn't quite explain. Using her God-given talent and love of running to help the people she loved most? That was more than she'd ever dreamed of. And so far, everyone had been more supportive than she'd expected. She looked forward to getting home, something that didn't usually happen when she was out for a run. But she was excited to sit down with her team and start ironing out concrete logistics and training plans.

She turned onto the homestretch, her watch beeping to alert her she was at mile eighteen. Only two left to go in her long run. She scanned her body from head to toe. Everything felt good. Not like she'd just jumped out of bed, but back-to-back double digit miles were feeling easier and easier. Ariel pushed the pace the last two miles to home, until her legs and lungs burned with the effort. As she cruised down the street towards home, the sky changed from midnight to indigo to a soft sherbet sunrise. By the time she made it to the driveway, the sun was peeking over the horizon.

Ariel smiled as she ground to a walk, resting both her hands on her head, surveying the scene before her. The corn fields surrounding their little property stood empty, now just collections of old stalks and churned dirt that steamed in the sunlight, the earthy smell of soil permeating the brisk air. Their neighbor's house silhouetted against the sunrise, her mom's tall grasses lining the property glowing golden. A slight breeze blew, sending a shiver down her spine.

"Hey, crazy!" Kyle yelled from across the street, jolting Ariel back to reality. He waved from his front porch. She jogged over to meet him.

"What're you doing up this early on a Saturday?" Ariel asked, her breath creating small clouds.

"I'm usually up this early, just not outside."

Ariel narrowed her eyes at him. "Somehow I doubt that."

"Yeah, you got me," Kyle chuckled, running a hand through his hair. Ariel felt a tug in her chest. "Just trying to impress the girl who seems invincible to cold and early mornings."

"They are two of my favorite things." Ariel laughed, flipping her ponytail over her shoulder. An awkward silence fell between the two, Ariel waiting for him to speak while he stared at his feet.

"So, what're you up to today?" Ariel asked, breaking the silence.

"That depends," he said, finally looking up to meet her gaze. "Want to go see that new Sandra Bullock movie that just came out?"

Her heart nearly leapt out of her chest. "Are you asking me on a date, Kyle James?"

"Yeah," he said with a nervous smile. "I think you've known that I've liked you for a while now. I haven't exactly been discreet about it."

Ariel smiled. "I mean, you haven't been that obvious either."

"And I've gotten the feeling you feel the same?" he asked, shoving his hands in his pockets. "Please tell me I read the mark right on that one."

It was Ariel's turn to stare at her feet. "You're right."

His bashful smile grew into a more confident one. Ariel held up a finger before he could say anything else.

"It's complicated though," she said. "I don't want to mess up our friendship."

"We won't," Kyle assured her, the excitement evident in his voice. "We'll just be best friends who also go on dates."

"After the race."

"After which race?" Kyle asked. "You're going to probably have several coming up."

"Haha, good point. After Leadville," Ariel said. "I can't lose focus on that."

"After Leadville? That's in August, that's practically a year away."

"Half a year." Ariel corrected him.

"I just want to spend more time with you," Kyle said, stepping forward and taking her hands in his. His hands were rough and warm, the warmth spreading up Ariel's arms and down her back. His touch was comforting.

"We spend a lot of time together already. You come over practically every day after school. And we're going to start having race crew meetings, so that's even more time we'll be spending together."

"You know what I mean," he said, drawing her closer so she could feel the heat radiating off his chest. "Time for just you and I."

Ariel's gaze dropped to the ground. "I don't know, Kyle. When do you suggest we'd spend time by ourselves? Like tonight, what time do you want to go to the movie?"

"There's a showing at seven."

"And it's probably two hours, so we'd be out around ten because the movie never actually starts at seven. Plus twenty minutes-drive time home and if we didn't sit around chatting or making out afterwards, I'd get to bed around eleven. Do you know what time I'm up for my morning training?"

"Not really."

"Four," Ariel answered. "So that means at most I'd get five hours of sleep which would mean I'd be exhausted for my training run which means the workout won't be maximized and my recovery will be compromised. I'd assume you'd want to go out once a week or so?"

"As many times as possible," Kyle said, trying to get a word in but Ariel cut him off.

"Take that times a few weeks, the sleep deprivation adds up, my workouts get worse, I stop improving, I get injured because I'm trying to train harder to make up for the poor performance and then I can't even get to the start line at Leadville because I'm injured. Do you see the problem here?" Ariel asked, desperate for him to understand.

"You think too much," Kyle said, squeezing her hands. "All of that is a what if."

"But it's a what if I have control over," Ariel said. "Training is priority number one right now. If something compromises it or gets in my way, it can't happen. I like you. A lot. But I can't give up this race for you."

"I'm not asking you to," Kyle assured her.

"I know it seems crazy, but I need to wait. Just until the race is over," Ariel said. "I want to give this my all. And I don't want to half ass a relationship with you, either."

Kyle's gaze fell. "Well, when you put it like that…"

Ariel squeezed his hands and brought them to her face, planting a kiss on his knuckles. "You give me butterflies, Kyle James. I love the time we spend together. Can we please wait until after I climb this mountain to give us a try?"

A crooked smile played at his lips. He pulled her close and wrapped his arms around her in a bear hug. She inhaled his woodsy scent. "Anything for you, Ariel Jane."

She pulled back and looked into his blue eyes. "Thank you." For a brief moment, she thought he would lean down to kiss her, but he loosened his hug and stepped back.

"Go get warm," he said. "I don't want my girl getting a chill."

Ariel's heart leapt into her throat at the words "my girl" and she nodded. "See you at the crew meeting later?"

"Wouldn't miss it for the world."

Ariel turned on her heel and dashed back across the street to her house, mentally screaming to herself the whole way there. She couldn't believe that had just happened. She shook her arms and legs when she got to the porch, working off the excess excitement so as not to tip off Mom or Sam about anything. This was just between her and Kyle.

A short hour later, Ariel was showered, dressed, and ready for the day. She rolled her yoga mat out in the living room and took a bite of her blueberry muffin, chewing as she stuck one leg out and stretched over it. Her phone buzzed in her pocket.

"You awake?"

Ariel rolled her eyes and texted Shelby back. *"Of course I am, come over."*

"Still in PJS, be over in 30."

Ariel set her phone aside and continued stretching, taking bites of her muffin in between. She was still in awe that Mom had found a way to sneak protein powder into her all-time favorite snack— while the carbs were good, she noticed she was needing more protein for recovery.

Ariel felt a warm feeling of immense gratitude for a mom who would put in so much work to make her daughter happy.

"Hey, good morning," Cheryl said as she walked into the living room.

"Hey yourself!" Ariel exclaimed. "Where have you been all morning? I was getting worried."

Just then, Coach Bobbi appeared behind her. "We went out for breakfast."

"And I wasn't invited?" Ariel said, her mouth hanging open in feigned shock.

"Sorry, adults only." Mom teased, plopping down on the love seat. "You wouldn't have given up your morning run for sitting around stuffing your face anyway."

"Your Mom's right," Coach said, cocking an eyebrow. "Plus, we need a break from all you crazy kids."

"I mean, you're not wrong, but you could've brought me back something," Ariel insisted.

"Who all's coming over this morning?" Cheryl said, diverting the conversation.

"Shelby and Kyle. Coach is already here so we're just waiting on the other two," Ariel said. She glanced at the clock on the wall. "Sam's supposed to come but who knows if she'll be awake in time."

As if on cue, a sleepy, messy haired Sam appeared at the bottom of the stairs, still rubbing sleep from her eyes.

"Hey! You're awake!" Ariel beamed.

Sam shook her head and shuffled to the kitchen. She reemerged a few minutes later with a steaming mug of coffee and tucked herself in beside Mom. After she'd sipped on the drink, she finally spoke. "Morning. You can never doubt how much I love you now."

"I know, waking up before nine on a weekend? I'm forever in your debt."

"Hell yeah you are," Sam said, holding the coffee mug close to her face, as if inhaling the steam would make the morning more tolerable.

Ariel rolled up her mat and returned it to its spot beside the TV. "Anyone want more coffee?"

All three nodded their heads in affirmation. "Geeze, it's like no one's a morning person around here." Ariel walked to the kitchen and retrieved three ceramic mugs, the pot of coffee, and a hot pad. She delivered the items to the living room and returned to grab creamer and the tray of mini quiches she'd made up last night.

"Wow, this is quite the spread," Coach Bobbi said as she watched Ariel lay out the goodies on the table.

"Oh, I've got more too," Ariel said with a wink, dashing back to the kitchen before returning with another serving tray. This one was full of blueberry muffins. "No official team meeting is complete without muffins."

"Your obsession is next level," Sam said as she leaned forward, taking a muffin herself. "Come to think of it, you're just obsessive all around."

"Eh, I know," Ariel shrugged. "Part of my charm."

As Mom was pouring coffee for herself and Coach, the front door opened and in walked Shelby and Kyle.

"Good morning, everyone!" Shelby said, clapping her hands together. Her slicked back ponytail bounced with her energetic steps. "Let's get this party started."

"Hey," nodded Kyle. Ariel noticed that he'd put on a new flannel shirt and dark blue jeans, despite it being Saturday. Most weekends he never left sweatpants. Ariel's heart fluttered when he looked her way and winked. She smirked at him. Somehow, their secret conversation they'd had earlier only made right now more fun. She looked away before her face aroused suspicion from the watchful eyes of Shelby or Sam.

"Come in, eat! Drink coffee!" Ariel said, catching her mom's sideways glance. Before, she never let the girls have caffeine but ever since Dad had died, she'd relaxed a little. She didn't say no this morning. Shelby and Kyle helped themselves to drinks and snacks while Ariel passed around blue notebooks and pens to everyone.

"Okay, are we ready to get this party started?" Ariel asked, clapping her hands together.

"Sure are," Coach Bobbi said, the only one close to mirroring her enthusiasm.

"Well then! Welcome to the first official meeting of 'The Crew.' I want to thank each and every one of you for being here today, especially those of you who are not morning people. Your support means the world to me. The point of this meeting is to outline crew roles and expectations, and to start a list of questions we all have. This is a huge learning curve for all of us, myself included, so no question is dumb. First item on the agenda, we need a team name. We can't just be 'The Crew'. We need something more original, more pizazz."

"I dunno, I like the simplicity of "The Crew"," Sam said. "No confusion on what we're about."

"Originality, though!" Ariel insisted. "We need a more fun name. Everyone, work on brainstorming ideas, and we'll go over them at the next meeting. Sound good?"

The group nodded, Mom and Shelby writing it down in their notebooks. Ariel grinned. She knew those two would be the logistical ones, and that she could count on Sam and Kyle for more of the creative things.

"Great. Now," Ariel said, turning to face Coach Bobbi. "Coach here has done some of these types of races before. Not only that, but she's coached me for nearly six years. She knows all my strengths, weaknesses, what motivates me, what doesn't, she gets me. Because of all these things, she's going to be our crew captain. On race day, what she says goes. If there's a decision that needs to be made, questions that need answered, she's your lady."

Coach Bobbi smiled, humbly nodding her head in acknowledgement. "Thank you, Ariel. I appreciate your trust in me. I want to be clear though, I'm not an expert at ultras. Not even close."

"You have more experience than any of us, so for all intents and purposes, you're the expert," Cheryl laughed playfully. "You really are the most qualified person to lead this little rag tag team." The rest of the group nodded in agreement.

"Perfect, glad we all agree. Every one of you is vital to this team," Ariel assured them. "Mom, you're the calorie counter and food expert. Come race day, you're going to be counting everything that goes in and out and convincing me to eat when I don't want to."

"Got it," Cheryl nodded, her face serious. "I've been doing that since you were little."

"Exactly." Ariel winked at her.

"Shelby, Sam, and Kyle," Ariel said, turning to her friends. "You're the hype and logistics team. We need to know which stations we can get crew to, what we can have there, estimated arrival and departure times, and knowing which roads to use to get there. I also need someone pep-talking me whenever I see you. Can y'all do those things?"

"Sure can," Sam said.

"No problem," Kyle nodded.

"You know I love a plan," Shelby said, not looking up from her paper as she furiously scribbled notes. On what, Ariel wasn't sure, but whatever it was, it was probably going to come in handy later.

"Awesome, so we're all in agreement of our roles on race day?"

Everyone nodded.

"Perfect. We'll go over them and refine them more the closer we get, but for now, we'll stick with that." Ariel said.

"What about pacers?" Sam asked.

"What about them?"

"Are you going to have any?"

"Well, Shelby, remember that conversation about you pacing me?" Ariel turning to face Shelby, whose eyes grew wide and terrified.

"Oh you were serious?"

Ariel put up her hands. "Of course, I was serious! But before you can say anything, remember, you won't be running anywhere near a hundred miles. I can't even have my first pacer until mile 62. You can do as small a section as you want, but it really would be helpful for me mentally and maybe even physically. Who knows how tired and loopy I'll be towards the end."

"She's right," Coach Bobbi said. "Pacers are race savers."

Shelby held Ariel's gaze for a moment before shaking her head. "Anything for you, girl. I'm not gonna like it though."

Ariel stood up and launched at Shelby, bear hugging her. "Oh thank you! You're the best!"

"I know I am," Shelby said, voice muffled by Ariel's sweatshirt.

"Coach, I'd like it if you'd be able to pace me too," Ariel said. "Maybe towards the very end, that way your crew chief duties will mostly be done?"

"Yeah, I think that's a good idea," Coach agreed. "I wouldn't want to do it any earlier. Usually people don't have their crew chief also pace them, but I think our situation is a little unique. I think it would work."

"Great. Plus what better way to bring in the race than by having my OG running Coach with me?"

"It would be pretty cool, I will admit," Coach Bobbi said, smiling. "Seeing you run around your backyard in diapers as a kid to running across the finish line of an ultra? You don't get more full circle than that."

"Stop it, you're gonna make me tear up," Cheryl said, gently slapping Bobbi's shoulder while blinking back little tears.

"So sentimental," Bobbi laughed.

"You'll be the same when you have kids, don't you worry," Cheryl chided.

"What if I wanted to pace a bit too?" Kyle asked. "I know I was never a cross star, but I think it'd be fun."

"Sure! The more the merrier," Ariel said, surprised at his offer. "I can have up to four pacers, so I'm down for whoever wants to pace." Kyle and Ariel's gazes met, sending a warm rush through her body. She shook it off and returned to the task at hand. "What questions do people have?"

"None at this time," Sam said. "Oh wait, yes I do. How early will we have to be getting up?"

"For the race?"

"Yeah."

"You don't wanna know," Ariel laughed. Sam groaned. "Just remember, it's only one day. The rest of the days you'll get to sleep in. And we'll make all future crew meetings later in the day from now on."

"Promise?" Sam asked.

"Promise," Ariel laughed. "Now any real questions?"

"I don't think so," Cheryl said, looking from side to side at everyone in the room who were all shaking their heads no. "But I'm sure we'll all come up with some as we go along. We don't know what we don't know yet."

"That's what I figured." Ariel pointed to the notebooks and pens. "That's why I gave everyone the notebooks. Write down your questions as they come to you and we can talk about them at our next meeting, which is next month after the holidays."

"In the meantime," Coach Bobbi said. "I've been looking at training plans and race schedules. Do you want to talk about that now?"

"Do I ever! Spill, what do you have for us?"

"Well," Coach Bobbi said, sitting on the edge of the couch and opening a folder in front of her. She removed several loose pieces of paper and placed them on the table in front of her. "Your training schedule will be determined by the races you might want to enter prior. You're making a huge leap, going from 5k to hundred miler. Ninety-nine percent of athletes do at least some races over marathon distance prior to tackling the really big courses."

"Do we have time for that?" Ariel asked, picking up one of the papers. It was a flyer for a 50k race in January in northern Iowa. "The weather here isn't really conducive for winter races, and we can't afford to fly to the coasts for anything."

"I know, that's making the situation a unique challenge, but not impossible. There's a few 50k and fifty-mile races in the Midwest this winter. I think the best one is the one you're holding there, Ariel. The Dubuque Winterfest. It's got a lot of climbing and would help introduce you to how these races function. It would also give us as a crew a bit of practice."

"I mean, it sounds like a great idea, but the ice on trails sounds like it could be a little dangerous," Ariel said, suddenly questioning their decision.

"Exactly," Coach said, smiling mischievously. "That's going to a big part of the training. You've got to learn how to run on more technical terrain. Leadville isn't highly technical, but it is trail and you've mostly been training on road. And here in Iowa, ice is about the most technical terrain we can find. If you can run on ice, you can run on anything."

Ariel knew she had a point. "Okay, I'm game. If we do this one, what does the training look like?"

Coach Bobbi and Ariel went over the training plan for the next hour in detail, hashing out little discrepancies here and there, starting to build a nutrition plan alongside it. To their credit, everyone listened intently, Shelby and Mom taking faithful notes even though this was the stuff that bored them to tears. Ariel appreciated their dedication and attention.

"Sounds like we've got a lot of work to do," Ariel said, sitting back on her heels. But despite admitting the long road ahead, her mouth parted into a grin. "I can't wait to get to work."

Chapter 13

"Good lord," Erin exclaimed as she dashed from the garage into the house. "I forgot how cold it is here." She jigged in place, pulling her thin coat tighter around her neck.

"Yeah, being away for fifteen years will do that to you," Cheryl said, hanging her coat next to the door.

"Hey, I've been back plenty of times since I moved to San Francisco. It's just always in the summers." Erin slipped off her shoes but left her coat on as she walked into the kitchen. Ariel and Sam appeared around the corner, their faces bright with smiles.

"Girls!" Erin said, stretching her arms out and embracing them all in a hug. Her long blonde hair smelled of flowery shampoo, a scent Ariel recognized from the last time she'd seen her. "I've missed you."

"We've missed you too," Sam and Ariel exclaimed in unison.

Erin stepped back and held the girls at arms' length. "I know everyone says this, but good lord you've both grown so much. How tall are you, Sam?"

"Five-seven," Sam said, standing up a little taller. "Tallest one in the family now."

"By half an inch," Ariel said, sticking her tongue out.

"And you," Erin said, turning to Ariel. "You've grown into such a young woman. And you both look so much like your momma."

They rolled their eyes. "We're going to start charging people when they say that. Use it for our college fund," Ariel laughed.

"Or we could enter the Mother-Daughter lookalike contest at the State Fair. Maybe we'd get a sponsorship or something," Cheryl teased.

"Maybe if they had prize money. I like to be compensated for my embarrassment."

It was Cheryl's turn to roll her eyes. She turned to her sister, slipping her hand through her elbow and pulling her towards the stairs. "C'mon, Erin. I'll show you to your room and help you get settled, then we can figure out dinner."

After Erin was settled into the guest room, they made a quick homemade pizza dinner. Erin was tired after her day of travel, so they made some tea and all four women cozied up on the couch.

"So, Ariel, I hear you have some big news to tell me," Erin said, glancing at her through the steam wafting off the mug.

"I don't know if I'd call it big news," Ariel shrugged. "But I'm going to be running my first ultramarathon next August."

"An ultra? That's huge!" Erin smiled. "Even I've never considered running more than twenty-six point two miles."

"You don't have to, you're so good at the
marathon you don't need to run further," Ariel laughed.
Her aunt was the only other runner in the family. She'd run
in high school and college as well, transitioning to
marathons after her collegiate career. She often placed in
the top ten of her age division and almost qualified for the
Olympics, missing the cut off by only thirty-two seconds.

"Which one are you doing?"

"The Leadville 100."

Erin's eyes widened. "Are you really?"

"Yeah, why?"

Erin glanced to her sister. "I was going to wait to
tell you all, but this summer I'm working an assignment in
Denver."

"Are you freaking serious?!" Ariel exclaimed,
rocketing off the couch. "Can I come live with you? It
would be so perfect for training, I'd have such a better
chance at winning, I'll help with all the housework, I can
get a part time job to help you with rent, I—"

"Whoa, slow down there for a second," Erin
laughed.

"Ariel, you cannot just invite yourself to stay with
someone," Cheryl scolded, her cheeks blushing. "Erin, I'm
sorry."

"Okay, first of all, you have nothing to be sorry
about. It's not rude at all. Second, Ariel, I think that sounds
like a fantastic idea. And don't worry about helping with
rent, that's the beauty of work assignments. They pay for
all of that."

"I officially want your job," Ariel nodded firmly. "But after this running thing. So I can? I can come out? When do you go?"

Erin laughed. "A million questions."

"This is normal," Cheryl laughed. "But Ariel, we have a lot to talk about. I'm not against you going, but this is a big piece of news. We'll talk about it more and see, okay?"

"Then let's talk about it right now," Ariel smiled.

"I'm down for talking more, but tomorrow," Erin yawned. "It's been a long day for me. But my assignment starts next June and goes through September. So we have plenty of time to figure out timeframes, logistics, all of that." Erin finished her last swig of tea and stood up, stretching her arms overhead. "Do we have any plans for tomorrow?"

Cheryl shook her head. "I'm just filling out job applications and have an interview that should be done by three, then I'll be home. I thought we could go grocery shopping afterwards, plan out some meals."

"Sounds fantastic," Erin nodded. She stood from the couch, stretching her long arms above her head. "Good night, everyone, I'll see you in the morning."

"Good night!" all three said in unison.

After she heard the door to the guest room close, Ariel whipped around to face her mom, an ear-to-ear grin on her face. "Mom! That's the universe."

"What?"

"Aunt Erin's trip! It's the universe saying I'm meant to run Leadville! It's literally so perfect, such a coincidence that it couldn't be anything else."

"I like your enthusiasm, Ariel, but I don't think the universe is doing things for you."

"It is," Ariel said, undeterred by her mother's skepticism. "I'm going to go to bed too so I can get my recovery run in early tomorrow morning." Ariel bent down and hugged her mom. "Love you."

"Love you too," Cheryl called after her daughter as she bounded upstairs.

The next evening, while Mom was cooking dinner on the stove, Ariel sat at the island with her laptop and two notebooks spread open on either side of her. She scribbled notes in one, then the other, comparing and contrasting training plans and nutrition strategies. Coach Bobbi had given her a few websites to comb through to start building a foundation.

"I was thinking this weekend we'd decorate the Christmas tree and do our cookie baking," Cheryl said.

"Finally!" Sam said from the living room. "I've been begging you for weeks."

"I know, I wanted to wait until your aunt was here."

"Cheryl, you didn't have to wait for me," Erin said, bumping her hip against her sister's. She was busy cutting up cucumbers and carrots for the salad.

"Can we talk more about going to Colorado this summer?" Ariel interrupted.

There was a long pause, the only sound the sizzling of onion on the stovetop and the chopping of the knife through carrots. Cheryl sighed. "I suppose. There's no way you're just going to let it go, are you?"

Ariel shook her head side to side. "Not a chance. So? Are you okay with me going?"

Cheryl didn't look up from the pan she was stirring. "I mean, Erin, are you okay with this? I know this is a big project for you and you'll be working a lot. Are you okay with having a teenager around?"

"I won't even be a teenager! I'll be eighteen, a full-blown, legal adult," Ariel interjected.

"Maybe, but you're still a teenager technically," Cheryl said. Ariel couldn't see her eyes, but she felt the eye roll.

"Of course I'm okay with having her around," Erin said. "It'll be nice to have the company, and someone to help with the dishes every now and then. Plus, we could even go on training runs together. But when you hit twenty-six miles, I'm out."

"That's fair," Ariel laughed. "As long as you'll join me for the last few miles sometimes."

"You've got yourself a deal."

Cheryl sighed. "If Aunt Erin is okay with it, and you continue to prove yourself a responsible young lady, then yes, you can go. But we need to talk about time frame."

Ariel swallowed hard. She knew this would be the one thing she might have to fight harder for. "I want to go from a week before the marathon until after Leadville."

That got Mom's full attention. She whipped around as if Ariel had just told her she was going to be a grandma. "Wait, what marathon? I thought this thing was an ultra?"

"It is," Ariel said, slowing her breathing to remain calm. "But remember Coach Bobbi suggesting that if I could, try to run a race at altitude before the big day?"

"Yeah, I remember," Cheryl reluctantly admitted.

"I mean, that makes sense," Erin agreed.

"So… the organization that puts on the hundred-mile race also puts on a marathon in June. What better way to prepare than to run a race on part of the course?"

Cheryl turned around, her brow furrowed. "That means you're gone the entire summer."

"Not the entire summer," Ariel corrected. "It would be the late June, like around the nineteenth and then until August twenty-third or something."

"I thought the race was August seventeenth," Cheryl said, eyes narrowed.

"It is, but I don't want to hop on a plane the day after I run a hundred miles. I'm guessing I'm going to need a few days to recoup and, if I win, I'll have media interviews and stuff in the area."

"That's a pretty big if," Mom said.

"Thanks for the vote of confidence," Ariel said, shrinking back a bit.

"I didn't mean it like that," Cheryl said, her face softening. "I don't want you gone all summer long. I know that's selfish of me, but…"

"Can I interrupt for a moment?" Erin interjected.

"What?"

"She's going to be going off to college in Colorado anyway, right?" Erin pointed out. "This would be a great way for her to get established in the community before school starts, and I'll be there for support. Kids that have family around when they go to college are proven to get better grades and land better jobs after they graduate."

Cheryl shook her head. "You always come in with all these scientific facts."

"That's what I do," Erin smiled. "I'm a scientist. That doesn't get turned off when I'm not at work. And, you're overlooking one other major factor."

"And what's that?" Cheryl asked, clearly peeved her sister wasn't exactly on her side.

"You can come and visit anytime," Erin said, poking her sister's shoulder. "The place they're setting me up in has three bedrooms. You have a place to stay for free, and the plane tickets to Denver are super cheap from Des Moines, and the flight is short enough that you can leave on a Friday after work and get back Sunday well before your work week begins."

Cheryl stared daggers at Erin, her mouth pressed into a thin line.

"She's right Mom," Ariel said, smiling at Erin, who gave her a small nod. "That would be so much fun."

"What about Sam?" Cheryl asked, finally thinking of something that hadn't been addressed.

"She can come too," Erin replied without missing a beat. "And she's got that job she's been working for a bit now, so she can pay her own way."

Cheryl threw her hands up. "I can't think of any other excuses."

Ariel leapt off her stool and threw her arms around her mom. "So that means I can go for the whole time? And that you'll come and visit me?!"

"I suppose it does," Cheryl said reluctantly. "We'll see about the me-coming-to-visit-you part. I'd love to, but I have so much to do here."

Ariel rolled her eyes before releasing her mom from the hug. She decided to ignore the comment, leaving that fight for another day. "Thank you, Mom. You have no idea how much my odds of winning, hell, of even just finishing, just went up! I've gotta go tell Coach!"

Ariel bounded off upstairs to make a phone call to Coach Bobbi, updating her on their training situation. Surely this opportunity would only serve to make the training easier. Just the other day, Coach had mentioned how attempting to train for altitude at their barely-above-sea-level area was the single biggest obstacle to success. And now, it seemed like that obstacle was now a thing of the past.

* * *

Ariel stared out her bedroom window, clutching her red and black plaid Christmas blanket around her shoulders to ward off the wintery chill. The sky was cloudy and grey, the type of slate sheet stretching as far as the eye can see. The kind that didn't show up until February, but here it was, making an appearance the week before Christmas. The spruce tree branches were bowing underneath the weight of a fresh snow, courtesy of a low pressure system that had parked over the Midwest for the past several days. School had been cancelled, blessing Ariel and Sam with an extra three days on their winter break. Today was the day they were going to finally make the house feel like Christmas.

Ariel was both excited and sad—this would be the first holiday season without Dad, and things didn't feel quite right, even with Aunt Erin there. Nothing compared to Dad's excitement about Christmas. He loved decorating the tree and always insisted on baking five different types of cookies. Cheryl would participate, just to make him happy. Ariel took a deep breath, held it for a count of four, and let it go slowly, willing herself to be the one to bring the joy today. Dad was here in spirit and the best way to remember that was to honor the traditions they loved most. She quickly exchanged her pajamas for running tights and a sweatshirt, along with a pair of fluffy socks, and headed downstairs.

Cheryl was already in the living room, sipping on her coffee and thumbing through the Bible in her lap. "Well good morning sleepy head," she greeted her, glancing at the clock. "It's nearly seven-thirty. I was starting to get worried."

Ariel rubbed her eyes. "I've been up for a while. I was reading in bed and didn't want to get up quite yet."

Cheryl furrowed her brow. "Aren't you starving? You always eat first thing when you get up."

"I'm so hungry I could throw up," Ariel said.

"Do you want me to make you something?" Cheryl asked, closing her Bible and setting it to the side.

Ariel shook her head. "No, I'll just make some toast. I'm trying to save room for all the goodies we're making today."

Cheryl cracked a small smile. "You need to eat more than cookies, you know."

"I know," Ariel said. "But I fully intend to indulge in all types of cookies. Do you want me to make you a piece of toast?"

"No, I already ate something."

"Okay," Ariel said. She kissed her mom on the head and headed into the kitchen to make herself something to eat. When she was done, she sat in the armchair opposite Mom and opened her book, reading while she ate.

A little while later, the rest of the household was awake and fed, everyone slowly waking up on the couches in the living room.

"What do we start with first?" Aunt Erin asked. She sat her empty coffee mug on the table and rubbed her hands together.

"Usually we divide and conquer," Sam said. "Two people do the outside decorations while the other two start on the inside decorations."

"I vote we all do them together this year," Cheryl chimed in before anyone could say anything. "That way no one has to stay outside in this bitter cold too long, and we all get to do a little bit of everything."

"You? Volunteering to do the outside decorations?" Sam said, taken aback. "You hate the outside stuff."

"Yeah, well, I'm trying to branch out," Cheryl said matter-of-factly. "Plus, I figured Erin would appreciate not being stuck out in the cold."

"Who's to say I would've been the one outside?" Erin scoffed. "You're too nice to let a guest get that end of the bargain."

"Wouldn't be too sure about that."

"Look at you, growing a spine," Erin teased, standing up. "Show me where the lights are!"

The four of them made their way downstairs to the basement where Cheryl had already pulled all the boxes of both inside and outside Christmas décor from the shelves: six large boxes in total. The women made quick work of transporting the boxes to the front porch, before returning inside to bundle up in warmer clothes. Despite there being no wind, a rarity for Iowa in December, it was a bitter ten degrees out. Armed with multiple layers of jackets and handwarmers stuffed in boots, they headed outside to start the decorating.

Ariel quickly grabbed her favorite box labeled "Reindeer and polar bear." She had begged for these decorations as a young girl after seeing them on a neighbor's lawn, and the following year, after her constant begging, they'd shown up as a Christmas present from Dad. She was surprised by the tears as she removed the cream-colored polar bear from the box. Ariel wiped the tears with the back of her sleeve, hoping no one had noticed.

"You know, that's the only Christmas present your Dad ever got you without help from me," Cheryl said, kneeling beside Ariel, resting a hand on her shoulder. She reached in and removed the reindeer. Ariel noticed she too had tears in her eyes. "You begged for months for these things."

"Yeah, cuz they're awesome," Ariel laughed, tears still falling from her eyes. "I miss him, Mom."

"Me too, sweetheart." Cheryl pulled her daughter close, wrapping her arms around her. "It's not the same, is it? Celebrating his favorite holiday without him feels… wrong."

"Dad would want us to celebrate though," Ariel said, wiping the tears away, wishing they'd stop coming. "I promised myself I'd bring the joy today and look at me now."

"I said the same thing to myself when I got up this morning," Sam interjected, joining the group. She held a small green wreath with red berries on it. She held it up. "This was the first wreath Dad gave me."

"Seems like he started all our obsessions with Christmas décor," Ariel laughed. "You have what, like ten wreaths?"

"Only eight!"

Cheryl put an arm around both her daughters' shoulders and pulled them in. "I love you girls. You know your Dad's still here, around us all the time."

"We know," Ariel and Sam said in unison.

Aunt Erin kneeled quietly beside them, tears brimming in her eyes as well. "You ladies are so strong. And you know what, your Dad also gifted me many Christmas decorations."

"What, really?" Cheryl asked, raising an eyebrow. "How is this the first I'm hearing of this?"

"It was back when I lived here, y'all were just dating then," Erin said, sitting down in the snow. "You guys had visited me in that crappy apartment, and he noticed all the fairy lights I had on the walls. Few months later, he gave me a whole box of Christmas colored ones."

"Of course he did," Cheryl laughed.

"His love of Christmas new no bounds," Erin said. "I'm glad we get to continue doing all this together. I know he's delighted as all get out right now."

Sam and Ariel smiled at each other, exchanging knowing glances. Today was hard but also healing. Ariel's heart was heavy and full of love at the same time. She didn't think she could ever feel sad and happy at the same time, but today, that's exactly how she felt.

"Do Californians decorate their houses like they do here?" Sam asked, nodding to the lights in Erin's hands.

"Mhm-hmm, just like Midwesterners do—with snowflakes, snowmen, penguins—but it never feels the same. Something about a penguin surrounded by desert sand and palm trees just doesn't feel as right as it would if there was snow on the ground," Erin laughed.

Together, the four of them worked to adorn the house with the Christmas decorations. The fresh snow added the perfect touch. Something about a white Christmas that somehow felt more in the spirit than bare trees and dormant grass. When they were finished, they stepped back to admire their work, huddled together for warmth.

"It looks beautiful," Erin said quietly. The other three nodded in agreement. The dark house looked a bit lighter all dressed up in the holiday spirit. Several light-up reindeer were arranged in a small herd, while the polar bear stood atop one of the decorative boulders, overlooking them. The garland with the lights strung about it glowed warmly, and the wreaths decorated every door and post on the porch.

"We did good," Sam said. "Now can we go inside and get warm? I'm freezing."

"Yes!" Erin and Ariel said in unison.

The four ran into the house, eager to get warm. Ariel kicked off her shoes and headed to the kitchen. She opened the cupboard and grabbed a large mason jar container filled with a brown powder, setting it on the counter next to the stove. She turned to take the kettle off the stove but found Sam had already done so and was filling it with water.

"Hot chocolate!" Ariel and Sam laughed.

"Did someone say hot chocolate?" Erin asked from the mudroom. "I haven't had that in years!"

"Yep!" Ariel replied, grabbing four ceramic mugs from the same cupboard. "Mom makes a huge batch of it every year."

"You make your own hot chocolate mix, Cheryl?" Erin asked, surprised.

Cheryl nodded, smiling. "I do! I started when the girls were little. I used it as a teacher gift. But it was so good, I couldn't go back to the Swiss Miss mix, so now it's a yearly thing."

"Do we have little marshmallows still? Can't have hot chocolate without those."

"Do we?" Ariels scoffed. "Upper cabinet on the left." Erin opened said cabinet and there was the promised jar of mini marshmallows. "Don't tell me these are homemade too."

"Haha not this year," Ariel laughed. "But we did make our own for a while."

"I got sick of doing the dishes after making them," Cheryl shrugged.

Erin picked up her mug, wrapping her hands around it to warm them. "I swear, Cheryl, you're like the modern-day little house on the prairie."

Cheryl picked up her mug and stirred it. She raised an eyebrow at her sister's comment. "Do you mean that as a compliment or a diss?"

"Compliment," Erin said. She took a ginger sip of the beverage but pulled back. "Ooo. This is so hot I burnt my tongue. It's good though. I'm gonna need my own supply to take home with me."

"I'll set you up," Cheryl said.

"Guys, c'mmon! We've gotta finish the inside decorations before I leave for work!" Sam called from the living room.

Erin and Cheryl rolled their eyes, grins on their faces.

They all gathered in the living room, continuing to decorate and reminisce. They spent the rest of the afternoon decorating, sipping hot chocolate, and telling stories.

As Sam left for work, Ariel realized that after opening the first box that morning, she'd gone the whole day feeling happy. There had been some sadness, but contentment and joy were the dominating emotions of the day. She smiled, grateful for the happiness returning.

"Hey, kid," Erin asked from across the kitchen. "What do you say we get out for a few easy miles? My legs need a stretch while those cookies bake."

"Say no more," Ariel said, downing the last dregs of her hot chocolate. "Let's go!"

In less than ten minutes, they were dressed and out the door, enjoying the last rays of sunshine of a beautiful day.

Chapter 14

"Push more! More!" Coach Bobbie shouted from the far side of the track. She cupped her hands around her mouth and repeated the command at the top of her lungs, doing her best to yell over the wind.

Ariel heard her and steeled herself to follow the instruction. One glance at her watch told her she was almost two seconds behind the goal time for her eight-hundred-meter sprint. She was on the back stretch of the last lap and this was her last repeat. After this, it was time for a cool down. She dug deep and willed her legs to move faster, faster, faster. The last two hundred was always the hardest, and she felt the nausea starting to creep up.

"You're almost there, push it!" Coach shouted as Ariel flew past. A few more feet, one last ditch effort and Ariel was across the finish line, pounding to a walk. She intertwined her fingers and placed them behind her head, closing her eyes and focusing on her breathing. "Breath in, breath out, don't puke, breath in, breath out, don't puke," She repeated the mantra in her head as she slowly walked the hundred yards back to where Coach was standing by the student section bleachers, hunkered down out of the wind.

"How'd I do?" Ariel huffed, her breathing still hard. "God I hate sprinting." She leaned forward, letting her elbows rest on her knees, her head hanging between her legs.

"I know you do," Coach said, patting her on the back. "Stand up, you're gonna pass out."

She stood up with a groan. "I feel like I'm gonna pass out standing up though." Her head felt light and she saw little black spots at the corners of her vision. She'd fainted enough times in the sultry Iowa summers to know when it was coming on.

"Hit the ground before the ground hits you," Coach said nonchalantly as she studied the times she'd written down on her clipboard.

Ariel crossed her legs and plopped to the ground. She'd learned the hard way that this advice was better followed than questioned: freshman year, she'd had a bump on her head for weeks after passing out and falling during an August practice. Since then, despite her best efforts, she always managed to faint at least once a year during the hotter months.

"How'd I do?" Ariel asked again, fiddling with her shoelaces.

"Only a few seconds off the goal," Coach nodded, clicking through her watch settings. "Which honestly is really good. I know it's not where we wanted to be, but that goal was ambitious anyway. I'd say we're right on track."

Ariel shook her head, her heart sinking. She knew she had given it her all, but she was frustrated with the slow progress. Her first 50k was only a few weeks away, and she wasn't where she'd hoped to be. Sure, she was fast in the 5k and even the 10k distance, but some of these workouts had her questioning her abilities.

"You'll get there," Coach assured her.

"I know," Ariel said. She pushed herself up off the ground, standing up. "Let me jog a mile to cool down and then we can get out of this cold."

"We're gonna jog a half mile and then we'll get out of here," Coach corrected her.

Ariel smiled. "Deal."

"Let's go," Coach said, starting to jog off down the track. "I'm freezing my ass off out here. That wind cuts to the bone."

"Right?" Ariel said. "That was the worst part, running straight into that." The two jogged around the track, chatting as Ariel's muscles relaxed and Coach's warmed up.

"The fact that you were able to get so close to goal pace despite twenty mile an hour, freezing head winds is actually pretty good."

"I probably would've been faster if it hadn't been for that," Ariel conceded. "The hard workouts make the biggest impacts. I gotta remember that."

"Yeah, you do," Coach nodded. "And speaking of things to remember, I want you to think about why you're really doing this."

Ariel glanced over at her. "You know why, to save my family's house."

"I know, and that's a noble goal. But I want you to have another goal. One just for you."

"What would that even look like?"

"That's up to you. Could be a certain pace or could simply be finishing."

"But—"

"Yes, I know the prize money is why you're doing it. But I want you to dig deeper. Because when the going gets tough, running for money? That ain't gonna cut it."

They rounded the corner in silence, the only sound the crunch of their feet on the dusting of snow the wind blew over the track. Ariel knew what Coach meant. She wanted her to have some loftier goal than winning money. Something like a personal best effort or discovering something about herself. And she knew that was important and all, but the problem was she couldn't think of anything other than saving her family home and helping her mom.

"Can I think about it?"

"You have to think about it," Coach said, throwing a smile her way. "This is a deep question. Deep questions require contemplation. Maybe it'll come to you at that 50k coming up."

"That's crazy it's so close now…" Ariel said in disbelief, shaking her head. It felt like she still had months before she'd toe a starting line.

"Yeah, it came up quick. Christmas in two days, New Year's, and then a 50k. Gonna be a crazy year."

"Crazy's where I thrive," Ariel grinned. At first, she hadn't been too excited at the idea of running thirty-one miles in the snow and ice along the bluffs of Northeast Iowa, but as the race approached, she got more and more excited.

"So, are we still on for our next crew meeting later this week?"

"Sure are! Kyle and Shelby are coming over and Sam will join us when she's off work. We gotta make sure we have all our ducks in a row."

"Sounds great. Your mom and I are still having our book club first though," Coach reminded her. "Remember, I do have a life outside of all this."

"What? No way!" Ariel teased. As they finished their last lap, Ariel's legs felt good and her mindset better about the workout. They gathered their things and walked to their respective cars.

"Take it easy the rest of the day, ya hear me?"

"I'll do my best. I'm heading home to shower, then do nothing but eat muffins and put my feet up."

"And stretch," Coach added.

"Hey, you told me to relax, so," Ariel held up her hands. "Just taking orders."

Coach Bobbi rolled her eyes. "You know what I mean."

"Just giving you shit," Ariel laughed. "See you in a few days. Have a good Christmas!"

"You too," Coach Bobbi said. They parted ways, Coach Bobbi to her car in the track parking lot while Ariel walked around to the front of the school to where her car was parked. She always liked to leave some extra steps at the end of practice to work off any extra energy or stiffness. The drive home was so quick, and she dashed to the house as soon as she turned off the engine.

"Hi, I'm home," Ariel called into the house. She slipped off her shoes and jacket before walking into the kitchen. No one was there and no one answered, so she figured Mom and Erin were off at the grocery store getting everything they needed for Christmas Eve tomorrow. Ariel opened the fridge and grabbed an apple before heading upstairs.

"Sam?" Ariel called out as she walked up the stairs. "Sam!"

"What?" Sam finally answered. "I'm watching something."

Ariel pushed open her sister's door and sure enough, Sam was curled up under a blanket in her bean bag chair, her noise canceling headphones over her ears. "Sorry. Where's Mom and Erin?"

"The store," Sam said shortly. "They'll probably be back soon. They left a while ago."

"Cool. I'm gonna hop in the shower."

"Okay. Wanna play a game after dinner?" Sam asked.

Ariel stopped and turned around. "Are you sick?" Ariel was always the one trying to get her sister to play games. Rarely did Sam agree and when she did, it was never with enthusiasm.

"Yeah, yeah, whatever. No, I'm not sick," Sam said, rolling her eyes to downplay the situation. "But I've been stuck alone all day which usually I love, but I wanna do something… family oriented."

Ariel grinned ear to ear. "You pick whatever game you want and we'll play it. I'm sure Mom and Erin will be down. It can be our new Christmas Eve Eve tradition."

"Don't go getting any big ideas," Sam warned.

"Oh you know me, that boat sailed as soon as you asked me to play a game. That's going in my diary."

"You're ridiculous."

"You remind me constantly."

"Yeah, yeah. Go shower. I'm hungry and I don't wanna wait on dinner for your thirty-minute showers."

Ariel smiled, knowing she was right. She did indeed take thirty minutes to shower: ten minutes to clean everything, twenty minutes to contemplate life and enjoy the hot water, especially after the amount of time she spent in the cold today.

Later that night after Mom and Erin returned from the store, they made a large bowl of popcorn and sprinkled it with mini M&Ms. As they played Pictionary and munched on the popcorn, Ariel felt that happiness she'd felt when they'd decorated the house last week. Maybe Christmas would be all right after all. Different, but all right.

* * *

The snow crunched beneath each footfall as Ariel ran down the quiet country road. The wind only a breeze as the sun started to peak over the horizon, turning the sky soft orange tones. Her breathing was even with her steps, the rhythm of running a meditation. She was on the last mile of her twenty-one mile run and her legs still felt fresh. Maybe it was the cookie carb loading she'd done yesterday, or maybe it was the training doing its work. She chose to think it was both. As she turned onto her street, she picked up the pace, sprinting with all her effort the last quarter of a mile. When she passed her driveway, she slowed to a walk and closed her eyes. She imagined the crowds at Leadville cheering her on, someone walking up to her to present her a finisher's medal as the announcer tells the crowd she's done it. She's the first woman to ever win the race.

"It's Christmas! Why are you out here running and not inside opening presents?" Kyle's voice interrupted her daydream. She turned around to see him sitting on his porch, wrapped in a red and black flannel blanket identical to one of her own. A fond memory of a Christmas from their childhood popped into her head: their parents had gotten them both special Christmas blankets for a bonfire where they'd toasted marshmallows and opened presents.

"Ain't no rest for the wicked," Ariel said, walking up his driveway. "I could ask the same for you. "Why the hell are you out here?" She leapt up the few steps and stood in front of him, sticking her leg out in front of her to stretch her hamstring.

"I saw you go whizzing by, thought your house might be on fire," he teased. He opened a corner of his blanket and nodded. "Want to get warm?"

Ariel raised an eyebrow and hesitated, but ultimately she sat down next to him. Kyle wrapped the blanket around her, his arm lingering for a moment before removing it. "I probably stink. I'm sweaty."

"You definitely stink." He pinched the bridge of his nose. "But I'm used to it."

She punched him in the arm. "Dick."

"Do you expect anything different from me?"

"No," she laughed. "Merry Christmas."

"Merry Christmas to you too," Kyle said. His chocolatey eyes glowed with the reflection of the sunrise as he looked at her. For a moment, Ariel thought he might lean in and kiss her. But instead, a mischievous smile played at his lips. "I got you something."

"What?" she asked, shocked. "You did not."

"I did too! Wait here." He stood up, leaving the blanket with her as he bounded back into his house. A few seconds later, he reappeared holding a small box wrapped in blue and gold paper. He handed it to her. She gave it a small shake. It was light, and it didn't rattle.

"What is this?"

"Just open it," he laughed.

Ariel eyed him skeptically as she pulled the string apart. She laced it around her neck and tore into the paper, revealing a nondescript cardboard box. When she opened the lid, she couldn't stop the smile. "Is this what I think it is?"

"If you think it's the same kind of shoelaces you had on your favorite shoes as a kid, then it's exactly what you think it is!" Kyle said, sitting up a little straighter.

Ariel removed the hot pink laces from the box and held them up, the silver strands of glitter woven into them catching the sunlight. "Now I just need the sparkly shoes to match."

"I looked and just couldn't find any in your size," Kyle teased. "I hope the laces are okay for now."

She smiled at him. "They're perfect. Thank you." She leaned over and hugged him, the smell of his woodsy cologne filling her nose. He squeezed her tight, for a few seconds longer than what felt friendly.

"Merry Christmas, Ari," he said as he pulled back, his hand still resting on her shoulder.

"You said that already," she teased, sticking her tongue out at him. His cheeks reddened a little, though she tried to convince herself that was because of the cold. "Merry Christmas to you, again." She glanced across the street at her house. She could see her mom putting a tray of cinnamon rolls into the oven through the window.

"You better get back inside," Kyle said, removing his arm so slowly it almost felt as if he didn't want to. "You're probably freezing with your sweat-soaked clothes.

She hadn't noticed it until now, but she was. Her fingers burned with cold and her nose threatened to drip. "Come over tomorrow? Lord knows we'll have plenty of leftovers."

"Can't miss that," he winked. Ariel threw one more smile his way before turning and jogging back to her house, pink shoelaces in hand.

* * *

Later that night, Ariel, Sam, Cheryl, and Erin sat around the fire, the only other light in the living room the soft glow of the Christmas tree lights. As was tradition, they were all cozied up in blankets, reading their new books, alternating between sipping hot chocolate and turning pages. Christmas music played softly in the background, the occasional pop from the fire adding to the ambiance. Ariel looked up from her book, a fictional story about the first woman to play in the NFL and surveyed the scene in front of her.

Immediately, she knew this was what she was running for. For quiet, homey moments with the people she loved most. For warm nights, warm drinks, and warm hearts. Her phone buzzed quietly beside her. It was Shelby.

"Merry Xmas bestieeeee!"

Ariel was about to text back when another text came in. "BTW I saw that little exchange between you and Kyle this AM. Don't think we won't be talking all about THAT tomorrow. I wanna see those shoe laces!"

Ariel's jaw hung open. How had Shelby seen so much detail from so far away? She texted back at lightning speed. "Do you have binoculars?!"

"… maybe. It's boring around here sometimes, okay?"

Ariel stifled a laugh and rolled her eyes. "Come over first thing tmrw. I'll dish all the dirty details."

"Can't wait," came the reply.

Ariel turned her phone to silent and tucked it away, not wanting to be pulled away for a moment longer. She wasn't sure how many more nights like this she'd get in this house. If things went according to plan, there were years to come. But, just in case, she wanted to savor every second.

Chapter 15

New Years came and went. Ariel and Sam returned to their first week of school, antsy for graduation far away in May. Cheryl continued her job search, hopeful that since this was a new year, companies would be hiring again. Christmas with Aunt Erin had been wonderful, Ariel missed her since she left a week ago but knew it was only a matter of time until she would see her again in Colorado.

But before she could think about this summer, she had to get through the next twenty-four hours of the freezing Iowa winter. The 50k race had come out of nowhere. It had always felt so far off in the future, and now suddenly it was tomorrow. Ariel had been watching the weather forecast for weeks, and while it had looked decent earlier, now it wasn't in her favor.

Channel 13 was calling for a "snow event." Not quite a blizzard, yet more than a dusting. This was her worst-case scenario. Not only did the cold hurt her lungs and make breathing hard, the chances of slipping and falling and sustaining an injury were high.

"What do you want for pre-race motivation?" Sam asked, scrolling the music on her phone. "Ooo, how about this?" She selected a song and started blaring Fetty Wap.

"I guess," Ariel said, too distracted by thoughts of tomorrow to care. "Do I race this like we'd originally planned? Or do I just try to finish at this point?" She asked Coach as she unpacked her small suitcase. She fished through her clothes until she found her race day outfit. With care, she laid out her black thermal top and matching tights, warm merino socks, and gloves. "Where are my hand warmers?"

"In the front pocket of your backpack," Cheryl said without looking up from her phone.

"We stick to the plan," Coach said from her perch on the bed opposite her. "This is everything we've talked about. Be mindful of your footing. Leadville isn't full of technical terrain, but it still has its moments. This is our practice. Don't let the nerves get to you."

"Yeah, if I don't get hurt."

"If you're that worried about getting injured, then slow down," Coach said. "You won't feel that way the whole time. This will be perfect practice in running smart. Now, what do you have packed for tomorrow?"

Ariel motioned to the outfit on the bed. "Clothes."

"Oh c'mon. You're so much more organized than this," Coach said, sliding off the bed and sitting on the floor. She pulled the larger suitcase in front of her and opened it up, revealing perfectly organized contents. "See? You're the only person I know who would pack a suitcase like this." Coach pulled out one of the containers and opened it, revealing perfectly folded clothes.

"Okay, you have a point," Ariel said, setting it next to her racing kit. "The crew bag should be in there, too."

"To the left and underneath your sweatpants?" Coach teased.

"Yeah, something like that," Cheryl laughed. "I'm the one who helped pack."

Coach removed the large bag labeled "crew" and opened it. "You know, when we get to bigger distances, we're going to have to have separate containers organized in the vehicle for things."

"How do you mean?"

"Like we'll have a box for shirts, a box for socks, a box for energy gels, and a box for food storage, camp stove storage," Coach Bobbi listed off.

"I wish we could've had all of that here so we could get a real practice run with the crew…"

"Don't worry about it," Coach waved her hand. "That's why you have me. Now, let's recheck everything for tomorrow and get you to bed."

* * *

The next morning's alarm was accompanied by the sweet smell of toasted bagels and coffee. Ariel rubbed the sleep from her eyes, grateful the hydroxyzine helped her sleep. She wasn't a fan of the pills, but she was grateful they eased her anxiety enough to let her get a good night's rest. She pushed herself up against the headboard and flipped on the bedside lamp. Mom emerged from the hotel bathroom moments later.

"Good morning, sunshine!" she greeted in her typical sunny morning fashion. "How'd you sleep?"

"Pretty good, actually." Ariel took the plate Mom was holding out in front of her. As expected, one large bagel spread with cream cheese and a little blueberry muffin on the side.

"The muffin isn't the greatest, but it was all the hotel had," Cheryl said, her face apologetic. "But when we get home, I'll make you some."

Ariel sunk her teeth into the bagel, savoring the goodness of her typical prerace routine. "This is divine. Thank you. But I sure won't say no to muffins when we're home."

"I figured as much," Cheryl chuckled. She sat down on the bed opposite Ariel and gently shook Sam, who groaned in protest. "T-minus one hour until we have to leave. Start waking up now."

Sam groaned again and rolled over, pulling the covers over her head. Ariel and Mom's gazes met and they shared a knowing glance and a laugh.

"Remember when we used to rock, paper, scissors for who had to wake her up from her nap?" Cheryl laughed, patting Sam's form under the blanket.

"Yes! I lost too many times, that's for sure. I hated having to go wake her up with all her crying and screaming."

"Some things never change," Cheryl smiled, shaking her head. "You two. One's up at the crack of dawn, the other doesn't get up until noon."

A soft knock at the door caught their attention. Cheryl uncrossed her legs and got up, opening the door for Coach Bobbi who waltzed into the room holding a drink holder full of beverages.

"Those all for you?" Ariel asked through a mouthful of bagel.

"Two of them are," Bobbi said, sipping on one. "The other two are for your mother."

"Nothing for me?" Ariel feigned disappointment.

Coach shook her head as she sipped on a steaming hot drink. "All your caffeine is coming through gels. We don't need to overload you and give you heart palpitations."

"I mean, I guess you have a point."

"That's why I'm the Coach." Bobbi winked. "You keep getting ready while Cheryl and I chat and wake up."

The next hour went by in a blur of coffee, getting dressed, and activating her handwarmers as they drove to the start line. As soon as she stepped out of the car, the prerace excitement was palpable. A small crowd of runners milled about, most jogging or stretching in an attempt to stay warm in the freezing temperatures. The smell of hot coffee and sugar wafted through the air. A local coffee shop had set up a cute stand in the back of an old-fashioned pickup, selling caffeine and pastries to the supportive family and friends who were there. The music over the loudspeaker blasted late 90s pop music, the perfect warm up vibe as far as Ariel was concerned.

"See you soon!" Ariel called, shutting the car door behind her as the rest of her family went to park the car. Ariel made her way towards the porta potties, where lots of runners were standing, all shifting back and forth, bouncing foot to foot in an attempt to keep warm. Everyone's breath turned to fog as they exhaled, sending little white puffs into the air around them, hands held close to their faces.

"Whoever thought it was a good idea to hold a race in January in Iowa was nuts," said the person in front of her in line.

"What's that make us then?" Ariel laughed. "We're the ones who showed up to run the damn thing."

"Hahah I guess you're right," the man laughed. He looked to be in his forties or fifties, but one glance at his legs told her he wasn't just a casual runner—the size of his calves rivaled baseballs. "I'm Tony."

"Ariel," she replied, shaking his outstretched glove.

"You done this before?"

"Nope," she said, shaking her head as she tucked her hands into her armpits. "And I'm cursing my coach right now for suggesting signing up for this thing."

"That's how we all feel at the start line," he laughed, stepping forward as the line inched closer. "Give it five or six miles and you'll feel great. Especially if you're a heavy sweater like myself."

"Well, that's good to hear because I sweat buckets." Ariel laughed. "Maybe I can save a few liters of sweat and salt this time."

Tony crossed his fingers and smiled before he took off for the next open porta potty. It wasn't long until another one came open and Ariel took it. When she came back out, Tony was nowhere in sight and her watch told her she had ten minutes until the race. She made her way over to the starting line, which wasn't hard to find on account of the bright lights and disco ball hung below the banner. It sparkled in the artificial light. Ariel was grateful the sun stayed away. Any melting of the already formed ice would make running that much harder.

"Racers, are you ready?" the announcer boomed over the megaphone. Ariel found her way to the middle of the pack, hoping to start at a decent pace.

"This is thirty-one miles, not three point one," she reminded herself under her breath. "Start slow, race patient."

A chorus of "yeses" and "hell yeahs" answered the announcer.

"On your marks, get set, go!"

And just like that, Ariel was off. Her first ever 50k had begun.

Chapter 16

"This is great!" Ariel cheered as she entered the first aid station. She slipped out her water bottles from her vest and handed it to the happy-faced aid station volunteer to refill. "It's a party out there!"

The volunteer grinned as she refilled the bottles, one with water, the other with electrolyte drink. Both had been completely empty. Ariel glanced at her watch, grinning. She was on track with her pacing, nutrition, and hydration. The aid station was busy—it was only five miles into the course, so the pack was still close together and people were chatting. The volunteer handed her back the bottles.

"Here you go, good luck out there!"

"Thanks," Ariel smiled, returning the bottles to their rightful place. She grabbed a paper cup of Gatorade and a paper cup of water, drinking them as she walked towards the end of the aid station. She chugged the dregs, tossed the cups in the trash bins, and picked up her jog again. She was in and out of the aid station in a little over sixty seconds. "Perfect," she thought to herself. That had gone exactly as planned. She knew later in the race she'd take a little more time, so she was doing her best to take advantage of feeling good early on and banking some extra time for later.

The course snaked through the snow-covered forest, the white powder crunched into a tightly packed trail beneath her feet that thankfully wasn't as slick as she had feared. The path widened a bit and she passed a slower runner, nodding to them. That was one thing she hadn't been prepared for— the bottleneck lasted the majority of the first lap. She did her best to be patient, passing only when there was enough space. Coach's voice echoed in her head-"We aren't racing this, we're running this."

"Wait a second, how are we going to know where we're going on the next lap without all these people around?" a voice behind her asked.

"Honestly, I don't know," his running buddy replied. "I hadn't even thought about it. I've just been following everyone else."

"That's not gonna work next lap. Most people are just doing the 15k," he replied, the worry evident in his voice.

Ariel laughed and smiled to herself. Getting lost had been one of her biggest worries. So much so, that the week before the race, she emailed the race director to ask how the course was marked. Thankfully, the director was gracious and had assured her not to worry.

"There're pink ribbons tied to trees along the route," Ariel said over her shoulder, slowing her stride a bit. The two men pulled up right behind her.

"Oh really?" one of them asked, "I haven't seen any but then again I've been staring at my feet."

"Look right there," Ariel said, pointing to a tree branch with a fluttering pink ribbon. It appeared right on cue. "That's what you're looking for."

"Well dang, all right," he laughed. "If I get lost, I can blame…" he leaned forward to read Ariel's bib. "Ariel."

"Well… Brett," Ariel laughed. "You can but everyone will know you're just shifting blame."

"Haha I suppose you're right," Brett admitted. "Thanks, either way!"

"Anytime," Ariel said. "I was so worried about getting lost I emailed the race director about it."

"Glad we weren't the only ones not quite sure what was going on."

"Nah, there's lots of us out here just winging it," a woman behind the little group laughed.

"See you out there," Ariel smiled. She picked her pace back up and slowly a gap formed between herself and Brett's group. She chugged along the trail, keeping up her pace as much as the crowds would let her, passing when she could. It was such a foreign thing to her, to just run and have fun instead of pushing herself until she couldn't see straight. She knew that time would come, but for now she was enjoying the easier effort.

And the views around her made it easy. The stunning snow-covered cliffs, the icy Mississippi River down below, cozy-looking houses nestled into the cliffsides. Suddenly, a thought popped into her head.

"Dad would love it out here," she whispered aloud, shaking her head and smiling. Not only did he love Christmas, he loved the entire winter season. She found herself grateful for the weather, finding the joy where she knew her Dad would have too. The sun shone high overhead, the wind mercifully still. The temperatures were a brisk twenty-five degrees, but the sun made it feel a touch warmer.

As she gained on the group in front of her, the trail narrowed to single track, bare brambly branches lining both sides almost as if to ensure no runners disturbed the resting woodlands beyond. She recognized the woman's dark brown braid, swinging in front of her bright yellow hydration pack.

"Hey, what's your name?" Ariel asked when she finally caught up to her.

The woman glanced over her shoulder, a smile revealing crooked, but sparkling white, teeth. "I'm Maddie, what's your name?"

"Ariel," she said. "We've been yo-yoing the whole race so far, and this single track goes for a hot minute, so I figured if we're going to be spending this much time together then we better at least know each other's names."

Maddie laughed. "I was thinking the exact same thing. I love your shoes. Where did you find that much glitter on a running shoe?"

Ariel beamed. "I glittered them myself."

"That's impressive."

"When I was little, my mom got me the sparkliest pair of shoes ever and that's what started my love of running. As I got older, it was harder and harder to find shoes with glitter on them and eventually they disappeared altogether. Which is like a crime against humanity. I still love glitter just as much at seventeen as I did at five."

"I totally agree," Maddie said. "I'm a hot pink kinda girly and even that's hard to find. All you get are those muted rose tones or reds."

"I'm glad you get it. I said, screw the establishment, I'm gonna make what I want. And I did!"

"I might just have to start dyeing my shoes hot pink," Maddie laughed. The two women turned a corner and were greeted with a steep incline that would've made a great sledding hill. They slowed to a fast walk, along with all the other runners in front of them.

"Oh boy, here we go," Maddie sighed. "I hate hills."

"Yeah, they're not my favorite," Ariel said, though she instantly questioned why. She loved hills. Why would she lie to this complete stranger?

As they trudged up the side of the hill, Ariel tried her best not to step on Maddie's heels. But the pace was so slow it almost made the ascent harder. A small pocket in the brambly bushes opened up and Maddie stepped to the side, motioning Ariel to go ahead.

"Unless you wanna push my ass up the hill, then I say you go first. You're way faster than I am," Maddie said between huffs of breath.

"Thanks," Ariel said sheepishly, stepping in front of her. "Sorry, I didn't mean to ride your ass."

Maddie laughed. "Don't be sorry at all! If it wouldn't DQ me, I would've just let you push me up."

"I actually love uphills," Ariel admitted. "I started doing hill workouts instead of sprints, 'cause I hate sprints.

And hills made me so fast and strong so quickly, after seeing those kinds of results I couldn't not love them."

"That's… a fair… point," Maddie said. "Maybe after this… I'll try that."

"I highly recommend," Ariel said. The hill finally crested, revealing just as steep of a descent on the other side. The snow shone, slick with semi melted snow and ice. Ariel stumbled to a stop, her heart catching in her throat. "What the hell do we do, slide down this?"

Maddie stopped behind her, pulling up just in time to not knock her over the edge. Other runners were descending, stepping sideways slowly, yet they were still slipping and sliding every which way. "I guess we just do what they're doing."

Ariel took a deep breath. "Okay, here goes nothing I guess!"

She began the descent, giving the runner in front of her a bit of a head start so if she were to fall, she wouldn't immediately take them out with her. The last thing they needed was a snowball situation down this mini mountain. Thankfully, the trail had been cut into a switchback, making it much easier to control her descent than if they had to bomb straight down it like you would if you were on a sled.

Ariel made it to the end of the first switch back and turned the corner, immediately starting down the next. Her thighs burned with the effort of braking herself against gravity, but they felt strong. A large root loomed in the path. She strategically planted her feet before picking one up to step down. She tested the ground, making sure she had a good foothold before lifting up her other leg to clear the branch. Suddenly, the ground slipped from beneath her and she flung her leg high as not to catch the branch and before she knew what had happened, she was on the ground.

"Ariel! Are you okay?" Maddie exclaimed, a few feet above her. She slid down, closing the gap.

Ariel sat up and shook her head. She hadn't hit it, but the whole situation had been a little disorienting. Tears welled in her eyes for reasons unknown. Nothing hurt. "Yeah I'm good, just shaken up."

"Yeah, I would be too," Maddie said, her voice concerned. "You sure you're okay?"

Ariel glanced at her right hand. Where she had gotten stitches a few months before throbbed. She removed her glove and studied her hand—it was in perfect shape. White, cold, the little pink scar forever a reminder of the race that ended her high school career. Maybe it remembered what happened the last time she fell. She shook it and returned it to the glove, silently thanking the person who invented handwarmers. She pushed herself up off the ground, dusting the snow from her leggings. "Yeah, I'm sure. That just scared the shit out of me."

"I bet," Maddie said, clearing the branch with ease. Lucky. "That's my worst fear."

"Mine too," Ariel said, starting to move slowly forward on the trail.

"That's great then!" Maddie beamed, close on her heels.

"How so?" Ariel asked, slightly annoyed. Suddenly, she wished she was running alone.

"Because, you just experience your worst fear and look! You're alive and just fine!"

Ariel moved ahead silently for a moment, letting the words sink in. She was totally right. She'd been most afraid of falling, more afraid of it than getting lost, and here she was, unhurt and still moving forward.

"Thanks, Maddie," Ariel said finally. She jogged the last few steps of the dreaded downhill, letting out a huge breath she hadn't realized she'd been holding. "Holy shit, I'm glad that's done."

"You and me both, sister," Maddie laughed. "I'm just glad I don't have to do it again. At least you'll know how to navigate it on your second and third laps!"

"Let's not think about that right now," Ariel said.

"Deal. So, what's your favorite food to eat after a race?"

The two women chatted as they made their way down the trail, the miles flying by with good conversation, commiseration over daunting downhills, warnings about tree roots, and general discussion of bowel habits. Before Ariel knew it, the notorious final downhill appeared around a bend.

"Wow, I need to make friends at races more often. That went so fast!" Ariel laughed to herself. "Let's get it!" Maddie and Ariel stopped at the top of the descent, marked with the usual pink flag plus a Halloween skeleton tied to the tree declaring they had stumbled upon "Nelly's Gnarly Descent." She peered down the hill, her eyes tracing the path of the rope tied between trees. Other runners were farther below, cautiously descending the steep and icy path with the rope's help. They slipped and slid, but thankfully no one went careening down.

Maddie took one glance down and stepped back. "Woah. That's steeper than I thought it would be… I don't like heights." Her face turned a paler shade of white.

"Hey, it's okay," Ariel assured her. "Just follow me. It'll be easier to go down backwards too so you won't have to look down. Watch." Ariel waited for the runner in front of her to start descending and put a good amount of space between them. When they were far enough ahead, Ariel grabbed the rope with both gloved hands, thankful she'd gotten the grippy gloves, and turned around to lower herself down. "See?"

Maddie eyed her skeptically. "I don't know…"

"How else are you getting down? You wanna run twenty miles back the other way? The finish line for you is only like fifty yards from the bottom of this hill."

"Ugh, you're right, okay." Maddie relented and followed Ariel, grabbing the rope, and very gingerly backing down the hill. "Don't laugh at me if I cry though, okay?" Her voice was shaky.

"I would never," Ariel swore. "Let's do this! One foot at a time." Ariel started lowering herself down, picking up the pace as Maddie joined her. While she didn't have the same fear of heights her newfound friend had, she wasn't the biggest fan either and did her best to make as quick of work of this hill as she could.

"There!" Ariel said, releasing the rope when she reached the bottom. "We did it!"

Maddie followed a few steps behind. When both her feet hit even ground, she let out a huge sigh, her shoulders visibly falling. "Glad I don't have to do that again."

"Yeah, lucky you," Ariel laughed. "Let's run this in!" The two women took off together, following the pink ribbons out of the woods. As soon as they cleared the last tree, the aid station/finish line appeared like an oasis in the desert.

"Thank god for the finish line!" Maddie sighed.

"Girl, it's not the finish yet! Just an aid station," Ariel laughed, nudging her in the ribs.

"No way. I'm only doing the 30k."

Ariel's face fell. "You mean I have to do the rest of this by myself?"

"Sorry!" Maddie laughed, shrugging. "I'll cheer you on from afar."

"Well, go on then, run it in!" Ariel said, letting Maddie take the lead. She crossed the finish line a few steps ahead of Ariel.

"Congrats!" Ariel beamed. "Here, give me your number." Ariel pulled out her phone and handed it to Maddie.

"I'll send you motivational texts from my warm couch," Maddie teased, handing her back the phone as a volunteer placed a finisher's medal around her neck.

"They'll be much appreciated." The girls nodded at each other and went their separate ways: Maddie to find the post-race food for runners, and Ariel to find the aid station and her crew. It didn't take much looking. Opposite of the finisher's tables and medals was the aid station, complete with paper cups of electrolytes and water, assortments of candy, bowls of pretzels and chips, two big coolers of liquid to refill runner's bottles, and folding tables for crew to set up. At the end of the nearest table stood Coach Bobbi, Cheryl, and Sam, along with Kyle and Shelby—who had driven up early this morning—all huddled around their set up in oversized jackets. Sam was the first to spot her.

"Ari! We're over here!!" Sam shouted, jumping up and down while waving her arms over head. The rest of the group turned and as soon as they saw her, did the same.

Ariel jogged over; smile plastered on her face. It wasn't often she got to see her mom get this excited about something. She removed the two empty bottles from her hydration vest and handed them to Shelby. Kyle got to work removing the wrappers from her vest pockets.

"How are you feeling?" Sam asked, shoving half a cheese quesadilla into her hand.

Ariel took a bite, its warmth radiating through her. "Honestly, I feel great. Nothing hurts. I'm breathing fine."

"That's great," Coach Bobbi said. "Think you can pick up the pace a little?"

Ariel nodded, mouth full of tortilla and cheese. "Yeah, I think so. I chatted with a gal almost the whole way which was awesome, but it did make me go a little slower than planned."

"Not a bad thing," Coach said, shaking her head. "Remember, this—"

"Isn't the race we're training for. I know, I know," Ariel said, rolling her eyes. "Can I get another one of those quesadillas?"

Sam handed her another.

"I can't believe you're actually doing this," Kyle said, excited. "You want four of these, right?" He held up different color packs of energy chews, two in each hand.

"Yes please," Ariel nodded. "And a bag of pretzels. My only potential concern is electrolytes." Ariel touched her face. Her cheek felt as though she'd left a sugar scrub on it overnight and had forgotten to wash it off. She scraped off some of the frozen sweat and salt from her face and held out her hand to Sam.

"Ew, that's so gross," she exclaimed, pulling her hand away like she'd touched something hot.

"You have salt tabs, right?" Kyle asked, raising an eyebrow. Ariel was grateful her cheeks were red from the cold so the extra heat in her face didn't show. She grinned at him, holding his gaze.

"They're in your big zipper pocket," Cheryl said. Kyle dropped his gaze to his shoes, but the smile on his face was evident.

"Yes, I do then," Ariel laughed. "Thanks Mom."

"Anytime."

Shelby handed her the refilled water bottles. "You ready to go? You're coming up on time."

Ariel finished off the last bite of quesadilla and took the bottles, shoving them back into the front of her vest. She patted her pockets, going through her mental checklist: hand warmers, energy chews, salt tabs, electrolytes, phone, headphones, lip balm. "Yep, I'm good to go. See y'all in ten miles!"

Ariel gave a little wave as she picked up her pace again, jogging out of the aid station. As the trail turned, she got one last glimpse at her family, everyone still waving and hollering until she disappeared. The field of runners had thinned out considerably. Most people were only doing one lap, like Maddie. Ariel settled into a fast clip, eager to focus on the race and push her pace.

Chapter 17

Everything was falling apart. The second lap had gone perfectly: she powered up the inclines, dominated the downhills, and kept a steady effort on the flats. She'd avoided all stray tree branches and hidden roots, and her feet were blister free and her stomach agreeable. When she'd seen her crew, everything had been fine. And now, only halfway through the last lap, nothing was fine anymore.

Ariel blinked back tears as she found a log to sit on. She couldn't take the pain in her foot a second longer. She removed her left shoe and sock, revealing her entire foot had erupted in angry red blisters.

"What the fuck…" she whispered to herself, trying not to panic. She fumbled to remove her pack, rummaging around for her tape and scissors. Her fingers struggled to bend, the cold playing mean tricks by making her feet burn and her fingers barely move as she did her best to tape and mend her foot before putting her sock and shoe back on. When she stood up, the pain was still there, but it was more manageable. She ran along the course, alone with her blisters and thoughts.

She'd done everything right: she'd changed her socks at the last aid station when they'd gotten too wet, her shoes were well broken in, her feet weren't slipping or sliding in the shoe. For the life of her, she couldn't figure out what had gone wrong. It was as if all of a sudden, her foot had decided it wanted to form blisters. Damn that foot.

The downhills made it worse. Even with the tape job, she felt each and every sore as she descended one of the steeper hills, each one feeling like a flame pressed into her skin. To make matters worse, she noticed a twinge in her knee that alleviated once she reached flat ground, but it didn't go away.

"Well… this is what I get, isn't it?" she said out loud to herself.

"What is what you get?" a voice asked from behind, making her nearly jump off the trail.

She turned to see a guy in his twenties behind her. "You scared the crap out of me!"

"Sorry," he chuckled as he pulled up beside her. They ran in stride. "I couldn't help but hear you talking to yourself."

"Don't tell me you don't do that out here," Ariel said, annoyed.

"I totally do. We all do at one point or another. You're not seeing things, are you?"

Ariel glanced at him. From what she could tell of his face, he was serious. When she didn't answer, he said, "Cuz you know, we save that for the hundred milers. A 50k is a little too early for that."

Ariel's eyes widened. "People hallucinate?"

"All the time," he laughed. "When I did my first one, I kept seeing a taco truck in the trees. It happens to a lot of people on account of the sleep deprivation and darkness."

What he said made sense, but it wasn't something Ariel had ever considered. Add it to the list of things she needed to research after this race. She tried not to beat herself up for not knowing; this was, after all, why she was doing this race: to learn.

"What's giving you grief?" the man asked, still matching her stride. "I had gnarly muscle cramps the last three miles but I figured that out. Just needed some salt tabs. Who woulda thought?"

"At least that's an easy fix."

"Your thing isn't?"

"Not unless you've got the magic answer for a foot covered in blisters," Ariel grimaced.

"I take it you already taped 'em?"

"Mm-hmm."

"Did you try tape and lube?" he asked, his voice brightening.

"Excuse me, lube?" Ariel asked, taking a wide sidestep to put some space between her and him.

He must've seen the look on her face because he immediately assured her that wasn't the kind of lube he was talking about. "Foot lube, it helps prevent friction and therefore, blisters."

Why in the world hadn't Coach Bobbi mentioned this? "People put lube on their feet?" she asked, skeptical.

"Oh yeah! All over. I haven't had blisters ever since I started doing it years ago. Do you want some? I've got some with me."

"Does it help if there's already a bunch of blisters?"

"Not if they're already formed, but you can put it on the skin around them that hasn't blistered to prevent anymore."

"It's just my left foot," Ariel said. "I don't know what happened, I was doing great, clean socks and everything and the last few miles it just blew up. My right foot is fine."

"Here," he said, pointing to a large log lining the side of the trail. "Let's sit here a second and you can put it on."

They dusted off a spot on the log and sat down. Ariel took her shoes off as the man took off his pack, removing a blue stick of something labeled "Squirrel's nut butter".

"If you're going to be giving me lube, I at least need to know your name," Ariel teased. This situation was so surreal. A stranger was giving her lube in the forest in the middle of January. What a life.

"Dan," he chuckled. "Nice to meet you. You are…"

"Ariel."

"Like the little mermaid!" Dan exclaimed. "Sorry, you probably get that a lot." He handed her the lube.

"Not as often anymore, but yes. What do I do with this?"

"Just put it on all your bare skin, don't be shy about it."

Ariel did as she was told and rolled the lube all over her right foot. "This feels disgusting. This is like I just dipped my entire foot in coconut oil."

"Yeah, it does take a bit of getting used to, but the blister prevention is worth it."

Ariel finished up and handed it back to Dan, pulling on her shoes as fast as she could. It didn't take long for the cold to set in, freezing up her toes just like it did her fingers. She stood up and took a few jogging steps. To her surprise, her foot didn't slip and slide in her shoes like she'd imagined. It felt the same, except a little softer. "All right, this isn't so bad. Thank you."

"Happy to help!" Dan said as he slung his pack back over his shoulders. "I'll see you down the trail. Just yell if you need more lube." He winked, then was gone as quickly as he appeared.

"Lube angel…" Ariel said under her breath as she picked up her pace again. "This is a weird day."

As she continued down the trail, the feeling of oily feet subsided, and the pain of the blisters stayed away. She said a silent prayer again for Dan the Lube Man, grateful for his timing. Her watch beeped, demanding her attention. Begrudgingly, she pulled another pack of energy chews out of her pack and forced them down.

They promptly came back up. Ariel veered to the edge of the trail, trying to not vomit until she was off the path and failing. She wretched, her stomach emptying itself of all the calories she'd just consumed and then some. Wiping her mouth on the back of her sleeve, she stood up and waited.

"What the hell…." This was getting nothing but worse. "Guess I don't need it?"

She started walking back down the trail, giving her body a few minutes. She'd thrown up after races before, and she'd fought off nausea in plenty of them. But she was always done running just a few yards after she threw up. She'd never had to keep going for miles before. Ariel wracked her brain for what Coach had said about it.

"Stomach and GI issues are very common in longer distances," Coach had said. They were in her office at the school, talking over differences between cross-country and ultra-distances, of which there were many. "Most of the time, you just gotta run right through it. The nice thing is, with longer races, you have longer to recover and turn things around."

"I'm supposed to run through this?" Ariel whispered to herself, spitting out some residual grossness in her mouth. "Why am I doing this again? That's right. We're running to keep the family together. Oh yeah, and we love it. I love it, I love it, I LOVE IT!"

Ariel laughed at herself, picking up a slow jog. "This is insane. I'm talking to myself in the middle of the woods, throwing up, and having the time of my life. What a day. What a freaking day."

* * *

"There she is!" Kyle yelled from the top of the final hill. He jumped up and down, glancing down the far side of the hill where the rest of Ariel's crew was setting up shop. "GO ARI! YOU'RE ALMOST THERE!"

The group stood to attention, hands gathered in front of their faces to keep them warm in the late morning chill.

Ariel didn't hear Kyle's cheers until she was halfway up the hill. She trudged up it, head down, hands on her legs as she gave the last climb all she had. She said a silent curse for the ignorant person who had dubbed the Midwest as flat. "Iowa ain't flat."

"Ari! You've done it! You're nearly there!"

Ariel looked up, craning her neck. The sight of Kyle jumping up and down at the crest of the hill made her heart soar, sending a surge of rejuvenating energy through her.

"You've got this!"

With one last push, Ariel reached the top of the hill, the crowd erupting in cheers on the other side as they saw her come into view. "Hey Kyle."

"You're amazing!" he said, throwing his arms around her without a second thought to her sweat-soaked clothes. She'd tell him about the vomit stains later. Didn't want to ruin the moment.

"Thanks," she said, blushing as he pulled away.

"Now go finish it out!"

Ariel took off without another word, bombing down the hill like she was on fresh legs. The crowd cheered as she got closer. She spotted her crew off to the right of the finish line, Mom and Sam clanking on cowbells and Shelby waving a sign that declared "Ari #1!" As she crossed over the timing mat, a wave of gratitude washed over her: grateful to have such great supporters, and grateful to be done,

Bobbi reached her first. She placed her hands on her shoulders and held her at arm's length, giving her the once over. "What's this?" she said, pointing to the wet spot on the front of her shirt. "Did you puke?"

Ariel nodded. "Yeah, but that's not all. You didn't tell me I had to lube my feet."

Bobbi's eyebrows scrunched together and then raised as her mouth formed an "o". "I've never had to lube my feet. But a bunch of people do. Did you get blisters?"

Ariel nodded again. "Just you wait. You get the honor of taking my shoes off, Coach." She winked.

"I didn't even think to mention it," Bobbi laughed, shaking her head. "Thank God for training races, right?"

"Right," Ariel said. "We'll figure out what went wrong with my stomach later. I want to sit down."

"Right here!" Shelby said, appearing out of nowhere with a folding chair she'd commandeered from the aid station. Ariel plopped down where she placed it but immediately regretted it.

"Let's move towards the heaters," Cheryl said, nudging the chair with her foot. "C'mon. Stand up before you freeze in place."

Ariel knew she was right, but the last thing she wanted to do was stand. Sam held out her hands and Ariel grabbed ahold of them. Sam pulled Ariel up and slung one arm around her shoulder, escorting Ariel towards the finishers tent where there were mercifully several transportable heaters. Runners and volunteers alike were huddled around them, but they all graciously made room for a chair and a freshly finished runner.

"Thanks," Ariel said, sitting and learning forward to get as close to the heat as possible. "This was a way better idea."

"I know," Cheryl beamed. "That's why you have me."

"If my brain is this bad after only thirty-one miles, it's gonna be nonexistent after one hundred…." Ariel said. She couldn't comprehend how much worse it could get.

"That's why you have crew and a pacer at the end," Bobbi said, squatting down in front of her. "But that's for another time. Drink this."

Ariel took the paper cup and downed its contents without question. Whatever it was, it was warm and salty and tasted like heaven. "Thanks," she said, handing her back the now empty cup.

"How do you feel?" Sam asked.

"Honestly," Ariel started, stretching out her legs and arms in a starfish shape. She rolled her neck in each direction. "Other than my feet and my stomach being a little off, I don't feel bad. I'm freezing and I'll be sore tomorrow but… that was fun."

A grin formed on Bobbi's face. "Didn't I tell you? Even when you race these things, they're like an adventure."

"That's exactly what it felt like," Ariel nodded, loosening the laces on her shoes. "Especially with Sled Hill."

"Sled Hill?" Kyle asked, raising an eyebrow.

"Yeah. And Nelly's Gnarly Descent. I have so many stories to tell you guys," Ariel laughed, smiling at the memory of the past few hours. "But for now, can we go back to the hotel and get changed? I'm tired and I'm pretty sure these clothes are going to be frozen on at some point if I stay out here too much longer."

"Yes, let's go," Coach Bobbi agreed. The crew gathered up all their things, Shelby and Sam helping Ariel. Her legs had stiffened up, making each step slow. They loaded the car and made their way back to the hotel room where room service was calling Ariel's name.

Chapter 18

The next few days were full of nothing but lots of rest, soup, stretching, and of course, as many blueberry muffins as Ariel could manage. On the third day postrace, the team reassembled at the Hart household. The kitchen table was set up with printed stats from the race, an excel spreadsheet with all the crew details, and snacks in the middle. Even though the meeting didn't start until one in the afternoon, Shelby had been there since last night's sleepover with Ariel and Sam. The girls were lounging on the couch while Ariel foam rolled her legs on the floor, a cheesy hallmark movie on the TV. The doorbell rang.

"Come in!" Ariel yelled from the floor through gritted teeth.

The door opened and in walked Kyle. "Am I late?"

"No, it was girls' night," Shelby said, not taking her eyes off the TV screen. "No boys allowed."

"Well, the real party starts now," he teased, slipping off his shoes and joining the group in the living room. "You guys watch this crap?"

"It's not crap!" Sam exclaimed, throwing a pillow at him which he expertly dodged. "This is cinema at its finest!"

"Whatever you say," Kyle said, rolling his eyes.

"You take that back!" Shelby lobbed another pillow at the back of his head.

Kyle made a pleading face towards Ariel. She returned his look with an unsympathetic shrug. "Don't look at me, I agree with them. And my mom has tons of throw pillows, so you might want to quit while you're ahead."

He held up his hands. "Fine, fine. It's not crap."

"Thank you for seeing the light," Sam said, sitting back against the cushions but with a pillow at the ready in her hands.

The front door opened and in walked Bobbi, bundled in a million layers. "Hey guys," she said, voice muffled by the thick scarf around her face.

Ariel stood up, setting the foam roller back in its rightful place next to the TV stand. "While you unwind yourself, Coach, I'm going to get things set up at the table. Now that we're all here, let's get this recap going! Where's Mom?"

"She's downstairs," Sam said. "MOM! MEETING!" Sam yelled so loud everyone covered their ears.

"Coming!" replied Cheryl's muffled voice from beneath them.

"Thanks for waking up the entire neighborhood," Bobbi laughed.

"It's one in the afternoon, if you're still asleep, you need to wake up," Sam said.

"I'll remember that when you yell at me for waking you up at noon," Ariel pointed out, raising an eyebrow at her sister.

"Well… that's different," she stammered.

"Yeah, uh huh, whatever you say."

A few moments later, everyone was gathered around the kitchen table. "First of all, I want to say a heartfelt thank you to each and every one of you for your support leading up to and on race day. And thank you for coming back yet again to go over everything."

"Well, we're here until August so…" Sam said under her breath.

Ariel ignored her sister's comment and moved on. "Let's talk about what went well. Mom, let's start with you and go around the table."

"I thought our organization was great." Cheryl started. "The bins were well labeled, it was easy to find stuff, and it was easy to put stuff back where we got it. Which everyone did, so thank you all for that."

"Coach?"

"We worked great together as a team. No one had any disagreements, people asked for help when needed. We jived well."

"Glad to hear it," Ariel said, making a few notes on her paper. "Sam? How was navigation and logistics?"

"Navigation was easy," she said. "We never got lost, we made it to all the spectator spots at the right time. And logistics, same."

"Shelby?"

"Cheering squad energy was on point," she said, a huge smile on her face.

"Agreed," Kyle said. "And I was able to float around wherever I was needed. That worked well."

"Sweet," Ariel said, jotting some notes on her paper. "Sounds like there were lots of things that went well. Now, let's go around again and talk about things we can improve upon. "Captain Coach?"

"First, I want to say I'm sorry for not mentioning lubing your feet. I seriously never even thought about it. I'm glad that runner was nice enough to share his."

"Wait, hold up," Sam said, leaning forward to look at Ariel. "Some guy shared lube with you in the middle of the woods?"

Mom's eyes widened and Ariel burst out laughing. "It's foot lube. Look." She pulled up a browser tab on her phone to show everyone. "See? Not as weird, but yes, it's hilarious and sounds sketchy AF. We're going to add this on the list of gear. I already ordered it."

"Good," Bobbi said. "We'll try pre lubing for blister management. We can also try toe socks if you want."

"That sounds awful," Ariel said, "But foot lube also sounded awful so I'll try anything."

"Other than the blisters, I know you had stomach issues," Bobbi said. "Tell us more about that."

Ariel recounted every detail of what she ate, when she ate it, how much, and how it made her feel.

"Ari," Cheryl interjected, "it sounds like you ate too much, too fast."

"But I just did a serving each time like all the packages say."

"Your mom's right," Bobbi said. "Next time let's try taking a little at a time. One chew, drink of water, repeat."

"That'll take forever…"

"But you probably won't throw up," Cheryl said. "You've always eaten too fast, ever since you were little."

"I mean…" Ariel knew she couldn't argue with her there. "Okay, okay. We'll do that too. I'd also like to try some more real foods. Those chews were good, but my lower GI was… let's just say my butt was on fire for 24 hours post-race."

"Oh we know," Sam said, making a face.

"Hey, in running, poop is an open topic," Bobbi laughed. "I've got plenty of stories—"

"Let's save those for another day," Shelby said, red faced. "Talking about… that weirds me out."

"Poop!" Kyle exclaimed.

"Poop, poop, poop!" Sam joined in, laughing.

"Okay, okay, y'all," Ariel laughed, enjoying Shelby squirming in her seat. "What else? What can we work on?"

Everyone looked from one to another, shrugging their shoulders.

"I think something helpful would be having a change of shoes," Ariel said. "That way if something happens, I don't have to worry about running in a bad pair."

"It might also help if you start having a nagging injury or blister or something," Bobbi added.

"Exactly. This distance I don't think it's that big a deal, but I was overhearing some people talking about racing hundred milers, and they all talked about multiple shoes. One guy said it saved his race. I just want to have that option in my back pocket."

"Added to the list," Cheryl said, scribbling on her paper.

"Now the fun part!" Ariel said, clapping her hands together. "Team name! What did we come up with?"

"Hartfelt Run Squad!" Shelby said. "You know, like a play on your last name."

"That's cute, it could grow on me," Ariel said. "Anyone else?"

Everyone shook their heads. "Well, there's your assignment for the time being. Next time we meet, everyone needs to have names to suggest. I don't care how bad they are, I just want something!"

"Okay, agreed," everyone around the table nodded.

"Perfect. Meeting adjourned!" Ariel said, smacking her hand on the table like a gavel. "Kyle, Bobbi, want to stay for lunch?"

"I made plenty of curry," Cheryl said.

"I'd love to," Kyle said.

"Already planned on it," Bobbi said, leaning back in her chair, interlacing her fingers behind her head. "Cheryl and I are hanging out today."

"How's the job search going, Mrs. Hart?" Shelby asked.

"I have a few leads," Cheryl said, standing up from the table. She walked to the kitchen, retrieving something from the oven. "I forgot how long it takes to get a job though. I'm trying to remind myself just to be patient."

"That sucks," Shelby said. "I'm sure you'll get something soon."

"Thanks, Shelbs. Me too." Ariel watched her mom closely. The small glimmer of doubt in her eye was unmistakable. It had been almost three months since she'd lost her job. Every day since, she'd spent hours perfecting her resume, searching and applying for job postings, going to interviews. She'd even taken up walking on the treadmill to try to add a little more "youthful energy for interviews". If Ariel could give her mom a job, she would. Thankfully, Sam was loving her gig at Panera and her paycheck was bigger than she'd expected so the amount she'd been able to contribute to the household was helpful. She nearly covered the entire grocery bill. Ariel felt the pang of guilt at not getting a job herself, but every time the subject came up, Sam and Shelby were quick to remind her that while she wasn't getting a paycheck right now, she was working towards the biggest paycheck of them all.

Chapter 19

Ariel's hand shook, her finger hovering over the enter button while her eyes eagerly watched the time in the bottom left of the computer screen. 6:28. Two more minutes. She bounced her leg, trying to think of other things to make the time go faster. Doing planks would be the only way to make the time go slower. 6:29.

"What if I don't get in?"

"You'll get in," Sam said. She was sprawled out in her beanbag chair, scrolling on her phone, undisturbed at her sister's anxious energy. Ariel was grateful for her steadiness.

As the clock turned to seven, a jolt of electricity shot down her spine, her stomach turning into a knot. She took a deep breath in and pressed the refresh button.

The page refreshed but didn't reload completely.

"Of course, now it's going to crash and I'm never going to know and I'm going to die from an anxiety attack." Ariel resisted the urge to smash every button on the keyboard until the screen loaded.

"Just get up and walk away," Sam said. "If you don't pay attention, it'll load. No need to be so dramatic."

Ariel threw a look her sister's way, staring daggers at her.

"Hey, chill. I'm just playing with you," Sam said, looking up from her phone.

"Not the time," Ariel said through her teeth. She stood up and paced around the room from the desk to the window and back again, trying to count to ten in her head. "I'm gonna throw up."

"Stop being dramatic," Sam teased.

Ariel peeked at the screen, ignoring Sam. It finally loaded. She rushed to the computer and scanned the first sentence in the paragraph on the screen. Her heart stopped. "I didn't get in."

"What?" Sam put down her phone, standing up and walking over to see for herself. "Are you sure?"

"It says so right here." Ariel pointed to the screen, her hand trembling. She read the text aloud. "Thank you for entering the Lifetime Leadville 100. It was a large pool of applications this year and while we wish we could welcome you all, we simply don't have the capacity. We're sorry to inform you, but you have not received a lottery placement. Thank you for applying, we look forward to seeing your name again next year.' I don't have next year, Sam. This was my only shot."

"I mean, you can run it any year you want," Sam shrugged.

Ariel punched her in the arm. "You know what I mean."

"I know, bad timing for a joke," Sam said, rubbing her arm.

"Duh."

"Well shit," Sam said under her breath. "Hold on."

"Hold on for what?" Ariel asked, standing up and starting to pace the room to keep from bursting into tears. What had been excitement a few moments ago had turned to despair.

"Just gimme a minute."

"I don't have time for a minute, I have to figure out what we're going to do next. I didn't get in. I didn't get in! That was the whole plan! God that was an awful plan…. I could try to get in and run Western States. They don't have the same prize money, but maybe I'd get sponsors. Maybe I can do a charity partnership for Leadville? I can reach out to some people from the homeless shelter downtown, maybe they can sponsor me? Or maybe a more local charity in Leadville?"

"Girl. Chill. Remember the Leadville marathon you were planning on doing?"

Sam's comment stopped Ariel's runaway thoughts in their tracks. "What does that have to do with this?"

Sam cocked her hip. "Do you really not remember this part? It's one of the races that has an extra mini lottery for the hundred miler. Here, look." Sam handed Ariel her phone where she'd pulled up the race pages.

Ariel thumbed through the information, her eyes scanning the small screen at lightning speed. The webpage detailed a list of races that would count as a qualifying race. Sure enough, the Leadville marathon was top of the page.

"You're gonna do that race, right?" Sam prompted. Ariel handed her back the phone.

"Yeah. We already have the schedule figured out."

"Exactly. We made that race schedule assuming you'd get in with this lottery. But you didn't and that's okay. Because the marathon has its own lottery and you have another chance at still getting into the hundred miler," Sam said.

Ariel let out a breath she didn't know she'd been holding. "I seriously don't remember talking about this at all."

"That's why you have a crew."

"I get it now…" Ariel stood up and stretched her hands above her head. "You're the greatest. What would I do without you?"

"Lose the house, obviously." Sam winked, flicking her hair over her shoulder.

"Yeah, that would be bad. Let's get signed up for the marathon then. I gotta get to bed, I have a huge build week tomorrow for workouts." Ariel sat back at the makeshift desk she'd set up on Sam's vanity. Her laptop was surrounded by Sam's makeup brushes and hair accessories, and the chair covered with outfits she'd tried on and decided against that day.

"What was that website again?"

Sam read the name of the race, and Ariel typed it into the search bar. Thankfully it was the first result that appeared, and the website was easy to navigate. Ariel made quick work of filling out the signup forms.

"Okay, are we ready?" she asked, hovering the mouse over the "submit" button.

"Yes, we're more than ready. I wanna go to bed," Sam moaned, laying back in her chair, covering her eyes with her elbow.

"Now who's being dramatic?" Ariel laughed. "Okay, it's done!" She pressed submit and the confirmation page appeared. She used her own phone to snap a quick picture of the page, just in case the email didn't make it into her inbox.

"That was a rollercoaster," Ariel huffed, falling back against the chair. "Hope, then the pits of despair, then hope again! I just wish I would've gotten in with the lottery, then I wouldn't have to worry about it. But I guess this is just as good because—"

"Ariel," Sam interrupted her. "Go relax. You've done everything you can, which is a lot. It's not really even a wrinkle in your plan because we'd planned for this anyway. Not ideal, no. But still totally fine."

Ariel smiled, hands on her hips. "Samantha Jean, you're so right."

"I always am," Sam said, pulling the covers over her head. "Now go away! I want to chill!"

Ariel stood up to retire to her own room. "If you insist. Night!"

"Night."

Ariel closed the door behind her as she left, skipping to her own room. She plopped down on her bed, a wave of relief washing over her. The past hour had been a whirlwind: the complete devastation of not getting the lottery traded for a renewed hope at a qualifying race. And the best part was, she didn't even have to have a certain time to qualify. All she had to do was show up and finish the race. Which was a big enough feat, seeing as how the marathon topped out at thirteen thousand feet. It would be a massive challenge. But with time and health on her side, she was confident she could do it.

Chapter 20

"Did you really fly on the plane in that?" Ariel asked, flabbergasted. Her sister stood in front of her clad only in a bikini and beanie.

"Sure did!" Sam said, tossing her shirt on the flannel bedspread. "Last one in the hot tub is a loser!" Sam dashed out the bedroom and down the stairs, blowing past Mom on the stairs.

Shelby and Ariel exchanged glances and burst out laughing. They grabbed their suits and put them on, joining Sam in the hot tub on the back porch fifteen minutes later. Ariel gingerly dipped her foot in before fully submerging it.

"Oh, this isn't that warm," she said, disappointed.

"I know, I had to turn it on," Sam said, shaking her head. "How dare Kyle and his family be good stewards of the planet's resources and turn off the thing when they're not here."

Ariel rolled her eyes and sunk into the water up to her chest. Shelby clambered over the side, forgoing the stairs in her eagerness. "It'll warm up fast, don't worry," she said, sighing as she settled into one of the curved seats. "This is a perfect way to end the day after a long school day and a flight."

"I could get used to this," Ariel smiled, agreeing. She leaned back, resting her head on the tub's head rest to gaze at the starry sky above. The sky was midnight, speckles of starlight and a bright half-moon illuminating the early Colorado evening. She still couldn't believe Mom had been on board with taking the week of Spring Break to spend it with Kyle and his family at their cabin. Everything was as she'd remembered it: the log cabin feel, the floor to ceiling windows in the living room, the plaid bedspreads. She had many fond childhood memories of Sam, Kyle, and herself chasing each other through the house, bouncing from couch to couch to avoid the floor that was obviously lava.

The back sliding door opened, and Mom appeared carrying a tray of drinks and snacks. Much to everyone's surprise, she was also in her bathing suit.

"Can this ole' lady join you girls?" she asked, doing a little gig.

"Hell yeah you can, Mrs. Hart! Please do!" Shelby said enthusiastically, splashing the water beside her. "We've got a spot with your name on it."

A youthful smile spread across Mom's face. She set the tray of snacks down on the table and pulled it within reach of the hot tub before she climbed in to join them. "The wine is for me, but you're welcome to whatever else you want."

"Damn, I wanted that glass of red wine," Sam said, feigning disappointment.

"When you're twenty-one," Cheryl said, taking a sip and raising her glass.

"So, what're we doing tonight?" Ariel asked, sinking down into the water up to her chin. The water was warming up, but the air was chilly around them, making her eager for it to become more than lukewarm bath temperature.

"Well, I thought we'd order delivery and watch movies. Maybe eat some ice cream?" Cheryl offered. "I peeked in the freezer, and they've got like six types of Ben and Jerry's in there. But no real food other than that."

Ariel laughed out loud, nearly spilling the La Croix she'd just opened. "That would be Kyle. Dude is obsessed."

"I mean, I'm not mad about it," Sam laughed. "But I agree, a frozen pizza at least would've been nice."

"They have tons of take-out menus in one of the drawers," Cheryl said. "In a bit I'll go grab them and we can order something."

"Ari, you're okay to eat take out?" Sam asked, jabbing her sister playfully in the ribs.

Ariel nodded. "Um, yes I am, thank you very much. I need all the carbs I can get. It helps with adjusting to elevation. I can't eat enough. And I need as much help as I can get for this training block."

"That must be tragic," Shelby said sarcastically. "Not being able to eat enough to keep weight on?"

"It actually sucks," Ariel explained, her tone serious. "I don't want to lose weight. If I don't eat enough, I lose muscle mass which is going to increase my risk for injury. Hey, if you want to eat whatever you want and not have to worry about weight, just start training with me every day."

Shelby shook her head side to side, sending her wet curls flying. "I'm enjoying running just my fifteen miles at the most, thank you very much. I like running, but not that much."

"No one likes it that much," Cheryl added. "Ariel's unique that way."

"I'll take that as a compliment, thank you very much," Ariel laughed, splashing water towards her mom.

For the next hour, the four women sat in the tub as it warmed up to a true hot tub temperature. They chatted about the week ahead, sights they wanted to see in Rocky Mountain National Park, restaurants they wanted to try, and how to structure it around Ariel's training runs. Eventually, Sam's stomach growled loud enough to be heard above the rumbling of the hot tub jets.

"I'll take that as my cue to get the takeout menus," Cheryl laughed. "I need to get out and pee anyway."

"Wait, you haven't just been peeing in here?" Shelby asked, wide eyed.

"Are you—" Cheryl started.

"Just teasing," Shelby laughed. "The look on your face was great though."

Cheryl didn't respond and just shook her head as she toweled herself dry. "I'll be back in a few with the menus. Anyone need anything?"

"We're good," Ariel said, glancing between Sam and Shelby, who nodded in agreement. Cheryl wrapped the towel around her waist and disappeared inside. As soon as the door closed, Shelby whipped around to face Ariel.

"Okay, while she's gone, let's pick up that convo we were having earlier in the car."

"What conversation?" Ariel asked, taken aback at the sudden one-eighty.

"About you and Kyle?" Shelby insisted. "And how there's totally something going on?" Sam leaned in behind Shelby, resting her chin on her shoulder.

"We all know there's something, so why don't you just spill?" Sam asked. "Spill or we continue this convo when Mom gets back."

Ariel sighed. There was no way she could hide it from her best friend and sister or play dumb any longer. She knew it and they knew it. "Okay, maybe. Maybe there's something there. And we've talked about it."

"What?!" Shelby yelled, smacking the water with her hands, sending droplets flying. "You've talked about it. Why did you not tell me?"

"Because I knew you'd react like that," Ariel laughed, motioning to her friend's outburst. "It's not a big deal."

"Not a big deal? Ari, I love you, but your love life has been severely lacking."

"It's been nonexistent actually," Sam pointed out. "Ever since freshman year when you dated Austin for a few months. And now we find out you and your best guy friend from kindergarten both like each other?"

Shelby nodded in agreement. "Exactly what she said!"

"Yeah, yeah, I know," Ariel said, smiling. She had to admit, it felt good to finally tell them about it. "I like him, a lot actually. But not enough to jeopardize my training. I have to be a hundred and ten percent focused on

225

it. I can't take a day off to go to a party, I can't take a night off to go to the movies. I don't have time for dating. Like… literally nothing can compromise this training. The odds are already so not in my favor. I'm not allowed any slip ups."

"I get that, but what if he's not a distraction?" Shelby offered. "What if it only helps?"

"Shelbs, you and I both know that romantic relationships are always distracting. Especially at first when you both are obsessed with each other. I've seen it happen enough times and in real life… I'm looking at you."

"What? Me? Get obsessed? No way!" Shelby feigned surprise. "Yeah, I know. It's not my best quality. But you're a different person than I am. You're so much more independent and shit."

"You really are," Sam said. "Didn't you and Austin break up because you wanted to have every Saturday to yourself instead of going on dates with him?"

"Yeah, that was part of it," Ariel admitted. "That and I just didn't like him all that much. Sloppy kisser."

"Ew, I don't need details," Sam said, waving her off. "But point is, you're very independent. I doubt dating Kyle would change that."

"I'm not chancing it."

"What did you talk about exactly?" Shelby pried.

"Just that we both have feelings for each other, but I'm not getting into a relationship right now because I'm completely dedicated to running this race and focusing on it and only it. He was a bit mopey, but he said he was willing to wait until after I win the race."

"Well, that's good. Guys don't usually take rejection well," Sam said.

"I think it helps we've been good friends forever. We have that solid foundation to lean on."

"Let's just hope he doesn't get impatient and resentful about having to wait, what… nine months?" Shelby said.

Ariel shrugged. "If he does, then I probably wouldn't have wanted to date him for very long anyway."

"You're so mature for someone who's only ever dated one guy," Shelby teased.

"Hey, I dated plenty in elementary school," Ariel laughed.

"Oh yes, the two-hour relationships we all had. Those were the days," Sam said, thinking back to her playground romances. They'd mostly consisted of chasing each other around the slides and sharing Cosmic brownies at lunch.

"Speaking of short relationships, what happened to you and Joe? I haven't seen you two around together at school and you haven't talked about him much lately."

"Yeah, I was gonna mention that," Shelby said, twirling a piece of her hair around her pointer finger. "We aren't really a thing anymore. He's kind of a dick actually, especially when he drinks. He's hot, but not hot enough to put up with that shit. And it was three weeks, so whatever."

"My bad," Ariel laughed. Shelby had always been popular with the boys at school, but none of the relationships seemed to last much longer than a month. Whether that was simply because Shelby knew exactly what she wanted, or had no idea about what she wanted, Ariel wasn't sure. But despite the rather quick turnaround, Shelby always seemed happy and content, never down and out when a relationship changed. Ariel figured as long as she was having fun with it and being herself, there was no harm. Just then, Mom reappeared with an array of colorful takeout menus in her hand.

"We've got lots to pick from," she announced as she fanned them all out on the table. The girls came to the edge of the hot tub and studied the fronts of them.

"Thai sounds great," Sam and Ariel said in unison. They glanced at each other and laughed.

"I like Thai food," Shelby agreed. "Mama Hart? You like Thai?"

Cheryl nodded. "Sure do. Who do you think turned them onto their drunken noodle obsession?"

"I thought maybe Dan had," Shelby laughed. The look on Ariel's face made her stop. "Oh shit, I'm so sorry. I didn't mean to bring him up…"

"No, it's okay," Ariel said quietly. "It's kind of nice to hear Dad's name. Sometimes it feels like the world forgets about him."

"I bet," Shelby said, her voice sympathetic. "I know he was obsessed with Chinese food, so I thought Thai would've been his wheelhouse too."

"Nope, that was all me," Cheryl said, a small one-sided smile appearing on her face. "He liked Thai food, but he always thought Chinese cuisine was superior."

"Aren't they practically the same?" Shelby asked, confused.

"If he heard you say that, he would be giving you an hour-long lecture on the many differences between the cuisines," Ariel exclaimed, giving her a playful shove. "They are vastly different."

"Dad and his lectures," Sam said, shaking her head. "Never thought I'd miss them."

Tears pricked at Ariel's eyes. "Me too."

Sam moved beside Ariel and put her arm around her wordlessly. Cheryl joined in and motioned for Shelby to do the same.

"I miss him," Sam whispered.

"Me too, honey," Cheryl said. "Me too. And that's okay."

"Shall we order both Thai and Chinese tonight in his honor? And I can have the education he would've wanted me to have?" Shelby quipped, trying to cheer them up.

"Done and done," Sam said, reaching for her phone off the table. "Do y'all know what you want? I'm starving, let's order."

The girls dried their hands on a towel and flipped through the menu while Sam dialed. After the order was placed, Mom rejoined them in the tub and they continued relaxing together. Exactly an hour and a half later, the girls were sprawled out on the large sectional in the living room with their Thai and Chinese food spread in front of them. Ariel dug into her Drunken Noodles as Sam scrolled through movie options on Netflix.

"13 Going on 30!" Shelby shouted, pointing at the TV with her chopsticks.

"Never seen it," Sam said nonchalantly.

"Are you fucking kidding me?!" Ariel said, head whipping around to stare at her twin. "How did we not see that together?"

Sam shrugged. "I was probably at gymnastics or something. I dunno."

"We're watching it," Cheryl decided.

"If you insist," Sam said. She obliged with the group consensus and clicked start on the movie.

"You can thank me later," Cheryl replied. "It's a classic." Shelby and Ariel nodded in agreement. As the opening credits rolled, Ariel felt a buzz in her pocket.

"Just landed, going to get the rental car and head your way. Be there around 10:30." Finally, the text from Kyle she'd been waiting for.

"Jeez, get delayed or something?"

"Yeah, an hour delay at Des Moines cuz the plane was late getting in," he replied instantly.

"Kyle and his family will be here around 10:30 tonight," Ariel announced to the group, setting her phone aside. "Said they got delayed earlier."

"Glad they made it here safe," Cheryl said, eyes glued to the screen. "It just sucks they couldn't take the early flight with us."

"His mom had to finish up something for work," Shelby explained. "Said something about needing to cover part of someone's shift."

"That woman," Cheryl said, shaking her head. "I know nurses are dedicated, but she's something else."

The rest of the night was spent watching the girl's night classic and eating a healthy dose of Ben and Jerry's ice cream. When it was over, Ariel was struggling to keep her eyes open. According to the time on the clock and Kyle's text from earlier, they were still about an hour away. She'd been looking forward to seeing him tonight, but with an early morning run looming on the horizon, she thought better of staying up and made her way to bed.

* * *

The scenery around them was stunning: snow-capped peaks in the distance against a baby blue sky, the foothills and evergreen trees rising around the shady running path. But it paled in comparison to the burn in their lungs.

"Oh…my… god.…" Ariel huffed as she chugged up a hill that seemed to never end. "I'm… never.… gonna.… be able… to … do… this.…."

Shelby grunted in agreement a few strides back, also struggling to surmount the elevation gain ahead of them. She was on mile twenty-eight of thirty, Shelby having joined her just a few miles ago to finish it out. The last several miles Ariel had felt her body struggling more than she was used to. She hoped and prayed it was simply the altitude making it harder to breathe. After all, it had been several months since she'd been above five-thousand feet and it took time to adjust. But she hadn't remembered her run with the Colorado State team being this hard.

"Maybe that's because it was only five miles, not twenty-eight," she reminded herself.

To distract from the pain, she started counting trees in the dense forest, trying to count as many as she could before passing one she designated as the marker, then repeating the process over again. It worked for the next mile, but her brain got bored and started focusing on the burn in her lungs and jelly in her legs again.

"On your left!" someone shouted from behind.

"The fuck you mean on your left?" Ariel huffed, turning over her shoulder and expecting to see Shelby getting a second wind and blowing past her. But instead, she saw an older woman wearing a running vest, her hair covered with a bright pink and yellow bandana running up the hill like it was nothing. She looked familiar, but Ariel couldn't place her. "Oh shit, sorry… thought… you were someone else."

The runner didn't say anything, just a polite wave and a hint of a smile played at the corners of her mouth as she sped past Ariel and disappeared into the woods around the bend just as quickly as she had appeared. Ariel slowed down and pulled up next to Shelby, exchanging wide eyed glances.

"She had to be in her forties, and she's kicking our asses," Shelby huffed. "God when will this be over."

A quick glance at her watch told her all she needed to know. "C'mon, just a mile left. And we just got passed up by an old lady. We can do better!" The older woman passing them turned out to be just the motivation they needed to get half of a second wind and finish the run strong.

"Holy shit, I'm gonna puke," Shelby said, leaning over and bracing her elbows on her knees. "That sucked."

Ariel rubbed her back with one hand, the other on her own head to open her lungs more to get as much oxygen as she possibly could. "Yeah, that was awful."

"You girl's run far today?" a voice asked from behind. The same woman who passed them on the trail reemerged from the other side of the woods. "You look beat."

"Yeah, we just finished twenty-eight," Ariel said, trying to stand a little straighter and not look like she could keel over at any second.

"Not me," Shelby huffed. "I just joined for the last eight. I'm not crazy enough to do what she does."

Ariel laughed off Shelby's dramatics. "What about you?"

The woman shrugged. "I just finished thirty. It was an easy day for me, so not too far." She winked, and Ariel suddenly recognized her. Her jaw dropped.

"Holy shit, you're Pam Riley." Ariel's hand flew to her mouth. "I'm so sorry, I–"

Pam laughed a hearty belly laugh. "I've heard much worse things yelled at me over the years. What's said during the run stays on the run."

Shelby looked from Pam to Ariel and back. "I'm sorry, but do you two know each other?"

"I mean, Pam Riley is one of the best women's ultrarunners ever. She's doing Leadville this summer," Ariel explained. "Pam, it's an honor to meet you. My name's Ariel, I'm a huge fan."

Pam smiled humbly and extended her hand to the girls, who both shook it. Her hand was small, but so was she. At only five-foot-one, Pam was the definition of the phrase "small but mighty". "I know who are, Ariel."

Ariel's eyes grew wide. "You do?"

"I heard rumor there was a young lady trying to be the youngest and first woman to outright win the Leadville 100, and I couldn't not look you up. You've had an impressive running career so far."

Ariel couldn't believe it. Pam Riley knew who she was. One of the sports biggest legends knew who she was and had spent time to look up more about her. She nearly fainted with joy. "Well, thank you. I'm shocked and honored you know who I am."

"You're easy to pay attention to once you hear your story," Pam said. "After all, I like to know my competitors."

Ariel was at a loss for words. "Do you train here often?"

"I do," Pam said. "Live here actually, the elevation gives me a training advantage."

"Yeah, I wish I could say the same," Ariel said. "Iowa's highest elevation is like sixteen hundred feet so it's not the best for that."

"Oof, yeah that sucks. My best advice? Up your carb intake and drink as much water as you can stomach. It really helps you acclimate faster."

"Thanks," Ariel beamed. She had just gotten running advice from the great Pamela Riley. Never mind she already knew that, but she wasn't about to look a gift horse in the mouth.

"Are you here for a while?" Pam asked, stretching her arms above her head and shifting her weight foot to foot. In true runner form, she couldn't stand still for long.

"Just for Spring Break to train, then I gotta go back to graduate. But after that I'm living out here for the summer," Ariel said. "So don't count me out just yet."

Pam smiled a toothy grin. "I'd never. I've got to get going, but I'll see you around. Nice meeting you."

"You too," Ariel said. And just as quickly as she'd appeared, she was gone, jogging down the hill to the parking lot and off to whatever else her day held. Ariel turned to Shelby and silently screamed.

"Holy hell, we just met Pam Riley!" Shelby exclaimed out loud, unbothered whether Pam heard her or not. "And she knows who you are!"

"Right?!" Ariel said, giddy. "A freakin' professional runner looked me up and knows who I am!"

"Not just a professional runner, one of the sports OG legends! And one of your biggest competitors come August."

The girls started walking toward the parking lot, their legs gassed enough for the day to forego jogging the last hundred yards. Maybe she actually had a shot at this. In her gut, Ariel had always doubted how seriously other people took her but after that moment, she realized if another runner thought she was worth looking up and keeping an eye on, maybe she had a better shot than she realized.

Chapter 21

The towering rock faces loomed above vast open valleys. Everything was covered in a fresh layer of snow from last night. Something Ariel hadn't accounted for was just how snowy the mountains were in late March. The thought had never crossed her mind, seeing as she was used to only intermittent snow cover at this point in the year. But she was determined to make the most of her time here. While running on alpine trails might not be an option right now, snowshoeing was, which is why she'd insisted the whole party give it a try.

"Why couldn't we have just gone skiing?" Kyle asked as they got out of the car. They'd parked in the large parking lot at Bear Lake, the starting point for popular snowshoeing trails. And it seemed they would be in good company as the parking lot was nearly full.

"Because, we don't get the same workout flying down a hill," Ariel insisted. "Plus, it's terrifying."

"Not to mention the ski lift tickets and rental equipment for all seven of us would've been over a thousand dollars," Kyle's dad, Bill pointed out. Kyle rolled his eyes and looked around. The skies were clear today, the bright blue hinting of warmer weather to come.

"It's beautiful here," Shelby said in awe. "Ari, if I don't end up going to Columbia, I might have to join you out here."

"I told you," Ariel said. The crew opened the trunk of the rental SUV and removed the rental snowshoes. Thankfully the person working the rental stand had demonstrated how to don the shoes and they made quick work of it. They trudged over to the big brown trailhead sign, indicating where to go.

Sam removed a map from her pocket. It was the same map, just smaller. "Looks like we're taking this one, towards Nymph Lake."

"Looks that way," Cheryl confirmed, nodding. "Lead the way!"

Ariel took off down the trail, followed by Sam, Kyle, and Shelby. Cheryl and Kyle's parents fell in behind them, content to hang back and chat while the kids tore ahead. After the first few hundred feet or so, the snowshoes started to feel less clumsy and Ariel found her groove. It wasn't running, but she felt every muscle in her legs working.

"Isn't this great?" she exclaimed, ogling the sights. The snow-covered conifers kept the trail quiet despite its many visitors at the moment. This was one of the most popular spots in the park, and for good reason. Between the trees and the lake set against the backdrop of the mountains, there was no shortage of beauty to take your mind off the workout that is snowshoeing.

"It's pretty cool," Sam admitted. While Ariel and Sam didn't share a love of running, they both loved the outdoors.

"I can't believe we've been out here so many times in the winter and never thought to do this," Kyle said.

"Well, your parents aren't exactly this type of outdoorsy," Shelby pointed out. "They're the kind of outdoorsy people that like to grill and sit outside on their back porch occasionally."

"You're not wrong," he admitted. "They're more outsidey than outdoorsy."

"Why the hell did they buy a second home out here then?" Ariel asked, looking back over her shoulder. She'd pulled away from the group a bit and waited until they caught up before moving ahead again. The parents were several paces behind them, engrossed in their own conversations.

"Dad was born and raised in Colorado. He wants to move back after I graduate, but who knows if they will. Mom likes it in Iowa."

"I see," Ariel said. "Well, if you move back here, I'll be here."

"Yeah, but you'll be busy with school."

"No one said you couldn't go to CSU too," Ariel commented. "They have a good psychology program."

"Sounds like you want me there," Kyle said, raising one eyebrow at her that sent a warm wave down her spine.

"Hey, look!" Sam said, stopping abruptly. "What's that?"

The group turned to look where she was pointing. Ariel squinted her eyes, trying to decipher what her sister was trying to show them.

"I don't see anything," Shelby said.

"There, towards the bottom of that tree," Sam wagged her finger to try to make it clearer.

Something moved at the base of a cluster of trees and Ariel finally saw it. There, hidden almost out of sight was a large brown animal, too huge to be a deer.

"Holy shit," Shelby said loudly. "Is that a moose?!"

"Shhhhh! You'll scare it away!" Ariel said, covering her friend's mouth with her hand.

Kyle turned to motion to his parents to hurry up. Looks of concern on their faces, the adults picked up their pace and quickly joined the teens. "Look! Over there is a moose."

"Oh wow," Cheryl said, astounded. "That's the coolest thing!" The snowshoeing party stood still, admiring the large animal going about her daily business with no care that there were lots of humans oohing and aweing over her every step. She was the largest animal Ariel had ever seen outside of a zoo, and she was graceful. Eventually, she wandered back into the woods out of sight. The entire group let out a breath none of them knew they'd been holding.

"Well that was magical," Kyle's Mom, Tanya, said. "We've spent so much time out here and yet this is the first I've ever seen a moose!"

Bill shrugged. "I used to see them all the time. But it's still cool to see them. Never gets old."

"Is it safe to keep going?" Sam asked, turning to Bill. "She won't get territorial?"

"Yeah, we're fine to keep going. She didn't have a baby with her and she moved away from the trail. She's probably so used to people she doesn't even notice us anymore." With Bill's reassurance, the group continued on around the lake. By the time they were back to the car a little over an hour later, Ariel's legs were feeling the effort. But she didn't have the workout she'd wanted.

As the others in the group were taking off their shoes, she stayed standing, crossing her arms in front of her chest and looking around. "Would you guys mind if I keep going for a bit? There's another lake a little further than the one we just saw."

"But we had plans to go to the lodge this afternoon for a ranger talk," Cheryl pointed out, tossing her snowshoes back in the back.

Ariel glanced at her watch. "I know. This won't take me hours. Please?"

Cheryl furrowed her brow. "I don't know if I'm comfortable with you out here by yourself."

"I won't be," Ariel said with a quick glance at Kyle. "He's coming with me."

A flash of surprise crossed his face, but he was quick to recover before Cheryl looked at him.

"You're going with?" she asked, slightly suspicious.

He nodded without missing a beat. "Yeah, we both wanted to do a bit more exploring if that's okay with you. Anyone can come if they want," he offered.

Sam and Shelby exchanged glances, shrugging at each other. "I think we'd both be better off if we got a little more running around in today," Shelby said. "After the plane yesterday, I have some steam I can burn off. Plus, if Kyle and I are going to be pacing this girl's crazy ass in August, we have to seriously start working a little harder."

"I'm all right with it if you are, Cheryl," Tanya shrugged. Her husband nodded in agreement.

Cheryl offered up her hands. "I guess that settles it then. We'll head to the lodge but we'll come back here to pick you guys up… say around three?" she glanced down at her watch. "That gives you three   hours?"

"Plenty of time," Ariel said, excited that they'd agreed. While she loved ranger talks, she knew she'd go stir crazy if she didn't get more exercise. "Put your boots back on kids, let's go!" She jogged a few steps away from the car, eager to get going. Luckily, Shelby still had her shoes on and it didn't take Sam and Kyle long to lace theirs back up.

As the parents piled into the car and made the short drive to the lodge and visitor center down the road, the group of teenagers started trudging down the path and back into the trees around the lake. Sam had her map out, studying it as she walked.

"Um, you realize this is like an eight-mile hike?" she asked, suddenly not so sure about this.

"Yeah, but I wasn't planning on doing the whole thing if you guys don't want to," Ariel said. "I would've gone by myself but I knew there was no way the 'rents would've gone for that."

"You're totally right," Sam said, shoving the map back in her coat pocket. "Mom would've been a hard no on that one."

"We'll just go until we don't want to go anymore," Ariel said. "No biggie."

The group marched on in silence, still awed at the beauty around them. Ariel didn't think this would ever get old. The soft crunch of their snowshoes, the occasional bird call as they flew from tree to tree in search of food, the random popping of branches breaking beneath the weight of the wet snow. It was every definition of a winter wonderland.

After a while, Ariel and Kyle had pulled ahead of the other two, their paces naturally faster. "Or maybe they're planning it—" Ariel thought to herself. She knew Shelby wasn't above scheming and neither was Sam. Put those two together and often they had a diabolical plan up their sleeves.

"I can't believe you get to come out here all the time," Ariel said quietly, almost unaware she'd said it out loud.

"Yeah, I'm pretty lucky," he said. He trailed off, leaving Ariel with the feeling something was on his mind.

"What're you thinking about right now?" she asked.

"Asking you to prom," he said quickly.

Ariel turned to him, her eyes wide with surprise that turned to skepticism. "Ha ha, very funny."

Kyle kept walking, his eyes on the ground. "No, I'm serious."

"Oh." Ariel went quiet, trying to keep the rising excitement in her chest under control. "Then ask me."

He looked up from his feet and looked at her, his eyes reflecting the light off the snow so they looked like they were lit up from somewhere deep behind them. "Ariel, will you go to prom with me?"

A large smile broke out across her face. She couldn't have suppressed it if she'd wanted to. "Sure."

Now it was his turn to smile, his cheeks red. Though she was pretty sure that was from the near subzero temperatures and the exertion of snow shoeing. "Cool."

"As a friend, or as a date to prom?" she teased, heart fluttering in her chest.

Kyle stepped in front of her and stopped. They were face to face, so close she could feel his body heat radiating off his broad chest. "As a date, Ariel Jane. We're great friends, but I'm excited to be more."

Ariel's knees nearly buckled. "Good."

He held her gaze, his eyes flitting down to her lips and back up again so fast she thought she may have imagined it. The crunching of boots on snow interrupted the moment. A glance over her shoulder revealed Sam and Shelby gaining on them. "Do I get to tell Shelby?" she asked.

"Well, she probably already knows," Kyle said sheepishly. "She's the one that convinced me to ask you."

Ariel whipped around, a mischievous grin plastered on her best friend's face.

"Did he do it?" Shelby squealed.

Ariel nodded, laughing and nodding her head. "Yes."

Shelby cheered and embraced her in a hug, nearly knocking her over. "You two are so damn cute. Just kiss already."

Ariel and Kyle both laughed nervously. "You're the worst," Ariel chided.

"Can we go back now?" Sam asked, "I'm freezing and tired."

"No! We just got started. We at least have to make it to Dream Lake. It's not that far," Ariel insisted.

They continued their trek onward, Ariel's mind buzzing with the idea of a date for prom and what other wildlife might cross their paths today.

Chapter 22

"How many times are you going to unpack and repack your running vest?" Sam asked, hanging lazily over the foot of the bed. She watched as Ariel organized all the pack's contents into neat piles for the hundredth time.

"As many times as it takes for me to feel confident that I have everything and it's in the right place," Ariel said, not looking up from her task. She pulled a caffeinated gel from her pack and set it in a pile of its own.

"Didn't you and your mom go over all of this twice yesterday?" Kyle asked. He sat on the floor across from Ariel, back leaning against the bed. He'd come over to do their physics homework together, but since they'd finished that long before dinner, Ariel had roped both Kyle and Sam into helping her prep for the weekend's race.

"Yes, but I swear I forgot something."

"Did you go through your checklist?" Sam asked.

"Yes."

"And did your mom agree with everything that was in there?" Kyle asked.

"Yes."

"Then you're fine," Sam and Kyle said in unison. Sam rolled her eyes and Kyle chuckled.

Ariel leaned back on her knees, exasperation on her face. "I don't know, I just feel like I'm forgetting something, but I can't figure out what it is. This race is so much bigger, you guys. This is the real test of how I do at longer distances, being self-sufficient, you guys being an effective crew…"

Sam gave Kyle a knowing look and mouthed the words "race nerves" to him. Ariel didn't usually get nervous, but Sam knew her sister well enough to recognize them the few times they popped up. Typically it only happened before firsts—her first cross country meet as varsity, her first time running at the State championship, Nike Footlocker Nationals, etc.

"A 100k is much more serious than a dinky 50k—"

"Would you have said that six months ago?" Sam asked, twisting around and sliding to the ground to sit beside Kyle so she was eye level with her sister.

"I don't know."

"Bullshit, yes you do."

"Probably not, okay?"

"Exactly," Sam said. "Then why are you saying it now?"

"That's thirty-one miles, Ari," Kyle pointed out. "That's insanely far. Most people on the planet would call you crazy for saying 'dinky' 50k. And Sam's right. Six months ago, you were freaking out about running that far."

"I know but—"

"No buts!" Kyle and Sam exclaimed together.

"We've gotta stop doing that, man. It's weird," Sam said, shaking her head in feigned disgust. "Anyway, he's right. I'm right. Who cares this one is further than the last? You do realize your end goal is to run a hundred freaking miles, right?"

Ariel's gaze dropped to her lap. Her shoulders shook with a soft laugh. "I guess that is a little crazy, isn't it?"

Sam breathed a small sigh of relief. Ariel didn't get flustered by much, but when she did it was bad. She was grateful they seemed to have avoided the worst of it.

"I'm crazy!" Ariel laughed out loud, a grin overtaking her face.

"Certifiably insane," Kyle teased.

"And yet you still like me, so what's that say about you?"

"Anyway," Kyle said, running his hands through his hair. "Can we repack now and go get some food? I'm starving."

"Let me finish this, and yes." Ariel agreed. The last thing in her pack was the water bladder, which she removed and set at the top of the grid she'd laid out before her. It was all here: water bladders, chews, gels, baggies for the real food she'd bring along, salt pills, electrolyte mix, Chapstick, band aids, precut blister covers, foot lube, peppermints. She couldn't get rid of the nagging feeling she was missing something as she carefully repacked everything into its rightful place in her running vest. The race was in two days, so she still had time to go through things again. Next time, she'd make sure Sam and Kyle weren't around to give her crap.

* * *

"All right, here you go," Coach Bobbi said as she helped Ariel slip her running vest into place. Ariel tightened and adjusted it until it was snug but comfortable. She patted all the pockets, finding comfort in the lumps that were going to be her lifelines the next few hours.

"It's all in there," Bobbi assured her. Her gaze softened. "I haven't seen you this flustered since freshman year."

Ariel shifted nervously on her feet. "I haven't felt this flustered since then. I mean, I was nervous for the 50k but not like this."

Bobbi shook her head. "Totally normal. I was so nervous I puked before my first marathon."

"You? Nervous?" Ariel eyed her skeptically.

"Mm-hmm. I used to get really bad race nerves all through high school. I finally chilled out once I wasn't competing anymore. But you? Competition is your thing. What evidence do you have for the doubt you feel?"

Ariel went quiet, staring at the shoes they'd decked out in sequins and glitter a few days before as she contemplated what Coach said. Finally, she looked up, meeting Coach's gaze. "None."

"Exactly. It's all just what ifs. And what do we say about those?"

"They're shit," Ariel said, grinning.

"Repeat that to yourself as much as you need," Bobbi said. "You're going to do great. This is the same thing you've always done, just a little longer. And you've proven that longer is no issue for you."

Coach was right in every way and Ariel knew she had no room to argue. She took a deep breath and did her best to believe it in every cell of her body. Coach noticed the change in her eyes and smiled, knowing she'd gotten through to her.

"Go get 'em. We'll be waiting for you at the second aid station."

"Thanks, Coach." Ariel turned and walked towards the starting line to test herself at the farthest distance yet.

* * *

She heard the aid station before she saw it, a raucous chorus of cowbells and hollering pierced carried across the open prairie. Ariel picked up the pace a bit, her legs and lungs still feeling fresh. As she entered the aid station, she scanned the crowd of volunteers and other runners' crews.

"Eighty-one," Ariel read off her bib number to the volunteer with the clipboard. Finally, she spotted Sam wildly running towards her and waiving her arms.

"We're over here!" Sam called. Ariel jogged over to her sister who led her around the edge of the aid station to a little patch of grass they'd set up on.

"What do you need?" Cheryl asked, presenting an array of food options. Ariel scanned them before grabbing the pretzels. Salt sounded good. As she ate a handful of pretzels, Sam removed her empty water bottles, and Shelby replaced them with full ones.

"Same as before, yeah?" Shelby confirmed as she slid the soft water bottle into its sleeve. "One electrolyte, one water?"

"Mm-hmm."

"No cramping, no nausea, no diarrhea?" Coach Bobbi asked, looking her up and down. She looked strong.

Ariel shook her head. "Nope. I feel great."

"That's a minute," Kyle called out the time since she'd been in the aid station.

"Damn, time flies," Ariel grabbed a few more pretzels and started jogging back toward the race course. "Eighty-one checking out!"

The volunteer marked down her time on the clipboard. Ariel waved to her crew. "See you at mile Forty!"

It would be a long time before she saw them again, nearly twenty miles. Thankfully, there were aid stations before then, just not ones the crew could access. That happened often in remote ultras due mostly to just that- the remoteness. Plus, races liked to minimize impact on the local areas and even with Leave No Trace principles, hundreds of people inevitably made an impact.

The morning was beautiful, and the miles ticked by. This race had fewer participants than the 50k she'd ran a few months prior and as such, she'd only seen one other person since mile ten. The field had spread out and she found herself missing the company of other runners. That was one of the best things about the 50k, you ran with people the whole time just like in cross country races. Having your competition around made you push harder, added excitement, camaraderie, and competition. It felt like a party on the trail. This was starting to feel more like a training run.

"But it's not, we've got a goal, we're racing," Ariel reminded herself.

Suddenly, the next aid station appeared. She glanced at her watch: ten miles in less than ninety minutes and she wasn't even hurting. A surge of adrenaline rushed over her while she simultaneously reminded herself she still had over half the race to go. This wasn't like short distances where she could get away with going hard the whole time.

"Respect the distance," Bobbi had constantly told her. "It'll be what takes you out."

With that sentiment in mind, she made it a point to go through the aid station mindfully. A volunteer had brought over her drop bag where she switched out her socks, refilled her water bottles, and replenished nutrition. When she went to return the bag, the volunteer had the biggest grin on her face.

"You're in first," she said, hopping up and down on both feet as she took the bag from Ariel.

Ariel's green eyes widened. "First? Like first woman?"

"No, first overall."

Ariel's jaw dropped. "Thanks for letting me know."

"Go get 'em! Show those guys where the real power is!" The volunteer cheered as Ariel entered the course again.

"Eighty-one out!" she called to the clipboard wielding volunteer guarding the course entrance.

Ariel had to make a conscious effort to slow down, but the adrenaline was surging. She was in first place, and not just first place woman, but first place of everyone. She loved it. This was the best news. But she knew she had far left to go and so many things can change over the course of that many miles. If this were a cross-country race, she'd put pedal to the medal and gun it the whole way home. But now? She didn't have enough gas in the tank to keep the peddle to the metal for nearly fifty miles.

"Smart is fast, fast is slow." Ariel repeated the mantra to herself until her paces matched the goal she had. "I guess that's why I wasn't seeing anyone, everyone's behind me!" She laughed to herself. Who knew it was this fun to run sixty-two miles?

At the next two aid stations, the volunteers eagerly gave her updates as to her standings in the field. She was still first overall, but now she knew she had nearly a two-hour lead on the next man and almost a four-hour lead on the next woman. As she pulled out of the latest aid station, she did a systems check: back, good. Arms, great. Feet, chilling and not sore. Calves, neutral. Knees, good on flats, a little tender on the downs. Quads, fresh. Hamstrings, a little tight but nothing bad. She was shocked at how good everything felt, particularly her feet. Once she got to her crew at the next aid station, it was time to race.

But before she got there, she had over two thousand feet of vertical climb to tackle. And the trail suddenly went from soft, single-track dirt to ground strewn with so many river rocks you couldn't step around them. "Yikes, this is prime ankle breaker territory," she said under her breath as she navigated the change in terrain. Soon enough, the incline was enough to slow her down to a power hike which was probably for the better. Didn't want to risk an injury at this point. It would be a slow and painful hop to the closest aid point. She powered up the incline in no time and was greeted with sweeping views at the top.

The late afternoon sun bounced off the blanket of humidity hanging over the corn fields, bringing an ethereal quietness to the vast openness. Dotted between fields were farmhouses with their cute red barns, the occasional cow mooing in the distance. It wasn't much, but it was home.

Now for the descent. As much as she'd done her best to train on technical downhill terrain, they were hard to come by in central Iowa. Thankfully, this didn't look too bad. The terrain was still rocky, but the incline was less than it had been on the way up. She took a deep breath and let gravity pull her down the Midwest mountain. She made quick, small steps, keeping her arms up. "Run like Jack Sparrow. Arms up, tiny steps." someone had told her when she'd asked how to run the technical downhills. She smiled to herself, her nerves easing.

Suddenly, a rock she'd placed her foot on moved, her ankle rolling unnaturally to the inside. "Ah!" she exclaimed, stumbling wildly to save herself from a tumble. She managed to stay upright and came to a halt. She looked at her ankle, no blood or scrapes. That was good. She drew circles with it in the air, moving it in all directions. That felt fine, too. She stood on it, no pain. She continued forward at a walk, testing out the ankle which remained pain free. After a few minutes, she picked up her run and let out a heavy sigh.

"Thank God, that could've been so bad." She sighed, relieved that she hadn't just damaged her ankle. She finally made it to the bottom of the hill and the trail got less rocky. Only three miles to go until she saw her people.

Thirty-two minutes later, she rolled into the aid station and immediately saw her crew. They'd managed a spot closer to the aid station this time which Ariel was grateful for. Any step off course she didn't have to take was a blessing.

"You're in first! You're in first!" they all chanted as she joined them. She slipped off her vest and handed it to Sam. Shelby replaced it with a new, fully stocked one as Ariel grabbed a triangle of quesadilla off one of the plates.

"I know!" Ariel said, grinning. "The aid station I got to after I saw you guys told me."

"How're you feeling?" Bobbi asked, cutting in through Sam and Shelby's excitement. "You're ahead of pace."

"Pretty good actually. I've been working really hard to not run away with it because believe me, the second I heard I was in first, I wanted to go guns-a-blazing."

"Well, you're not not going gun- a-blazing," Cheryl said, looking at the clipboard she had in front of her with split times and ETAs at aid stations. "You're a full three hours ahead of where we predicted you'd be."

"I feel great, you guys," Ariel said. Bobbi eyed her skeptically. "Honestly. My knees are a little sore on the downhills, but perfect otherwise. My feet are getting a little sore, but I don't have any hot spots or blisters to my knowledge. I did roll an ankle but—"

"You rolled an ankle? Which one?" Bobbi asked, immediately crouching down and running her hands down Ariel's calves much like a vet does to a horse when they're checking for lameness.

Ariel threw her head back in laughter. "Oh my god, Coach. I'm not a horse. It was the right one, and it doesn't hurt anymore."

"After all the work we've done to strengthen your feet and ankles, that hypermobility just won't quit, will it?" Bobbi shook her head, feeling all around the affected ankle. "There's no swelling or anything."

"It comes in handy sometimes," Ariel shrugged. She finished off the last of the quesadilla. "Hey, hand me my headlamp. I don't have one in the drop bag."

Kyle found it and tucked it into the back part of the pack. "I added some quesadilla there too."

Ariel's shoulders sagged under the extra weight. She shook her head. "That's too heavy. Give me pancakes instead."

Cheryl elbowed past Kyle and swapped one food item for the other, tucking it next to the headlamp. She zipped it shut and patted her on the back. "You're good to go."

"You haven't had any stomach issues?" Bobbi asked, one eyebrow raised.

"Not yet," Ariel said, crossing the fingers on both her hands.

"Girl, you gotta get outta here," Sam said. "Two minutes."

Ariel went through the mental checklist as she made her way back onto the course. "Okay, see y'all at the finish line!"

"Woohoo! Go get 'em, Ariel!" Sam yelled after her.

"Let's win this thing!" Cheryl cheered.

"Remember this isn't the main race we're training for!" Coach Bobbi's voice of reason cut through the cheers and Ariel did her best to remember that. This wasn't the ultimate win she was chasing. Sure, it'd be great if she was the first to cross that tape, but she had to keep it in perspective. She couldn't risk it all to win this one: she had to save that for Leadville.

Chapter 23

As the miles continued to tick by, the adrenaline coursing through Ariel's veins rose. Once her watch beeped and alerted her that she'd just past mile fifty, the brakes came off. It was go time. She had no idea how far back the next competitor was. All she knew was that she wasn't going to find out. The sun was low in the sky, casting long shadows and turning the bare early spring tree branches into silhouettes against a sherbet sky. Only twelve miles left to go. She chuckled to herself. What crazy person said *only twelve miles* left like it was nothing?

Then ten, nine, eight, seven, six, five, four, miles left to go. She could practically taste the finish line. Her legs were tired, her right knee ached on any downhill, her feet throbbed. But nothing was so bad it was stopping her. She kept her eyes trained on the ground in front of her. "Now's gonna be the time I actually twist an ankle or something," she mumbled to herself, carefully picking her way along the trail. She ran through the grassy meadow between forest clumps. One glance behind her proved there was no one else in sight. Finally, she let herself smile.

This race was hers.

When she entered the last bit of forest, the trees greeted her with reflective spinners, Halloween decorations, and cheeky signs declaring "You're Almost There!" For a moment, she thought she might be hallucinating the 12-foot-tall skeleton holding a pumpkin at the side of the trail.

"It's springtime, why are there Halloween decorations?" she whispered to herself out loud. She reached out and touched it as she ran past, confirming it was indeed real. "Thank god. If I hallucinate this easy, the hundred miler is gonna suck."

She ran the last three miles with a smile plastered on her face. As with every aid station on the course, she heard the finish line before she saw it and when she finally rounded the bend and it came into view, the noise erupted in cheers and the DJ turned up the music, deep base thumping through the ground. Even though no one was in sight, Ariel kicked hard and ran as fast as she physically could to cross that finish line, silky ribbon of the banner brushing against her arms as she broke through.

Tears erupted from her eyes as the tiredness consumed her legs, causing her to sink to her knees and sit back on her heels. She held the finish line banner above her head in victory, laughing through the happy tears rolling down her reddened cheeks. The crowd surrounding her cheered, cowbells clanked.

"Ladies and gents, Ariel Hart is our OVERALL winner of this year's 100k! She beat every single man and woman out there with a time of eleven hours, three minutes, seventeen seconds!" the announcer boomed over the sound system. "Congratulations, Ariel! I'd like to mention, Ariel is also our youngest ever finisher AND winner at the ripe old age of seventeen." The crowd clapped and cheered. Suddenly, Ariel's crew appeared in front of her, emerging from the crowd, bringing a whole new wave of happy tears.

Sam and Shelby got to her first, knocking her over with their bear hugs. "You did it! You freaking did it!"

"I never had any doubts!"

Cheryl sunk to the ground, joining them. Coach Bobbi and Kyle stood over them laughing.

"They're ridiculous," Bobbi laughed.

"They've always been a family that loves out loud," Kyle agreed. "It's cute."

"I suppose," Bobbi shook her head. "I can appreciate it."

When the bear hug finally broke up, Sam helped Ariel to her feet. "Are you exhausted? Can you even walk still?"

Ariel took a few tentative steps to confirm. A white-hot pain shot up on the outside of her knee, but it lessened with the next step. Her feet were worst of all. Each step felt like nails were being driven into her soles. "Sore, yes. But I can still function."

"Let's get you back to our little camp," Bobbi said. "Remember what I always say—"

"Recovery starts the second you cross the finish line," Ariel said, repeating what Bobbi always yelled at them after a cross-country meet. "I've been your athlete long enough I know the drill."

"Just making sure all those miles didn't go to your head," Bobbi teased.

"I'm sure they will. I'm just too tired right now. Wait until I get that first-place award. Then it'll go to my head," Ariel laughed, glancing back over her shoulder and winking at Coach. Bobbi laughed and shook her head. Mercifully, they'd managed to set up their crew station fairly close to the finish line aid tent.

"Your throne, milady," Sam said dramatically as she helped Ariel sit in the camping chair at the center of the blue tarp.

"Thank you, peasant."

Sam just rolled her eyes and shoved a bag of chips into her sister's hand. "Eat."

Just the sight of the chips turned her stomach. Ariel shook her head and handed them back. "What else do you got? 'Cause these ain't it."

Cheryl turned around and glanced over the assortment of food they'd spread out. "How about noodles and broth?"

"That sounds doable," Ariel said, getting comfortable in the chair. She sprawled her legs out in front of her, resting her head on the back of the chair. "Kind of. Nothing sounds good."

"You gotta get something in," Coach Bobbi said as she kneeled down in front of her. Slowly, she untied each shoe and removed them as well as the socks, exposing Ariel's feet. Bobbi inspected them with a careful eye. "You only have one blister. Amazing."

"Only one?" Ariel asked in disbelief, she tried to crane her neck to get a better view. "Why do they hurt so bad then? I was convinced I had one on the bottom of my little toe and on the ball of both my feet." Mom handed Sam the soup, who handed it to Ariel. The warm cup felt good in her hands.

Bobbi reexamined them. "You might have ones under the calluses on the balls of your feet, but I can't really see them. I suppose we'll find out in the next day or so."

Kyle appeared at Bobbi's side with the foot kit, wet wipes in hand. "You take one and I take the other?"

"I'm not turning that down," Bobbi laughed, taking one of the wipes from him.

"Kyle, you don't have to do that," Ariel said, suddenly self-conscious of her feet. But she was too tired to protest more and he didn't hesitate.

"I've got it. Eat your noodles," he instructed. He glanced up at her, their eyes meeting in a tender gaze. His cheeks turned a shade of bubblegum, and he gave her a bashful smile before turning his focus back to her feet. Ariel took the first bite of the broth and noodles and thankfully, it felt good to her stomach.

Shelby pulled up a chair and sat next to her with the tablet in her hand. "So do you want to see your predicted splits and where you actually ended up?"

"Yes, but I don't think it's going to stick so you'll have to remind me tomorrow."

"That's fine," Shelby said eagerly. "Look." She held the tablet so Ariel could read it as she pointed out each difference in the splits. "So overall, you were three times faster than we thought you would be."

"You better have written down every single thing we did so we can do it again at Leadville," Ariel said. "Cause apparently we got it right this time."

"Oh don't worry," Shelby said, switching to a different spreadsheet that was an array of dark lines, colors, and blocks of text. "I've got it all right here. I call it the MasterBoard."

"Good lord," Ariel said, shocked at the organization of it all. "I'm glad y'all are type A because I could never."

"I did all the formatting and color coding, Sam was our information geek," Shelby said.

"It's true," Sam agreed. She walked back over to join them after mixing up a bottle of sports drink. She handed it to Ariel. "Drink this too. You're not going to be able to eat enough calories to really help your muscle repair so this will help."

Ariel took the bottle in her free hand and eyed her sister skeptically. "Who says I can't eat enough calories? Usually, I'm ravenous after I run. Check back with me in an hour or two."

"How's those noodles coming?" Sam asked, pointing to the still full cup with her chin.

"Shut up. I said in an hour or two." Ariel finished half of the cup before her stomach started to turn sour on her. She set it down in hopes of finishing it later. "I'm ready to go to sleep."

"Not before we get you out of those nasty clothes," Cheryl said, poking her in the side.

"We're done with your feet," Kyle said, sitting back on his heels as he drenched them with hand sanitizer.

"Where are my fuzzy socks?" Ariel asked, leaning forward to scan the area. "I'm freezing."

"Right here." Kyle pulled them out of his back pocket and slid them onto her feet. "And here are your crocs." Ariel slipped her Christmas-socked feet into the black glitter crocs, tapping her feet on the ground.

"Thank you."

"Now, let's get you up and changed," Cheryl said, standing in front of her daughter, arms outstretched. Ariel took them. "One, two, three, up!"

"You know, this is gonna be me with you when you're old," Ariel laughed as she struggled to stand. "Holy shit I stiffened up fast." Her legs that had felt tired but loose just thirty minutes before suddenly felt like metal rods.

"That happens," Bobbi said. "You feel great as long as you keep moving, but the second you stop? Seized up legs. That's why when you're done, we're foam rolling."

"Nooooo," Ariel whined. The last thing she wanted to do was use that torture device.

"Focus," Cheryl said. "Change, then worry about that."

"Fine," Ariel conceded, too tired to argue. Ariel let her mom help her change in the back of the car, every movement difficult.

"I appreciate your help, Mom," Ariel said as her mom helped slip her pant legs into place.

"Honey, I'm so proud of what you can do. It's inspiring. I'm grateful I get to be a part of it."

"You are?"

Cheryl stopped what she was doing and looked her daughter in the eyes. "Of course, I am."

"Thank you," Ariel said, tears building in her eyes again.

"Awe, these races bring out your emotional side," Cheryl teased, wiping away a single tear with her thumb.

"Yeah, I don't know what that's about," Ariel laughed, shaking her head.

"I like it," Cheryl laughed. "Do you want me to pull your hair back?"

"Yes please," Ariel said. "I don't have the energy to deal with it."

Cheryl grabbed the hairbrush and tucked it into her sweatshirt pocket. "Let's go sit by the fire ring they have set up, shall we?"

Ariel woke up a little at the idea. "A fire sounds amazing. And we can watch the finishers!"

"Exactly. Let's go!" Cheryl held out her hands and helped Ariel stand up and take her first few steps. After a few steps to shake off the stiffness, Ariel found she could walk just fine except for the growing pain in the outside of her knee. The little group moved to the fire rings the race director had set up and gathered around.

"Hey Sam," Ariel called out. Mom was standing behind her, brushing her hair into a high messy bun. Sam appeared at her side.

"What's up?"

"Can you bring me an ice pack? Two actually."

"Yeah, what for?" Sam asked, a hint of concern in her voice.

"Just want to be nice to my knees. They're fine, but ice won't hurt."

"Roger that, be right back." And off she went, returning moments later with two premade ice packs. Ariel balanced them on her knees and leaned back. Just as she started to doze off, the finish line erupted in more cheers.

A runner appeared at the edge of the forest, their headlamp bouncing in the twilight. Ariel stood, clapping and cheering. As the runner crossed the finish line, she saw it was the first male finisher. He held the banner above his head, shaking it in victory. The crowd whooped and hollered. The man was joined by his crew.

"Our first-place male finisher is Brad Duhane from Ames, Iowa with a time of thirteen hours, eleven minutes, and fifty-four seconds. Congratulations, Brad!" As the announcer boomed the runner's accomplishment, a look of confusion came over his face. Ariel could see him mouth a question to his buddy.

"First male?"

His friend nodded and pointed over to where Ariel was standing. Ariel waved, the biggest smile on her face despite the fatigue and soreness setting in. "This is the best feeling in the world," Ariel said, nudging Sam who was standing next to her.

"Yeah, it is! Look at his face," Sam laughed. It was obvious Brad was having difficulty processing the fact he'd been beaten by a woman. That a woman had beaten everyone out there. This. This was what it was about. Well, partly anyway. Brad and his few friends joined them around the fire ring.

"You won?" Brad asked, extending a hand to Ariel. She took it and he shook it so vigorously Ariel almost laughed out loud.

"Sure did. Congrats on being the first guy to finish," Ariel said. "Brad, right?"

"Yep. You are…"

"Ariel."

"Nice to meet you," Brad said, massive grin plastered across his face. "I'd love to chat, but I'm wiped so I'm going to go to the car. Maybe we can catch up after the awards ceremony later? I gotta know how you did it!"

"Yeah, sure," Ariel said, a little surprised. "That'd be cool."

"Sweet, see ya later!" He waved as he turned and made his way towards the lot of parked cars.

Ariel and her group watched them walk away. As soon as they were out of earshot, Ariel and Sam exchanged glances and immediately broke into belly laughter. Bobbi, Cheryl, Shelby, and Kyle all broke out in the same.

"Haa-hah, he was so excited!" Shelby heaved between bouts of laughter.

"He was way nicer than I thought," Sam laughed, "When I saw him coming up to you, I thought for sure he was gonna be cranky and complaining about losing to you."

"Blown away is what that was," Bobbi cheered, slinging her arm over Cheryl's shoulder. "I hope you're proud of your daughter."

"Always have been," Cheryl assured her. "But that was a special moment."

"That's living rent free in my head for the rest of my life," Ariel said.

"So during Leadville," Bobbi said, turning to Ariel, suddenly serious. "When you want to lie on the side of the trail and die at mile eighty-eight. When your stomach turns south and you throw up every few minutes, this. This right here is what you need to think of."

"Okay," Ariel laughed, trying to calm her fits of giggles.

"I'm serious," Bobbi said. "Those times will come. And you must remember this moment."

"I will. Promise. Cross my heart and hope to win," Ariel said with a wink.

"Good. Now let's go get you that medal."

Chapter 24

After the 100k, time flew. The schoolwork came easy, as most of the hard stuff was finished before Spring Break for the seniors on account of the teacher's knowing senioritis was about to hit hard. Ariel's training continued steadily: long runs, sprint workouts, recovering with lots of calories and stretching. Her days were regimented, and she liked it that way because after graduation, things were going to get chaotic. For now, she wanted to hold onto the routine of her high school career. Before she knew it, the weekend of prom had arrived.

"Hold still," Sam said through clenched teeth.

"I'm trying!" Ariel gripped the door frame as Sam used her knee to brace Ariel's back and tighten the corset laces as tight as she could. "Ugh, jeezuz."

"That's what you get for getting a dress with a corset bodice," Sam said. She gave the laces another tug and started tying them together. "There. Got the last one. Can you breathe?"

Ariel took the biggest breath in she possible could. "Yes, but not well. Hopefully it'll loosen itself over the course of the night."

"I dunno, I tied it pretty tight. It shouldn't go anywhere."

"Girls! Are you ready for pictures?" Mom called from downstairs. "Shelby's here!"

"Yeah! Be right down!" Sam yelled back. "Look at us!" Sam grabbed her sister by the waist and pulled her into the view of the full-length mirror on the back of her bedroom door. Ariel had to admit, they looked great. Sam was stunning in her ruby red A-line gown. She looked like a regal, Old Hollywood beauty ready to walk the red carpet of her blockbuster hit. Ariel was wearing a beautiful midnight black ball gown, the tulle woven with glittery thread and the bodice full of crystals.

Sam laid her head on Ariel's shoulder. "Do you think Dad would approve?"

"Most certainly." Ariel felt a knot rising in her throat.

"Girl, don't cry. We just spent so much time on your makeup!"

"You brought up Dad, that's your fault," Ariel laughed as she tilted her head back in an effort to hold in the water works.

"Not my fault you're a cry baby," Sam teased, bumping her with her hip. "You ready to go downstairs?"

Ariel nodded, not trusting her voice.

"Are you ready, Mom? Here we come!" Sam yelled out.

The girls descended the stairs together, and Mom and Shelby were both waiting for them at the foot of the stairs, her phone recording their grand entrance.

"You girls are stunning!" Shelby squealed.

"Thanks, we know," Sam said, one hand on her hip, the other in her hair.

"So are you!" Ariel said, gushing at the sight of her best friend all dolled up. She wished they'd been able to get ready together, but Shelby's mom had insisted they spend some quality mother-daughter time together. Shelby was dressed in a large yellow ball gown that made her look like a sunbeam.

"So humble, too," Cheryl said sarcastically, shaking her head and ending the phone recording. She hugged both her daughters. "You're so grown up."

"I don't feel grown up," Ariel laughed.

"Haha, even I don't feel grown up sometimes, so get used to that feeling," Cheryl laughed.

Just then, the doorbell rang, making Ariel's heart jump.

"Come in!" Cheryl called out.

The door opened and in walked Kyle. Ariel caught her breath. Usually, Kyle wore jeans and an old t-shirt, tennis shoes if he was feeling fancy that day, otherwise it was always cowboy boots. But tonight, he was in a sharp black tuxedo, no tennis shoes in sight. His tie matched the navy undertones of Ariel's dress perfectly, and his pocket square was pure silver glitter.

"You look nice," Ariel said, understating what was going through her mind. She could feel Shelby starting at her but didn't give her the satisfaction of looking her way. She had eyes only for him at this point.

A hint of red crossed his cheeks. "Thanks, so do you."

"You two are adorable," Sam teased, causing them both to blush.

They spent the next half an hour getting pictures before they climbed into the limo and off they went. Cheryl waved at them until they disappeared over the hill.

"This limo is sick!" Sam said, touching every surface she could in the fancy interior. The stretch limo was modern, with sleek interior design and leather seats. "Aw, they didn't leave these filled for us?" She pointed to the empty wine glass rack.

"Unfortunately, no." Kyle said, laughing. "But at the afterparty there will be plenty."

"Woo!" Shelby cheered. Ariel was a little surprised. Her friends didn't typically drink, but at parties Shelby was known to indulge. The limo ride to the high school was quick. As they pulled into the parking lot, they joined a sea of other limos and fancy cars people either rented or borrowed from their car-collecting family members. When it was their turn, Shelby and Sam exited first.

"After you," Kyle said, offering her the door.

"Thanks," Ariel said. She gathered her dress in her hands and scooted towards the door. As she passed him, he gently grabbed her arm and pulled her close.

"You look incredible," he whispered into her ear, so close his lips brushed her ear lobe, sending shivers down her spine.

She pulled back just slightly to look at him, not caring her face was probably bright red. "So do you." They lingered close for a moment, Ariel's heart nearly bursting out of her chest. But when he didn't move in for a kiss like she hoped she would, she pulled back and continued out the door and into the crowd.

Prom was Hollywood themed this year, so she stepped out onto a red carpet to a sea of flashing lights. The junior class had a done a great job hiring paparazzi to take pictures of their arrival, an idea that Ariel thought elevated the rather stereotypical prom theme. Kyle stepped out after her and they posed in front of the limo for a few pictures before making their way up the carpet and into the building.

The high school gym normally used for jogging laps and shooting hoops was unrecognizable. The lights were dim, the music was bumping from the DJ stand in the corner. A wooden dance floor was laid out, and people were already grooving to the Top Forty Hits that were on. On the right side near the bleachers was a row of tables and chairs. Sam waved them over, having already secured a spot at the edge of the table.

"Best seat in the house," Sam said proudly. "Close to the dance floor, photo booth, and bathrooms!"

Ariel set her clutch down, and Kyle removed his jacket, draping it over the back of the chair. Shelby motioned to the punch table. "Let's go get drinks!" Ariel dashed off with her, and a few moments later they came back with four cups of red punch.

Kyle took a swig of his and made a face. "Too bad no one's spiked it yet."

Shelby jerked her thumb back towards the table. "Doubt they will. Mr. Behrens is standing guard all night. Said his sole job is to guard the bowl."

"Aw, that's a good job for him," Sam said. "He hates talking to anyone and I doubt he can dance. So silently standing guard over the punch is right up his alley."

"Yeah, he didn't seem too upset about it," Shelby shrugged. "Let's dance!" The group moved onto the dance floor just as a new song was coming on and all started dancing together in a group.

The night that followed was perhaps the most fun that Ariel had had in a long time. For the entire night, she let go. She didn't think about her training, the race coming up, going off to college in a few short months, or the fact that her dad wasn't there to see any of it. Instead, she got to dance her heart out with her best friends, all the while knowing she came here with Kyle.

The song changed from fast to slow, and the dance floor emptied out except for the couples. A few girlfriends grabbed each other and started dancing together, which is what Sam and Shelby did. As they walked away from Ariel and Kyle, Shelby gave her best friend a wink. Ariel just rolled her eyes and brushed her off.

"Do you want to dance?" Kyle asked, looking at his feet. He'd never been a shy person, but apparently this uncharted territory was bringing it out in him.

"I'd like that," Ariel said, trying her best to reassure him. She liked Kyle, but she liked the confident Kyle she knew. She didn't want him to change just because there were more-than-friends feelings between them now.

Kyle took her hand and led her into the middle of the dance floor, away from the prying eyes of Sam and Shelby. They meant well, but it was nice not to have spectators while they figured this out for themselves. In one smooth move, he moved his arm wide, guiding her in a circle around him before pulling her close and resting his hands gently on her waist. She placed her hands on his shoulders, bringing them close together but not so much so that her head was resting on his shoulder. They swayed to the music together in silence, unsure of what to say.

"Are you having a good time?" Kyle asked, breaking the silence between them.

Ariel looked up and into his eyes. "Yeah, I'm having a lot of fun."

"Sorry we aren't really getting much time to ourselves," he said. "I'd like to spend more time with you… you know, one on one."

"I know, I'm looking forward to when we can do that, too," Ariel asked, her tone teasing and playful. "But for now, I'm loving tonight."

"Me too," Kyle said, lightening up a bit with her playfulness. "Wouldn't it be great if we didn't have to wait? Which, we technically don't, you know."

"You remember what I said a few months ago, right?" Ariel prompted. "Anything that detracts time from my training has to wait. But we're getting closer every day." She felt his shoulders slump beneath her hands. She knew he was disappointed she brought it back up. He hadn't liked it then and she suspected he liked it even less now.

"Yeah. But I'm not asking you to. It's just one little date," he explained, not ready to let it go as easily as he had before. He paused. She felt his hands tighten a little around her waist, drawing her body closer to his. She didn't resist and adjusted her hands so that they were clasped behind his neck. "I still really like you, Ariel Jane."

Her heart did a somersault with the use of her full name. "I still really like you."

He smiled a warm, hearty grin that lit up his eyes. "Then will you be my girlfriend?"

Her heart did somersault in the opposite direction. "Kyle, we've talked about this. I don't want to officially be anything until after August."

His face steeled. "Why not?"

Ariel stared at him, doing her best not to let her face betray what she was really thinking. "I've told you this several times. Being official is too exciting, it'll distract me from my training, and I can't have that. I still like you, like, a lot. Like a lot a lot. Then in August, after I cross that finish line, you can sweep me off my feet and we can go on our first date as boyfriend and girlfriend." She smiled up sweetly at him, but the excitement and love were no longer on his face.

"If you cross the finish line…" he said, almost so quiet she couldn't hear.

Now it was her turn to pull back. "What did you just say?" She felt a well of fire growing in her stomach.

Instant regret flashed across his face, but he didn't recant his statement. "I just mean that—"

"No, I heard what you said," she said, her voice loud. "And I know exactly what you mean by it."

He sighed, flustered. "Ari, you have to admit, you don't have a good chance at winning this. So, like… why bother waiting? We're just wasting time."

Her jaw hung open, ears ringing with anger. "You think I'm wasting my time trying to achieve my goals? I'm wasting my time trying to save my family's home?"

"That's not what I'm saying," he said. "I'm just saying you won't win. So why not go on a date now?"

Ariel removed her hands from him as if she'd just touched hot iron. She recoiled, backing away from his grasp. He held onto her dress, but she shoved his hands off. "You don't believe in me? You've just been lying to me this whole time. For what? To get in my pants?" she spat.

"No, not even close," he insisted, shaking his head. "I want to believe in you, but you're dreaming too big."

By now, Shelby and Sam had appeared at her side, having seen the commotion. They stood behind her in case things escalated, and she needed back up, whether verbal or physical.

"I have a newsflash for you, Kyle James," she said, spitting his name at him as if it were an insult. "If my dreams are too big for you, then you're not good enough for me. As a boyfriend, or a friend." She spun on her heel and stormed off before he could reply.

It didn't take long before they found her in the bathroom, dabbing at the mascara running down her cheeks with a wet tissue. "I can't get this off," she said through the tears to Shelby when she walked in.

"That's why you have me," Shelby said softly. She opened her clutch and retrieved a small packet of makeup removal wipes. She wiped her friend's cheeks gently, clearing the black stains. "There. All better, see?"

Ariel looked in the mirror and while the black mess of mascara was gone, she didn't feel like anything was better. Her eyes were red and puffy from crying, and her heart felt like it was in a million pieces, scattered all along the dance floor. Sam pulled her sister into a long hug, Shelby wrapping her arms around them both. When they pulled away, Sam asked. "What happened?" Ariel briefly recounted the conversation.

"Honestly I'm shocked," Sam said, shaking her head in disbelief. "Kyle's always been such a genuine guy. He's always been down for everything we've ever done."

"I know," Ariel said, her voice quivering with the potential for more tears.

"It's because his dick can't have what it wants," Shelby said matter-of-factly. "It's a tale as old as time. Man wants to get dick wet, woman says no, man kills woman. Well, in this case, lashes out at all your hopes and dreams to metaphorically kill you."

Ariel and Sam burst out laughing, bringing much needed levity back into the night that was supposed to be nothing but magical. When they'd recovered from their belly laughter, Shelby took Ariel by the shoulders.

"Are you ready to go back out there and reclaim the night?"

Ariel sighed. Her heart still hurt, and she didn't feel much like celebrating, but she was more angry at the thought that she'd given a stupid boy the power to ruin a special night like this. She stood up tall, rolling her shoulders back. "Let's do this."

Sam clapped her on the back. "Hell yeah, let's go." The party of three left the bathroom just as another group was entering, and Ariel was grateful she was blessed with the best sister and best friend a girl could ever ask for.

Chapter 25

In the weeks between prom night and graduation day, Kyle and Ariel hadn't spoken a word to each other. He'd tried to initiate small talk in the hallways between classes, but Ariel had given him the cold shoulder. If he really wanted to talk, the first thing out of his mouth had to be an apology, not some wisecrack about their English homework or what the school cafeteria served that day. And so far, he'd made no effort to mend the fence that he broke and as far as Ariel was concerned, that was his responsibility, not hers. When she ran by his house after school on her training runs, she'd sometimes see him standing in the window. She wondered if he watched her run, and she always made it a point to run fast anytime she suspected he was around. She was going to prove him wrong in every sense of the word.

The gymnasium was transformed into something unrecognizable once again. A sea of blue and white replaced the wooden floors, though it still smelled faintly of sweaty socks and rubber dodge balls. The bleachers were filled with doting parents and family members, everyone armed with a camera or cellphone to record what was perhaps the biggest moment of all their short lives so far. As they stood in the line waiting to get the signal to begin the ceremony, Ariel glanced down the line of classmates: eighty-six kids she'd spent the last twelve years of her life with. Some of them were her best friends, some of them were rivals, some were teammates, and others were simply classmates, but they all held a special place in her heart. Held together by the bond of a small high school class, she knew there wouldn't be another group of people like this ever again. Sure, there'd be important people and groups in her life, but none quite like this one. The music from the band started, and a hush fell over the audience as well as the students standing in line, anxiously wanting to get the show on the road.

Principal Patterson gave the cue and the line started moving, walking as slowly as they could down the makeshift aisle between folding chairs. Their blue and white gowns made a satisfying swishing noise, the girls' heels making the lovely clack-clack noise Ariel loved so much. When they all were standing in front of the chairs, and the music ended, Principal Patterson motioned for them to sit.

The ceremony went by in a blur, and before they knew it, Ariel and Sam were standing, throwing their graduation caps in the air and walking out triumphantly, leaving the gym as high school graduates.

Sam nudged Ariel and pointed up into the stands to where Mom was standing, waving both hands above her head. In the empty seat next to her was a framed photo of Dad, one twin on each hip. An old shirt of his was draped across the bleacher.

"Is she trying to make me ruin my makeup?" Sam asked, her voice tense as she choked back tears.

"Waterproof mascara, it's fine," Ariel said, not even bothering to try to control the tears. "She made sure he was here."

Sam laid her head on Ariel's shoulder. Together, each girl held up one hand forming half of a heart. Cheryl smiled, wiping away her own tears before forming a heart with her hands too, returning the gesture.

"C'mon, let's go before I turn into a puddle," Sam sniffled. Ariel followed without protest. When they made it back to the library, the designated staging spot, Ariel and Sam hugged.

"We did it!" Sam said, her voice giddy. Her eyes were still wet with tears, but there was brightness now. "Dad would've been proud. God, I'm so excited not to ever do homework again."

"Um, I'm pretty sure you get homework in college," Ariel laughed.

"Maybe, but we'll deal with that when we get there."

"Hey, congratulations, ladies!" Kyle said, sauntering up to them with outstretched arms. He was acting as if nothing had happened. "Who's ready to party?"

"We are, but not with you," Sam sassed.

Kyle's face flashed rejection, but he recovered quickly. "C'mon you guys, I'm trying."

"Do you think my dreams are still too big?" Ariel asked bluntly.

"I, uh—"

"Then keep moving," Ariel said, no time for his hesitation. She wasn't accepting anything less than an immediate "you can do anything you want and I fully believe you, also I'm sorry I was so stupid at prom."

Kyle looked at Sam, hoping for a softer reception. But she didn't give it to him. "You heard her. Go on, git."

She shooed him away with her hands like an old lady would a child trying to steal cookies from the cookie jar. He rolled his eyes and muttered something under his breath as he walked away.

Shelby popped up out of nowhere. "Are we still icing out Kyle?"

"Basically," Sam said.

"You know he feels really bad about what happened at prom," Shelby said hesitantly.

"Since when have you talked to him?"

"Last week," Shelby said. Ariel and Sam's eyes widened but Shelby continued before they could start in on her. "He approached me after school. Said he wanted advice on how to make it up to you, Ariel."

"Did you tell him to come up and be all like wazz up, wanna party?" Ariel asked, crossing her arms in front of her chest.

"No, I have no idea where that came from but it definitely wasn't from me."

"What did you tell him then?" Sam asked.

"That he needed to say he was sorry, and that he believes in you whole heartedly. And I told him not to bother with it unless he meant it," Shelby said, grabbing both of Ariel's hands in hers. "I figured that's what you'd want."

"That's exactly what I want him to do," Ariel admitted, her tone softening. She'd missed having him around the past few weeks. But every time she thought about reaching out to him, the painful memory of his betrayal at prom came rushing back.

"Too bad that's not what he did," Sam said, rolling her eyes.

"Guys, I swear. So stupid. Anyway, where are we going to party?" Shelby said, draping her arms around each of her friends.

"Our house," Sam answered. "We'll eat cake while we have our crew meeting!"

"It'll have to be a quick meeting too," Ariel interjected. "I've got a weight session I still have to squeeze in."

"Really? Isn't this a cutback week or something?"

Ariel rolled her eyes. "Yes, but I'm still working out. Just running less miles."

"You can't take even one night off? Just one night to party and let your hair down?"

"I will!" Ariel said. "For a few hours. You know I—"

"Yeah, yeah, yeah, I get it. You can't take a day off, blah blah blah," Shelby said, miming a talking face with her hand.

"Then let's quit yapping, grab our diplomas, and get outta here so we can maximize party time for you," Sam said, steering Ariel towards the table where one of their teachers was handing out diplomas.

An hour later, they were all sitting around the table at the Hart household, graduation gowns draped on the backs of the chairs.

"Welcome everyone to another pre-race meeting!" Ariel said, standing at the head of the table. She glanced around at the faces surrounding the table. Bobbi and Cheryl sat together, their elbows on the table, hands cradling their eager faces. Shelby was scribbling something on her notes, and Sam lounged back, arms crossed as per usual. The empty chair where Kyle would've been was a small stab in her heart. It was a hard feeling to explain. She was hurt he didn't believe in her, angry he hadn't apologized, and sad she didn't have one of her oldest friends by her side all at once. She shook her head, shoving those thoughts aside.

"We've had some changes to the team, and some shifts in the roles everyone is playing. What questions do you all have?" Ariel asked, pulling her chair in and sitting down. She caught Cheryl and Coach looking at Kyle's empty seat and exchanging a knowing glance.

"Any questions about the race, I mean?" Ariel clarified before anyone could grill her about things she wasn't ready to talk about yet.

"Team names," Shelby said, opening the notebook laying in front of her. "I've been hard at work on them and I want to run some by you."

"This'll be good," Bobbi laughed.

"Muffin Mavins."

Ariel snorted. "Because I eat a lot of muffins?"

"Exactly! It's like, your signature thing," Shelby said, her face serious. "No one eats muffins like you do. And lots of people are known for what they eat. Tara Dower, aka Candy Mama, for example."

"I don't hate it actually," Ariel said, contemplating it. "What else do you have?"

"Honestly that was my best one, but I've also got Scrambled Legs, Hart and Solers, Hartbeaters, and Hart over Heels."

"I like Hart over Heels," Mom said.

"Yeah, I'm partial to Hart puns myself," Sam said.

"I like them all, but none of them make me say 'that's the one'," Ariel said. "Keep those, let's all think on them, and we'll come back around to that. Coach, can we talk about pacing?"

"Love to," Coach said, sitting up taller in her chair. "Everyone take one of these." She passed around copies of a printed excel spreadsheet filled with colored boxes and numbers.

"These are Ariel's estimated paces and split times between the aid stations. This upcoming race is going to really be a test not only of Ariel's fitness, but also of our ability to operate effectively as a crew. A hundred miler is a lot more reliant on crew and this race is a bit remote, so we'll be relying on navigation with minimal mistakes, watching her tracker, and great time management."

"All things you did great at in the first race," Ariel pointed out.

"True, but now we're going to be remote and chasing you around a course. You aren't coming right to us," Sam said. "This time we have a chance at getting lost."

"I'm going to be the primary driver," Coach Bobbi said, "so Shelby and Sam, I'm going to need you on your Google Maps A game. We won't have time to scout the course beforehand, so we'll be flying by the seat of our pants a bit. And Cheryl, nutrition is also gonna be a bigger part of the race this time.”

“Everything is going to be a bigger part. What was it you told me, Bobbi? The longer the race, the less about running it is?” Ariel said.

“Mm-hmm. Running is still important obviously but the longer you go, the more important your nutrition and hydration gets. We’ve gotta be on point.”

“Oh, don’t worry about that,” Cheryl said. She leaned down, disappearing beneath the table as she retrieved something. “I’ve got a run down for y’all.”

She stood up and placed a large, plastic box full of an assortment of food, books, hydration mixes, and more. She handed a pile of papers to Sam on her left. “Take one and pass it down.”

“I’ve been doing a lot of research on sports nutrition and Ariel and I have been talking a lot about what works and what doesn’t for her. And I want everyone to be on the same page so when she comes into aid stations, we all know what to do and can fill that role if I’m occupied with something else,” Cheryl said.

“Look at you, Mrs. Hart!” Shelby said, looking her up and down. “Maybe you should go back to school to get your nutrition degree.”

“Haha, maybe, let’s see how the race goes first.”

Cheryl spent the next hour delving into their nutrition strategy, Ariel giving her input when needed. By the time she was done, everyone was on the same page and learned a lot about race nutrition.

"I hate to say it," Bobbi said, glancing up at the clock on the wall. "But I've gotta get going. I've got a teachers' meeting."

"Sounds good," Ariel said. "I think we could all stretch our legs. We'll reconvene for part two in the hotel room before the race. We've covered all the major things and I think we're prepared!"

"Ariel, we're tabling your lifting session," Coach Bobbi said, placing her hand on Ariel's knee as she attempted to stand.

"What? Why?" Ariel asked, eyebrows scrunched in confusion.

"Because it's your graduation day!" Cheryl said, clapping her hands together. "Wait right here kids."

The two adults left the room, leaving the freshly graduated teenagers exchanging confused glances. Moments later, Mom and Coach reappeared with their arms full of food. Cheryl placed a beautifully decorated cake on the table and Coach laid out several pizza boxes from their favorite pizza joint.

"We're celebrating tonight. Both of us are immensely proud of all three of you," Cheryl said, her voice cracking ever so slightly. "There's been lots of ups and downs the past few years… but we've all stuck together and grown. It's been an honor seeing you grow from little babies to independent young women."

"You're all going to do great things in life, we're excited to see your next chapter," Coach added. "We have one more thing." She disappeared and reappeared in a flash, this time toting a green bottle and five champagne flutes.

"You're letting us have champagne!" Sam exclaimed, nearly jumping up and down with excitement.

"Sparkling cider," Cheryl said, giving Sam a look. "We'll break out the champagne a few birthdays from now."

Sam rolled her eyes and smiled at Ariel, who shook her head. Coach passed the glasses around and Cheryl filled the glasses.

"To our ladies," Mom said, raising her glass.

"May the road rise to meet you, always." Coach said.

"And may your running shoes never come untied," Ariel added with a laugh.

"Hart on three," Shelby said, standing up and holding out her free hand in front of her.

Everyone did the same, stacking their hands one on top of the other.

"One, two, three, HART!"

Later that night, Ariel was helping Mom clean up from the party.

"So do you want to talk about what's going on between you and Kyle?" Cheryl asked without looking up from the dish she was scrubbing.

"Not really," Ariel said, wanting to avoid a lecture.

"I've missed having him around," Mom said to no one in particular.

"Me too," Ariel said. "It's not my choice to not have him around."

"Oh?" Cheryl didn't pry when Ariel didn't answer right away.

"He asked me to be his girlfriend and I said after the race and he doesn't like that," Ariel admitted, the words spilling from her before she could stop them.

"Oh, I see," Cheryl said, glancing sideways at her daughter.

"Mom, have you ever had a boy try to tell you what to do?"

Cheryl laughed out loud. She covered her mouth when she saw the look of horror on her daughter's face. "I'm sorry, honey. I'm not laughing at you. I'm laughing because god, have I ever. It's all boys seem to like to do sometimes."

"Okay, so I'm not imagining it," Ariel said, sighing a breath of relief.

"No, most certainly not," Cheryl said. "Kyle's young and eager. It'll take him a little while to grow up. But I'm proud of you for not letting him boss you around, even if you do like him."

"Whoever said I did?" Ariel asked, her face flushing.

Cheryl cocked an eyebrow at her. "You're fooling no one."

"No?" Ariel laughed, taking the wet plate from her and drying it with the terry cloth towel. "I thought I hid it pretty well."

"Maybe from a stranger, but not from your ole' Mom," she laughed. "Just do me a favor and don't let this sour you on him or anyone else, okay? Love is hard. Especially at your age."

"I know, Mom," Ariel said, rolling her eyes. "But thanks." The finished the dishes in silence, but Ariel felt the support of her mom. She felt better having talked to someone about it, her thoughts less racing. Now the only thought in her head was the race looming ahead this weekend.

Chapter 26

The cold, biting wind ripped through her soaked rain shell. She would've pulled it off by now if it hadn't been underneath her hydration vest. Her arms couldn't bend that way and if she walked, the shivers started to take over.

"Just keep running, just keep running, just keep running," Ariel repeated to herself through clattering teeth. Her headlamp illuminated a small circle of the trail, doing just enough to keep her moving in the right direction. Every now and then, the edges of the light caught the edge of a reflective course marker, bringing a wave of relief each time. One glance at her watch sparked tears in her eyes. "Goddammit." Today hadn't gone right from the start. Her legs had felt like lead since the first mile, her stomach rejected anything except Honey Stinger chews and strawberry freezies since mile twenty, and now her stomach wasn't taking anything. And to top things off, this freak thunderstorm wouldn't let up. Hours behind her goal time, it took every ounce of strength to not just crawl into a puddle and close her eyes.

She glanced up into the night. She hadn't planned to be running into the dark, but alas, here she was. Headlights bobbed ahead and above her. The final hill. That had to mean the last aid station was right around the corner. She couldn't hear anything except the pounding rain, no aid station cheers or cowbells.

"Head down, keep working. Keep running, keep running," she encouraged herself. She leaned into her poles to propel her forward despite it being flat ground. Taking a page from the Nordic ski book, she figured she'd conserve every ounce of energy she had left and give herself a break.

Suddenly, her headlamp caught the edge of another reflective marker, but this time it was a sign.

"Skwirl Bah-rittos ahead!" proclaimed a spray-painted cardboard sign.

She shook her head and read it again. It still said the same thing. She pinched herself, but her arm was so numb from cold she couldn't tell if it was real or not. "Am I hallucinating?" She kept moving and another sign appeared, this one advertising "Redneck Pedicures" with a poorly drawn nail trimmer and K-tape plastered on it. If she was hallucinating, it at least had a theme. The trail started to lighten and she could see more than her headlamp allowed.

The aid station.

She looked up and sure enough, there it was. A hundred feet ahead was the bright oasis in the dark. Two large blue tents were decorated in Christmas lights and plastic flamingos. People milling about, but Ariel's vision was too blurry to tell if Mom and Coach Bobbi were there. The aid station gave her a bit of renewed strength, and she jogged in, the cowbell clanking sounding as if it were behind a door. "That's not normal," Ariel thought to herself. The sudden brightness was disorienting, and she looked around the tents without really seeing much.

"Ariel! Ariel, hey." Coach Bobbi appeared suddenly in front of her, her hands on her shoulders.

"Squirrel burritos?" Ariel asked. "Are there really squirrel burritos?"

Bobbi laughed, but her eyes were still. "If by squirrel you mean, pulled pork, then yes. This aid station is redneck themed. Come with me." Bobbi threw a space blanket around her shoulders. Ariel did as she was told, stumbling over her feet as Coach Bobbi led her to a camping chair placed around a portable propane firepit. It was crowded, but as soon as Ariel made eye contact with them, nearly all of them got up and offered their spots. "That's weird." Ariel thought to herself.

"Hey, Ari!" Sam exclaimed, appearing on the other side of the fire with a burrito in one hand, her phone in the other. "Oh." Sam stood wide eyed for a moment before snapping a quick picture. "I'm going to go get the soup. Unless the burrito sounds good?"

Ariel shook her head as she lowered herself into the chair with Coach Bobbi's guidance. Nothing sounded good. Soup, maybe. Something warm to hold. "Can I have handwarmers?"

"You've already got two in your hands," Bobbi said gently. Shelby appeared at her side.

"Hey, go keep your Mom occupied," Bobbi whispered to Shelby. "Tell her she's fine, Ariel wants some privacy with her Coach."

"Pretty sure she's napping in the truck."

"Will you just make sure?"

"On it." Shelby nodded and trotted off to find Mom before she could glimpse the state her daughter was in.

Bobbi reached into her backpack and procured several more handwarmers. "Here, lift up your arms." Ariel did as she was told, her gaze fixated on the fire. Bobbi placed two handwarmers under each of her arms. "Now let them fall." They plopped into her lap like a ragdoll. She opened two more and rubbed them in her hands to activate them. "I'm going to put two of each of these right on top of your femoral artery, okay? I'm going to place them—"

"On my groin?" Ariel asked, her voice monotone.

"Ha, yes," Bobbi said. "Is that okay?"

Ariel nodded and Bobbi quickly placed the handwarmers in the crease between Ariel's quads and pelvic bone. Sam and Shelby reappeared, each toting cups of steaming hot liquids.

"What does she need?" Sam asked Bobbi, squatting down next to her.

"She needs to get warm," Coach Bobbi said. "She's hypothermic."

"But it's summer, can that happen?" Sam asked, confused.

"Sure can." Coach replied. "When I did the Midwest Madness 100k many Junes ago, it was a bad weather year like today. Plenty of runners dropped from hypothermia."

"Is that why she's acting like a zombie right now?" Shelby asked, her voice quiet.

"Mm-hmm. Runners can get delirious just from being tired, but this is from the cold. She's soaked to the bone. Her lips are blue."

"Ariel, do you want minestrone soup or chicken broth?" Sam asked, placing a hand on her sister's knee.

"Broth," Ariel whispered, her teeth clattering so loud Sam almost missed what she said. Ariel reached out for the cup, her hands shaking violently.

"On second thought, I'm going to help." Sam repositioned herself next to Ariel and spoon fed her the first mouthful. "How's that?"

"Warm," Ariel said, a small smile playing on her lips. "More please." Ariel ate the soup as fast as Sam could feed it to her and finished it off.

"Here, I have more," Shelby said, handing Sam the cup she held.

Ariel shook her head and sat up in the chair. She shrugged off the warming blanket and tried to stand, but to no avail. "I have to get going. How long have I been here?"

"That's not what we're worried about right now, Ariel," Coach Bobbi said. "Put that space blanket back on."

"I'm cold, but I'll be fine," Ariel said, attempting to stand again. This time, she was successful, but wobbled as she got her balance. Sam stood slightly behind her, her hands hovering just in case.

"No," Coach Bobbi said, standing. Her voice was kind, but firm. "Ariel, your lips are blue. You have to warm up before you can leave the aid station."

"I'm an adult now," Ariel said, her face scrunched together. "You can't tell me what to do."

Coach stifled a laugh. "Just because you turn eighteen today doesn't mean I'm no longer your coach.

Coaches get to tell you what to do no matter how old you are. Now let's change your clothes."

Ariel glanced down at her sopping wet outfit. "Okay, yeah. Let's do that."

Shelby fished out the beach towel they used for privacy and Sam pulled out Ariel's designated change of clothes.

"Coach, will you hold this?" Sam asked, holding the towel out to her. "I think I'm going to need to help her." They both watched as Ariel struggled and failed to get her arm out of the rain shell.

"I agree," Coach Bobbi said, taking the towel from her. Together, Shelby and Coach held up their makeshift privacy tent as Sam helped Ariel change.

"Girl, sit down," Sam instructed. "Let me help you."

"I'm not a baby," Ariel whined, falling back into the chair.

"Put your arms over your head," Sam instructed, ignoring her comment.

Ariel did as she was told and Sam tugged the rain shell off, followed by her shirt and bra.

"I'm freezing," Ariel said, wrapping her arms around her naked chest. Her body shivered so much it worried Sam.

"I know, I'm sorry, I'm fixing it. Put your arms through here," Sam instructed, holding out the arms of the sports bra for Ariel to fit into. With much pulling and twisting, Sam managed to get her sports bra in place. "You gotta adjust the girlies though. I know we're sisters, but…"

295

"I have some dignity, you know," Ariel said, rolling her eyes as she adjusted the sports bra to the right place. "Can I have those hand warmers back? That felt nice."

Sam handed her the warmers she'd had tucked under her arms and Ariel shoved them into the sides of the dry bra. "Now put this shirt on." Ariel put her arms through the holes and Sam helped pull it up over her head, adjusting the long sleeves. "Now this sweatshirt."

"I'm not running in that," Ariel said.

"Put it on. You're not running until you're warm," Coach Bobbi commanded from outside of the towel tent. Ariel did as she was told. They repeated the process with her shorts, Sam replacing them with insulated running tights and fuzzy socks. She made sure to put the handwarmers back over her thighs.

"And to finish it off, put this on," Sam said, tugging a knit beanie over her sister's wet braids.

"Thanks, Sammie," Ariel said, tears pricking at her eyes. "Not many sisters would dress each other."

Sam snorted. "We're not like most sisters."

"We're twins," they said in unison.

The towel tent fell and Ariel made a face.

"It was way warmer with that up. Can I have another blanket?" Immediately, two fell into her lap.

Coach Bobbi squatted down in front of her. "If your lips are still as blue as they are right now in thirty minutes, we need to talk about what to do next."

"I'll be fine in thirty. I feel a lot better after having on dry clothes," Ariel assured her. "Especially if I get more soup."

"On it!" Shelby dashed off for a refill.

Thirty minutes and two cups of soup later, Ariel's lips were still just as blue as the moment she'd stumbled into the aid station. When the timer went off, Ariel threw off the blanket and stood, her enthusiasm nearly toppling her sideways.

"Let's finish this thing! Only seven more miles to go," she declared, glancing at her watch and adjusting something on it.

"Take a few steps for me," Bobbi said.

Ariel wobbled with each step. Her head spun. Her thoughts were cloudy. She turned back to face Coach. "I don't feel great, but I feel better than when I got here!"

"I know you do but look at this." Coach Bobbi held out her phone with the camera open to selfie mode.

Ariel's face dropped when she saw herself. "Did Sam put blue lipstick on me?"

"I'm mean, but I wouldn't be that mean," Sam laughed.

"Let me see your hands," Bobbi said. Ariel held them out. "Can you bend your fingers?"

Ariel tried, but they didn't move.

"Hold this," Bobbi said, handing Ariel her phone. Ariel promptly dropped it.

"And you're still shivering. Honey, for your health and safety, we need to stop."

We need to stop. Those words were a knife through the heart. "I don't want to."

"I know you don't, but is finishing this race your biggest goal?"

Ariel was silent for a minute, her head hanging low. "No."

"What is?"

"Leadville."

"That's not what your biggest goal is," Bobbi scoffed. "What's your biggest goal?"

Ariel picked her head back up, tears quietly falling down her cheeks, leaving little tracks through the dust accumulated there. "To win the Leadville 100."

"And in order to do that, you have to stay safe and healthy. Continuing to finish the last seven miles of this race will put that ultimate goal in danger. More importantly, it puts yourself in danger."

Ariel knew she was right, but she desperately wanted her to be wrong. Sam slung an arm over her sister's shoulder on one side and Shelby did the same on another. "We've done what we came here to do, girly. You've done what you needed to do. Now it's time to rest and recoup, because you've still got a lot of miles ahead of you."

Ariel leaned her head to the side, resting it atop Sam's. "Okay. This is a shit way to celebrate our birthday."

Sam grinned. "That's the sanest thing you've said all day. So why don't we get you warm and then go celebrate our first day as adults doing something that's actually fun."

Bobbi breathed a sigh of silent relief that Ariel agreed. "Let's go find the aid station captain." The little group made their way over to where the aid station captain sat and spoke with them about their situation. The medic at the aid station took Ariel's vitals and did a quick assessment, agreeing that it was best to pull her from the race. When they cut off her wrist band, a new wave of tears flowed from her eyes.

"Where's Mom?" Ariel asked, looking around.

"She was taking a nap in the van," Shelby said. "We'll tell her when we get back there."

As they made their way back to the van, Ariel was overcome by a wave of gratitude for her amazing support system. This wasn't the race she'd wanted, but she was thankful for their teamwork and dedication to keeping her safe and focused on the real goal.

"We're going to Fuzzy's Tacos, right?" Ariel asked, her voice muffled by the blanket she had wrapped around her head.

"Duh," Sam said. She opened the passenger door on the van and helped Ariel inside. "You get free tacos on your birthday. And then we're going to Baskin Robins for our free ice cream."

"Ugh, will they heat up the ice cream for me?" Ariel asked. "I can't stand to think of anything cold."

"Well, I'm not sure how well that'll work out, but we sure can ask them," Shelby laughed.

* * *

The next weekend, the team met back up at the Hart House for a debrief session.

"What was the number one thing we learned at this race?" Coach Bobbi asked.

"Hypothermia sucks!" Ariel shouted. Thankfully, she'd made a full recovery.

"Yes," Bobbi chuckled. "And what are we going to do to prevent it? Leadville is known for getting late afternoon storms. It's not likely, but there is the chance you could get soaked."

"Those handwarmers were super helpful, especially on my legs and in my armpits," Ariel said. "I think adding more of those to my pack when we're worried about rain or cold coming would help me be better prepared."

"I agree," Bobbi said.

"We'll have more soup ready for you too," Sam said. "That seemed to help a lot once you reached us."

"Yeah, and I feel like at the aid station before you dropped out, you were already sort of cold," Shelby pointed out.

"I was, but it just felt like normal cold, ya know?"

"So next time, if you start to feel even a bit chilled, we should change out any wet clothing you have. Your sports bra was probably wet at the first station, yeah?"

"Oh yeah, it's usually wet just because of how sweaty I am. But it never bothers me or causes issues."

"Let's have you pick out more changes of clothes, that way, if we're worried at all about weather or you're already cold, we can start combating it earlier. It was too late by the time you came into the last aid station," Shelby said.

"I agree, I'll add it to my list," Ariel said, writing down the information.

"And I'll stock up on soups and handwarmers," Mom said, typing it into the list she kept on her phone. "Next time, can y'all wake me up for the action? I'd like to be involved if my daughter is hurt."

"I wasn't hurt, Mom," Ariel said, rolling her eyes. Ever since they'd gotten back, Cheryl hadn't let it go that they hadn't woken her up.

"Cheryl, there's a reason family members don't usually crew their runners, especially moms," Coach Bobbi said, raising an eyebrow. "Ariel's going to look pretty rough later in the race, especially to a mother's eye. We're going to be able to fix it most times, so you need to trust us that when we ask you to step back, it's for Ariel's race's best interest."

"I get it… I don't like it though," Cheryl laughed.

"I'll stay with you, Mama Hart," Shelby offered.

"I appreciate that," Cheryl said, reaching out and squeezing Shelby's shoulder.

"Any other things we need to make adjustments too?" Ariel asked.

"Can we get an organizing bin with a lid on it for your shoes?" Sam asked. "My car still reeks of feet."

"It isn't that bad, but fine," Ariel rolled her eyes. "Organizing bin. Done. Now, what went well from the crew side?"

"Our teamwork," Shelby said. "Especially when you came in looking like a zombie. Like, a real dead zombie. Bobbi gave clear orders, we executed them, and worked together to keep you alive."

"I gotta say, Sammie, you're really good at dressing people," Ariel teased. "Seriously, thank you."

"Anything for you," Sam said, rolling her eyes.

"And we did great at navigating," Cheryl added. "Even out there in the middle of nowhere and my history of getting lost, we didn't get lost once and always made it to the aid stations on time."

Ariel smiled. "Good. I'm glad to hear we've got a good thing going. Now, can we go eat? I'm starving."

Chapter 27

It was barely summer and already the sun was intense. When they pulled off at a rest stop to stretch their legs, the sun warmed Ariel's face despite the cool wind blowing across the planes. They were close enough to see the mountains in the distance, barely visible along the horizon. But they were there, Ariel could almost feel them. The mountains had a different presence than the flat plains or the gently rolling hills in Southern Iowa. They were big, imposing. And you could sense them hundreds of miles away.

"You ready to get back on the road? We've only got about two hours left," Cheryl said as she stretched her arms over head.

"Yeah," Ariel said. "Do you want me to drive?"

"No, I'm good. I like driving."

"You like driving twelve hours straight?"

"I mean, there's things I'd rather do," Cheryl said as she opened the car door. "But if it's ride for twelve or drive for twelve, I'd rather drive."

"Fair enough," Ariel said. She had to admit, road trips weren't exactly her jam, at least not the way her family did them. She wanted to stop at all the roadside attractions, check out the kitschy signs that said "World's Largest Ball of Yarn, this Exit!", and try the divey restaurants along highways. But her dad barely allowed bathroom breaks and food stops at gas stations during road trips.

"Hey, remember when Dad got mad at us for having to stop and pee after that nineteen-hour day in the car?" Ariel asked as they pulled back onto the interstate.

"How could I forget? Sam was in tears because she was about to pee her pants. Dad was yelling, you were pulling your hair out," Mom laughed. "I grabbed your father's shoulder and squeezed so hard I bruised him. It was one of those road trip horror story moments."

"That's what makes them memorable!" Sam exclaimed. "No one talks about the road trip where nothing happened."

"This is true. I just wish I would've known that in the moment because I was ready to lose my marbles," Cheryl laughed.

"Afterwards he apologized and we went to Denny's the next exit over," Ariel said. "Remember those huge shakes they gave us?"

"Still the best milkshakes to this day," Mom said, reminiscing.

"Can't believe the last time we were out here was for your college tour last fall," Cheryl said after a long silence. "Seems like that was years ago now."

"Right?" Ariel agreed. "Oh, that reminds me, Coach Angela called me yesterday."

"Whoa, what did she say? You never told me that."

"I'm telling you now. She just asked how I was doing. Apparently she's been following some of my racing and was curious to know if I was still planning to run with CSU in the fall."

"And what did you say?" Cheryl asked, her voice rising ever so slightly.

"I most definitely am still running with them in the fall. Especially now that the NCAA ruled college athletes can get paid, I'm in the clear! No need to worry."

"I think it's funny she's following your races," Cheryl chuckled. "Why is she so obsessed with you?"

"Because I blew her off to hang out with Kyle," Ariel laughed, quoting Sam's favorite movie. "No, she's just being a good coach, following up with her new recruits."

As they drove the last few hours into Denver, the mountains grew larger and larger. It was hypnotic, watching them go from pinpoint bumps on the horizon to massive beings that rose far above Denver's tallest downtown skyscraper. The traffic thickened as they went through the outskirts of the Denver suburbs and made their way out to the town of Boulder, where Aunt Erin was staying. When they exited the highway, the houses grew bigger and fancier.

"I heard they have a Ben & Jerry's test kitchen here," Mom said as they pulled up to a stop light.

"Are you serious?" Ariel asked, wide-eyed.

"Mm-hmm. Want to check it out later after we get you settled?"

"Uhm, is that even a question? Of course we're checking it out!"

They drove through the neighborhoods, following the GPS directions until they turned onto the last street. No directions were needed, as Aunt Erin was sitting in a beach chair in the middle of her driveway reading a book. The house was a small white cottage but had an ample front porch with a full set of wicker furniture on it. Yet, Erin was sitting in a beach chair in the middle of the driveway, soaking in the full sun. Mom honked as they pulled in, making Erin jump. She waved and stood up, closing the book that was open on her lap.

"Hey guys! How was the drive?" she asked, running up to the car.

"Long," Ariel answered as she climbed out of the car. Despite having stopped just two hours ago, her legs were stiff, and she was beyond grateful to be out of the car. "But worth it. It was beautiful the last few hours."

"Yeah, the first six kind of suck. Nebraska's the worst," Cheryl said.

"Oh, yeah, I forget about that part of the drive," Erin said. "Mostly because I've never driven it. And since you're staying with me for the summer, and the rest of y'all are going to visit me, I don't have to. Thank you for that."

"Anytime," Cheryl said, opening the trunk. She grabbed the two duffel bags out of the back and closed it. "You know me, I'm always down for a road trip."

"More like a road run," Ariel said, rolling her eyes. "Trips are meant to be fun. This wasn't fun. This was a mad dash for the finish line."

"Oh hush," Cheryl said, waving her off. "Take one of these and let's get settled." Ariel picked up one of the duffle bags and they followed Erin. The inside was just as charming as the front porch: dark wood floors stood out against bright white walls. The hooks in the mudroom were antique wrought iron, and the walls held tasteful abstract artwork with bright colors, bringing a warmth and playfulness to the room that otherwise could've leaned the way of feeling like a doctor's office.

"Your bedroom is in the back to the left," Erin pointed down the hallway. "My casa is your casa. Settle in and feel free to explore."

Ariel grabbed the other pack out of her mom's hand. "You two go catch up while I unpack. Erin, Mom said there's a Ben and Jerry's here?"

Erin nodded. "Sure is, and we can walk there from here."

"That's dangerous. We're going there later," Ariel said, wiggling her eyebrows. She turned and walked off toward her bedroom, leaving Erin and Cheryl to catch up.

"Sounds like a plan," Erin said

An hour later, Ariel emerged from her room in a fresh set of clothes, wringing her hair in a towel, to find her mom and aunt indulging in a glass of red wine on the couch. "Are you two drunk? It's not even five yet!"

"It is somewhere," Erin laughed, raising her glass.

"No, we're not getting drunk. We're just having one glass. The Europeans always have wine with lunch," Cheryl said, winking.

"Okay, whatever you say," Ariel said, rolling her eyes. "Looks like you don't mind that I took a shower. I had to wake myself up a bit."

"The thought of fresh Ben and Jerry's ice cream wasn't enough to keep you awake?" Mom asked, her mouth agape in feigned shock.

"Nothing is enough to keep me awake on three hours of sleep," Ariel laughed.

"Fair enough," Cheryl said. She finished off the last of the wine in her glass and stood up. "Shall we get some ice cream?"

"Yes!" Erin and Ariel said in unison. Cheryl put the wine glasses on the counter and exchanged them for her purse. "Then let's go!"

Later that night, after dinner of popcorn and the pint of ice cream they'd brought home, they settled into their beds. Before she fell asleep, Ariel shot a text off to Sam.

"You're still comin out for the race, right? Sucks you couldn't get off work."

Sam replied almost immediately. *"Of course. Was the trip weird without me?"*

Ariel smiled and shook her head. As much as she hated to admit it, she missed her twin immensely. *"Yeah. Mom played her weird songs and wouldn't stop."*

"Don't miss that."

"Yeah, you were lucky. Txt you tomorrow. Have fun at work."

"U know I will."

Ariel set her phone down and rolled over. She closed her eyes and hoped sleep would come easily. There was only a week and a half until marathon day, her last chance at a shot to run the Leadville 100. She moved her ankle around in circles, testing it out. There was no pain, no clicks, no tight spots. While she wished she was doing the fifty miler, she reminded herself the main point of this run was to gain confidence and win that coveted lottery spot. Tomorrow would be her first big training run back at altitude. And she had no illusions about how hard it would be.

* * *

Ariel's lungs were on fire. Aunt Erin was about ten yards ahead of her on the trail, seemingly unaffected by the lack of oxygen at five thousand feet. Ariel willed herself to keep up, but the distance between herself and Erin kept growing, until Erin was over the hilltop and out of sight. Ariel skidded to a walk, trudging up the hill with her hands on her knees, trying to force more energy out of her tired muscles. The familiar churning of nausea played with her stomach, threatening to throw up the breakfast she hadn't eaten to avoid this very situation. But despite her best planning, she was still there. When she reached the top of the hill, she was greeted with a stunning view of the town below, bathed in the pink light of the sunrise.

The sun was barely over the flat eastern plains of Colorado, and the pink turned to gold in moments. The town below was alive with cars filling the streets already, despite it being only five thirty in the morning.

"Beautiful isn't it?" Erin said from somewhere off to the left, making Ariel jump.

"Jeezuz, I thought you were farther down trail."

"I was, but when I didn't see you, I circled back," Erin said. She wasn't even out of breath, and her forehead was only slightly beaded with sweat. Ariel was flabbergasted. They'd been doing mile speed repeats uphill. How was her aunt not feeling this? "Are you doing all right?"

"Yeah," Ariel breathed, still trying to catch her breath. "This elevation is kicking my ass though. Maybe speed work was a terrible idea."

Erin patted her on the back. "Give yourself a break. You haven't even been here a full day. And besides, don't you always say that speed work is your worst work?" Ariel nodded in agreement. "See? Don't beat yourself up. You'll adjust in no time."

"Maybe you should run the marathon."

"God no, I'm not in shape for that in the slightest."

"Aunt Erin, you could run and place in your age group tomorrow," Ariel said. "Don't give me that."

Knowing she couldn't argue, she just laughed and shook her head, pushing the pace a little faster.

By now, the sun was fully above the horizon and the daylight had set in, already warming the foothills of the mountain. By noon, it would be close to ninety degrees. A record that Ariel hoped wouldn't be repeated anytime soon, especially not on race day. Altitude was enough to contend with, she didn't need hot temperatures to battle as well. Because then, the race might be over before it even had a chance to get started.

"Ready to finish strong? I'll race ya back down."

Ariel shook her head. "I'm not racing you for nothing."

"Why not? It'll be good practice for ya. Teach you how to be a loser," she teased, poking her in the side.

"C'mon, let's go!" Erin took off at pace down the back end of the loop trail they were running, leaving Ariel no choice but to follow suit.

Thankfully, the last half of the run was downhill, so the perceived effort was less and she was able to finish feeling stronger than she did at the top of the hill. When she stopped her watch, she was surprised to find that her splits had been right on point.

"See?" Erin said, looking over her shoulder at the watch times. "You're fine. It just felt hard."

"Because it was hard," Ariel laughed.

"Still, you hit your goal. You did your workout successfully. Now let's get back, I've got to get to work." The two women jogged back to the house for a cool down. Erin's house was situated about half a mile from the trail they took, which as far as Ariel was concerned, was the most perfect location anyone could ask for in a house. Half a mile from Ben and Jerry's and a super cute downtown area, half a mile from a trail that took you miles and miles into the Rocky Mountain foothills? Sounded like the perfect spot to Ariel. She made a mental note to keep an eye on real estate in the area for after graduation.

When they got back to the house, Mom was already dressed and lounging on the porch, a book in one hand and a coffee in the other. Ariel smiled. It had been a long time since she'd seen her mom so relaxed. She secretly hoped she'd take the hint and stay that way. "How was the run, girls?"

"I've got a long way to go," Ariel lamented, dramatically jogging the last few steps in the driveway as if she were about to fall over.

"She's exaggerating, she'll be fine by race day."

"I'm sure she will be," Cheryl said. "Now, you ladies go get changed. Erin, you're sure you can't get off work today?"

"Unfortunately," she said with a shrug. "But I'm excited, we've found some native artifacts from the BC era we're digging up. So it won't be a bad day."

"Fair enough," Cheryl lamented. "We'll just have to do another spa day later."

Ariel still couldn't believe that her mom had splurged and gotten them a full day at the spa, especially when Sam wasn't here. "Sam is gonna be so mad, Mom."

"She was certainly not happy when I told her on the phone," she laughed. "But I promised we'd go when she got here, or when we got back to Des Moines, so then she was fine with it."

"Ahh, I see what you did there," Erin said. "You get to go twice now."

Cheryl acted as if she was offended by the suggestion. "Who? Me?" The three women made their way inside, excited for the day ahead.

* * *

Ariel was in the middle of a deep sleep when she felt something pull at her covers. She pulled back, tucking them underneath her chin.

"Cover hog. Share," said a familiar voice.

Ariel's eyes blinked open. "Sam?"

"The one and only, now share the damn blankets, will ya?"

Ariel relented, but only slightly. She rolled over and flopped her arm over her sister. "Welcome to Colorado. Missed you."

"Yeah, yeah, missed you too," Sam said, patting Ariel's arm. "I'm deadass tired, can we catch up in the morning?"

"At five in the morning?"

"If you wake me up at 5am, you're getting slapped," Sam grumbled, turning her back to Ariel.

"But I'll be racing by the time you get up," Ariel whined.

"Ugh, fine. We can talk before your race," Sam relented. "Just don't be mad at me if I'm grumpy."

"Deal. G'night, Sammi. Glad you're here."

"Me too," Sam said.

Ariel fell back asleep, relieved to know Sam had made it safe and sound.

Chapter 28

Ariel wove in between people, finding her way through the pack as she focused her mind. The air was tense, the smell of adrenaline intermingling with the pine bark in the crisp morning air. It was still dark, the starting area lit by flood lights, a harsh contrast to the inky sky. She stared at her feet, the glittery threads of her laces catching the light and dancing it away. "I should've changed these," Ariel thought to herself, shaking her head. She loved them, but she hated being reminded of Kyle and his betrayal. Today wasn't about that, it was only about her and the race she had to run.

She lifted one of her legs in front of her and shook it, loosening her quads. Despite having just raced 100k a few weeks ago, they felt fresh and light. "This is just a training race, remember?" Coach Bobbi had reminded her this morning in the car. They'd picked her up from the airport and headed straight to the race start line. "Our focus here is speed at elevation, we're acclimatizing, not trying to win. Stay strong, run smart."

"And the Leadville token," Ariel added.

"Yes, the whole reason you're running this race: Finish to get the token that'll hopefully win the post-race drawing for entry. Keep that in mind. We're not winning here— we're snagging a token. Stay strong, run smart."

Ariel repeated the mantra in her head as she watched the other runners around her, wondering what thoughts were racing through their minds.

Some of them danced in place, bouncing around as if their shoes were filled with springs. Others jogged around the edges of the crowd, occasionally leaning forward to stretch out a hamstring or calf muscle. A few were sitting in open grassy patches, eyes closed with ear buds in, no doubt trying to center themselves like she was.

She glanced at the large digital clock next to the start line, which showed she had exactly six minutes until the gun went off. She left the crowd of runners and jogged toward the porta-potties lined up to the left of the starting chute, back behind the registration tables. There were a bunch of them thankfully, so the line was short and moved quickly.

After peeing, the nerves lessened, replaced with excitement. She had fueled as best she could with her traditional night-before-dinner of spaghetti heaped on garlic bread, and this morning's breakfast had been simple with an asiago bagel and hummus. She patted her pockets as she walked back towards the starting line: filled water bottles, gels, chews, chap stick. Everything was where it should be. Fall Out Boy's "Centuries" started blaring in her headphones. Perfect timing. This was always the last song she listened to before a race. It was her magic. As the song played in her ears, she danced a little, jogging in place and moving her hips to loosen up and redirect her nerves.

"T-minus two minutes!" the announcer boomed over the loudspeaker, interrupting the violin music. Ariel popped her headphones out and tucked them into the small, zippered pocket on the front of her tie-dyed fanny pack.

She never raced with music, but she did practice with it sometimes. People told her she should kick the habit, but she needed something to help the endless miles of Iowa cornfields pass by otherwise she wasn't sure if she'd be able to pound out back-to-back double digit runs weekend after weekend.

Ariel found her way towards the front of the crowd, not on the starting line but within sight of it. She'd never been a competitive racer in the sense that she hated to be passed, but she didn't like to start from the back and get left behind in the beginning of the race. That inevitably made her go out faster than she should, which all runners know is the biggest mistake to make on race day. Luckily, she had learned that early on, and Coach Bobbi had trained that habit out of her.

"One minute!" the announcer warned, readying his starting bell. The countdown began on the red time clock to the left of the starting line. Ariel settled to the left of the field, three rows behind the starters. They were almost exclusively college-aged men, a few older ones, in tiny running shorts sans a shirt despite the temperature being in the upper forties. They were hopping in place, pulling their knees up to their chest mid jump, trotting in place when they landed. Ariel took a more stoic approach, simply shifting her weight between her feet, left to right, right to left, all in time with her breath. Inhale for four, exhale for eight, repeat. When she started running, her breathing would sync up with her feet but for now she kept them separated. It was a mind exercise in control.

"Thirty seconds!"

Now she was getting excited. She looked up from her feet, taking in the beautiful morning surrounding her. It was the perfect weather for a run. Sunshine on the horizon, the high for the day was sixty with no wind. You really couldn't ask for better weather.

The gun went off and the group of runners came to life.

"Go, go, go!" the announcer boomed through the megaphone, his little confetti cannon going off and showering the runners with paper sparkles. She couldn't contain her smile as she took her first official steps of the race. It didn't take long for the front of the pack to pull away from the rest, and Ariel found her groove on the left side of the road, letting all the faster runners pass her as she settled in.

"Woohoo, let's go!" she thought, excited to be here. She had worked so long and so hard, and now all she had to do was run. And it was the shortest distance she'd raced in a long time. Today was simple: run, drink, eat. Repeat until crossing the finish line. Simple didn't always mean easy, but with the amount of work she'd put in, she hoped it would be easier than a lot of other things given this distance was now on the shorter side of her long runs. But she was under no illusions- there was a lot of elevation in front of her. Only time would tell how her body would respond. Thankfully, she knew how to deal with most problems. She just prayed she wouldn't have to.

The energy of the crowd lining the streets was contagious- when she glanced at her watch she noticed she was a couple seconds faster than she was supposed to be. She knocked back her pace just a tad until her timing matched up with what she wanted.

The course started out on pavement, winding through the streets of downtown Leadville and out into the surrounding foothills. Ariel inhaled mountain air deep into her lungs, savoring the relatively flat ground and thick air.

It wouldn't be long until the air grew thin and the terrain steep. Seeing as how all she had to do was finish this race to get a chance at a token, Coach Bobbi had decided the best strategy would be to use the first few miles as a warmup instead of tacking on extras and risk burning her out. Her weekly mileage was nearing ninety, mileage burnout could be quite high and injuries were a real possibility. Wanting to avoid them at all costs, Ariel had agreed.

The crowd started to thin as they headed out into the foothills, the ground beneath them starting to rise into an incline. Ariel did her best to focus on the beauty around her, not the increase in incline she felt with each step or the thinness of the air she was breathing. She'd only been here a few days, and they weren't even that high up yet. She had a long way to go and the air would get much thinner. Instead, she watched the swish of the ponytails and braids of the runners in front of her, the swing of their legs. She was always fascinated by how everyone's natural stride was different. That's the beauty of being human, she supposed.

The oak lined path opened into a green grassy valley, the shade disappearing and the sunshine warming the cool morning air. For late June, it was awfully cold by Ariel's standards. But she was grateful for it- she did her best running in the cold. To her left, she saw the first water station.

As she came upon the first aid station, a bright yellow flag indicated she'd already reached mile eight. A quick glance at her watch told her she was right on track with her timing- not too fast, not too slow. She grinned. Maybe all the speedwork was paying off after all.

Without missing a stride, Ariel coasted in and swooped a paper cup of red liquid off the table, downing it in one swig. She tossed it in the bin at the end of the table and repeated the process at the next table with the water cups. She smiled at the volunteers and nodded her thanks before she pulled away from the aid tables and found her spot in the middle of the path again.

This was fun. A joy filled her chest that she hadn't felt since cross country season. She hesitated to say it was better, but she dared to guess that it was because here, she felt all the joy cross country had brought her and none of the nauseated, jello-legged feeling that she always had at the end of races. "I'm sure that will come later," she thought. As she rounded a corner, she saw Coach Bobbi, Cheryl, and Sam standing on the sidelines, waving little pink rally towels. Ariel perked up when she saw them and waved. Coach Bobbi held up something in her hand, waving it around and pointing at it. Ariel squinted, then laughed and nodded back.

"I've already had two gels!" she shouted without breaking stride.

Coach Bobbi gave her two thumbs up. Ariel waved as she passed, feeling rejuvenated having seen her family. She couldn't help but laugh at Coach, of course she'd check in to make sure she was eating. As much as Ariel despised gels, she choked them down religiously. "Nutrition is a big factor the longer you go," was practically the tagline to any marathon or ultradistance blog. Her watch told her she was on pace, and she was on track with calories. She felt a renewed sense of confidence this race would go fine.

And it was. Until mile twenty.

Try as she might, Ariel had fallen behind off her target pace by fifteen seconds. Her lungs burned. No matter how fast or how deep she breathed, it felt like she was breathing through a straw. Her legs felt like lead. Protesting every little movement she asked of them. She knew her support crew would be right behind the next bend, and the last thing she wanted to see was the disappointment on Coach Bobbi's face.

"God I wanna quit," Ariel thought.

"You can't quit," someone behind her said.

"Shit, did I say that out loud?" Ariel asked, glancing over her shoulder to see who was behind her. A middle-aged woman thin as a rail and wearing a Nike sponsorship bib that declared her name as Renee pulled up next to her, matching her stride for stride.

"Sure did," the woman laughed. Her long brown ponytail bounced from shoulder to shoulder. Clearly this lady was feeling great. Ariel was jealous. "You can't quit."

"And why not?" Ariel asked, feeling indignant this stranger thought she could tell her what she could and could not do.

"Because, I've been trying to catch you all race and here you are. If you quit, I have no one to race against and then what was this all for?"

"Ha, you're funny."

"No, I'm serious. I've been trying to catch you from so far back all day. I'm honestly surprised I caught up."

"Yeah, well, the elevation is kicking my ass more than I thought it would," Ariel huffed.

Renee laughed. "It did me the first time too. I was visiting my sister in Denver from Florida, and I ran the Denver marathon, and I DNFed it."

"Really?"

She nodded. "Really. This your first race here?"

Ariel nodded silently, saving her breath and energy for her legs.

"Give yourself a break then. You'll get your second wind," Renee assured her. "Look over there, I see your team's cheering you on." Renee pointed out to the right side of the path where Erin, Coach Bobbi, Cheryl, and Sam were standing with big smiles on their faces, waving their rally towels like their lives depended on it.

Ariel smiled wearily. "Thanks, Renee."

"Anytime," Renee said, smiling a toothy grin that stretched from ear to ear. "I'll race you to the finish." She winked and continued as Ariel pulled aside for a quick pit stop with her crew.

"You've got this," were the first words out of Coach Bobbi's mouth.

"Excuse me," Ariel said, shaking her head as if to clear water from her ears. "What did you say?"

"You've got this," she repeated. "All you gotta do is run through the wall."

"Ha! Just run through a wall, got it," Ariel laughed, shaking her head.

"See you at the finish," Sam said, pushing her shoulder away. "Now go! Catch that lady you were talking to! Go go go! You only have six more miles."

"Six? I thought I still had nine more to go."

"Nope!" Cheryl interjected. "You passed those markers. six more to go!"

"Holy shit," Ariel said, energy surging from her center. She could do six miles in her sleep. Without another word, she was off and running, the lead suddenly lifting from her legs. Apparently, her family and Renee's pep talk did the trick, putting just enough air back in her lungs to rejuvenate her effort. She put her head down and got to work, willing her legs faster and faster until her watch showed her right on pace with her goal time.

She wasn't likely to make her original finishing time, but that was okay. All she had to do was finish. Finish, finish, finish, she repeated to herself in her head. She knew she had to keep the real goal in sight so as not to get overzealous, push too hard, and lose all her goals all together because she'd overshot.

"Finish, finish, finish," she repeated with each step she took. The mountains opened up before her, looming large and glorious with the midmorning sun reflecting off what little snow was still held on their highest peaks. A dark blue bird flew in front of her—a Stellar's jay. She smiled. This was more than she'd dreamed of.

The field of runners had really thinned out now. As the race wore on, people had forged their own paths. Some of them had met their goals, others had fallen short, others had surprised themselves. Up ahead, Ariel spotted a familiar long brown ponytail.

"You're a hard woman to catch," Ariel called out.

"You found me!" Renee laughed, turning over her shoulder while still running forward. "Wait, you never did tell me your name."

"Ariel," she said, pulling up next to her. They matched stride for stride. "Your pep talk was really helpful."

"Glad you didn't quit."

"Me too," Ariel said. "I'll see you at the finish line." She winked and pulled ahead. She could hear Renee laughing behind her but didn't hear her pick up the pace.

"You got it!" she called.

Ariel pumped her fist in the air as she continued.

The mile markers ticked by—twenty-one, twenty-two, twenty-three, twenty-four, twenty-five—and finally, the coveted twenty-six.

"Holy fuck, I'm gonna get there," Ariel huffed to herself. "Only point two to go. That's less than two laps around the track."

As she turned the corner, the whole vibe of the race changed. The finish chute was lined with red, white, and blue flags. People were packed in behind the flag tape, holding signs, blowing whistles, and yelling loudly for their loved ones and for anyone who simply had had enough gumption to make it this far.

Tears pricked at the backs of her eyes and her legs moved faster. She didn't have to will them anymore—they just went. She didn't notice where her team was cheering her from, but she knew they were there. Her eyes were fixated on the finish line and the ticket clock above it. 3:31:11… 3:32:19…3:33:52….

Ariel broke the finish line and stumbled to a halt. The burning in her eyes had turned to full on tears of gratitude. She bent over, resting her knees on her elbows, more so to catch her emotions than her breath. When she stood up again, the crowd was cheering for her and she waved to all of them.

"Ariel Hart with a finishing time of three hours, thirty-three minutes, and fifty-two seconds in the marathon. Congratulations, Ariel!" the MC boomed over the loudspeaker system. "You're our first-place woman!" The crowd roared a little louder, and she smiled, waving with both hands. A volunteer stepped in front of her and held out a race medal.

"Thank you!" Ariel beamed, taking the medal. "Did I really place first woman?"

The volunteer gave her a smirk and a shrug. "If the big man says you did, you did. Congrats."

She ran her thumbs over the metal engravement. It was a beautifully designed mountain with a runner, the words "Leadville Marathon" embossed in gold on it. She placed it around her neck and stood a little taller.

Not only had she finished, she took first woman overall. A podium spot had never entered her mind. She'd simply wanted to finish as fast and as uninjured as possible. She started walking towards the sidelines, getting out of the way of the next wave of runners who were coming in to finish. The crowd was dense, and there was no way she'd find her crew in here, so she started moving towards their designated meeting spot—the refreshment tent.

The tent was set up a block away from the finish line and provided the runners with all the post-race goodies they could ask for: bananas, apples, pizza slices from the local pizzeria, pies, and a huge assortment of bagels and toppings along with coffee, teas, water, and sports drinks galore. She didn't spot her mom or Coach Bobbi anywhere, so she headed into the tent and loaded a plate full of as many snacks as she could grab. She didn't have an appetite at the moment, but she definitely would later and she wasn't about to miss out on all the goodness they were offering.

When she emerged from the other side of the tent, she posted up on the left side and waited. Eventually, Mom emerged from the crowd and spotted her, all smiles on her face.

"You did it!" she cheered. "I'm so proud of you!!" She ran up to her daughter and embraced her in a hug.

"Thanks Mom. I'm just as shocked as you are."

"I'm not shocked at all," she said, standing back at arm's length. "I knew you could do it."

"We all knew you could," Coach Bobbi said, appearing behind her. "But first place? Damn, good work kid."

"Thanks," Ariel nodded. "Look at this medal!" She held it out for everyone to admire.

"You made that look easier than I thought," Sam commented.

"You want to do one with me next time?" Ariel asked mischievously.

"Hell no," she laughed, letting the medal go. "It'll be a cold day in hell before I run a marathon."

"Here, why don't you sit down?" Cheryl said, pointing to a soft patch of grass underneath a tree a few yards away.

Ariel shook her head. "If I sit down now, I'm not getting back up."

"You're that sore already?" Coach asked, a hint of concern in her voice.

"No, but I am that tired," Ariel laughed.

"Well let me take this plate, and you head over to that med tent," Coach Bobbi said, taking the paper plate gingerly from her hands. "They've got the local college students giving free sports massages."

"Ughhh do I have to?" Ariel asked. She hated sports massages. They were more painful than any race she'd ever run. But she had to admit, she recovered much quicker when she had them.

"Yes. Go," Coach shooed her away. Ariel obliged, not looking forward to the least relaxing massage of her life.

"Pick a table, any table," the young man wearing a purple polo greeted her. "Any health conditions or medical issues?"

Ariel shook her head. "Nope. Just tight muscles and my Coach ordered me over here."

"Smart coach," the man said. "We'll have you feeling great and recovered in no time."

Ariel got on one of the empty massage tables on her stomach, turning her head to the left.

"Renee!" she exclaimed. "What are the chances!"

The brunette woman turned her head, her huge smile still on her face. "Oh wow! Hey Ariel! I guess we really meant it when we said we'll see each other at the finish line."

"That we did," Ariel laughed. "What was your time?"

"Three hours, fifty-five minutes, and fifty seconds."

"Nice!"

"All right, racers and families!" The man on the loudspeaker boomed, interrupting their conversation. "T-minus one hour until we draw for the coveted Leadville 100 lottery spot!"

"Oooo, that's exciting," Ariel said. "Ow!!!" She winced, clenching her hands into fists as the man dug into her calves with his elbow.

"You tell me when to stop," he said.

"I will," she replied through gritted teeth.

"I take it you really want to qualify for the ultra?" Renee asked. Her massage therapist was working just as hard on her legs, but she didn't even flinch.

"I do," Ariel said, wincing again. "It's the whole reason I came here. Have you ever done it?"

Renee shook her head. "Nope. And I have no desire to either. I like my marathon and I don't have any desire to run any more than that."

"Really? Then why run this?"

"Because I love the scenery. I live nearby and it's a great race."

"Fair enough."

"Why do you want to do the ultra?"

"I'm going to win it," Ariel said without hesitation.

Renee chuckled. "You've got quite lofty goals."

"I know. Trust me, I know I'm crazy. Enough people have said it enough times, I get it. But it's what I want to do. It's what I have to do."

"I don't think you're crazy at all. I think you're ambitious. I wish I had that gumption when I was your age."

"Yeah, well sometimes it's not all it's cracked up to be," Ariel lamented.

"Here," Renee said. She reached back into her side pocket and pulled out a little blue token. She held it out to Ariel. "Take this."

Her eyes widened. "No, you can't be serious. I can't take your lottery token."

"Why not? I don't want it anyway. Someone who wants to run it might as well have it. And if anyone deserves two chances to win, it's you."

Ariel tentatively took the coin from her hand, turning it over in her fingers. "Are you sure?"

"I'm doubly sure."

Ariel stared at it, not believing her luck. "You're an angel, you know? First you pep-talk me during a low moment, and now you're giving me your token?"

Renee's massage was over, so she sat up on the table, swinging her legs over the side. She shrugged. "What can I say? I'm just doing what feels right and somehow things always work out."

"Thank you. Thank you, a lot."

"Of course. Good luck." Renee grabbed her runner's swag bag off the floor and slung it over her shoulder, walking towards the exit of the tent.

"Hey wait," Ariel called to her. Renee stopped and turned around. "If I get in, you better come spectate the hundred miler!"

Another one of those toothy grins spread across Renee's face. "I wouldn't miss it."

An hour later, Ariel was chowing down on a bagel loaded with hummus, spinach, and a slice of teriyaki flavored tofu while Cheryl, Sam, and Coach Bobbi paced about. They were standing in front of the announcers stand along with every other runner who'd received a lottery token. The crowd energy was an interesting one. The buzzing excitement and anticipation of the starting line mixed with the exhaustion and gratitude of the finish line. A hush fell over the crowd as the brightly dressed announcer ascended the stage.

"Good afternoon ladies and gentlemen!" he said. His voice confirmed this was the same man who'd been announcing finishers all day as they crossed the finish line. "First and foremost, I want to congratulate every one of you for your amazing accomplishment today. Even if you only got to the starting line, you accomplished more than what most people will ever accomplish. Only one percent of the American population will ever run a marathon, and you, ladies and gents, chose one of the hardest."

The crowd clapped and cheered.

"Now, to what you all have probably been waiting for since you crossed that finish line."

"Since before I got here!" someone yelled from the front. The crowd laughed in agreement.

"Or since before you got here!" the MC laughed. "Either way, let's get down to brass tax and start pulling the winning lottery numbers!"

A cart was wheeled on stage with a large, caged sphere on top, just like the kind they use at bingo halls or to select the lottery numbers on TV. The MC stepped up to it and started spinning. "I'm going to pull out twenty numbers at random. If your number is called, please come to the stage and one of our volunteers will assist you with getting signed up for the ultramarathon. We found that this cuts down on missed registrations. All right, here we go."

The crowd waited in silent anticipation for him to pull the first number.

"Sam, take this," Ariel said, hanging her the blue token Renee had gifted her.

"Why?"

"Because I can't read two numbers at once," she whispered.

He finally pulled one of the ping pong balls and read off the number. It wasn't either of Ariel's.

"Remember, you've got nineteen more chances."

As the MC kept pulling numbers, none being Ariel's. They were down to the final three.

"Number 5430!" he yelled out. The camera zoomed in on the numbers he was reading. "Number five, four, three, zero."

A cheer came from somewhere behind where Ariel and her family were standing. A young man in his twenties bounced up and down before making his way to the stage to claim his number. Now Ariel was getting worried. What if her number wasn't called? It was too late to become a charity runner. This was it. This was literally her last chance…

"Number 3319!" the MC called.

Ariel glanced at the token in her hands—3397. Close, but not close enough. Her heart sank.

"Number 3319!" he repeated.

Sam nudged Ariel in the ribs.

"Can you not?" Ariel said, annoyed her sister was deciding this was the time to be a pain in the ass.

"I can, but only if you want to lose out on your lottery spot," Sam said, "Look." She held up the token and read the numbers out loud. "3319."

Ariel ripped the token from Sam's hands. "Holy shit, 3319. 3319! Guys! Guys! I'm 3319!!" she shouted, going from annoyance to elation. She jumped up and down, despite her legs protesting against it. The people surrounding her cheered for her, clapping her on the back as she made her way in a blur towards the stands. She handed her token to the MC, who checked it against the ping pong ball.

"Here you go, lucky lady. Congratulations," he smiled, handing her the token back and shaking her hand. "You can step to the side here and a volunteer will get you all squared away."

Ariel smiled, too shocked to say anything. She started making her way towards the volunteer smiling at her from the sidelines but turned around.

"Can I keep the ping pong ball?" she asked. She didn't even know why she was asking it.

The MC looked surprised, but he handed it to her.

"Thanks," she nodded, kissing the ball and holding it skyward. She said a small prayer of thanks to her Dad before tucking it into her pocket next to the token. Ariel went with the volunteer to complete the paperwork to sign up. The entire process was a blur, so she was grateful the woman gave her copies of all the documents and said she'd get emails about it as well.

When she returned to her family, they were eager to hear the details. She just handed them the packet of information in exchange for her bagel. As Coach Bobbi and Mom looked over the packet, Ariel plopped down on the ground, savoring the food.

She'd done it. She'd gotten into the Leadville 100.

Thank god for Renee.

Chapter 29

The week following the marathon, Ariel rode the post-race high. The massive weight of uncertainty had been lifted off her shoulders, and the night after the race she slept twelve hours without waking up.

For the first time in a long time, she felt like her goal was within reach. She spent most of the week taking it easy and enjoying the time with Mom, Sam, and Coach Bobbi while they were in town. They spent many happy hours exploring the town and surrounding nature, and in the evenings, they soaked in the hot tub until their fingers were wrinkly. Aunt Erin joined them when she was off work, and she even took a day off to explore a local museum and tea shop with them. A local paper had caught wind of her story and had called, asking Ariel if she'd be willing to sit down for an interview to be run in the paper. It had been a pleasant experience. The reporter was nice and it felt great to talk about her goals and accomplishments. At the end, she'd been told that it would run on the eighth page of the sports section, which to the best of Ariel's knowledge was the second to last page.

Come Sunday morning, Ariel picked up the paper that had been tossed into their driveway and opened it. There, on the whole bottom half of the front page, was her name.

Iowa Runner Ariel Hart Youngest Ever to Enter Legendary Race

"Holy shit," she said under her breath. She sprinted into the house, the door slamming behind her. "Mom! Mom!"

"What?" she asked worriedly. "Did you hurt yourself?"

She shook her head and shoved the paper into her hands. "I'm on the front page!"

Cheryl glanced over the black and white print. "Wow, this is incredible. Erin! Ariel made the front page!"

Aunt Erin walked into the living room, nursing her morning tea. Cheryl held up the paper for her to see. "Look!"

Erin glanced at Ariel. "I thought they said it was going to be buried. Just kind of a puff piece?"

"A puff piece that someone's editor liked!" Ariel said, giddy. She grabbed the paper out of their hands. "I'm waking up Sam." Ariel took off down the hallway and barged into Sam's room.

"I made the front page!" she shouted, waving the paper above her head.

"Cool, now get the fuck out," Sam mumbled from underneath the covers.

Ariel hopped on top of her and pulled the covers back, shoving the paper in her face. "Look!"

"Good God," Sam moaned. She blinked the sleep from her eyes and studied the paper. "Okay, that's kind of cool actually."

"Right?! Okay, you can sleep now." Ariel hopped off the bed and closed the door on her way out, leaving just as quickly as she'd come. When she returned to the living room, her mom and aunt were sitting on opposite couches, scrolling on their phones.

"Do you and Sam have to leave today?" Ariel asked, sitting down in the love seat by the window. It was always bathed in natural light, so it had become Ariel's favorite spot to sit.

"We do," Cheryl nodded. "I have to get back to searching for work. But we'll be back in a little over a month for your big race."

"That's so far away," Ariel moaned, dramatically sprawling out on the chair. "Why can't you stay all summer? We'd have the ultimate girls' summer here."

"I know, I wish we could," Cheryl said solemnly. Ariel felt a twinge of guilt. She knew her Mom would stay if she could. "But we'll be back. And next time we're staying for two weeks."

"And besides, we'll be plenty busy," Aunt Erin said. "You've got a lot of training still and then it's my duty to make sure you don't do anything crazy during your taper. The time will fly by."

Ariel knew Erin was right, but that didn't take away the fact she didn't want to see her mom and sister leave today. The rest of the morning was spent savoring their company until it was time to go to the airport. After an emotional goodbye, Erin and Sam drove back to the condo in silence. When they got back to the house, Ariel grabbed a protein bar from the counter and hugged her aunt.

"I'm feeling really drained after today," she admitted. "And with training starting back up tomorrow, I'm going to turn in early."

"Okay," Erin said softly, stroking her hair. "You okay?"

"Yeah," Ariel said, pulling back from the hug. "I'm just a little sad. I bet it'll be gone tomorrow morning."

"Or when you look at your front-page news story again," Erin teased, tapping the newspaper that was right next to them on the counter. This got a grin out of Ariel. "There we go. See? I told you. These next few weeks will fly by and before you know it, you'll be at the starting line again."

The next morning, the alarm went off way too early. Ariel had slept great in the days immediately after the race, but after day four, she'd been tossing and turning to no avail. She silenced the alarm clock and rubbed her eyes, getting out of bed through sheer willpower. It was still dark out, so she turned on the bedside lamp to get dressed. As she always did, she had laid out her running gear the night before, so she made quick work of getting dressed and throwing her hair up into a ponytail. She made her way quietly to the kitchen and popped bread in the toaster. While she waited for it to be done, she laced up her shoes and donned her running jacket. According to the weather app, it was a cool forty-four degrees this morning, so for good measure she pulled on her ear warmers. The last thing she wanted was a cold ear headache after the run. It would make functioning the rest of the day extremely difficult. Once the toast popped, she grabbed it and slathered on some peanut butter. Instead of sitting in the kitchen to eat it, she munched as she walked out the door and started down the street.

Today was the first of her last set of back-to-back long runs: twenty miles today, thirty miles tomorrow. She patted down her vest and pants pockets, ensuring she had enough water and snacks for the first leg, and then that her phone was fully charged so she'd be able to call Erin when she needed a refill or if, heaven forbid, she got herself into a predicament out in the mountains. When she was sure everything was in order, she set off into the starting of the sunrise.

By now, this routine was familiar. She took the trail out of town and up into the mountains she went. With each little gain of elevation, the sun crept closer to the horizon until eventually it rose, bringing in the day. And with it, warmer temperatures. Gratefully, she removed her ear warmers and tucked them in the pocket of her leggings. The desert evenings were heavenly, but the days in the summers were brutal. Iowa may not have given her the elevation advantage, but Ariel was no stranger to running in the heat. As she rounded a bend to bring her above the tree line, she heard the familiar sound of crunching gravel underneath running shoes behind her.

A quick glance over her shoulder revealed two runners coming up the switchback below her—two men. Her stomach did a little twist. The warnings that'd been ingrained in her since she could run: don't run by yourself, run with your keys in your hand, have a rape whistle, don't run with music, run in public places. She shook her head, trying to make the negative thoughts go away.

"They're just other trail runners," she told herself. She put her head down and kept her pace up the mountain pass. The crunch of their shoes got closer until they were close behind her. This spot of the trail was narrow and rocky with no spot to let other runners pass, so they would just have to wait. Ariel wasn't about to interrupt her run to get out of their way. A few minutes later, the trail peaked and opened in an alpine meadow flush with greenery and wildflowers.

"On your left," said a runner in a bright blue tech shirt as he pulled up beside her.

"Thanks." Ariel glanced up at him. He was young, probably in his mid-twenties, with dark brown hair that curled around his ears. Something about his deep-set eyes was a little unnerving.

"You training for something?" he asked, matching her stride to keep pace with her. "Not many people run up here unless they are."

"Yeah, Leadville." Ariel didn't want to be rude, but she didn't want to encourage too much conversation. She knew all too well the dangerous line between being nice and being mistaken for flirting.

"No shit! Me too," the other man said, pulling up on the other side of Ariel so that they were running three wide. She didn't like that one bit. "I'm Scott."

Ariel threw a quick glance over at him. He too was probably in his twenties and by the looks of him, he spent more time in the gym than running. Her stomach clenched, a knot building in her chest. She fought the urge to smile at him, instead remaining straight-faced with her gaze trained on the trail ahead of her.

He smiled, revealing blindingly white teeth. "What's your name?"

Ariel didn't look in his direction. "Jane."

"You done Leadville before?" Scott asked.

"First time," she said shortly.

"Is that so?" he asked. Out of the corner of her eye, Ariel saw him look her up and down, his gaze lingering in certain spots that made her skin crawl. "Pretty little thing like you doing a big, hard race like that? I'd love to see it."

That was it. Without thinking, Ariel took off at a dead sprint, putting as much distance between herself and the two men as possible.

"Hey, I didn't mean—" Scott called after her.

Ariel didn't look back, but thankfully his voice was far away and not breathless, so she knew they weren't sprinting to catch up to her. She kept going at lightning speed, not caring if it bit her in the ass the last few miles of the run. She had to get as far away from these two as she could. Maybe they were harmless jocks, but she had no desire to find out, lest she end up as a different type of headline.

The rest of her run was uneventful and several grueling hours later, Ariel came down the last stretch of hill into town. She finished her run strong, pushing until she crossed the rock she used as her finish line and stumbling to a halt. She resisted the urge to lay down, and instead forced herself to walk slowly, her hands on top of her head. As she slowly walked the last half mile back to the house, she focused on controlling her breathing. As her breathing slowed to a more regular pace, the ache in her legs started to grow as did a sharp, stabbing pain in her foot. She wiggled her leg, did some skipping to loosen up. Her muscles were expected to be sore, but by the time she crawled up the porch steps and into the house, the pain on the top of her foot was unbearable. Each step felt like her tendon was being run across a hot knife. That wasn't good.

"What did you do?" Aunt Erin asked, concern in her voice. She was on the living room floor on her yoga mat in warrior pose, so there was no sneaking past her into the kitchen.

"My foot just hurts, that's all," Ariel said, sitting down on the love seat closest to her. Her legs practically sighed with relief at having her weight taken off them. She gingerly removed her left shoe, wiggling her toes to ensure they all still functioned properly. They did, but the whole top of her foot burned with the movement. She repeated the process with her other foot with the same results. When she removed her socks, she noticed a small lump on the top of her foot. "That explains some of it." She held up her foot over the counter for Erin to see. "What's this about?"

"That's disgusting, put your foot down," Erin laughed. "It looks like swelling on your tendon. Are you running in new shoes?"

Ariel shook her head. "They aren't that new. I've been running in them for a few days, but apparently I misjudged how broken in they are."

"Ice it, don't wear shoes for a bit," Erin shook her head. "That's probably not great this late in the game."

"Well, it sure isn't ideal," Ariel said, standing up. "But like you said, nothing a little ice, elevation, and rest won't fix. Besides, I'm officially in my taper period, so it's not that big of a deal. It'll be perfect by race time in a few weeks."

Erin side eyed her skeptically. "You better watch it like a hawk. And keep an eye on those shoes. I've had more than one race ruined by a little blistered skin and irritated tendons."

"Gee, thanks for the positivity," Ariel said sarcastically.

Erin held up her hands. "Just speaking from experience."

"I know," Ariel smiled. "I'm going to go take care of this. And then we can eat? I hope you made me a whole separate lasagna because I bet you twenty bucks I could eat that whole thing."

"I made two," Erin winked.

"You're the best." She was incredibly grateful for an aunt that understood the phenomenon that is runner hunger.

Ariel retreated to the bathroom to fix some of her blisters and when she reemerged, Aunt Erin had already set up dinner. She felt bad she hadn't been more help. While she'd been out running all day, her aunt had been hard at work at a nearby archeological site digging through the dirt for twelve hours. Ariel was sure all Erin wanted to do was sit down and not get up for a bit.

"Do you mind if we eat in the living room?" Ariel asked, knowing her aunt would appreciate the comfier chairs. "I really want to elevate my feet."

"I'd love it. My back is killing me after today."

"Cool, you sit down, and I'll bring over everything." Ariel said, bumping her out of the way with her hips. She donned the potholders and grabbed the lasagna out of the oven.

"But—"

"I insist," she said firmly. "Sit your ass down."

Erin smiled and did as she was told. "Do you talk to your mother like that?"

Ariel laughed. She made quick work of plating a large helping of lasagna for each of them and brought them out to the coffee table. The two women enjoyed the dinner in silence, both exhausted from their days. As they were cleaning up the dishes, Erin spoke up. "What's your plan for the weekend?"

"I was actually hoping you'd go up to Leadville with me," Ariel said. "I've been here all summer and I haven't spent much time up there. It'd be good to get at least some taper runs in."

"Sounds like a good idea to me," Erin said. "I could use some time away from the city. I don't get to play in the mountains all day like you do."

"You play in the dirt at dig sites though! Isn't that practically the same?"

"You'd think, but when you have to deal with lots of scientists' egos, it kind of ruins the ambiance."

"Guess that's fair," Ariel smiled. She hadn't even thought about that aspect of her aunt's job. Ariel toyed with whether or not to tell her about what had happened earlier today on the trail, ultimately deciding she should. At the very least, someone else would know about those two—just in case—"   .

"I met some creeps on the trail today," she said casually.

"Wait, what?" Erin exclaimed, almost dropping a dish. "What happened?"

"Nothing, they were just… creepy. Their vibe was off, which was whatever until one of them said something super creepy—"Ariel explained. It was hard to put into words, that feeling every woman knows.

"No, what did they say?"

"Well, it was more a combination of what they said and how they said it."

"What was it, Ariel Jane?"

"'Pretty little thing like you doing a big, hard race like that? I'd love to see it,'" Ariel said, doing her best to imitate the sultury tone with which Scott had first said the line.

Erin shook her head back and forth. "No, absolutely not. And he said it like that?"

"Oh yeah," Ariel chuckled. "I was outta there. I sprinted the next two miles, thankfully that was the end of it all, but still."

"No, no, no. That's so bad. What would've happened if they'd try to keep up with you?"

"Then I would've bear sprayed them in the face, or stabbed them with my pocketknife," Ariel shrugged, taking another bite of lasagna. "I always have that stuff with me."

"Good," Erin said, the tension leaving her shoulders. "Lord knows I've had my fair share of bad encounters with creepy dudes, but it's always been on the road, not out in the middle of no where."

"It's the first time something like that has ever happened. Hopefully it's the last, too."

"Uh, agreed," Erin said.

"At least he sounded skeptical that I could actually run Leadville. I love proving people wrong."

"Good," Erin laughed. She walked over to the island and picked up her glass of wine, swirling the red contents around it. "He'll be jaw on the floor come race day. Him and tons of others. You've got all the edge in the world."

Ariel raised an eyebrow. "Yeah? What edge? Like the fact that my crew is a bunch of amateurs? Or that I have no sponsorships? Or maybe that this is my first hundred miler ever?"

"Hey, don't discount beginners' luck," Erin nodded knowingly. "First time I ever gambled in a casino I won five grand. Then next time I took my friend to the casino and she won six grand. I had a coworker that had never played golf before, and he hit a hole in one."

"I mean, that's pretty impressive," Ariel admitted. "Remind me that when this is over, I need to go to the casino with you."

"Exactly, don't discount beginner's luck. People say it's cheating, that it nullifies your accomplishments somehow. But I disagree. A win is a win no matter what, as long as it isn't actual cheating like cutting the course or doping."

"I like it. If you dare to be a beginner, you deserve a little something-something for that bravery."

"Exactly," Erin nodded. "Now let's finish these dishes and go to bed."

Chapter 30

"We're here!" Cheryl announced as they pulled into cute downtown Leadville. The street was lined with beautiful, log-styled buildings similar to what you'd find at a ski resort town. There were people walking all about, rather busy for the time of day on a Wednesday.

Ariel slapped Shelby's thigh, startling her awake. "Girl we're here!"

Shelby grumbled something in audible and sat up, glancing out both windows in the back of the car. "That was fast."

"Time flies when you're sleeping," Sam added. "You missed a pretty drive."

"I'll see it on the way back," Shelby said, unbothered by the fact she'd missed the beautiful drive up the mountain roads. It was a typical Colorado summer day—clear and sunny. There wasn't much breeze, cool air coming down from the mountains.

"There're already so many runners here," Ariel said, watching the groups of people meandering along the sidewalks and through the small-town square. They were mostly young people in groups of three to five. And a lot of them were tall and lanky wearing sporty apparel. Definitely distance runners.

Coach Bobbi rolled her window down and let her arm hang out. "Most likely. A lot of the professionals who don't live here move in a few weeks before the race starts."

"That would've been nice," Ariel said.

"Nah, I'm not worried about it," Bobbi clarified. She twisted in her seat so she could face Ariel, her eyes serious. "Remember. You've done all the hard work. You've earned your place here. Now, it's time to rest, relax, and enjoy the fruits of your training. Got it?"

"Got it," Ariel nodded in affirmation. And she meant it. On the drive up to Leadville, she'd reflected on her journey the past several months. From the first summer practice for cross country, the disastrous last race that cost her the state title, to the threat of losing her home, and then coming up with a plan to save it, she was confident she'd done everything within her control to set herself up for success. She'd learned and she'd put in the work, no matter how hard it was. And that she was proud of.

"You're running up there?" Shelby said to no one in particular as she gazed out the window at the looming mountain peaks. "No wonder there's a fifty percent fail rate."

"Ha-ha, thank you Captain Obvious," Ariel said. "What're you lost in thought about over there?"

"Sorry, just waking up," she said, rubbing her eyes with her palms. "Can the first stop be a coffee shop?"

"Our first stop after we check into the hotel, yes," CHeryl said, pulling into the parking lot of a small, nothing-special motel.

"It's cute?" Sam offered. The building was a mix of old red brick and brick walls painted black, the old red peeking through where the paint had started to fleck off. There was a courtyard with a firepit, surrounded by rustic wooden chairs.

Mom parked the car and the women got out, grabbing their backpacks. "Let's check in and then we'll get the rest."

The group walked into the lobby, where a smiling Asian woman greeted them. "Hi! Welcome. Checking in?"

"Yeah," Cheryl said, walking up to the counter. "We got early check in."

As Cheryl checked into the rooms, Sam and Shelby posted up on the nearest couch and Ariel checked out the fireplace mantel in the middle of the lobby. On the stone mantel were a series of pictures in sleek black frames. Each picture was in black and white, the first one was a group of young men standing underneath the banner that proclaimed, "Leadville 100, 1960." The subsequent pictures were of the same group of men throughout the years up until 2016.

"These must be the founders," Ariel said. "This is cool."

"Interesting," Sam said from her post on the black cushiony couch. The large window wall at the front let the sunlight pour in, bathing the room in beautiful natural light.

"All right," Cheryl said, waving several hotel keys around. "Let's go settle into our rooms." She handed each a key and they walked back out to the car, grabbing their luggage. They walked around the back, through another courtyard with a fireplace.

"Two-oh-two… right here," Ariel said, stopping in front of the door with golden numbers that matched the numbers written on their room cards. She inserted her key into the lock and opened the door.

The room was exactly what you'd expect at a cabin in the west, thought it was admittedly more modern than most western motifs. The wall with the door was mostly large front windows, in front of which sat a dining table with four chairs. A small kitchenette with a full-sized, stainless-steel fridge was on the far wall across from a small living room with a futon, a loveseat, and a large screen TV mounted on the wall. The bathroom was off the far wall, and two large French doors separated the living from the sleeping area.

"Wow!" Ariel said, mouth agape. "You went all out!"

Mom shrugged, plopping her bag down on the luggage cart at the foot of the bed. "I figured it's our big vacation this year, and it's a special event. We're gonna go all out for it! Plus, we need somewhere to keep and manage all the calories you're gonna need."

"But… can we afford it?" Sam asked, her voice quiet.

"Oh, honey," Cheryl said, pulling Sam into a hug. "Yes, we can. Plus, I wanted to wait until after the race to tell you, but… I got a job!"

"What?!" Ariel and Sam exclaimed in unison. "You got a job?!"

Cheryl laughed. "Yes, I did! I'm going to work at Iowa Orthodontics as their bookkeeper. It's not glamourous, but I figure we spent so much money there on you girls' teeth that I can earn some of it back from them.

Plus, it's a short drive, the benefits are good, and there's potential for growth."

"That's amazing!" Ariel cheered, bear hugging her mom. "Why on earth were you waiting to tell us?!"

Cheryl shrugged. "I didn't want to detract from your special day!"

"You're not detracting anything," Ariel assured her. "Now we'll have even more reason to party!"

"Proud of you, Mom," Sam said. "I'm so glad you got something."

"Me too," Cheryl said, her voice cracking. "I was getting worried there for a bit."

"Understandable," Sam said. "But no more worrying! Except for how this race is gonna go."

"Let's not worry about that either," Ariel said. "I'm trying to avoid that. Speaking of, where's my stress-eating food?"

"In the cooler," Sam said, nodding to the blue container in the corner. Ariel sauntered over and removed a bag of spinach leaves. She shoved a handful in her mouth and chewed.

Mom and Sam exchanged a glance before bursting out into laughter.

"You're the only person I know to stress-eat spinach," Cheryl said, wiping the tears from her eyes.

"Me too," Ariel said. "I appreciate some fresh food in addition to all the junky stuff."

"I think you're the first runner in the history of runners, no, first person in the history of people to not just want to eat all the junk food possible. You're literally running one hundred miles, you can eat whatever you damn well please," Sam said.

Ariel shook her head. "Nuh uh, I have to eat healthy stuff otherwise my gut feels like a brick and I run like crap. Trust me, if I felt as good after eating a pan of brownies the night before as I do after eating something healthier, I'd always take the brownies."

"Meh, I guess. Whose bed is whose?" Sam asked as she flung open the French doors. In the next room were two queen sized beds with spotless white duvet covers and copious amounts of pillows.

"I want the one on the left," Ariel said, poking her head over her sister's shoulder. Shelby appeared on the other side of Sam, doing the same. "Does that mean that's our bed?"

Ariel gave her a side-eye as she walked into the room. "I need to sleep, thank you very much."

Shelby gave her a pouty look. "But we always sleep in the same bed at sleepovers."

"This ain't a sleepover," Ariel pointed out. She flopped back onto the bed and sunk into the softness. "I need to actually sleep."

"You can sleep with me," Sam offered.

"But where'll Mom sleep?" Ariel asked. Mom was the one footing the bill for all of this, it was hardly fair to expect her to sleep on the floor of the nice hotel room she booked.

"Oh, I'll be sharing a room with Erin and Bobbi," Cheryl said, wiggling her eyebrows mischievously. "You girls get this one all to yourselves."

The three girls exchanged glances. They couldn't believe their luck. "Thanks, Mom!" Sam said, hugging her around the waist. "Let the party commence!"

"Mom, you didn't have to do that," Ariel started to say, pangs of guilt tightening her chest. This couldn't have been a cheap lodging option, and she knew how tight money was. Especially if she didn't win on Saturday.

"I'm happy to," Cheryl smiled sweetly, walking over and gently kissing Ariel on the forehead. "We've got to give you the best chance at winning, right? I figured a nice, comfy place to sleep and relax would help out with that."

"I mean, it sure does make things easier."

"Good. I'm going to go put my things in our room right next door." Cheryl grabbed her bag off the couch and started walking towards the door. "You girls come over when you're done settling in and we'll go walk around town."

"Sounds like a plan," Ariel said. She was excited to get to explore Leadville a little more. She hadn't gotten up to visit the town as much as she would've liked, but she was determined to make up for lost time.

The girls unpacked a little, settling into their homebase for the next few days. As Ariel hung up her clothes, she pulled out the shirt she would wear on race day: an airy, yellow t-shirt that hung loosely on her frame. It was her favorite training shirt, and the one she'd been wearing when she ran the Leadville marathon a few weeks ago. That race hadn't gone exactly how'd she'd imagined it, but in the end she had been lucky enough to win her entry into the ultra, so she considered this her lucky shirt. If it brought her luck the first time, she was sure it could do it again. She laid out her pants on the dresser, folded neatly. She was still undecided if she wanted to wear long shorts, spandex shorts, or maybe even running tights. The last thing she wanted was chafing, but then again the pants might be too hot. Oh well, that was a decision for later. She made quick work of unpacking the rest.

She glanced over to see Shelby pulling out an orange and white dress from her suitcase.

"What's that for?"

"So, I can look cute when we go out to dinner," she said simply. She hung it gently on the hanger and placed it in the closet.

Ariel laughed, typical Shelby. Sam had decided not to unpack, instead leaving her things in the suitcase with the top open. She was laying on her belly scrolling through her phone, impatiently waiting.

"Are you two done yet?" Sam asked, tossing her phone aside and grabbing her stomach. "I'm hungry."

"I'm done." Ariel said. Shelby nodded in agreement. "I'm hungry too. I wanna go check out that Mexican place we saw on the way in."

"Ooooo chips and salsa sound great," Shelby agreed. "Let's go to the adults' room."

"Perfect, then we can walk around town afterwards," Ariel said. She grabbed her jacket off the couch and headed out the door behind Sam and Shelby. Despite it being late in July, it was still brisk at this elevation. Something she thankfully remembered from last time she was here. But the sun was shining bright overhead, bathing the entire mountain range in sunlight. It was cool, but the golden rays warmed Ariel's black coat. The air smelled of pine, with a hint of the fast-food restaurants down the street which added an aroma of French fries to the mix. The grass was incredibly green, and the white puffy clouds provided the most picturesque of locations.

The room next door was propped open and without even thinking to knock, Sam waltzed inside.

"You do realize their room could've been on either side of ours, right?" Shelby laughed, following in behind.

"No, I knew it was this one," Sam explained. "I saw Mom walk to the left after she walked out of ours."

Ariel was glad she'd seen that instead of just having the confidence to waltz into any open hotel room she saw. Cheryl and Erin were standing around their small kitchenette, trying to get the Keurig machine to work.

"We're all hungry," Sam said unapologetically.

"Perfect, we can get coffee there," Erin laughed. "We'll figure this out later."

Coach Bobbi emerged from the bedroom. Her dark hair was gathered atop her head in a messy bun, her crossbody bag slung over her shoulder. "Man am I ever ready for food. My friend raved about this place."

The group made their way out of the courtyard to the front, which put them on the main street leading through the relatively small town. Lots of people milling about looked as though they she'd be seeing them at the starting line in a few days. A lot of women wore thick, boho headbands paired with a puffer vest, long sleeve compression gear, and running tights with either tennis shoes or hiking shoes. The men looked similar, but instead of running tights they had Carhart-type pants, and thick long sleeve crew neck sweatshirts with baseball caps, many of which had the Patagonia logo emblazoned on them.

Ariel smiled. This was it. This was everything she'd been training for since last fall, and she was excited. This world was different from her cross-country world— the people were full grown adults with their own lives, own stories, own goals and bills to pay. They weren't her teammates. Instead, she had her teammates on the sidelines with her, supporting her the entire way. She just hoped she could make some connections in the runner's field. Suddenly, she felt more like a kid than she had in years. She'd hadn't particularly liked being a kid. In her house, kids didn't get much of a choice, always had to follow and do whatever anyone else told her to do.

But she wasn't a kid anymore. She was eighteen, and she'd worked hard for where she was today. She'd trained for months through rain, sleet, scorching temperatures, wind, and heartbreak. She'd been meticulous with her recovery training too: eating well balanced, healthy meals, making sure she got enough sleep, not going out with friends, not drinking alcohol. All the things the professionals were doing, she was doing too.

The week flew by. Ariel spent her mornings doing very light training runs with Coach Bobbi, followed by a foam rolling and massage sessions. They finished each day with long soaks in the hot tub, strolls around town, and through it all, dining on the yummiest food they could get their hands on.

Chapter 31

When Ariel awoke the morning before the race, she felt a small tickle at the back of her throat. Like the one you get the day before you wake up with a cold that takes you out for a few days.

"Oh no, no, no, no," she mumbled to herself as she threw back the covers and tumbled out of bed.

"What?" Shelby asked groggily, lifting her head from her pillow. Sam didn't stir beside her, still fast asleep.

"Nothing, just super thirsty," she said, not wanting anyone to freak out. She was doing enough of that and didn't need everyone telling her it was in her head. She hoped it was though. She walked into the next room and put a tea packet into the Keurig machine. As she waited for it to brew, she walked around the little apartment. She threw back the curtains, letting in the early morning light. When the machine beeped, she retrieved her cup and inhaled the peppermint-scented steam.

"It's fine, it's nothing," she thought, willing herself to believe it. A few moments later, Shelby joined her in the kitchen.

"What time are we headed to the expo?" Shelby asked as she set up the Keurig to make her own   cup of hot beverage.

"It opens at ten, so, ten," Ariel said. She took a cautious sip, testing the temperature, then took a long drink, the hot tea soothing whatever ache was in her throat.

"What exactly is an expo, again?"

"It's a bunch of vendors set up when you go pick up your race packet," Ariel explained. "Like a mini running convention."

"Oh, dope. Do you think your mom and Erin are up yet?" Shelby asked, hyper focused on the coffee maker. The Keurig sputtered and she removed her coffee cup, taking it to the fridge to add the sugary creamer they'd picked up. As Ariel watched her pour it, she wondered if she even tasted the coffee.

"For sure. Both of them are up earlier than me usually."

"Early bird-ness must run in the family."

"It does," Ariel nodded. "The gene skipped Sam though."

"She'll wake up eventually," Shelby laughed. She sat down on the couch next to Ariel and pulled one of the throw blankets across her legs. "Have you heard from Kyle recently?"

Ariel gave her friend a look. How on earth could she have guessed Ariel's phone currently held thirty-seven unread texts from Kyle? "How did you know?" There was no way Shelby could've known.

Shelby gave a halfhearted grin. "When you don't reply, he texts me, ya know."

"Are you serious?" Ariel asked, sitting up wide-eyed. "I had no idea."

"He wants to make sure you're okay," Shelby said, her tone more sympathetic than Ariel appreciated. "He still really likes you."

Ariel shook her head sharply. "If he really liked me, he would've been supportive. I was very clear about everything, and he decided it wasn't good enough. I don't have time for that shit."

"I know, I know," Shelby said, trying to diffuse her friend, "But you guys have been friends for so long… don't you at least want to salvage the friendship?"

Ariel knew she was right. And she did miss Kyle, there was no doubt about that. She missed exchanging wisecracks in the hallway at school, waving to each other as she passed his house on a run. But she especially missed going over to his house whenever she just wanted to shoot pool or watch a stupid movie. "Maybe after the race. I won't have any of his doubt around me. This—"

"It's hard enough as it is," Shelby said, finishing her sentence. "I know. And I respect that. I just wanted you to know he still asks about you. What did he text you?"

"Just said he wanted to wish me luck, asked how I was feeling," Ariel shrugged. She was happy when his name had popped up on her phone screen, but when she saw the text didn't contain any semblance of an apology for his lack of support, the disappointment returned and she tossed her phone aside. "Let's go bother the adults and get them to make us pancakes."

"Sold," Shelby said mid sip. She threw the blanket to the side and stood up, offering her hand. Ariel took it, being careful not to spill the tea. "Should we wake Sam?"

"Hell no," Ariel shook her head and made a beeline for the door. Shelby followed behind and the two knocked on the adjoining door.

"Come in!" Mom's voice called from within. Ariel opened the door, the smell of bacon already filling the air.

"Looks like we're late for breakfast!" Ariel exclaimed, pretending to be mad. "Why didn't you come get us?"

"Sometimes we like to have some peace and quiet before your chaos starts," Cheryl teased.

"We just started," Erin laughed. "Come join us."

The morning was spent eating pancakes and bacon, sipping tea and coffee. Ariel was anxious to get to the expo but did her best to be present. As soon as the clock struck ten, she stood up off the couch.

"Who's coming to the expo with me?"

"I thought we were all heading there,?" Cheryl asked, looking around the room. Coach Bobbi and Sam had joined them at this point.

"Just making sure," Ariel said. "Let's go! It started five minutes ago."

Coach Bobbi just laughed. "Yeah, and it's open until like seven o'clock tonight."

"I want to get there, see what I want, get my packet, and then chill the rest of the day," Ariel said, shifting her weight from foot to foot.

Coach smiled knowingly. "This taper's really getting to you, isn't it?"

Ariel held her arms wide. "Ya think?"

Cheryl looked at Bobbi confused. "What do you mean?"

"It's a well-known fact that when endurance athletes decrease their mileage before a big race, they start to go a little stir crazy," Bobbi explained. "Especially athletes as high strung as your daughter here."

Cheryl gently took the coffee cup out of Ariel's hands, glancing at its now empty contents. "You didn't add caffeine to this fire, did you?"

"No, just herbal tea," Ariel assured her. She swallowed a few times, testing to see how sore her throat was. She wasn't sure if it felt any better, but it didn't feel worse so for now, she was counting that as a win. "Can we please go or are you all just going to torture me and make fun of me?"

Erin slapped her knees as she arose from the couch. "We're coming." The party gathered up their coats and purses and headed out the door.

"How's your tendon?" Coach asked, noticing that Ariel had slipped on flip flops instead of tennis shoes.

"It feels great, I'm just playing it safe," Ariel shrugged. "Don't want to make it mad walking around the expo."

"Flip flops aren't great either," Coach said.

"We won't be there that long. two hours tops, then I'm off my feet the rest of the day," Ariel said, winking at her.

The day was bright and sunny, not a single cloud in the deep blue sky. They could see the crowds on the streets, all heading towards the expo building. When they entered the building, it was bustling with activity. Apparently, a lot of the other runners had the same idea Ariel did: get in, get what they wanted and needed, get out and relax the rest of the day.

"I'm going to go get my packet," Ariel said. "Then I'll come find you guys."

Cheryl and Erin nodded, and they headed off to check out what freebies the Gu Energy Lab booth was handing out. Ariel wove her way through the crowd and found the line for packet pickup. The line moved quickly, and she was at the front before she knew it.

"Name?" the volunteer behind the counter asked.

"Ariel Hart," she told them. The volunteer immediately got to work digging through one of the many boxes that filled the folding tables.

"Ariel, I thought that was you," said a familiar woman's voice from behind her in line. When Ariel turned around, she smiled.

"Hey Pam! Nice to see you here."

The older woman smiled kindly. "I'm glad you got your lottery placement. Last we spoke you were just hoping for it."

"I got so lucky," Ariel said, remembering just how lucky she was. Had it not been for Renee, she wouldn't be here right now.

"I'm excited to race with you tomorrow," Pam said. Ariel could tell from the kindness in her eyes she really meant it.

"Same here," Ariel said, standing up a little taller.

"Here's your packet, Ms. Hart," the volunteer said, handing her the manilla envelope.

Ariel took it from her hands, running her fingers over the smooth paper. She finally had it, her ticket to race. "Thanks."

Pam stepped up and gave her full name. As she waited for the volunteer to find her packet, she turned to Ariel.

"Do you wanna walk around together? I know the one of the reps at the Salamon table, I can score us some goodies."

Ariel had to do her best not to do a happy dance right then and there. Pam Riley was asking to hangout! "Sure, as long as you don't mind my family showing up at some point."

"Not at all, I'd love to meet the woman who raised such an incredible runner," Pam said.

"Well, be sure to tell her that when you meet her, she'll love it." Ariel and Pam started off in the direction of traffic, clockwise around the vendors. As they looked around and talked with the people in the booths, they met many people who recognized them. And Ariel realized slowly that the people who knew Pam, also knew her. The idea that her name was already well-known was sinking in and adding just a bit of pressure to race day. But ultimately, she was honored.

Chapter 32

Bing, bing, bing.

The phone alarm chimed next to Ariel's head from its dedicated space on the nightstand. She reached over and slid the bar to snooze, even though she knew she wouldn't fall back asleep. The little green numbers on the clock read two-thirty in the morning. Even for her, this was a bit early.

"*Today's the day.*" she whispered to herself in the dark. Dad would've been proud. He would've thought she was insane, probably would've even tried to dissuade her from doing it, citing joint damage, exhaustion, sleep deprivation, etc. She would've laughed it off, disappointed he wasn't supportive, but grateful he wasn't unapproving.

The ache of grief tugged at her heart, letting her know it was still there. At this point, she figured it always would be. A lot had happened the past year. Starting with the tragic death of her father, followed by grief and growing up, it had been filled with highs and lows. The amount of highs surprised her. They'd been some of the best: setting race records, being scouted by some of the best colleges in the country, graduating high school, becoming an ultrarunner, and getting into the Leadville 100. All those accomplishments and milestones helped make some of the lows more worth it.

But not all of them. She'd give it all back in a heartbeat if it meant her dad was still around, that losing the house wasn't even in the picture. That was the reason she'd started this crazy adventure, but as she thought about it, it wasn't the reason she was still running it. She wanted to run it because she wanted to prove to herself that she could. That she could hold her own amongst some of the best runners in the world, and against one of the most notorious courses. She wanted to experience a hard thing, to know the land intimately, to die out on that course and be born again, a transition from her teenage years into adulthood. It felt like a new beginning and a perfect way of closing out her childhood.

Bing, bing, bing.

The alarm went off again. This time she slid the bar to the off position. It was time to leave the comfort of bed and get ready. She'd already laid out everything the night before: her numbers pinned onto her race jersey; her socks already laid out atop her shoes. Even her hairbrush, hair ties, and headband were laid out on the bathroom counter ready for her to throw her hair into its traditional French braid. She made quick work of changing from her pajamas to the racing gear, sneaking into the bathroom so as not to wake Shelby or Sam. But when she looked over her shoulder to see if the creaking door had made them stir, she saw their bed was empty. Puzzled, she decided to pee before searching for her.

When she emerged from the bathroom a few moments later and walked into the main living area, she smelled freshly brewed coffee with a mug placed on the counter next to the machine. But no Shelby or Sam anywhere. Ariel walked over and poured herself a cup, scouring the area for a note but not finding one. It took her a moment to figure out they were most likely next door. She slipped her feet into flipflops and opened the door. The fresh air felt great, removing any grogginess leftover from the little sleep she'd managed last night. Or maybe that was the first few sips of caffeine at work. She'd specifically stayed away from caffeine for weeks before the race, on a hope that it would make her more sensitive. Seems her plan had worked. She could see the light on around the edges of the curtain draped across the window of the room next door, so she used her keycard to let herself in.

"Happy race day!!" The whole group shouted, waving noise makers, and clanging a bell. Ariel about dropped her coffee. The room was brightly lit with streamers hung over the pendant lights, a beautiful array of breakfast foods on the island below.

"Thanks, guys!" she said, beaming. "I can't eat all this though."

"Oh, who said it was for you?" Erin scoffed, popping a strawberry into her mouth. "Your crew needs all the fuel we can get. We've got a thirty-hour day ahead of us!"

"These are for you though," Mom said, handing her a plate already made up of her tried and true pre-race food: an asiago bagel with cream cheese and a scrambled egg burrito. Ariel happily took the plate and dug in, being careful to keep a close eye on the time.

"What time did y'all get up?" Ariel asked through a mouthful of bagel.

"Not that long ago," Bobbi said, her hands cupped around her tea mug. "Thirty minutes or so before you did."

"You didn't have to do all this."

"We know, but we wanted to!" Shelby said, hugging her best friend from behind. "This is stupidly early to be awake. We got to make it fun somehow. What's that thing you were saying earlier, Coach?"

"That ninety percent of the race is all in your head?"

"Yeah, that. We figured this would help get your head in the right space so you don't freak out," Shelby said, giving her a knowing sideways glance.

"Who? Me? Never!" Ariel laughed. "It is helpful, thank you."

"Do you want to go over what all we have packed for you?" Coach Bobbi asked, motioning to a duffel bag resting on the sofa.

"Um, yes please," Ariel said. She brought her plate with her and sat it on the coffee table within arm's reach as she knelt down and started to dig through the bag. She wanted eyes on all the contents but was careful not to undo the systematic packing job Erin and Bobbi had devised. There were plenty of running gels, mac and cheese packets, oatmeal, granola bars, Twix bars, and Combos. "This looks great. I don't think you missed a thing."

"Is there sunscreen in there?" Cheryl asked.

"No!" Erin exclaimed. She dashed into the bathroom and emerged waving the orange and white bottle in the air. "We about gave you the worst sunburn of your life!" She tossed the bottle to Bobbi who placed it in the bag.

"I think you're over exaggerating a little bit there," Ariel laughed. She finished off the last bit of her bagel and coffee. "But I appreciate the enthusiasm."

"Hey, we're not about to let the fact we aren't a professional crew affect your ability to win this thing," Bobbi winked at her. "Speaking of, Shelby, how're you feeling?"

Shelby did a little jig and stretch. "Great! I'm ready to run some miles."

Ariel smiled. Running with her friend again was one thing she was looking forward to most about this race. That and running with Coach Bobbi. Sure, she'd run some of the practices with them, but this would be different. They'd be equals on a totally different running field. Sure, by the time the two would take turns pacing her, she'd be in a world of pain, but that was something to worry about later. "I still can't tell you guys enough how excited I am that it's you who'll help pace me."

"Wouldn't have it any other way," Shelby teased. "Well, if I had it my way, we wouldn't be running this thing at all, but I'm a good friend so here we are."

"And you two," Ariel said, turning to face her mom and sister. Sure, they weren't into running like Shelby and Bobbi and Erin, but they were integral to her success. "The heart and soul of this crew. The logistics masters. We really wouldn't be able to do anything without you."

"Thanks, we know," Sam said, flicking her hair over her shoulder. Ariel glanced at her watch.

"Well, are we ready? Because it's time to head out to the starting line."

"Let's do this!" Cheryl said, wiping her hands on her pants to rid them of any leftover bagel crumbs. "Everybody in." The team gathered around, each placing their hand into the middle of the circle.

"Hart on three," Cheryl said. "One two three-"

"Hart!" they all yelled at the top of their lungs, not caring who they woke up. Ariel pulled her headlamp over her head and clicked it on, stepping into the throng of people making their way towards the starting line. An excited energy buzzed through the air, everyone moving about restlessly. With only five minutes until the gun went off, Ariel made her way towards the front of the pack. She wove between several men and found another woman to stand beside. She looked to be in her mid-forties, her eyes glued to her watch face as she shifted her weight nervously from foot to foot. Ariel lined up right behind the elites, doing her best to keep her own nerves under control.

"Go out quick enough to beat the bottle neck—" she thought to herself, going over the race strategy in her head. "Then settle into pace. The race doesn't really start until mile sixty."

"Runners, are you ready?" the announcer boomed.

The crowd cheered before settling into a hushed lull, but the excitement electrified the air.

"Five, four, three, two, one, Go! Go! Go!" The announcer yelled through his megaphone as he fired the starting gun overhead. The crowd surged forward, off into the night. This was it. Ariel had just begun the biggest adventure of her life.

Chapter 33

The sky was fading from blue to sherbet. "Okay, here we go," Ariel mumbled under her breath, steeling her nerves against the setting sun. This was the hardest part of the race, and she was ready for it. All she had to do was keep her mindset right, run smart, and keep eating. Her body would take care of the rest as long as she stayed out of her own way.

The orange hues painting the sky contrasted against the cold blue mountains, now casting long shadows over the barren trail, giving the illusion of shade. It was silent above the tree line, no birds in sight. The only animals she'd seen since rising above the tree line were marmots, which provided a cute distraction from the ever-present ache in her legs. The ache wasn't painful, so Ariel knew it was nothing to worry about. Instead, she focused on the changing shades of sky: orange, yellow, to red, to purple and navy once the sun sunk below the horizon beyond the mountains. There were a few headlamps bobbing in the dark up ahead of her. It was comforting to know she wasn't truly alone out here, even if the only other people around were the ones she was trying to beat. She knew the next aid station was coming up and her friends would be there eager to greet her. They might be tired, but they'd be eager.

The crunch of gravel beneath her shoes was her symphony, breaking up the silence that engulfed the air around her. To the best of her knowledge, there were four runners in front of her with forty-four miles to go. Four had never been her lucky number, but in that moment, she decided it was going to be.

Four runners, forty-four miles left. She could do it. Her legs were tired, but she felt great. She imagined herself sitting on the porch at home, her finisher's belt buckle displayed on the table beside her as she sipped her tea and watched this same sun set. She imagined the smile she'd have, the utter feeling of completeness and wholeness as she reveled in her home that she literally had run a hundred miles to keep.

"Woop, shit," she said out loud, an ill placed rock bringing her back to the present moment. "Don't do that again." She smiled and shook off the almost disastrous incident. Out here, it only took one wrong step and the race was over. The last thing she wanted was to get within the last few miles of the race only to have an injury take her out. A glance at her watch told her she had five more miles until the aid station. Five more miles until she got to pick up her first pacer.

* * *

The glorious beeping of car horns sounded in the near distance. Almost there. God it had been a hard five miles. She went from feeling on top of the world, to crying and wanting to lie down on the ground and sleep. Every runner she talked to said this is what happened at this point in the race, and she was exactly where she was supposed to be. It didn't mean she liked it though.

As soon as she rounded the corner, she spotted her crew. Wide awake, Shelby and Erin were waving their arms above their heads. Ariel couldn't help but laugh when she saw Coach Bobbi standing on the end of the tailgate waving glow sticks around and hollering at the top of her lungs. "Here she comes!"

Ariel stumbled into camp, Shelby catching her with a chair before she collapsed. "Guys, I'm so tired."

"Obviously," Bobbi said, jumping down from the tailgate, Gatorade in hand. "You've run sixty-one miles. Drink this."

"I don't think—"

"Nah uh, we don't think here. We're just doing now," Shelby said, squatting down in front of her. "No thinking, just doing. Are you hurt?"

Ariel shook her head.

"Are you so tired you can't put one foot in front of the other."

After a pause, Ariel shook her head.

"Damn straight," Shelby said, patting her leg. "What do you wanna eat? PB&J? Pizza?"

"Mac and cheese," Ariel said without hesitation.

"Mac and cheese it is!"

Cheryl had anticipated Ariel's request and already had a packet of easy mac mixed with tofu ready to go. The warm cup felt like heaven in Ariel's cold hands. She was damp with sweat, the night chill creeping into her bones now that she'd come to a standstill. Erin draped a space blanket around her shoulders, trapping in what warmth she had.

"Thirty-nine miles to go," Bobbi said, sitting next to her on the ground. "You've done training runs longer than that. Only four people in front of you. The third-place runner is only about fifteen minutes ahead of you. And second place didn't leave but ten minutes before her. You're still well within this race."

Ariel nodded, her mouth full of cheesy noodles. "Who's in first?"

"Zach Mc'Daniel."

"The guy who won UTMB last year?" Ariel commented, eyes wide. "Great."

"Don't think about him yet. There's a lot of race to go," Bobbi said.

"How're you doing mentally?" Shelby asked, kneeling in front of her.

"I'm okay," Ariel lied. "Just tired."

"No mental break downs yet?"

"Nope." Ariel figured it couldn't hurt to fake it until she made it. After all, that's the exact phrase more than one coach had told her and countless other athletes. "Tired and exhausted, can't wait to be done."

"That's the spirit! Just thinking about how badly you want to be done, put one foot in front of the other, and that'll get you there." Aunt Erin encouraged as she repacked Ariel's water bottles.

"Thanks, for the sage words of wisdom." Ariel rolled her eyes. She knew Erin was trying to be helpful, but her incessant bright energy was a little grating considering she was coming up on twenty-four hours of no sleep. She figured she'd be forgiven for not being her typical bright and bubbly self. "How're you guys doing?"

"We're great, it's a lot of fun, actually." Shelby said. "It's like a camp out where we have to keep tracking down one of our drunk friends. But that drunk friend knows what she's doing and is about to win half a million dollars, so this is way cooler."

"You still might find me vomiting in a bush somewhere," Ariel said.

"Have you been throwing up?" Bobbi asked, wide-eyed.

"Only once and that was a while ago. I've been great ever since. Pretty sure it was the Mountain Dew I picked up at one of the aid stations."

"I told you, if you didn't train with it, don't race with it," Bobbi laughed, but her face was stern. "I'm glad that's the only thing that's given you trouble. At the last aid station, we saw a runner drop because of GI issues. I felt so bad. You could smell him from three cars over."

"Ohmigod, that's awful," Ariel said, scrapping the last bits of mac and cheese off the sides of the bowl. "

"Now, we gotta move, girly," Coach Bobbi said, tapping the back of the chair.

Ariel knew Coach was right, but the last thing she wanted to do in that moment was stand up and keep going. How good would it feel to just lay down in the back of the sedan, her belly full, and finally get to close her eyes.

"Not as good as it will feel when you cross that finish line, that's for sure," a familiar voice said. The hair on the back of Ariel's neck stood up. She glanced around, knowing she'd never find her dad standing there but knowing nonetheless she'd heard his voice clear as day. He'd always had a knack for saying the exact right thing when she wanted to quit and it seems he hadn't lost that quality in the afterlife.

"Ari, you good?" Sam asked, raising an eyebrow. "What are you looking for?"

"Nothing." She handed the empty bowl to Erin and stood up, giving Sam a hug so she wouldn't see the tears threatening to fall. "Thanks gals. One more, and then we're home free."

"Hell yeah we are! You've got this. Eyes on the prize. You got enough water in your pack?" Coach asked, going through the checklist.

"Mm-hmm."

"You have gels?" Cheryl asked.

Ariel patted the front of her running vest and her shorts pockets. "No, good God! Good catch," Ariel said, her heart nearly skipping a beat. Those gels were the only thing keeping her going mile to mile. With it being so dark, the scenery wasn't a distraction anymore, so she'd been using the cherry-flavored gels not only as fuel to physically keep her going but as mental candy to keep her moving along and feeling like she got somewhere.

Mom ducked behind the back seat of the car and dug through a bag until she found the gels. "How many are you taking?"

"Gimme… ten, I don't know," Ariel said, grabbing a handful and counting them out.

"I wasn't asking you," Cheryl said, reemerging with a handful of colorful packets. "I was thinking out loud. You're taking these." She started tucking the gels away in Ariel's vest pockets, leaving the last one in her daughter's hand.

"Okay. Now I'm ready to go," Ariel said, nodding firmly. "What would I do without y'all?"

"You wouldn't be here right now, that's for sure," Shelby laughed, bouncing in place to warm up her calves. "Between almost forgetting your gels, to nearly forgetting socks, you would've been in a lot of pain after mile thirty."

"Thanks y'all, love you and see you soon!" Ariel said. "Bobbi, you ready?"

"Sure am," she said, grinning. She looked fresh— clean running gear, a spotless pack filled with all her fluids and nutrition. "I've been ready to go for hours!" They jogged out of sight as the crew cheered them on. The light from the aid station faded, the darkness of the forest at night enveloping them in the small bubbles of their headlamps. Bobbi suddenly jumped up and clicked her heels together. "Hell yeah! We're doing the thing!"

"Yeah, this is the energy I'm gonna need," Ariel laughed. "I'm okay at the moment, but I know I won't be forever."

"That's not for you to worry about right now," Bobbi said, clapping her on the back. "We're just here to run and have fun. I think this will be the first time we've ever raced together."

"How crazy is that?"

"It's kind of surreal. I still remember you as a freshman who had no idea how to pace herself."

"Ha! Ain't that the truth," Ariel laughed, remembering.

"I'll never forget your first meet where you went out guns a-blazing—"

"And then I crashed and burned so hard I came in second to last?"

"That's the one," Bobbi laughed.

"Thank God you've taught me well," Ariel said. "Because that's not happening today."

"Damn straight it's not," Bobbi said. She opened her phone and checked the tracker, not breaking stride. "Well would you look at that, we've got—"

Suddenly, Ariel heard the familiar crunch-crunch of someone's shoes on gravel. They'd only just left the aid station. But a glance at her watch informed her they were already three miles in. "Shit, I haven't eaten anything since leaving."

"That's my bad," Bobbi said, her head snapping to attention. "Gel. Now."

Ariel was already on it, tearing the top off the mango flavored one with her teeth. She ate the whole thing as fast as she could, choking down the gloopy texture. "Done."

"God, I'm failing at this," Bobbi laughed. "I was excited we already caught someone!"

Ariel kicked herself for zoning out so well she'd missed her fueling marks. But on the other hand, she was grateful to have zoned out for those three miles. It was like falling asleep on a long road trip to suddenly wake up and miraculously find you've arrived. The crunch-crunch of the shoes didn't go away and as soon as they rounded a slight bend in the trail, they spotted a headlamp not too far ahead on the trail.

"Wanna go get him?" Bobbi egged her on.

"That's what I came here to do," Ariel said. Without another word, they steadily continued forward, their pace inching faster.

"Try to sip on another gel to make up for the calories we missed out on," Bobbi instructed.

"Okay." Ariel took out another packet and slowly took a sip.

It wasn't long until they were on the heels of the runner and his pacer.

"Hey, Ben," Bobbi said as they came up on the heels of his pacer.

"Ben Staple? Holy shit. Professional ultrarunner, I didn't think I'd gain on him this early." Ariel thought to herself.

His pacer looked over his shoulder. "You scared me," he laughed, not breaking stride. Ben didn't turn to look behind him, but kept on trudging along, head down.

"Hey, it's you. You're the teenager everyone's been talking about," his pacer noticed.

"Surprise," Ariel smiled. "And I'm a legal adult, thank you." It never got old having the professionals and adults surprised by her presence. Especially now. Now, no one could say she didn't have what it takes. She was in the end stretch of this massive race, and she was in the top of the pack. And she was about to overtake one of the best men's ultrarunners in the world. "Bet you didn't expect to see me here."

He shrugged. "I didn't not think I'd see you here. I'm not one of your naysayers."

"I didn't think you were."

"I wish I would've had your dedication at your age. I was more focused on partying and having fun than getting serious about being a runner. I admire your grit."

"Thanks, it makes me not popular."

"I wasn't even popular. There are no rules of what'll make you popular, and you usually aren't happy if you follow them. In all my years, I've only met one person who was popular in high school who deserved to be."

"Wow, sounds like you might be a bit jealous," Ariel teased, knowing full well a very similar popular girl at school.

"She's my wife, actually," he smiled. "Like I said, she deserved every bit of it."

They fell silent for a moment, continuing along the single track. Ariel knew Bobbi was just waiting for an opportunity to pass. For a moment, Ariel had forgotten that they were competitors. That was the beauty of running, the people made the sport everything that it was. But this was still a race, and there could only be one winner. And Ariel wasn't about to let her friendliness cost her everything. She noticed the pace increasing: Ben was trying to drop her.

"Not today, buddy," Ariel thought to herself.

"You ready to go? It's gonna open up right here," Bobbi said in a low tone.

"You know it," she said, her eyes laser focused on the terrain in front of her. As if on cue, the trail widened into a double track.

"On your left," Bobbi announced, edging ahead of the pacer.

Ariel took a big breath through her nose, inhaling the sharp mountain air and pushed her legs harder. She kept her eyes to the ground in front of her. As she pulled up next to him, she could tell Ben was pushing to match her. She should've known he wouldn't give up so easily. But one quick glance at her watch told her that this was the perfect time to push her pace up to the next notch and she could hold it, especially with the support of Bobbi.

The next few miles the two kept pace, suffering in silence as they each tried to gain on the other.

"Eat!" Bobbi called back to her. Ariel did as instructed, taking this gel more slowly as her stomach was starting to slosh a bit. Bobbi glanced back at her, eyebrows raised.

"Let's go," Ariel mouthed to her.

Bobbi nodded and the pace picked up again. Ariel willed herself to pick it up a few more notches. She was done running with him.

"Good luck out there," Ben said, suddenly breaking his silence.

"Thanks, you too," Ariel replied. "I'll see you there."

With a final nod, Ariel slowly pulled ahead, leaving Ben behind. The darkness was empty, but the sky clear. In between the dark outlines of the trees, the night sky shone through with an inky blue dotted with bright pinpricks of stars. The moon was off to the left, a milky crescent in the sky not offering much light but looking beautiful, nonetheless. An owl hooted off in the distance, completing the midnight ambiance.

The world was simple out here. All the animals in the woods were doing the same, and so were the plants. Something about being part of the natural rhythm of nature was soothing and made the rest of the world's problems melt away. Out here, there was no concern about starting college or picking up a second job just to make ends meet and put food on the table. There was still grief, that tightness around her heart, but it somehow felt lighter, more natural. There was no worry about elections, wars, gas prices, family dynamics, college futures, running contracts, or anything else. Out here, the only things that mattered were staying warm, staying full, and staying connected.

But she did have to worry about puking. Despite her best efforts at sipping the gel, her stomach churned.

"Hey, the gels aren't gelling anymore," Ariel said.

Bobbi slowed a few steps to run next to her. She held out a piece of pancake. "Try this."

Ariel took it and smelled it. When the smell didn't immediately put her off, she took a bite and held it in her mouth until it dissolved. When she eventually swallowed, she waited with bated breath to see what her stomach would say.

"Hey, stop focusing on it," Bobbi instructed. "That's going to make it worse."

"Distract me then," Ariel said, curt.

"What's the next hundred miler you want to run?"

"Really? That's your distraction? Asking me what hundred miler I want to run when I'm at mile eighty-five of the current hundred miler?"

"Yeah, bad question. Forget I asked. If you had half a million dollars what would you do with it?"

"Buy my house." Her stomach was tightening. She tried to focus on her breathing, sending the breath to her stomach to help it relax.

"Well duh, but what else? That house isn't half a million dollars."

"Pay for college."

"Ugh you're such an adult," Bobbi laughed. "If you were to spend it on something fun, what would you buy?"

A painful cramp wracked her stomach, a wave of nausea threatening to eject the bite of pancake. "Honestly, I'd invest half of it in index funds. Then use whatever I needed to travel Europe for a year."

"Index funds? Investing? Where did you learn that?! I know for a fact Mr. Montgomery doesn't teach that in his business class."

"I needed something to keep me entertained while I ran countless miles on asphalt surrounded by cornfields, so I listened to podcasts. Tori Dunlap taught me everything I needed to know to be an uncontrollable woman, aka be great with my money." Ariel explained.

"How does being an uncontrollable woman make you rich?" Coach asked, skeptical.

"Other way around. Having money makes you an uncontrollable woman," Ariel laughed. "Money is power and I want to be able to do what I want with my life."

"So how do you get rich? Get lucky in the stock market?"

"Not really, a lot of the financial dude bros you hear about make it sound that way. But it's way simpler than that. You take your income, invest as much of it as you can in index funds via your retirement and brokerage accounts, and let it grow. Your money makes more money while you have fun and live your best life!"

"But you'll lose all of it if the stock market crashes, won't you?" Bobbi asked, genuinely curious.

"I thought adults knew all this stuff," Ariel said, shocked. Her stomach sloshed uncomfortably.

"No one taught me," Bobbi said.

"I'll send you her podcast then. She'll teach you all you need to know about the stock market. And there's this other podcast I love called The Frugal Friends. They talk about spending as a skill and it's not bad to spend money."

"Now that's a new take."

"Right?! You just have to spend on what you value, not what other people think you should value. Like me. I value running and the prize money, so spending five hundred bucks on this race is worth it where other people would think I'm crazy."

"Girl you are crazy," Bobbi laughed. "We're running a hundred miles, talking about investing. Who even are we?"

"Who knows," Ariel laughed. "Tiredness makes you do funny things." Suddenly her stomach had had enough of being ignored and the nausea overwhelmed her. She skidded to a stop and vomited on the side of the trail.

"Where did that come from?" Bobbi asked, holding her braid out of the way as she puked.

When the retching stopped, Ariel straightened up and kept walking down the trail. "Who knows. I've been feeling nauseated, but that came out of nowhere."

Without a word, Coach whipped out a packet of peppermint candies. "Put one of these in your mouth. Don't chew it, just suck on it. Can you keep running?"

Ariel unwrapped one of the candies and plopped it in her mouth, tucking it into her cheek. She nodded.

"Then let's keep trekking," Bobbi said firmly. "We're not that far behind first place woman, only two behind first place man."

Ariel took a deep breath to steady herself, the vomiting session had left her a bit shaky. She did not come this far, run this many miles, get this many blisters, lose this many hours of sleep just for her to lose it all because her stomach decided to act up.

"Let's do it."

Chapter 34

"Right this way, ladies," Sam said, leading the way to their crew sight. Ariel speed walked behind Sam, desperate to get off her feet.

"Sit." Bobbi ordered. Ariel obliged, more falling into the chair than sitting in it. Her eyes were glassy.

"We need a change of shirt and a smoothie," Bobbi said. "Ari, a smoothie still sound good?"

Ariel nodded wordlessly. She leaned forward in the chair, resting her elbows on her knees, her head in her hands. "Trash can."

Bobbi swiftly scooted the small trash can underneath Ariel's tripod stance with her foot. Just in time too as Ariel threw up what little bile was left.

Mom and Sam exchanged wide eyed glances. "How long has this been going on?" Cheryl asked Bobbi.

"Almost since we last saw you guys," Bobbi said, shaking her head. "We've tried everything, but her stomach just says no."

"Any water? Electrolytes in?"

Bobbi shook her head slowly. "We've gotten four peppermint candies in."

"Woof," Cheryl said, hands on her hips. After a brief pause, she jumped into action. She pulled out a smoothie she had premade and added a watermelon chunk with salt on top. Kneeling in front of her daughter, she placed a hand on her knee.

"Honey, look at me."

Ariel looked up with tired eyes. "I'm so tired, Mom."

"I know you are. It's okay that you're tired. Drink this." She positioned the straw so she could sip on it. Ariel took a small sip and stopped.

"My stomach, I've literally been throwing up while I run. Like, take a step, puke, take another step, puke."

"That sounds miserable," Cheryl agreed. "But you're still going, aren't you?"

"Yeah, but—"

"No buts. Just drink this. It'll help, I promise."

Ariel made a face. The idea of putting more in her stomach just so it could be thrown up again was almost as bad as the throwing up itself.

"Drink. This is what you'd always have when you were sick."

Begrudgingly, Ariel obliged and took a sip. Suddenly, memories of laying on the couch watching weird day time TV flooded her brain.

"Why does this drink make me think of teenage girls named Heather murdering each other?" Ariel asked, laughing. "What did you put in this, Mom?"

Cheryl burst out laughing. "Oh honey. Remember that week you had mono and you couldn't get off the couch? We watched the movie Heathers and you probably drank 4 of those smoothies in a day."

Ariel held out the cup in front of her, as if studying the drink would make her understand. "You know how they say taste the rainbow? It's really more like taste the memories, huh?"

"Taste the memories sounds like a Fallout Boy Song," Sam laughed as she massaged her sister's shoulders.

"We should write them and tell them we've got a great new hit for their next album," Ariel chuckled. "God where is my brain."

"Any hallucinations yet?" Aunt Erin asked, kneeling in front of her.

"I guess not if my memory of the teen girl murders is real," Ariel shrugged. "I'll keep you posted." Ariel continued to slowly sip the drink as Shelby and Bobbi worked on her feet. She was grateful for the fire and the space blanket someone had wrapped around her shoulders as the cold mountain air was quick to set a chill.

"What's the update on our place?" Bobbi asked, leaning over to whisper in Mom's ear. "My tracker hasn't updated in ages."

"Three people have already been through. First place woman left here about twenty minutes ago." Cheryl said. "She's not that far ahead and she wasn't moving great. Is your tracker updating, Sam?"

"No, the service here sucks," Sam said, reappearing and standing next to Coach. "The only way we know is because I keep bugging the ham radio guys, they're a cranky bunch."

"Ha, probably because you keep bugging them," Cheryl said.

"Well, if their equipment worked and their trackers did what they said they'd be doing, I wouldn't have to bug them. Not my fault their equipment sucks." Sam craned her head to see how much of the smoothie Ariel had managed to finish. "Girl, don't chug that whole thing. It's gonna come right back up."

"But it feels good on my throat," Ariel said, her voice hoarse with trail dust.

"I know, but vomit won't," Sam said, easing the cup out of her hand. "Let's take a break for a second. Ready to change your shirt?"

"Ready Freddy," Ariel said. "You're helping, right?"

"Of course," Sam said. "Tent, ladies!"

A well-practiced team, Cheryl and Bobbi held the towel tent in place as Sam helped Ariel change her shirt and sports bra in a matter of minutes. A timer beeped on Cheryl's watch.

"Time to go, ladies!" she said, folding up the towel. "Take that smoothie to go."

"It hasn't been ten minutes," Ariel insisted.

"Yes it has. And that's three more minutes than we'd planned for."

"I don't know—" Ariel started to plead.

"Yes you do know," Cheryl said, her voice sterner than Ariel had ever heard it. "You're going to finish this race, and you're going to kick ass. You've got two people to catch. Go get them."

"But my stomach—" Ariel said, her eyes welling with tears as her upper lip trembled.

"You haven't thrown up in 10 minutes, that's improvement! You have calories on board, electrolytes on board, and guess what?"

"What?"

"You've already proven to yourself you can run and throw up at the same time," Cheryl laughed.

Ariel smirked halfheartedly. Mom took Ariel's head in her hands, resting her forehead on her daughter's. "You can and you will. Say it."

"I can and I will."

"That's my girl." She kissed her forehead and pushed her forward. "No, go catch first place woman. She's only twenty or twenty-five minutes ahead of you."

"Mom!" Ariel exclaimed, eyes wide as saucers. "Why didn't you lead with that?!" She stood up so fast she knocked the camping chair over. "Shelby, we gotta go!"

"We're goin'!" Shelby laughed, shoving a few last-minute things into her own running vest pockets.

"You got her, Shelby?" Coach Bobbi asked. Part of her wanted to keep pacing, but the other part understood she needed a pacer with fresher legs for the last leg.

"She's in good hands, Coach. You've taught me well," Shelby assured her. "Let's go, go, go!" Shelby shooed Ariel back towards the trail.

"We'll see you at the finish line!" Ariel waved. The crew cheered.

"Ohmigod, I'm so nervous," Sam said, biting her nails as Ariel and Shelby disappeared into the night.

"Me too," Coach Bobbi said, vibrating with nervous energy.

"Number sixty-two, checking out," Shelby called to the aid station captain who marked her down.

"Let's finish this thing. You wanna go win half a million dollars?" Shelby asked, her voice full of excitement.

"Hell yeah I do," Ariel said. She didn't feel great, but between the smoothie and her Mom's kind words, she was energized. Only eleven miles left to go. She could run eleven miles in her sleep.

"Keep sipping that smoothie if your stomach is liking it," Shelby reminded her.

"Okay, Coach," Ariel teased, rolling her eyes. "I've never seen you like this."

"Coach made me promise to take the job seriously, so here I am," Shelby said. "You get the rare Serious Shelby."

"You'd be a good Coach yourself, some day," Ariel laughed.

"Well pretend today's that day, cuz I'm here to make sure you get to that finish line come hell or high water."

"Mhmm," Ariel said, amused to see this new side of her best friend. "Has your tracker updated?"

Shelby looked at her phone and by some miracle, it had updated five minutes ago. "First place woman is only two miles out. She's stopped."

Ariel finished the smoothie and handed off the silicone bottle to Shelby who tucked it into her pack. "Let's do it." Heads down, Shelby and Ariel picked up the pace and steadily made their way down the trail, the only sound between them their footsteps on the soft ground.

"How's your stomach?" Shelby asked after a while.

"I don't want to jinx it," Ariel called back to her. "Just take the lack of throwing-up sounds to be a good thing."

Shelby chuckled. She checked her tracker again and what she saw made her heart jump. She looked up, her head on a swivel.

"Holy shi—" Ariel yelled, leaping to the side of the trail as if something had bitten her ankle. "Sorry, you startled me."

Ariel and Shelby stopped in the middle of the trail. Along the side, a runner was perched on top of a rock, head between her knees while her pacer rubbed her back. It was the woman currently in first place.

"Are you okay?" Ariel asked, crouching down to look her in the eye.

She nodded silently. Ariel stood back up and addressed the pacer. "Hi, I'm Ariel."

"Melissa," the woman said curtly.

"Can we do anything to help you guys? Salt tabs? Leukotape? Pickles?"

"No, we've got everything we need. I think we just need a few minutes."

"Okay," Ariel said. "Good luck."

"Thanks," Melissa said, barely audible.

Ariel looked at Shelby who shrugged and nodded her head in the direction of the trail. Ariel turned and picked her pace back up. Taking over first place woman didn't feel like she thought it would. She was elated to be leading the pack of women, but her heart ached for the woman she'd passed. The race hadn't gone her way and that sucked. Ariel knew that feeling too.

As if she could read her mind, Shelby spoke up. "It's okay, we passed her when she was in a low moment. You did the right thing, you offered help and kept going. Very classy sportswoman of you."

"Thanks," Ariel said. "That was me less than an hour ago, and now I'm feeling great. That smoothie was magic."

"And that's how it goes in these ultras. They really show how time changes everything."

The two ran in silence for a while. Ariel focused on the small spot of trail she could see with her headlamp. The crunching of gravel and the chirping of crickets were the perfect running cadence metronome.

"Turn off your head lamp," Shelby suddenly said.

"What? But it's dark! I can't see," Ariel said, confused.

"Just do it. We'll hike for a second while our eyes adjust."

Ariel did as she was told and turned off the lamp. At first, everything was so dark she couldn't see her hand in front of her face. But slowly her eyes adjusted, and the bright light of the full moon ahead illuminated the path ahead just fine.

"This section is smooth and open. This way he won't see us coming," Shelby said, picking up her run again with Ariel falling in behind. Her feet burned and one knee ached, but nothing bad enough to stop her.

"That's a genius idea, actually," Ariel said. "How did you think of it?"

"I was reading a lot of blogs and a lot of runners do it."

"You studied for this?" Ariel was touched by her friend's dedication. "I feel so loved."

"Because you are, dummy. Now shush, we aren't going to be much surprise if they can hear us coming."

The two continued on, Shelby constantly searching the hillside for a sign of the second-place runner. "Looks like they may have turned off their headlamps too."

"That's okay, we'll just scare the crap out of each other when we come up on them," Ariel laughed.

"Holy—well that was good timing," Shelby laughed up ahead. "Hey Todd."

"Where the hell did you two come from?" Todd, the pacer, asked, whipping his head around.

"Behind you," Shelby shrugged. She pulled alongside him. His runner Scott was only a few steps ahead, he looked over his shoulder and smiled.

"Hey," Scott said.

"Hey, Scott," Ariel called back. She wanted him to know it was her. "We're passing on your left."

Silence from him, but his pacer nodded a thanks. Shelby led the way. As Ariel passed Scott, he looked at her and they made eye contact. A look of surprise flickered in his eyes.

"You're the girl I saw running up on the mountain."

"It's me." Ariel winked.

Scott shook his head but didn't say another word. His arrogance fueled her, lightening the weight that had settled in her legs. "Good luck." He didn't acknowledge her again and she pulled away, following Shelby into the night. She was booking it, and they quickly lost sight of Scott and Todd.

"Second place overall, baby," Shelby cheered once they were out of ear shot. "And first is only two miles ahead."

"That's farther than I'd like…"

"You've got nine miles to catch him," Shelby said. "He's hurting. You're hurting. Everyone is hurting at this point. He's moving slow on the tracker. We're faster."

"No way, you're kidding me."

"Nope," Shelby shook her head. "We're way faster."

A smile spread across Ariel's face, a tingle through her shoulders and down her back. "I'm faster. I'm faster! Let's go!" Ariel dashed ahead of Shelby, arms held out to the side like an airplane. "Am I supposed to be having this much fun right now?"

Shelby laughed, wide eyed. "This is that runner's high you never got running cross country."

"Well damn, guess it only takes me 90 miles to find it," she laughed.

Suddenly, her stomach lurched, and the smoothie came back up. Ariel kept running, turning her head to the side of the trail as best she could—"Well shit."

Shelby pulled up next to her. "Just breathe. How do you feel after that?"

Ariel did a quick inventory. "Actually, I feel a little better now."

"Okay, good. Let's try to keep it at just one," Shelby said. "Take a deep breath, we've got this."

Unfortunately, it was not a one and done situation. Ariel dry heaved frequently, and her pace slowed.

"Ugh, Shelby. Why?!" she cried between heaves.

"Because a hundred miles and altitude, that's why," Shelby said, her voice sympathetic. "But you've got this. Throwing up ain't nothing!"

Ariel did her best to keep up her pace, but each time she had to throw up on the side of the trail, she slowed. "Are we falling behind?" she asked, straightening up as she wiped her mouth with the back of her sleeve.

"No. You're throwing up constantly and you're still faster than him. You're a beast."

"Imma beast," Ariel repeated, her voice monotone. "Come against me that's a no no, yo, cause imma beast!"

"What the hell are you singing?" Shelby laughed, glancing over her shoulder to make sure her friend wasn't losing her marbles.

"The Tech9 song! The Beast!" Ariel exclaimed. "You can't tell me you've never heard Sam blasting that at a pool party before."

"I try to tune out her rap music," Shelby laughed.

"Same, but that one's kinda catchy."

They kept running down the trail, Ariel humming the tune to herself, too out of breath to sing anymore. The soft flat trail turned into a gentle up hill, almost like salt in the wound.

"There he is!" Shelby whisper shouted to Ariel. She grabbed her arm and pointed ahead at the crest of the hill where a hunched figure was slowly ascending. "He's right there. And he looks awful. You can get him."

"I can and I will. I can and I will. I can and I WILL!" Ariel yelled. She dug deep, searching for the last bit of strength her body had. This was it. This is the moment she'd been working towards the past year. All the four am wake up calls, carb counting, late night sessions at the track, countless hours of race planning, it all came down to this.

The hill felt like a mountain as she climbed it, Shelby running on her heels cheering her on. She crested the hill and below was the beautiful, sleepy town. But despite it being the wee hours of the morning, it wasn't sleepy at all. There, in the middle of the town, was the finish line adorned in flood lights, colorful signs, and a surprising number of dedicated fans. A mile to go. This was her specialty.

"Run it like it's state!" Shelby yelled from behind. "It's state and and you've gotta catch that bitch Danielle who stole your title from you! You can and you will. Go, go, go!"

Ariel glanced at her palm, the little white scar from her stitches burning with the memory from that disaster so many months earlier. She pulled ahead, leaving Shelby behind as gravity pulled her down the hill. She closed the gap between her and the first-place runner until she was on his heels. The crowd saw them coming and the cheering turned deafening. She ran beside him, head down and focused. She felt him look at her and pick up his pace. It was going to be a dead sprint to the finish.

As they turned onto the main street, Ariel took the inner corner, gaining a bit of ground. She couldn't let up now. She pushed harder than she'd ever pushed before. Her arms pumped, her chest leaned forward. Her stomach cramped and she felt the heaves come but she didn't break stride. The crowd suddenly sounded far away, the cowbells as if they were off in the distance. Her vision narrowed.

"Focus, focus, focus," she thought. She zeroed in on the "F" of the finish line banner and set her sights on that, the rest of her vision blurring. The last person she'd been chasing, Zach, was by her side, on her heels. And then he was gone. Suddenly, the "f" of the finish line banner disappeared, too. Stumbling to a stop and falling to her knees, she felt something draped around her waist. She looked down to touch it and it felt smooth. Her vision was so burry she could only make out colors, but she instantly recognized the black and gold script of the finish line banner.

She glanced around for a race official. "Did I win?" she asked the closest person to her.

"It was a photo finish, my dear," he said, squatting down to eye level. She couldn't make out his face, but he had a beard and wore a black beanie. "But I do believe you did."

"I won?"

"I think so," he repeated, "but they're confirming right now. Here, take this while you wait." He handed her a cold metal object: the finisher's belt buckle.

Tears welled in her eyes. "Thank you." She sat back on her heels, too exhausted to stand. "Can you tell my crew I'm here?"

The man chuckled a hearty belly laugh. "They know good and well you're here. Let's get you up and to them." He helped her to her feet and slung one of her arms over his shoulders as he escorted her to the side of the finishing line where her entire crew was eagerly waiting. She hadn't noticed until now the roar of the crowd.

"Hold on," Ariel said, suddenly feeling the urge to throw up. She turned her head away from the crowd as best she could. After a few moments, the feeling subsided. "Well, guess that was a false alarm."

"You good?" a familiar voice asked from behind. "I've got this, thank you sir."

Ariel turned around to see Coach relieve the kind volunteer of his duties of holding her up. "I'm good, I think. He couldn't tell me if I'd won."

"It was a photo finish, girly," Shelby squealed, appearing at her side. "Most exciting thing I've ever seen in my life! My heart is about to burst! They're reviewing the photographer's pictures to confirm before they make an official call."

"I don't think there's ever been a photo finish that needed review in the history of hundred milers," Coach Bobbi laughed.

"Congratulations," Zach said from behind her. Ariel turned around to face him. Her vision was slowly returning, but the edges were still a bit blurred. Thankfully, he was hard to miss in his bright yellow running kit.

"Hey, thank you," Ariel said, extending a hand. "You gave me a run for my money."

"You did the same for me," he said, laughing as he shook her hand. "I knew you'd been hot on my heels for a while. It's what kept me moving."

Ariel smiled. "I'm honored."

"Go sit down and enjoy your victory," Zach said. "We'll catch up more in a bit. I'm gonna go throw up and take a nap."

Ariel laughed out loud. "Same."

"Are you nauseated again?" Sam asked, jumping in front of her twin's face with a green barf bag in her hands.

"No, I feel amazing!" Ariel playfully flipped her braid over her shoulder. "Shockingly."

The group giggled, giddy with the adrenaline of her heart pumping finish. Suddenly, the announcer's microphone crackled to life.

"Ladies and gentlemen, I have an update for you all." A hush fell over the crowd. Ariel held her breath. "After reviewing all finish line photographs, we can confirm that your overall winner of the Leadville 100-mile run is Ariel Hart. History has been made today. Not only is she the first woman to win the race overall, she's the youngest ever winner. Our first male winner is Zach Gavin who ran a hell of a race. Stay tuned for your awards ceremony Sunday at noon. Let's applaud our champions!"

As the crowd erupted into a chorus of applause and cheers, Ariel fell to her knees in tears.

She'd won.

Chapter 35

Later that night, Ariel lay wide awake in the hotel bed. Despite her eyes burning with exhaustion, her body wouldn't let her sleep. She tossed and turned, trying to relieve the deep ache in all of her muscles. Hunger pains would strike followed by waves of nausea. She glanced over at the clock. Three thirty in the morning. She'd been at this for hours. Frustrated, she got out of bed and padded across the floor, careful not to wake Sam or Shelby. She grabbed her new finisher's hoodie off the coat rack, slipped on her sliders, and quietly opened the door.

The brisk night air was refreshing, easing the exhaustion just slightly.

"Wow…." She craned her neck up to see the sky. The entire town was dark, allowing the inky black show off the millions of stars sprinkled overhead. It was more than she'd ever seen. Ariel walked across the gravel to the small garden area in the middle of the courtyard where she scoped out a bench. She sat, laid back, and stared into the sky.

What a journey the past year had been. Now that the race was done, she wasn't quite sure what to think. It still didn't feel real, that she'd run the race or that she'd actually won the whole thing. Though every ache in her muscles told her, yes, we did indeed run one hundred miles.

"I wonder what Kyle's doing right now?" she thought to herself. She pulled out her phone and dialed the number she'd dialed a million times before.

"Hello?" a groggy voice answered on the other side of the line.

The sound of his sleepy voice made her heart lurch. "I won."

Silence.

"That's amazing," Kyle said, the sleep fading from his voice ever so slightly. "I was rooting for you."

Ariel squinted her eyes but stayed silent.

"Ari?"

"Yeah?"

"For what it's worth, I'm sorry for what I said at prom."

Finally. He finally said those two little words she'd been desperate to hear all this time. Tears pricked at the edges of her eyes.

"I always knew you could do it," he continued.

"Then why did you say it? And why did you try to convince me this wasn't important?" Ariel asked, leaning forward so her elbows rested on her knees.

"I dunno, because I like you and I wanted to spend more time with you," Kyle said. "You were always busy running and training."

"I made the time when I could, Kyle," Ariel said, a little confused. They'd seen each other at school every day, half the days they'd hung out afterwards doing schoolwork, she'd gone to prom with him, and they'd gotten together throughout the month at the ice cream shop. "What more did you want?"

"More time, I guess," Kyle said. "I wanted to spend every hour of every weekend together. And now that your race is over, we can."

"What happens when I want to spend a day with Sam and Shelby, instead? Or when I have a big cross country meet for school? Or when I'm cramming for a huge final at CSU? My life isn't going to slow down, Kyle."

"I understand school," Kyle said, his tone tense. "And you can still hangout with your friends, just—"

"Just what?" Ariel asked, a hot flash of anger coursing through her veins. This is not how she thought this conversation would go. "Just when you're okay with it?"

"No, that's not what I meant."

"Then what do you mean? Because that's what I'm hearing right now."

Kyle was silent, the only sound a heavy sigh. "I don't know. I don't know how to explain to you that all I want to do is spend time with you. All my time."

"Kyle, I like you, a lot. I've missed you these past few months," Ariel admitted. "But I'm not going to give up my whole life for you. I have a lot I want to do, and I'm just getting started."

"I guess that's that then," he said curtly.

"Goodbye, Kyle," Ariel said. "See you around."

"See ya." He hung up before she could.

Ariel stared at the dark phone in her hands. When she'd first heard his apology, her mind had dreamt of their first date back, that first tender kiss. But then he'd revealed his true intentions. Part of her was flattered he wanted to spend every waking minute with her, but the other part felt smothered. The idea of not seeing her friends, family, of not having a long run or of being tied to him instead of her cross-country team in the fall was revolting. A tear slid down her cheek.

"Why can't he just be reasonable?" she whispered into the night.

"Hey, are you okay?" a soft voice asked, startling her.

Ariel whipped around to see Pam Riley walking towards her, blanket wrapped around her shoulders. "What're you doing up at this hour?"

Pam grinned as she sat atop the picnic table next to Ariel. "I never sleep well after races."

"I thought I was the only one," Ariel said, wiping her cheeks dry with the back of her sweatshirt sleeve.

"Nah, most people don't sleep well for a few days afterwards," Pam explained. "I get about three or four hours of sleep, then I'll be awake. Usually takes me until day four to sleep more than six hours at a time. By the second week I'll sleep fine though."

"Good to know this doesn't last forever," Ariel said, rubbing her eyes. "I'm exhausted but so awake at the same time."

"Horrible, isn't it?"

"Yeah."

"So when are you signing up for your next race?" Pam teased, nudging her.

"I've got my eye on a few things, but nothing solid picked out yet," Ariel laughed. "This is addicting."

"It really is. Congratulations, by the way. I tried to find you at the finish, but I think you'd already left."

"What place did you get?" Ariel asked. "I stuck around as long as I could, but I was so tired."

"I got fifth," Pam said, disappointment in her voice. "My achilles gave me a lot of problems after mile fifty-one, but I managed top ten, so it wasn't a total loss."

"You managed top 5," Ariel said, raising an eyebrow. "Sorry your achilles decided today wasn't the day."

"Eh, I'll get the next one. When you've been in this for as long as I have, you get more used to the lows and the highs. And now, I kinda just run for fun and to see if I still got it. Not as much pressure as 10 years ago when I had something to prove." The two were silent for a moment, gazing up at the stars in the night sky.

"It's beautiful out here," Ariel said, breaking the silence. "Makes being up this early not so bad."

"It's a magic hour," Pam agreed. "Especially the night after a race. No one's awake, the world is yours, and you get to soak in all those post-race endorphins."

"And aches and pains," Ariel laughed. "I'm not sure I'm going to be able to stand up from this table. I don't understand how you and runners like Tara Dower,

Sally McRae, Courtney Dauwalter can run two of these races in a span of like six weeks."

"It gets easier," Pam said, chuckling. "The more you do them, the faster you'll recover. The next time you run a hundred miler, I promise, you'll feel back to yourself much faster."

"That's good to know because as of right now, I don't think I'm running for two months."

"You take all the time you need. The worst thing you can do is rush back into it."

"You sound like my Coach," Ariel laughed.

"Your coach knows what she's talking about. Was she on the ultra-scene ever?"

Ariel shook her head. "For a bit, but she realized she liked middle distance better. She's done a few road marathons, but that's as much endurance as she does these days."

"She did a helluva job with you. You got lucky."

"I know, she's the best."

Pam stretched her arms overhead and yawned. "Looks like my tiredness is coming back. I'm going to take advantage of it while I have it." She hopped off the table and shook out her legs as she fished her phone out of her pocket. "Hey, just in case I don't see you before you leave, what's your number?"

Ariel rattled off her number.

Pam's fingers flew over her phone. "Just texted you my number. Call me, text me anytime. If you have questions, want some running advice, or just want to go get a bite.”

Ariel sat up a little straighter, trying to make sure her smile didn’t reveal the dance she was doing inside her head. “Thanks, I’d like that. Sleep tight.”

“You too, when you can!” Pam waved and turned on her heels to head back towards her room. When she disappeared around the corner, Ariel waved her hands overhead in an excited, seated dance.

“Pam Riley is gonna be my mentor!” she whispered to the stars above.

She laid down on the picnic table, soaking in everything. This time, it was tears of gratitude wetting her cheeks.

Chapter 36

Four weeks later

"You should do the honors," Cheryl said, pushing back from the desk. She stood up and motioned to the chair. "You're the one that earned it."

"I mean, yeah, but you're the one who did the really hard work of working jobs and raising kids that got us the house in the first place," Ariel said, hovering around the back of the chair. Cheryl gave her a gentle push and she sat down, scooting it in so she could reach the keyboard.

On the screen was the bank's webpage. In the top right corner was the total balance owed on the mortgage and in the center of the screen were the big red numbers showing them how behind on payments they were. That would all change with the click of a single button.

"Is it this one right here?" Ariel asked, hovering her mouse over a button in the bottom left.

"Yep. And I've got everything set up, so all you have to do is press it."

"I feel like we should say something before we do it," Ariel laughed. "This has been a long time coming. It's quite the momentous occasion, really."

"Be right back," Sam said, disappearing out of the office. She heard kitchen cabinets opening and closing, followed by the clinking of glasses before Sam reappeared a few moments later. In her hands were three champagne glasses and a bottle of sparkling apple juice. "This was for today anyway, might as well start the party early!"

Sam distributed the glasses and poured them all a drink. She held hers up high. "A toast. To the amazing Ariel, who put her life on the line to save our house."

"That's a little dramatic—"

"Hush! It's my toast, I can be as dramatic as I want to be," Sam declared. "And to this little family of ours. We've been through a lot, but through it all we've stuck together. And to this house, thank you for protecting us. Cheers!"

"Cheers!" Cheryl and Ariel echoed, clinking their glasses together before taking a sip of the sweet bubbles.

Sam tossed her head back and downed her glass in one go, refilling it for a second time. "Jeezuz, Sam," Ariel laughed.

"What?" she shrugged. "I like bubbly apple juice."

"Press the button already, would you?" Cheryl interrupted, jigging in place.

"Okay, okay!" Ariel said, placing her glass on the coaster to the side. "Here we go, one… two… three!" She pressed the pay button and the screen went blank.

"Uh oh, we broke it," Sam said.

"It's just loading," Ariel said, holding her breath. Thankfully, the webpage reloaded in full and the new balance on the mortgage showed $0.

"The house is ours!" Cheryl squealed, throwing her hands up in the air. "It's ours forever and ever! We don't owe anyone anything."

Ariel and Sam exchanged glances, smiles on their faces. Ariel picked up her champagne glass and downed it all at once before holding it out to Sam to refill.

"Now that's what I'm talking about!" Sam cheered. "Woooo!"

"I'm gonna tell Shelby to come over," Ariel said, whipping out her phone to shoot off a text. "You should invite Coach Bobbi."

"You know, that's a good idea," Cheryl said.

"Yeah!" Ariel cheered, mirroring her mother's enthusiasm. The moment felt less climatic than she'd expected, but the relief on her mom's face was worth every minute spent training. It didn't feel real yet—that the house was fully theirs and no bank would ever slap a foreclosure notice on the door again. And that she'd been the reason that'd happened. But she was grateful.

The sound of the door opening and slamming brought her back to reality.

"Geez, that was fast, Shelby," Ariel laughed, shaking her head. But the person who appeared at the top of the stairs wasn't Shelby. Kyle stood there, hands shoved in his jean's pockets, his head low so that his tousled hair fell into his eyes.

"Hey, Kyle," Sam said, her eyes darting between him and her sister.

"We're gonna go downstairs and put a pizza in," Cheryl said, pulling Sam behind her by the hand. Kyle and

Ariel were alone for the first time since prom. She glared at him, her arms crossed across her chest.

He kicked at the carpet with his foot. "You look good, happy."

"I am," Ariel sighed, her arms falling to her sides. "I really am. It's the happiest I've been in a while."

"Glad to hear it," he said. "You're beautiful when you smile."

Ariel's cheeks flushed red as her eyes darted toward the ground. "Thanks."

Kyle took a step towards her and reached for her hand, but when Ariel shifted her weight backwards, he stopped.

"Nothing has changed since our phone conversation, Kyle." The hurt in his eyes pulled at her heart strings. A part of her wanted nothing more than to run to him, hug him, and say she'd love to spend every waking moment with him. But the other half told her to hold strong. "I do miss you though…"

"What do you mean?"

"I miss being friends," Ariel said, sighing. "I still like you, but like, as a friend. I want to come over and complain about Sam when she makes me mad, and I miss your stupid jokes."

Ariel could've sworn she saw his eyes well up with tears, but his face remained stoic. "I'm sorry I ever doubted you," he said, finally looking up from his feet to meet her gaze. "I was stupid to ever think that."

"Yeah, you were," she said, scoffing. She watched his face closely to see where he was going with this.

"I'm really, really sorry," he continued. "I'm going to regret doubting you for the rest of my life. Please, let me make it up to you."

She raised an eyebrow. "How would you go about doing that?"

"Let me buy you dinner."

Ariel's jaw dropped before she could catch it.

His face remained serious for a beat before breaking into a mischievous grin. "I'm just playing with you. About the dinner thing, not about being sorry for doubting you and me wanting to try to make it up to you."

She picked her jaw back up and launched a playful punch into his muscled shoulder. "Kyle James, you are a certified jerk."

"I know, I know, you remind me constantly."

Ariel smiled at him, the weight on her shoulders easing ever so slightly. "Do you wanna stay for dinner? Mom's making her homemade grilled pizzas."

"Say no more," he said, hands in the air as if surrendering. The two rejoined the rest of the group who'd gathered in the kitchen around the large wooden dining room table. The same table where they'd held many meetings the past few months, the table that led to this very moment.

"Ari! Mom told me the good news! Your house is yours and yours alone!" Shelby exclaimed, jumping up from the table and wrapping her arms around Ariel's neck in a bear hug. Ariel smiled.

"It is! All those miles and long days paid off!"

"Yeah, they did! Where's the bubbly?" Shelby asked, nodding to the glass Ariel was still holding.

"Sam has it, if she hasn't finished all of it by now."

"It's right here," Sam said, producing a nearly empty bottle. "Don't worry, we have more." Ariel joined the group and they all sat around celebrating together. When the pizza was done, they all ate around the same table they'd spent months planning around, laughing as they shared war stories from the trail.

"I'm still shocked I couldn't eat normal for a week," Ariel said through a mouthful of pizza. "And I still can't look at a pancake the same."

"Oof, hope that doesn't last forever," Shelby said.

"I know, right?"

"It'll come back," Bobbi said. "I once couldn't eat spaghetti because I threw it up, but ten years later I can eat it again!"

"I hope it's faster than ten years," Ariel said with a huff.

"It will be," Cheryl said. "Who wants brownies after this? I made a special pan of them."

"A special pan?" Sam asked.

"Different kind of special," Cheryl rolled her eyes. "They're the double fudge caramel ones."

"Those are better than special brownies," Bobbi said, hopping up to go to the kitchen. "I'll get them."

Ariel's phone buzzed on the table and she leaned forward to see who was calling. She raised her eyebrows and fumbled to answer it.

"Hi Coach Angela," Ariel said. The whole room fell silent, all eyes on her. She'd left a message with the college coach a week ago but hadn't heard back since. Ariel stood up and walked out of the room, not wanting her every word and expression to be scrutinized.

"Hey, Ariel," Coach Angela replied, her voice raspier than she remembered. "Sorry it's taken me so long to get back to you, I've been out with the flu. Still getting over the last of it but I feel better."

"That sucks you've been sick, glad you're on the mend though," Ariel said, desperate for her to get to the point.

"I got your message. And of course, I saw your race. I watched the live stream and it was in the local newspaper the next day."

"Really? It was in the Denver newspaper?"

"Well, The Coloradoan—"

"Any newspaper is amazing, honestly," Ariel laughed, twisting a strand of her hair around her finger.

"Anyway, I wanted to say congratulations on your big win. You're really turning heads in the sport. From the rumors I've heard, you've got lots of sponsorship deals to juggle. Are you even interested in still running for CSU?"

"I am," Ariel said, a little too quickly. "I mean, I love running and if I can make a career out of it, great. But I also want to go to school and become an environmental scientist. Running for CSU would make both of those dreams happen."

"Are you sure you want to run shorter distances? You know we don't have hundred milers at the collegiate level," Coach Angela laughed, which turned into a cough.

"As long as you'll still have me and I have a scholarship, I'd like to run."

"The spot's still yours," Coach Angela said, her smile audible through the phone. "I won't keep you, and we can talk more next week. Hopefully by then I'll be over this flu for good."

"Okay, sounds great. Talk to you later." Ariel hung up the phone and did a silent happy dance before returning to the living room where everyone looked at her expectantly.

"So?" Sam asked. "Don't keep us hanging, what did she say?"

Ariel's face broke out into a huge grin. "I'm still running for CSU! I get to keep my scholarship!"

Everyone in the room cheered for her.

"You do know you don't need that scholarship for school anymore, right?" Sam asked as Ariel sat down next to her. "With your winnings and a sponsorship deal, you can afford to pay on your own."

"Yeah, but now I get my scholarship so I can invest the race winnings and save the sponsorship money."

"I raised you right," Cheryl laughed, raising her glass.

As the night wore on, Ariel grew more and more tired but refused to go to bed. She fell asleep on the couch to the sound of her loved ones chatting away.

Chapter 37

Six months later

The sky started to fade from midnight black to navy to cobalt, to the light pinks and oranges of sunrise, to bright orange and yellow as the top of the sun crested the horizon. The few puffy white clouds in the sky turned softer hues of the sky where they sat. The corn stood tall in the fields, their deep green leaves soaking up the moisture of the humid air surrounding them. The gentle breeze did little to alleviate the heavy air. It was clear the day would be hot even before the sun fully crested the horizon.

Ariel was sitting in the wicker rocking chair on the front porch, watching the sun rise with a full and grateful heart. She brought the coffee cup she was holding to her face, taking a sip of the hot brown beverage. She sipped it slowly. She still wasn't the biggest coffee fan, but she was loving the waves of nostalgia each sip conjured. It took her back to the morning of Leadville when her and Mom shared a cup in the quiet before the chaos started. And while it hadn't been her favorite taste, that moment she would forever savor.

The smell of warm dirt and freshly mown grass filled the air. The smell of home. The spruce trees her parents had planted along the edge of the property stood tall, working hard to grow taller. It would be years before they were tall enough to fulfill their role as wind break and living privacy fence. The grass on the front yard was browning, evidence of the dry summers. The planters at the base of the porch buzzed with bees feeding on the nectar of the alyssums and petunias she and Mom had planted in April when she'd visited for break.

Being back for the final weeks of summer before she went off to college was a blessing. While she was loving Colorado, her heart would always bring her back to Iowa, to the home that had raised her and made her.

The front door opened, and Mom stepped out, holding her own cup of coffee in one hand the whole coffee pot in the other. "Need a refill?"

Ariel held out her cup to be topped off and Mom obliged, then set the pot on the glass topped table. She took a seat on the lounge couch next to her daughter. They sipped their coffee in silence for a few moments, enjoying the quiet breeze and the calls of the mourning doves perched on the power lines along the road. A few red winged black birds landed next to them, adding their songs to the mix.

"It's nice to have you home," Cheryl said. She reached over and grabbed her daughter's hand, giving it a squeeze.

"Me too. Though I will say, I miss seeing the mountains on the horizon."

"Me too," Cheryl laughed. "And I didn't even spend as much time out there as you. If we could just pick up one of those mountains and drop it off in the distance here so I could look at it every morning, that would be ideal."

"Wouldn't it?" Ariel agreed. She imagined the scene in her head—what the sunrise would look like above both the corn fields and the mountains. "I like it the way it is though."

"I agree," Cheryl nodded. "How long do you have until your next race?"

"About two months. Are you going to come out for it?"

"I am."

Ariel's eyes widened and she shook her head. "Wait, what? Say that again?"

Cheryl laughed. "I'm coming out to see it. I had such a good time when I was with you and Erin in Colorado… it was the first time I felt kind of… normal, since your dad died. I want to be that way again."

"Do you feel normal now? Like… here in this house?" Ariel asked. That had been her biggest fear, that staying in the home they'd all shared as a family would be too painful for her mother, make it difficult to move on with her life and find happiness in the new normal.

"I do. Some days are harder than others, but I think I'd feel that anywhere. Just… going to Colorado with you for Leadville just gave me a reset. It got me out of my funk and showed me what life could be again. That I could be happy. I felt like myself. And when I came home, I felt a little down. But I found myself seeking out things that I used to enjoy like going out to my favorite cafes. Hell, I actually reached out to a friend and we went and got dinner."

"Oh Mom, I'm so glad to hear that," Ariel smiled, her heart warm. It was great hearing that her mom was taking an initiative. Even before Dad died, she hadn't been the most active and didn't have many friends. But Ariel was happy to hear she was finding herself and making her way back into the world. "Of course, I hope that doesn't keep you from visiting me at college…. Or from coming to help crew my races.”

Cheryl smiled and shook her head. “Of course not. I’m going to be at every race I can, work permitting.”

“Good. Because you’re an integral part of the crew team. And, if I keep doing well, I’m sure it won’t be long before Salomon starts paying the members of my crew team if you know what I mean.”

“That would be a pretty cool addition to my resume,” Cheryl laughed.

The porch door swung open and Sam walked out, coffee cup in her hand. “That’s where the coffee pot went,” she said groggily.

The coffee pot sat empty on the glass topped table. Cheryl and Ariel looked at each other and laughed. “Sorry, I didn’t think you’d be up for a while.”

“I’m full of surprises,” Sam rolling her eyes. “I found the extra coffee pot from the old machine in the basement and used that to make another pot. So, there’s more if y’all want some.”

“Ingenious,” Ariel smiled. “Also, Mom, you should probably clean out the basement if there’s just old coffee pots sitting around.”

“Want to help? That’s been on the to do list for ages.”

“I don’t have any other plans for today,” Ariel said. “And it’s kind of fun going through old boxes.”

“I’m free too,” Sam said, as she blew the steam off the top of her cup. “Ooo, can we have a garage sale? We could make good money. Put it in our trip fund."

"I didn't know we had a trip fund," Cheryl laughed.

"Oh, we do," Sam said. "Ariel and I started it last summer. Since we were graduating, we wanted to make sure we still got to take family trips. And… we kinda figured it would be a good way to honor Dad."

"Aw, girls, that's so sweet," Cheryl said softly, her gaze falling to her hands in her lap. "He was always wishing we traveled more…"

"So we'll honor him and do exactly that," Sam assured her, reaching out to squeeze her hand.

"But for now, our day is planned out. We've got plenty of coffee, leftovers in the fridge. Let's clean the basement!"

"We'll talk vacation and travel planning while we go through boxes," Ariel said, hopping to her feet. She was full of hope for whatever the future brought her next because no matter what came her way, she could always come home. Because the house was saved, and history was made.

"Maybe the Grand Canyon next summer?" Cheryl offered as they made their way inside.

"Love that idea!" Sam and Ariel said in unison.

About the Author

When not dreaming up new adventures for her characters to go on, CR (also known as Casey) can be found having adventures herself. From horseback riding to running 100 mile races, to eating her way through the streets of Italy, Casey's down for it all. While her day job is in healthcare, she's been filling notebooks with stories and computers with manuscripts since the 4th grade. A Midwesterner at heart, Casey has lived all across the country and currently resides in sunny San Diego. Check her website, crbaumberger.com or her Instagram @crbaumberger for the latest updates on her next book and all her adventures.

Leave a Review

Book reviews are the life blood of indie authors like myself. If you enjoyed *The Race Through the Sky*, I would be honored if you took one more moment of your time to leave a review on a platform (or all of them!) *The Race Through the Sky* is available on Amazon, Goodreads, and of course all social media platforms! If you didn't enjoy it, please email me directly at casey@baumbergers.com to tell me how I can improve the next one.

Acknowledgements

I like to keep this page short and sweet. Biggest thanks to my mom, Sarah. Since the first book I wrote in 4th grade (which she had bound for me!) to when I published *Breaking the Pocket* to all the stories in between. Thank you for always believing in my writing and encouraging me to keep going.

Also by the Author

Breaking the Pocket

And a whole lot more on the way… check crbaumberger.com for details!